Kirsty Moseley's debut novel *The Boy Who Sneaks in My Bedroom Window* was one of ten finalists for the 2012 Goodreads Choice Awards, Best YA Fiction, and she is also the author of the novel *Always You*. Kirsty lives in Norfolk with her husband and son.

Visit Kirsty Moseley online at:
www.kirstymoseley.com
www.facebook.com/authorkirstymoseley
www.twitter.com/KirstyEMoseley

FIGHTING TO BE FREE

KIRSTY MOSELEY

Mix
Paper from
responsible sources
FSC® C104740

Piatkus
An imprint of
Little, Brown Book Group
Carmelite House
50 Victoria Embankment
London EC4Y 0DZ

An Hachette UK Company
www.hachette.co.uk

piatkus

PIATKUS

First published in the US in 2016 by Forever,
an imprint of Grand Central Publishing
First published in Great Britain in 2016 by Piatkus

1 3 5 7 9 10 8 6 4 2

A CIP catalogue record for this book
is available from the British Library.

ISBN 978-0-349-41337-2

Printed and bound in Great Britain by
Clays Ltd, St Ives plc

Papers used by Piatkus are from well-managed forests
and other responsible sources.

For Lee
Your support knows no bounds,
and I absolutely do not deserve you.

ACKNOWLEDGMENTS

There are so many people I want to thank, so please bear with me!

First and foremost, to my amazing family. You all have no idea how much your support, encouragement, and belief in me helps, so thank you for always having my back. To Dad, cheers for not ringing me while I was working. To Mum, thanks for not letting Dad ring while I was working. To Toni, you're still a nugget but you're my nugget. Special shout out to my husband, Lee, for never being mad that I spend hours on end at the laptop and neglect him (and the housework, but that's nothing to do with writing, I neglected it before). As I said in my dedication, I absolutely do not deserve you. Another special mention to my son for being the most amazing and supportive little boy I could ever dare hope for. I adore each and every one of you!

Secondly, to my agent, Lorella, thank you so much for championing Jamie and Ellie from the get-go and for all of your hard work in turning my dream into a reality. You're amazing and I'm lucky to have you. Your passion for your work and clients is awe-inspiring. Hugs. x

Stephany, my US agent, thank you for your support and hard work! Drinks are on me when I come to your side of the pond!

I have to shout out to my own personal cheerleading squad who are always on the end of a message when I need them: Chloe Meyer, Kerry Duke, Natasha Preston, Terrie Arasin, Adelaine Saria, and Hilda Reyes. Also to my Facebook street team "Moseley's Minions" who are an incredible bunch of girls (and one man, mustn't forget Darrell), I'm privileged to have you all!

To all bloggers, yes, *all of you*, you guys are my rock stars. Thank you for all of your support over the years, it means more than I can tell you. x

To the readers of Wattpad, whose feedback, messages, and comments helped shape it into the book you're reading today. You guys rock and always have done. x

Special thank you must go to the team at Forever, especially to the design team that absolutely smashed it out of the park with the stunning cover for the book, also to the editors, formatters, and everyone else behind the scenes, thank you for everything. Special mention to Megha, my editor at Forever, for falling in love with Jamie and Ellie and seeing their potential. Also to Anna at Piatkus, my UK publisher, thank you for loving my words.

And lastly to you, dear reader, thank you for picking up this book. I really hope you enjoy it and the journey within. Remember to always fight for what you want every single day. xxx

FIGHTING

TO BE

FREE

PROLOGUE

THERE ARE SIGNIFICANT moments in life that shape the way you see yourself. Some sort of shift in the balance, a throwing off the equilibrium. Moments that, in hindsight, you can look back on and pinpoint as exactly when things changed either for better or for worse. This was that moment for me. Everything hung in the balance; everything was uncertain, undecided, and unwritten.

This was my second shot, my chance to come out of the darkness and into the light. With every cell in my body I was planning on fighting to be free of this life, even if it killed me.

The trouble was, it was out of my hands. Maybe I would try my hardest but wouldn't be accepted; maybe I would never be good enough. Society had its ideals, and a guy like me didn't fit in with those at all.

Every now and again something comes along that ignites your desire to be the person you strive to be, the better person. When I stripped everything else away, peeled off the dirty, raw, and damaged layers, all that was left was hope. Hope for a better life, for a brighter future. Just hope for a chance.

Suddenly, with that fire in your belly, a *what if* becomes a possibility. What if you threw ideals out the window? What if you dismissed everything you ever knew? What if the bad guy could be the hero of the story for a change?

I guess what it all boils down to is this: My name is Jamie Cole, and I'm a murderer.

CHAPTER 1

TAKING A DEEP breath, I stepped tentatively over the threshold, leaving the place I vowed I would never return to. I was free; finally, after serving just over four years in juvie, I was free to start over. Stuffed deep in my pocket, so it wouldn't get lost, I had just under two thousand dollars—my wages for working kitchen duties while I carried out my sentence. Nestled next to it was the address of the rooming house that my parole officer had arranged for me to stay at, some sort of shitty convict rehabilitation accommodation block by my understanding.

As the door slammed shut behind me, panic set in for a second because I wasn't entirely sure I wanted to be free. But that was when I saw it. Outside. Not the exercise yard, which was the only "outside" I usually got to see, but freedom. The January sun was shining, there were no walls with barbed wire on the top, just a clear, open view of a road and a yellow cab parked a hundred yards away, obviously waiting to pick me up and take me to my new place. Nervous excitement built in my stomach.

I shouldered my bag, which contained the only possessions I had to my name: a few sets of clothes and one photograph of my little sister, Sophie. As I took the first few steps away from the gates, my heart was beating out of my chest; it felt weird to be walking away from the place I'd considered home for the last few years. I was waiting for the alarms to sound and someone to tackle me to the ground and start smashing me with a baton. They didn't. I walked quickly toward the waiting cab. I didn't look back; I'd never look back. This was my fresh start. This place had saved me, and I was hoping that it had changed my life and had at least given me a fighting chance. I didn't want to go back to the life I'd led before all this happened; I couldn't live like that any longer. I was determined to change.

"Hey, Kid!" someone shouted just as I pulled the cab door open.

I turned around, and my heart dropped down to my feet as I spotted a familiar figure just getting out of a shiny black Mercedes that was parked across the road and down a little way.

"Ed?" I hadn't seen this guy since I was sent down, and I didn't want to see him now.

Ed jogged over and pulled me into a hug, slapping my back enthusiastically. "Good to see you again," he greeted me happily.

Ed looked no different than I remembered; he was still a smarmy, overdressed jackass. "What are you doing here?" I asked, flicking my eyes around nervously. I didn't even want to be seen talking to guys like this again.

"Boss wants to see you." Ed nodded toward the car about thirty feet away from the cab that I was so desperately trying to get into.

"I can't right now, I need to go get checked into my new place," I rejected, trying to think of a better excuse. But I knew it was useless; if Brett Reyes wanted to see me, he'd see me conscious or unconscious.

Ed smiled. "Boss wants to see you now, Kid. You can check into your place later." He turned and walked off toward his car without looking back.

A scowl slipped onto my face. I hated being called Kid. They had all called me that when I worked for Brett. I guess it was because when I started working for him, that's what I was. I was eleven years old the first time I did a job for him—dropping a manila envelope full of cash through the window of a parked cop patrol car. Bribe money. The cops turned a blind eye to his activities, and in return they got a nice little payout. Perfect.

I closed my eyes and sighed dejectedly before leaning into the cab and smiling apologetically at the driver. "Sorry, I won't be needing you." I didn't wait for an answer, just slammed the door and followed behind Ed, climbing into the passenger side of the Mercedes.

I felt sick. There was no way out of this. I probably wasn't going to survive the rest of the day. So much for the fresh start I wanted. I wasn't even going to see the sun set. To say that my life sucked right now would be the understatement of the century.

Resting my head back against the expensive leather, I looked out the window, watching the streets change and turn more urban as we headed deeper into New York City and toward, I assumed, Queens, where Brett usually conducted his business. I sighed inwardly and wondered why I'd dared to hope that things could be different. There was no way Brett would let me live, I knew too much about him. The things I knew could put him away for years, but I would never tell. I'd been offered a deal so many times when I was going down: reduced sentence, a high-class juvie instead of the craphole I was sent to, even a cushy little job when I was inside. But I never once considered turning state's evidence and standing against him, never.

* * *

About forty minutes later, we pulled up to the warehouse that I had spent so much time in as an adolescent. The place hadn't changed at all. My stomach clenched as I thought about what was probably going to happen to me inside. I just prayed that it would be quick and painless. Brett surely respected me that much, at least.

"Come on then, Kid, let's go," Ed urged, climbing out of the car.

The sounds of the angle grinders and welders from the warehouse chop shop were like familiar music to my ears. I'd spent way too many hours of my childhood here, learning how to remove serial and chassis numbers so that we could sell the cars that I stole to order. I was the best car thief in Brett's organization. People placed their orders, Brett found the cars, and I stole them. Easy. I'd never even come close to being caught. We didn't steal any old car, though; they had to be top end. We didn't take anything worth less than a hundred thousand.

"Hey, Kid. Long time no see!" someone called.

I glanced over to see Ray lifting his welding mask from his face. He was the one who'd taught me everything I knew about cars. I walked over and gave him an awkward hug while he patted my back affectionately.

"Hey, Ray. How's it going?" I asked, discreetly eyeing the silver Porsche 911 on the ramp.

"Things are great. I have a daughter," he answered proudly, pulling off one of his thick leather gloves and running a hand through his sweaty brown hair.

"No shit, really? Congrats!"

"Thanks. We called her Tia. She's two," he gushed, grinning.

I slapped him on the shoulder; he'd always taken care of me, and would make an excellent father. "That's awesome, man, nice." Ray deserved to be happy. He was one of the best people I knew.

"Thanks. How you been?" His eyes drifted over me slowly, probably checking for any cuts or bruises.

I shrugged. "I'm good. I'm about to go see Brett. I'll talk to you later; maybe we could grab a drink or something?" Now that I was trying to go straight, I wanted nothing to do with anyone in this world anymore, but Ray was the exception. I thought of him as a big brother, and would love to keep in touch with him. Well, if I survived the next few minutes, which was highly doubtful.

"Absolutely. Here, I'll give you my number. Call me and we'll sort something out. You have a place to stay? You could come and stay with me and Samantha, she won't mind. You can meet Tia," he offered, already scribbling his number onto a scrap of paper and holding it out to me.

I stuffed the number in my pocket as I spoke, "It's okay, I've got a place. But thanks anyway."

"Kid, come on, you know Boss doesn't like to wait!" Ed called behind me.

Sighing deeply, I gave Ray another man hug before following Ed. I felt like I was taking the long walk to my death.

I thought about my life as I climbed the stairs. My eighteen short years of life. Wasted. A pile of shit. What was the point in even bothering? To be honest, for about fifteen of them I'd wished I was dead anyway, so maybe this outcome wasn't too bad after all. At least this way I wouldn't have to try to change. Changing would be hard, probably the hardest thing I would ever have to do. Maybe I should be grateful that I was about to bite it.

I stopped outside the office door, waiting as Ed knocked.

"Come in!" Brett shouted through the door. The sound of his deep, husky voice made my shoulders stiffen.

Ed smiled and twisted the handle. "See you after, Kid. We'll catch up," he said, opening the door and slapping me on the shoulder.

"Sure, Ed, whatever," I replied dismissively, rolling my eyes. Why he was bothering to act like he didn't know what was coming was beyond me.

Holding my breath, I forced myself to remain calm. My eyes swept the large office; it was still done up exceptionally, just like I remembered. Brett's overly large antique oak desk still had pride of place in the center of the room. There were expensive vases and statues behind him, and even the houseplant on his desk looked exotic. Brett Reyes liked the best, he always had.

Brett stood up from behind his desk, smiling warmly at me in his expensive gray tailored suit. "Hey, Kid! Good to see you," he said, coming around the desk and engulfing me in a hug.

"Yeah, you too," I lied, trying to control the slight tremor in my voice. I knew how this was going to end; I just prayed he liked me enough to do it quickly. A nice shot to the face, or, even better, the back of the head so I wouldn't see it coming.

Brett pulled back and smiled at me, his blue eyes soft and friendly. He'd aged considerably in my absence. His forehead was lined with wrinkles, and his dirty-blond hair had receded. Although he'd aged quite a bit since I last saw him, he still didn't look as old as he was. He was easily in his midfifties, but people often thought he was early forties.

"So, how was it?" he asked, gripping my shoulders as he waited for my answer.

"It was okay." Glancing around, I saw two guys sitting on the sofa off to the side. The older, dark haired one I didn't know, the other was a guy I knew from juvie. Shaun. He was a real nasty piece of work, and I'd seen him make many peoples' lives a misery in the year that we were inside together. I myself had had a fair few run-ins with him, the last of which had ended when I'd smashed his face into a table not long before he was released. I held in my groan. "Hey, Shaun," I greeted him stiffly.

Brett snickered and slapped me on the shoulder as he strutted back around to his side of the desk. "Yeah, I heard you two had some problems inside," he mused, still chuckling. "Maybe you should kiss and make up."

I snorted. "He can kiss my fucking ass if he wants," I retorted, looking at Shaun warningly as he glared at me and stood.

"You little shit...I swear to God, I'll—" he started, but Brett held up a hand, silencing him.

"Enough! I won't have you two fighting. Shaun, you've been here for the last three years, so I've seen how you operate, but trust me, you don't want to be having a problem with the kid," he warned.

I clenched my jaw. I didn't want to get into a fight, but I knew I could defend myself if I needed to. I'd always been proficient at taking care of myself—probably because I'd learned how to block out pain. Of course, I still felt it, but I just didn't care. Pain made you strong; it meant you were still alive. Pain could be your friend when you thought you were dead inside.

I smiled a challenge at Shaun, daring him to go against Brett's orders. He sneered at me but sat back down, so I turned my attention to Brett.

"So then, Kid, I've set up an apartment for you. I thought you'd like a few days off to get settled, and then come back to work Friday night," Brett said, rummaging through the top drawer of his desk. He pulled out a set of keys and tossed it to me. "Here, it's a two-bedroom. We'll sort out rent and stuff later."

I set the keys on the desk and shook my head. "Brett, thank you for going to all this trouble for me, but I can't. I don't want to do this anymore. I'm going straight from here on out."

He visibly recoiled at my words. "Kid, I *need* you here. No one can boost like you." The throbbing muscle in his jaw told me he was growing angry.

"I'm sorry, Brett, I am. But I just don't have the motivation that I used to. I'm not doing this type of shit anymore," I replied sternly. I'd made up my mind: Either I went straight, or he would have to kill me. I didn't need this anymore; the reasons I'd had to do it had died the day I became a murderer. Everything changed on that day: my outlook, my priorities, everything.

His fist slammed down on the desk, making his plant shake from the blow and a pot of pens tip over, scattering across his desk. "You think you can just walk away? For more than three years I looked after you and showed you my business! Three years I spent training you, and you think you can just walk away? You can't!" he ranted, his loud voice echoing off the walls.

"Brett, I want out of this life. I just want to go straight. I won't do it, I'm sorry." I shook my head and looked him right in the eye, showing him I wasn't going to back down.

He sighed, the muscle in his jaw clenched again, and then he nodded to the two guys behind me. I closed my eyes, waiting to die. In unison, they grabbed my arms, pulling them behind my back as I was slammed face-first into the desk. Someone's arm went across the back of my neck, pressing down, making it difficult to breathe.

I didn't open my eyes when something hard pushed against my temple. As the safety was clicked off, I waited for my life to flash before my eyes, or the epiphany you were supposed to see before you died, but I didn't see anything as the gun pressed harder into my skin, causing my jaw to ache.

"Kid, you know the rules. If you want out, you *earn* it. You still owe me for all the time I invested in you," Brett growled angrily.

I forced my eyes open and saw that he was the one holding the gun as he leaned over the desk, glaring at me. I didn't bother struggling; I was dead either way, there was no way I was getting out of here.

"Just kill me if you have to, because I'm not doing it," I said, awkwardly shaking my head.

"I don't want to kill you, Kid. You're amazing at what you do. The best I've seen. It'd be a waste," Brett said, looking at me hopefully.

The arm across my neck pushed down harder, making me groan as I struggled to draw breath. "No!" I choked out.

Brett growled in frustration. "I need you to do a job. It's five cars, one night. One job, then you're out."

Just one job? But would it actually stop at one? The thrill of boosting cars was like some sort of addictive high. If I started again, would I be able to stop? I wasn't convinced I would.

"Can't do it," I said ignoring the metallic tang of my own blood as I chewed on the inside of my cheek. I knew what was coming, and it wasn't going to be painless.

But instead of delivering the slow, brutal death I was envisioning, the gun was withdrawn and Brett stepped back. "You should think of your mother, Kid. She's so screwed up. Having her daughter murdered like that, then her son getting sent down. She kind of went off the rails. I've been looking after her for you. It'd be a shame if something awful happened to her after all she's been through already." He shrugged casually as if we were talking about the weather.

The son of a bitch is threatening my mom? I thrashed, managing to get one of my arms free so I could push myself up, but before my attempt could accomplish anything, I was slammed back down on the table roughly.

"Don't you fucking dare!" I shouted acidly.

Brett chuckled. "Kid, I like her, honestly. I don't want to have to hurt her. One job and I'll leave your mother alone," he bartered.

I squeezed my eyes shut. As much as I hated my mom, she was

still my mother at the end of the day and I didn't want her hurt, especially not the type of hurt I'd seen Brett inflict on so many other people.

Awkwardly, I nodded in agreement. Air rushed back into my lungs as I was yanked up to standing by the back of my shirt. Shaun smiled wickedly at me as he patted the top of my head. "There's a good boy," he teased condescendingly. I gritted my teeth, trying not to react.

Brett clapped his hands, rubbing his palms together excitedly. "Great! The job is in three days. Here, take this cell and I'll call you with the details, I had it all set up for you. And take the apartment, too." He slid a cell phone and the apartment keys across the desk.

I grabbed the phone and shoved it deep into my jeans pocket. "I've got a place. One job is what we've agreed to, so I don't need the apartment. Thanks anyway," I said, trying to be polite even though I actually wanted to maim him.

"Okay, Kid. Whatever you want."

I turned to leave but caught sight of Shaun arrogantly smirking at me. Before I could stop myself, I raised my arm and threw a punch into his face. The satisfying crack of his nose made me smile as blood instantly spurted from his nostrils. He yelped, shocked, his hand shooting up to his nose to staunch the flow.

"Don't ever touch me again. There's a good boy," I growled angrily, using his words. I turned and strutted out the door, ignoring Brett roaring with laughter behind me.

CHAPTER 2

THIS IS IT," the cabdriver announced, cautiously locking his door with his elbow as he stopped outside a filthy-looking, dilapidated apartment block.

Trying not to turn my nose up at the place the state had arranged for me to stay upon my release, I handed him the requested money and stepped out. Instantly, the sweet aroma of burning weed assaulted my nose from where several people milled around outside smoking joints in broad daylight. The cab sped away almost as soon as my door closed, leaving me standing there among the scummy-looking people, who were all looking at me like they wanted to beat and rape me to within an inch of my life.

As I made my way up the sidewalk toward the front of the building, a barely legal girl stepped forward and set her hand on my chest. Her eyes were bloodshot, her hair was wild, and she looked like she hadn't washed or changed her almost nonexistent clothes in about a week. "Hi there, handsome, you looking for someone?" she purred.

"No thanks," I replied quickly, shrugging away from her hand as I continued to the front door.

Once inside, I walked toward the little reception desk, my feet sticking to the cracked tile floor with each step. I had to laugh when I realized that the guy was sitting behind chunky thick bars with what looked like bulletproof glass behind them. He even had a handgun sitting on the side of his desk.

He sneered distastefully as I approached. "Yeah?" he grunted, muting the TV show he was watching.

"Hey. I'm Jamie Cole. I was told I had a room here."

"Cole? Let me see…" He shifted in his chair, causing it to squeak from the pressure, and shuffled through some papers.

I turned subtly so that I could see up the hallway, making sure no one was sneaking up on me from behind. I'd gotten pretty adept at staying out of trouble. As long as you saw it coming, you could either face it head-on or walk the other way.

"Yeah, here you are." He ticked my name off some sort of list, then sniffed and wiped his nose on the back of his hand as he pushed himself up from his swivel chair and padded over to a little cabinet mounted on the wall. He pulled down a set of keys and waddled back to me, plopping down heavily. Everything looked like too much effort for him. The guy was carrying about fifty pounds of sheer fat around the middle, so no wonder life seemed taxing.

He threw a couple of forms and a pen into a little metal drawer and shoved it hard so that the drawer popped out on my side of his protective bubble. "Sign on the bottom and it's all yours," he instructed as I retrieved the registration forms from the drawer.

I scribbled my name and passed the papers back to him.

Barely glancing at my forms, he tossed them to the side. "Okay, so there aren't very many rules here. Just try and stay out of trouble. Make sure you lock your door, even when you're in the room. Take anything valuable out with you, or lock it in one of the safes here inside the office," he advised, waving his chubby hand at the row of little safes built into the wall. I nodded, and he continued, "You have a front door key. The door gets locked at ten p.m.; after that you'll have to let yourself in. Your room is 234." He shoved the drawer back through to me.

I grabbed the set of keys from the bottom and shifted my bag on my shoulder.

"Second floor, turn left at the top, and good luck." He smirked, and I silently noted the amusement in his tone.

"Right," I mumbled. On the way to my room I avoided touching the railings and walls, covered in years of grime and dirt. If Brett didn't kill me, then I'd probably die from some incurable infection I'd catch from this place; I could practically taste the germs with every breath.

I found my room easily, unlocking the door and shoving it open. The room was bare save for a couple of bits of furniture; on the upside, the mattress looked clean, and the sheets piled at the end looked new, so at least I wouldn't have to sleep in other people's filth.

In the corner, next to a door, was a little sink; I headed over to the door and opened it to find a toilet and the tiniest shower stall I'd ever seen. *I could kill two birds with one stone, and shower while I'm taking a leak. Now that's a time saver!* I snorted before outright laughing at my predicament. The place was so awful that I kind of wished I were back in juvie; at least it was clean and familiar there.

Dropping my bag, I flopped on the bed and stared at the ceiling. All I could hear was shouting and fighting from outside, and people banging around in the room next door. I closed my eyes and thought everything through. I needed to get a job, and I needed to get a car, and then I could get the hell out of this place.

One job for Brett would make my mom safe; after that I could move on like I'd planned.

When the sounds of girlie moaning and headboard banging started in the room next to mine, I pushed myself up and decided that I might as well go and start the job hunt now.

I left the rooming house in quite high spirits and headed to the nearest stores, starting to ask around for a job. A couple of people seemed interested, right up until I told them where I was staying, and then they backed off right away. It was obviously common knowledge what kind of people lived at that place—scum of the earth, murdering losers, just like me. By the third place I asked, I was lying and telling people I was in the process of moving. But I still didn't manage to swing an interview.

A little way out of the neighborhood, a junkyard caught my attention. I decided to try to fulfill my second task—getting a car.

I headed toward the little white office trailer, but a guy stopped me on my way there. "Hey, what you looking for?" he asked politely, wiping his greasy hands on a rag. He was wearing oil-stained gray overalls and had a Yankees baseball cap covering his black hair; he was probably not much older than me.

"Oh, hi. Uh…I'm not sure. Do you have any cars that need work to get them running? Ones that you want to get rid of cheap?" I inquired.

A smile crept over his lips. "You know about cars?"

"Yeah. A thing or two," I answered. There wasn't much I didn't know about cars, actually.

"Okay, well, I'll show you what we've got. None of them run, though." He shrugged and walked off behind the trailer. I followed behind, barely able to contain my excitement. I hadn't had my hands on a car engine for what felt like forever.

Around the back of the office, he stopped. "These are the ones we use for parts; the others we crush. They're okay, except they don't run. None of them are complete now, though. You could make a car out of the parts of the other ones and what we have around the yard," he stated, nodding to about ten beat-up, scratched, and rusted cars parked there.

"Can I have a look?" I asked, heading over to the first in the row. I instantly dismissed it because the chassis was rusted to hell. I hated welding. After looking at a couple, I settled on a pickup that had probably started its life as dark green. It had no wheels and no bumper, but those were probably lying around here some-where. "This looks good. Can I turn it over?"

He grinned and nodded, obviously thinking I was crazy as I jumped behind the wheel excitedly.

The keys were already in it, so I pumped the gas as I turned the engine over, hearing the whine and slight ticking noise. It was perfect. It sounded like the problem was with the alternator, easy enough to fix *if* I could find the parts in the yard somewhere. I popped the hood and jumped out to look at the engine. As I clipped the hood above my head, I smiled. It didn't look too bad at all; it just required a little cleanup and a few new parts. All she needed was some love and care. I shoved my hand down the side and pulled out the alternator cable. "You have a rag I could borrow?"

The guy's smirk grew wider as he threw me the rag he'd been wiping his hands on. I cleaned up the cable and plucked a stone from the ground, scratching the inside of the head slightly to give some friction before putting it back.

"Can you turn it over for me?" I requested.

He burst out laughing. "Look, man, this truck's been here for almost a year, it's probably rusted solid. I've tried to get this one going, it's not just gonna be the alternator."

I shrugged. "Worth a shot, right? That's just a temporary re-pair, I'll have to change most of the fixings, but it should be okay."

He rolled his eyes and climbed in, clearly not expecting anything judging by the look on his face. As he turned the key, the truck spluttered to life for a split second before cutting out. It was loud as hell, but it was perfect. The guy stepped out, his mouth agape.

"So how much you want for it? I'll need the parts, too. New wheels and bumper. I'll replace all of the plugs, clips, and cables as well," I stated, taking another look into the engine.

He pursed his lips in thought. "Call it...two hundred bucks?"

I raised one eyebrow. "Two hundred is a little steep. You said yourself you can't get it going. I'll take it, and the parts, for one fifty," I bartered, knowing I would pay the two hundred and it would still be cheap as anything.

He rolled his eyes. "One seventy-five?"

I nodded. "One seventy-five it is then. You think I could maybe fix it up here? I won't be any trouble; I'll stay out of the way, I promise. It's just, I don't have anywhere to do this..." That was a lie, I could easily get the truck to Brett's warehouse, but I didn't want to owe him anything.

"Sure, why not," he agreed

"Awesome. I'm Jamie, by the way." I stuck out my hand to him.

"Connor," he replied, shaking it.

After paying for the truck, I made arrangements to come back the following day to make a start. On the way back to the hellhole that I now called home, I grabbed a sandwich from the corner store. As I headed into the building I ensured I steered clear of the drug dealer and the two prostitutes who had set up camp outside the door.

★ ★ ★

The next couple of days passed quickly. Other than a quick visit to my parole officer the day after my release, the rest of my time was mostly spent down at the junkyard; I was doing extremely well with the car. Connor was a likable guy; at twenty-one, he was fairly close to my age, as I'd guessed. His dad owned the yard, and Connor ran it for him most of the time. The day I finally finished fixing up my pickup, I was more than a little proud of myself.

Connor sauntered out of the office, carrying two steaming mugs of coffee. "I can't believe you did this. I tried with this one. I'm pretty good with cars, but this one was dead."

I took a sip, wincing at the slight burn on my tongue. "You know, I could have a look at the others if you want. Maybe fix them up so you can sell them?" I offered. I'd been thinking about this a lot recently.

He frowned skeptically. "Yeah? And what would you get out of that?"

I shrugged. "What would you sell them for in the state that they're in?"

His lips pursed as he thought about it. "I don't know. Hardly anything. No one's crazy enough to buy a car that doesn't work. Present company excluded, of course," he joked, laughing.

"Okay, well how about this: I fix them up, you sell them, and I get half of the profit," I suggested.

"Half?" he repeated.

"Only half of the profit," I clarified. "So, for example, if you buy the car for a hundred bucks and sell it for two, then I'll get fifty. That way you're still making more than you normally would and I get some, too. Plus, they won't just be worth two hundred when I'm done; you'll probably sell them for closer to four or five hundred."

"Um...I'm not sure, Jamie. I like the idea, but I'm not sure how feasible it is. We've never been into selling working cars, only parts."

"Tell you what, how about a trial run?" I looked around and pointed at the car that, in my opinion, needed the least work to get going. "It'll take me a couple of days to get it running but if I do, how about you stick it in the auction next week and see what happens?" I offered hopefully.

He frowned over at the car. "I don't know, I'm not sure my dad will be into the idea."

I shrugged. "What do you have to lose? If it doesn't sell, then it doesn't sell."

He chewed on his lip, obviously thinking about it before he finally nodded and stuck out his hand to me. "All right, deal."

I grinned, shaking his hand. "Deal!" I hoped with everything inside me that this worked out. I'd get to fix cars and make money at the same time.

"Wanna go for a drink tonight?" Connor offered, sipping his coffee.

"Sure, I'd like that." It was nice to have someone to talk to, and I could certainly use a drinking partner.

Just as I was about to arrange the details, my cell phone rang. Other than Connor, only two people had the number: Brett and Ray. I pulled the phone from my pocket roughly, hoping for it to be Ray. Unfortunately, it wasn't.

"Hey, Brett," I answered, forcing politeness.

"Hey, Kid. I'm just about to send you the list for tomorrow night. Be at the warehouse at nine. I've done the scouting, so it should be easy."

"Sure. See you then," I answered, ending the call, cussing under my breath.

"Problem?" Connor inquired.

I shook my head quickly. "Nothing I can't handle." I was trying desperately not to look forward to tomorrow night, but I just couldn't help it. The thought of doing a boost was growing more appealing every day. The high I got from boosting was one of the only pleasurable things I'd ever had in life, and I'd missed it.

My phone beeped with a new message, so I opened it, eager to see the list of cars I was to steal. I stared at the screen, shocked. The excitement that I was trying to keep at bay was bubbling over as I looked at the last car on the list.

1. Audi R8 Spyder
2. Alfa Romeo 8C Competizione
3. BMW Z4
4. Porsche Carrera GT
5. Bugatti Veyron

I laughed in disbelief. I was in real trouble. A Bugatti Veyron was an amazing car, and the price alone was enough to make me weak at the knees. They cost a cool $1.7 million. Even the Alfa Romeo was pretty rare. This boost would be incredible. I could feel myself being sucked back in at the thought of driving them.

Later that night I went for a couple of drinks with Connor. It was good to let loose for a bit. But when he spotted a couple of people he knew and proceeded to try to hook me up with one of his friends, I made my excuses and left, going home to my empty room. It wasn't that I wasn't interested in girls, I just wasn't looking to get into anything with anyone. Not again.

I'd had experience, quite considerable experience, before I was sent down. Though only fourteen, I'd caught the eye of Star—not her real name, I'm sure, but that's what she called herself. She'd been older than me and liked to hang around near the workshop, flirting with Brett's staff. Some girls were just attracted to bad boys, or so she'd told me. At seventeen she'd held my hand and shown me the dos and don'ts of sex—though, with her, there were more dos than don'ts. Being a fourteen-year-old boy, full of hormones and exhilarating car-boosting highs, I'd casually hooked up with her…a lot. It was good for a while, until one day I'd overheard her talking to a group of her girlfriends about my body while they all speculated about what had happened to me. Girls can be fucking cruel sometimes. Thanks to Star and her bitchy friends, my already low confidence crashed through the floor and I decided I would never suffer that humiliating experience again.

So that was it for me, no more hooking up. Period.

From then on I rebuffed all advances from the opposite sex and vowed that I always would because my past was clear across my skin, and I didn't want anyone else to see it and ask about it. No one knew the truth, and I wanted to keep it that way.

CHAPTER 3

WHEN I ARRIVED at the warehouse the following night, my insides swam with excitement. As I walked in, I saw Shaun sitting there with another guy I recognized from when I used to work for Brett.

"Hey, Enzo," I greeted him warmly. Enzo had been on a lot of boosts with me in the past.

"Hey, Kid," he replied, getting up and slapping me on the back. It was incredibly easy to fit back in with these guys because they didn't care where I'd been or what I'd done; it was just easy acceptance.

"You on with me tonight?" I asked, looking around for anyone else.

"Yeah. I'm driving, and Shaun, José, Aaron, and Steve are with you," he answered, rubbing his hands together excitedly.

Shaun's with me? Great, well tonight's going to be fun then...

I looked at Shaun. He had a cut over the bridge of his nose and two fading black eyes from where I'd punched him. "Awesome. What happened to your face, Shaun? Looks bad," I teased, smirking at him.

He stood up, glaring warningly. "That's two, Kid. You won't get three."

"No, trust me, you don't want three." I snorted, shrugging and turning away from him. If Shaun wanted to attack me he wouldn't do it from behind, that was a code we had around here. If you wanted to start something, you had to be man enough to do it face-to-face. "Hey, where's my package?" I called over to Ray. He pointed to his desk so I stalked over to it and grabbed the manila envelope, ripping it open and sitting down to read it through.

Inside were all the details of the boost: the location of each car, the owner's routine, and any security on the cars that could be easily viewed by walking past, such as alarms and immobilizers. There were also photos of each car. I stopped at the Bugatti. It was incredible, and my hands started to sweat just at the thought of it. It was a beautiful one too, black with red doors, not even your run-of-the-mill showroom car, this one was custom made. Even the Porsche was sleek, classy, and probably priced at over four hundred thousand.

"You see this list?" I asked Ray.

He grinned. "Hell yeah I saw it. I can't fucking wait. Don't scratch that Bugatti, Kid; I want to see it in all its perfect glory. I've never seen a real one," he gushed.

"I won't scratch it. What do you think I am, some sort of half-baked idiot like Shaun?" I asked, grinning, making Ray laugh. From the corner of my eye I could see Shaun staring at me like he wanted to rip my head off.

At nine o'clock, Brett came down and slung his arm around my shoulder. "I appreciate you agreeing to this, Kid. We haven't been able to go after cars like this since you've been gone. This is an extremely big score, as you can probably see from the list." He squeezed my shoulder affectionately.

"Sure, Brett. This is it though, right?" I checked. His cell phone rang before he could answer, and he turned away to take the call, talking quickly. I frowned, hoping that he'd keep his word and I would be allowed out after this boost.

He turned back to me a minute later. "Right then, boys, get going. Do them in whatever order you want; I don't care as long as they all get here tonight. I have a couple of transporters coming to pick them up at six o'clock," he instructed, patting me on the shoulder before disappearing up the stairs.

"You have my old stuff, Ray?" I asked.

He nodded and headed to his desk, pulling out the gray duffel bag that contained my "car-stealing kit," I guess you could call it. I rifled through the bag, checking that everything was in there, and then nodded to Enzo, who led us to his car. I jumped in the front, making Shaun, José, Aaron, and Steve all squeeze into the backseat.

"So, what order are we doing them in?" Enzo asked, starting the engine.

I shrugged. "Let's just go to the closest first. As long as the Bugatti's last, I don't care." I hated that I was so excited to be boosting again.

Enzo pulled out and headed to the nearest car, the BMW Z4. He parked a couple of spaces away, and I turned to face the guys in the back. "I'll drive it a few streets away. Shaun, you can take it back to Brett's," I ordered.

He frowned, obviously not liking being told what to do. "I want the Alfa Romeo," he retorted angrily.

I raised one eyebrow at his attitude. "I don't give a flying fuck what you want. I don't want you near me any longer; I can feel your stupidity lowering my IQ with every passing second. I need you away from me as soon as possible, before I forget how to tie my shoes." I smirked at him, making Enzo and Aaron laugh.

"Cocky little shit," Shaun growled.

I ignored him and jumped out, looking around cautiously at the dimly lit, deserted street. As quietly as possible, I made my way over to the car, selecting my window bar from my bag. As I stopped next to the Z4, I shoved the bar down the side of the window and caught the locking mechanism, swiftly pulling the bar back out. My heart was crashing in my chest, and I couldn't keep the smile off my face. I jumped in and quickly disabled the immobilizer. There was a steering wheel lock, so I grabbed my slide hammer and shoved it in, slamming my hand on the end to release the lock. As it clicked free, I pulled it off and threw it on the seat next to me before yanking off the steering column. Wire cutters made quick work of the sheath of plastic that covered the internal wire, so I sparked the metal fibers together, grinning as the car came to life with a sexy little growl.

As soon as the engine purred, my excitement ramped up. I'd missed this so much—the high, the rush, the knowing that I was so skilled at something that I wouldn't get caught. This car was a thing of beauty, but on the scale of what I was doing tonight, it was probably ranked number five, which was why I was giving it to Shaun. I knew he'd want one of the better cars, and I had just wanted to piss him off some more.

I sped down the road, turning my lights on when I was safely off the street, and pulled over after a couple of minutes. I left the car running and jumped out, watching as Shaun climbed out of Enzo's car.

"Try not to scratch it," I teased, strutting back to the other car.

José grinned at me as I climbed into the passenger side. "Kid, I forgot how kickass you are at this. That was incredible. Immobilizer *and* steering lock in less than a minute," he enthused, looking at me in awe.

I shrugged, ignoring the thrill running through my veins. "Let's get to the next one."

The second and third cars went the same as the first. No surprises. Easy. Steve and José drove those two back to the warehouse. The fourth car was a piece of cake, considering the team had found out the VIN for it and had simply purchased a new key from one of their contacts in the Porsche dealership in town. It was almost a waste of my time, as one of the other boys could have done that on his own.

The fifth one was what I was waiting for. The car of my dreams.

Enzo pulled up outside the warehouse where the Bugatti was being stored and turned toward me, killing the engine. "See you after, then. Good luck."

I slipped on a pair of latex gloves and pulled up the hood of my jacket, covering my head. There were security cameras here that I'd have to disable. This car required a lot more effort than the others, but nothing I hadn't done plenty of times before. "I don't need luck," I told him confidently. "Wait until I'm out, then meet me back at the warehouse."

Shouldering my bag, I quickly climbed out of the car and ran over to the electrical box on the other side of the street. Once I reached it, I grabbed my dent puller, shoving it into the lock of the box and pulling it. The lock popped out, clanging to the ground at my feet. After prying off the protective metal lid, I looked inside the box. Hundreds of wires crisscrossed and trailed across it, all fused in to little connectors. This box alone controlled the electrical flow for a four-block radius.

I dropped my bag on the ground and pulled out a detailed drawing of the inside of the box. Brett had people everywhere, so it was easy for him to get hold of things like schematics for the utility grid. After checking the plans, I quickly found the wires that controlled the warehouse across the street and cut them cleanly. I glanced up just in time to see the lights go off in the parking lot and the cameras stop moving. I'd probably have about two and a half minutes before the generator kicked in. I shoved the cover back on the box, ramming a screwdriver in the side and bending the metal so it would stay in place and not fall off.

I sprinted over to the fence and looked up at the security camera, praying that it was off. It wasn't making the slow sweep across the lot like it should be and the red light wasn't flickering, so I knew I was safe. I grinned triumphantly. *Too fucking easy.* I made my way to the warehouse door, shoving the dent puller into the lock, then yanking it out and letting it drop to the concrete floor. There wasn't much need to be careful here, and I had to be fast. Once inside, I shined my flashlight on the alarm system mounted on the wall before cutting the wires at the bottom and attaching the code breaker machine to it. My toe tapped on the floor, counting the seconds as I waited for the little machine to go through the thousands of combinations to find the matching six-digit code. I needed the code in order to open the garage door, otherwise when I raised it all hell would break loose, and the alarms would wake the whole damn neighborhood.

As I waited, I glanced around the warehouse, waving my flashlight so I could see. Brand-new cars were parked everywhere, but I couldn't take my eyes off the Bugatti. The light bounced off the black-and-red paint job, the beam sparkling against the window. It was truly a thing of beauty. My palms were growing slick inside the latex gloves; I was desperate to touch it, smell that new car smell, and slide my ass into the luxurious leather seat.

Finally the code was found, so I tapped it in and the light turned green. I headed to the roller door and lifted it up so I could get the car out. I held my breath as I jogged over to the car, so excited that my stomach was clenching with nervous anticipation.

Unable to resist touching it, I took off one of the gloves and ran my hand over the hood lovingly, feeling the slick paint job under my fingers. It was perfect.

I forced myself to stop admiring it and shoved the bar down the side of the window, unlocking it easily and climbing in. After disabling the alarm, I eased the plastic covering off the dash and used my wire cutters to carefully slice through the exposed wires. Reaching into my pocket, I pulled out the code breaker and attached it to the wires. The Bugatti started by a button that was activated only when the door was opened with a special chipped key card—which, of course, I didn't have. Without the ignition activated, this car was a $1.7 million useless lump of metal. I left the code breaker to do its thing while I checked all over for a kill switch. Nervously, I glanced at my watch; by my calculation, I had about thirty seconds left before the generator kicked in and the security cameras came back on. When the code finally worked, I pressed the ignition button and heard the little purr of the engine.

I whooped like a little kid and slid into the driver's seat. My breath came out as a low groan of appreciation as my hands gripped the leather wheel. Tentatively, I put my foot down on the gas. The car lurched forward, making the hair on the back of my neck stand up as the force pressed my body back into the softness of the seat. As soon as I was outside, I stopped and jumped out, running back to the roller door and pulling it shut. That way, when the cameras kicked back on, there was a good chance that any security guards that had access to the video feed wouldn't see anything amiss or notice that the car was gone until morning.

I jumped back in the car and sped off down the road, not bothering to wait for Enzo; he'd just meet me back at Brett's. "Shit yeah!" I shouted excitedly.

The interior of the car was red leather; the smell of it was intoxicating. I ran my hands over the wheel lovingly as I drove. The forty-minute drive was way too short, in my opinion, and I was devastated when I pulled in.

Ray was practically bouncing on the spot as he looked at the car through teary eyes. He traced his hand across the top. "Oh, baby, Daddy loves you so much," he purred, making me and the rest of the guys laugh. Ray was almost as car mad as me.

Brett slapped me on the back, beaming proudly. "You still got it, Kid."

"Yeah, I still got it," I admitted. I knew I was good at this; I didn't need to be told. I had a certain knack for stealing cars. Ray had once joked I was a car whisperer, coaxing them to start when no one else could. It definitely made me proud to know I was explicitly good at something—that was where most of my high came from. I'd never been good at anything else, but stealing cars was something it felt like I was almost destined to do.

"Here." Brett held out a thick manila envelope that I knew would be filled with five thousand bucks, my old nightly fee.

"Thanks." I nodded, turning the envelope over in my hands, appreciatively feeling the weight of it.

"Money tempting you back in?" he asked, grinning wolfishly.

I shook my head in response and shrugged. "It's just money, it don't mean shit to me anymore."

He gripped my shoulder, regarding me as if I'd lost my mind. "Look, Kid, you know you won't be able to get a job now, don't you? This is it, this is your life, and you're damn good at it. You sure you want to leave all this?"

No, this wasn't my life; that life ended four years ago. This was my new chance. I just needed to stay strong.

"I'm sure." I stepped away from him, hoping he'd be true to his word and let me go now that the job was done.

He sighed deeply. "Well, if you change your mind about the

boosts, you know I'm always here. Maybe you could do the occasional job?"

I would love to do that, but I knew that if I kept doing it I wouldn't be able to stop. I could feel the pull already. "I don't think so." I pulled out the cell phone he'd given me and held it out to him.

He shook his head in rejection. "You keep it. I've got plenty of them. That way I can call you from time to time and see how you're getting on. Why don't you stop down at the club tomorrow night and check it out, first round of drinks is on the house."

"Sure, that'd be great," I agreed.

After saying my good-byes, I made my way back to my place. It was after four in the morning already. My bed looked so incredibly inviting that I flopped down onto it as the exhaustion took over. I didn't even bother to change out of my clothes or take off my shoes. The boost was done, my debt was paid, so now I was free to start over with Brett's blessing. Just as I fell asleep, I couldn't help but wonder if I could ever truly be free, though. Would I always feel the call to the adrenaline rush of a boost? Could anybody ever defy their destiny? I wasn't sure, but I was damned well going to try.

* * *

The next night I took Brett up on his offer of free drinks at his club, and met up with Ray. I'd already had a tour of the club from Brett and was happily downing my fifth drink when Ray nudged me in the ribs.

"Holy shit, look at that!" he hissed, staring at something over my shoulder. I turned and spotted a pretty blonde with extremely long legs and a short skirt.

I laughed. "She's too young for you, married man."

He rolled his eyes. "Yeah, but she's perfect for you," he enthused.

"Nah, not my type at all," I shot back, shrugging. In total honesty, I tried not to look at girls too much; I didn't want to start thinking about what I was missing out on.

"Kid, seriously, you need to go hook up with that girl, because wow, seriously, *wow*." He was still ogling her, totally fucking her with his eyes.

"She's not that hot." I glanced over at her again, taking another sip of my drink.

The blonde was now standing and laughing with another girl. I almost choked on my drink as I looked the other girl over. She had long, curly red hair that hung around her flawless face. Her nose wrinkled as she rolled her eyes, pushing her friend playfully as they both laughed at something. This girl was stunningly beautiful. The little black dress that she was wearing clung to her perfectly sculpted body, showing off all of her curves, but in a classy way that made my mouth water and my hand itch to trace up the side of her leg.

Now she's *hot!*

I couldn't take my eyes off her; I'd never wanted a girl more in my life.

CHAPTER 4

ELLIE

I GLANCED AT myself in the mirror, squinting through the haze of alcohol that clouded my brain. The girl that squinted back at me looked a mess, even to my own eyes. Bending down, I wet my hands with cold water and then touched my cooled fingers to my cheeks, trying to calm myself a little. My head felt fuzzy and my stomach still quivered, even though I'd just emptied it into the toilet behind me.

When my heart had slowed down to a normal pace again, I looked back into the mirror at myself, rubbing a finger under each of my gray eyes to wipe away the mascara smudges. My usually pale skin looked even paler in the seedy light of the club bathrooms. The only decent thing that I could see about myself was my hair. Somehow, even though I'd stood in the chilly wind for almost an hour to get into the club and then proceeded to whip it around while dancing for the last few hours, it still held a lot of the loose curls that I'd teased in with the curling iron earlier in the night.

I hiccupped and quickly held my breath, wondering if I was going to vomit again. I couldn't hold my liquor at all, and even though I wasn't old enough to be in the club anyway, I'd been dragged out tonight by Stacey and a couple of other friends who thought tonight was a great time to test out the fake IDs we'd recently purchased. According to them, the timing was perfect because, apparently, I needed a girls' night out to help me get over my broken heart. Well, they all *thought* I was brokenhearted—my friends were actually more upset about my breakup than I was.

I tried not to let my thoughts drift to Miles, but I just couldn't help it. As I looked at the short, slinky black dress that Stacey had insisted I borrow from her and wear tonight, I silently wondered what he would say about it if he could see me now. No doubt he'd have a few choice words for me. In fact, he would have insisted I change and said I looked like a slut.

Things hadn't started out like that between us, though. At the beginning of our two-and-a-half-year relationship he'd been sweet and would go out of his way to make me laugh. Unfortunately, things had changed after a while; he'd become more concerned about status and image and less like the sweet boy I'd fallen for. By the end, I was pretty sure I was nothing more than a trophy girlfriend to him, something to hang on his arm and make him look good. I was everything society—and his parents—thought he should have to complete him. On the outside our relationship was perfection, love's young dream. Inside, not so much.

In all honesty, Miles could be a real jerk when no one else was around. After a year of dating he'd turned from cute, thoughtful, slightly lanky kid to overbearing, possessive captain of the football team and every girl's desired man. I didn't think he knew he was being controlling or possessive of me; when he'd belittled me, I didn't think he did it with vicious intent, it was just the way he was. He wanted to be respected, he wanted people to look up to him, and that meant everything had to be his version of perfect.

Reputation was everything to Miles—but I'd finally grown

tired of it yesterday. So when he'd accused me of flirting with one of his teammates at last night's postgame party, shouting at me in front of several of the attendees, ruining his own perfectly carved façade, I'd seized the opportunity and broken it off with him in front of them, knowing the story would spread around the school like wildfire and I wouldn't be pressured into taking him back.

It was a relief; it had been exhausting walking on eggshells all the time, trying to be the perfect girl he wanted and not upset him. I actually couldn't be happier about the breakup. Since I was fifteen I'd been one half of "Miles and Ellie, super couple," and I couldn't wait to find out what it was like just being Ellie.

I smiled to myself just as the bathroom door opened behind me, the drone of music growing louder for a couple of seconds before it swung closed again. I looked over my shoulder in the mirror and smiled as Stacey frowned over at me. "Ellie Pearce! I've been looking everywhere for you," she slurred accusingly.

I giggled and rolled my eyes, turning to face her but still keeping my grip on the sink in case my stomach took another nose dive. "Oh, really? I wasn't in that guy's mouth?"

She chuckled sheepishly. "Surprisingly not, but I had a good look." She winked at me. I shook my head at her fondly. Stacey liked to hook up a lot when she was single. I, on the other hand, had only ever been with Miles and had never even kissed anyone else.

"I just threw up." I admitted, swallowing a couple of times at the memory.

"Ew! Here, have a mint." She giggled, passing me a tin; I gratefully took one, trying to get the horrible taste out of my mouth. "Come on, come and dance. Maybe you should hook up with someone tonight to take your mind off Miles. It'll help you get over him," she said sympathetically.

I sighed. I'd never told anyone what Miles was actually like, so everyone truly thought we had been the perfect couple. Stacey really did think I was devastated at the breakup. It was easier to let her believe that than explain that Miles wasn't all everyone thought he was. "Okay, I'll dance, but I'm not hooking up with anyone."

"Whatevs. I'm thirsty, let's get another drink, then we can go find the others." Her hand gripped mine as we walked out of the bathroom.

As soon as the door opened again the volume of the club music made my head throb. The place was dark, hot, and extremely crowded. I couldn't really see where I was going and everything was just a mass of bodies grinding up against each other. I let Stacey lead me blindly along and prayed that she could remember the layout of the club, because I sure couldn't. Finally, after two pinches to my behind and one crude, suggestive comment, we made it through the crowd to the bar and I felt as if I could breathe again.

Stacey grinned wickedly at me before turning to the bar. "Hi, can I get four vodka shots?" she shouted to the bartender, who was totally checking her out. Stacey was what you'd call a stunner. She had long, natural blonde hair, blue eyes, and legs that seemed to go on forever; she modeled part-time and actually made decent money from it.

"You can get anything you want," he replied, grinning. She leaned in suggestively and started flirting with him.

Not particularly wanting to see her get her flirt on, I turned away and looked around the packed club. She'd already dumped me three times tonight to make out with different guys, so I knew how this exchange would probably go down. I didn't mind, though; she truly was a great friend, and I wouldn't change her for the world. She was in a relationship that was constantly on and off, so when it was off she let loose and flirted her butt off.

Feeling a nudge to my arm, I turned and Stacey handed me two shot glasses. Not wanting to hold two drinks, I downed one immediately, wincing as the colorless liquid burned my throat. I shuddered, grimacing at the vile taste.

"I hope that's not your sex face," a voice purred in my ear. Whipping my head around, I locked eyes with a guy who was probably in his late twenties. He was quite good-looking—if you liked the older-guy look.

"Well, you won't find out," I replied, turning to grab Stacey's hand, meaning to pull her away, but she was too busy flirting with the bartender again.

"My name's Sam. Remember it, you'll be screaming it later." The guy smirked and winked at me confidently as he put his hand on the small of my back, leaning in. I could smell the alcohol on his breath as it blew across my face.

Yuck, as if! "I don't think so." I shied away from his hand, getting a little personal space back.

He laughed, his blue eyes twinkling. "What's your name?" He grinned at me lopsidedly, obviously not knowing how to take a hint.

"Look, I'm not interested, so just go find another girl to flirt with, okay?" I suggested, frowning. I really didn't need this right now. All I wanted was a lovely, comfy bed to climb into and maybe the pizza that Stacey had promised would come later in the night.

Mr. I Don't Know How to Take a Hint laughed again and stepped closer to me, making me step back so that our bodies didn't brush together. "Don't be like that. I could make you feel better," he flirted, his eyes dropping to my chest. I looked around uncomfortably for some sort of escape plan, but Stacey was still leaning over the bar talking animatedly to the barman.

Suddenly a heavy arm slipped around my shoulder. "Hey,

babe, there you are. Sorry I'm late." Male, unquestionably a male—with a decidedly sexy voice to boot!

I looked up, shocked, because I was now pinned against a stranger's side. As soon as I laid eyes on him my heart took off in double time. The new arrival was the most gorgeous man I'd ever seen in real life. A quick estimate put him at about twenty-one; he had short brown hair shaven into a buzz cut, a chiseled chin, perfect kissable lips, and dark brown eyes that sparkled mysteriously. Where I was pressed against him, I could feel hard, taut muscles. I took all this in quickly and all I could think was: *Wow*.

My mouth was dry as I struggled to remember how to string words together in a coherent sentence. "Uh, yeah, no problem, you're here now," I mumbled, playing along.

I couldn't take my eyes off him as he turned his head to the side, smiling and holding out his right hand to the guy who'd been hitting on me seconds before. "Hey, I'm Jamie. You a friend of my girlfriend's?" he asked.

From the corner of my eye, I noticed Sam step back and shake his head, but I couldn't tear my gaze from the beautiful boy who was still pinning me close to his side. "Nah, man, we were just talking. I'd better go find my friends," he said quickly before skulking off into the crowd.

Almost instantly the new guy lifted his arm off my shoulder and smiled down at me, exposing a row of perfectly straight white teeth. His smile was incredibly sexy and caused a little dimple to form on his right cheek. I fought hard against my urge to trace that little indent with my finger.

I smiled back gratefully. "Thanks."

"No probs, you looked like you were having trouble getting rid of him," he said easily. "I'm Jamie." He bent down slightly to talk to me; that was when I noted how tall he was. He was easily six foot one, much taller than my five foot five. I was wearing three-inch heels, yet he still towered over me. I quite liked the way he made me feel small.

"Ellie," I muttered, trying to pry my eyes away from his face.

"What you drinking there, Ellie?" he asked, nodding at my drink.

"Um...I think it's vodka." I frowned at it distastefully. He grinned that little dimpled smile again and his hand gripped my elbow, tugging me gently toward the bar, where he proceeded to order two more vodka shots. I winced, knowing I needed to drink the one I already had so that I didn't look rude by refusing his drink. Holding my breath, I chugged down the other one Stacey had purchased before pushing the empty glass onto the bar.

Jamie turned back and passed me another shot glass of clear liquid. He raised his glass at me in silent cheers before downing the contents. I gulped and then did the same with mine. I genuinely didn't want to drink any more. Already I felt a bit weightless, which meant I'd drunk more than enough to make my head pound in the morning. I silently prayed I didn't throw up again tonight.

Behind Jamie, Stacey was staring at me with wide eyes. She dramatically fanned her face while mouthing the word *hot* as she nodded at Jamie's back. I giggled and nodded in agreement.

Jamie smiled and leaned in closer to me, his hot breath fanning across my face as he spoke. "Wanna dance?"

I didn't even need to think about that one. Hell yeah I wanted to dance with him; then I would have the perfect opportunity to touch his body without making myself look like a deranged pervert who felt up hot guys in clubs for a hobby.

"Sure, why not." I looked at him through my eyelashes, flirting my ass off.

He grinned and his hand covered mine. It was warm and fairly rough, like he worked hard for a living. Without saying anything else, he turned and pulled me close to his back as he started to weave through the crowd.

The dance floor was packed with bodies everywhere making it extremely hot and humid as he stepped up close to me. His smell filled my senses: manly, rugged, and kind of woodsy. My eyes slid over him as we started to dance. He had on low-slung ripped jeans and a checked red button-down shirt that he wore slightly open at the top and bottom, the sleeves rolled up to his elbows. I felt someone dancing close to me from behind, but before I could react, Jamie reached out, gripping my hips and pulling me forward into his body. He frowned, his hands still resting on my hips almost possessively. Flicking a quick glance over my shoulder, I saw a guy dancing behind me, his eyes glued to my ass. Inwardly, I cursed the borrowed dress.

The song changed, and when I realized what it was, I felt a grin slip onto my face as the beat took over, weaving its spell on me. Closing my eyes, I started dancing properly, grinding into Jamie and swaying my hips to the sexy drumbeat of the familiar song. My chest was rubbing against his, making my scalp prickle and butterflies swoop in my stomach. His hands moved from my hips to my back, one of them sneakily trailing down to rest on my behind. I took my chance to press my face into the side of his neck, breathing in his delicious scent. He genuinely smelled good enough to eat.

I pulled back to peek at him. The flashing green lights of the club danced across his face, making him look inhumanly beautiful as his dark, brooding eyes locked onto mine. I could easily have been dreaming up this moment because this guy just looked too good to be true.

Slowly, his head moved toward mine, his lips brushing against mine gently, so gently, in fact, that I barely even felt it. He pulled back and looked at me curiously, as if waiting for my permission to continue. Lust was written clearly across his face. My body was burning at the sight of it. My stomach flipped. I'd probably never been this excited by a guy, ever. Miles had never made me feel like this. It was almost as if I wasn't in control of myself, like some force was guiding me along, making me press closer to him, making me trace my hands up his hard chest to loop around his neck. That force, though, was, of course, just my raging and uncontrollable hormones.

When my palm rubbed against his short hair, I moaned breathily at the soft, silky feel of it. I knew right then and there that I could do that all night long and still not get tired of it. He shivered against me. The movement made my breath catch in my throat as I eagerly guided his mouth back down toward mine again.

As his lips touched mine, I felt something deep in my stomach: a longing, a burning need, and it was spreading to every part of my body as the kiss deepened. His kissing was demanding, masterful, and sexy as hell. If I hadn't been hot for him before, I undoubtedly was now.

He pulled out of the kiss too soon. "Wanna go somewhere?" he asked huskily.

My body stiffened at his question. I'd broken up with my long-term boyfriend only yesterday; I couldn't go and have a one-night stand with a sexy-ass stranger . . . could I? Looking at him, I desperately wanted to. This was my chance, the perfect opportunity to do something a little wild for once in my life, to do something just for me instead of what was expected of me. My hormones were urging me forward.

Should I?

He seemed to sense my indecision and shook his head, smiling apologetically. "Sorry, I shouldn't have asked." His hand moved off my ass to rest on the small of my back, holding me against him as if he thought I would slap him and run away any second.

Before I could speak, or even figure out what I wanted to say, he pressed his lips to mine again, tangling one hand into the back of my hair as he pulled me closer to him.

My body was about ready to spontaneously combust...and my mind was made up. I'd be bold for once, daring, instead of the goody two-shoes I usually was. I broke the kiss and quickly stepped back, taking his hand and heading toward the exit. I almost ached with anticipation of what was to come tonight. After a second he obviously caught on to my intentions. His hand moved in mine, adjusting so that his fingers interlocked with mine more intimately. As I stalked toward the doors that led to the lobby beyond, I pulled out my phone from my cleavage and dialed Stacey. I knew she'd answer. It was one of the girls' rules for when we went out; the phone *had* to go down the cleavage so that we could feel it vibrate if we needed one another.

"Hey, girl, where are you?" I heard her shout through the earpiece.

I smiled, knowing she was going to freak out any second. "I'm leaving, I'll see you later. Stay with the girls, Stace, and don't drive for goodness' sake."

She gasped. "You're leaving? With that sexy-ass boy?"

"Yeah. I'll speak to you later." I disconnected the call, grinning as excitement and lust simmered in my tummy.

Jamie's hand tightened around mine as he pulled me to a stop by the coat check, handing over his ticket. Moments later, the lady gave him a black leather jacket. "You have one?" he asked me, pointing to the desk. I shook my head in response. None of us girls had brought coats; one of my friends had had the stupid idea that our fake IDs would be less likely to be questioned if we were showing a little skin...I was about to suffer for that decision.

Jamie frowned at that but didn't say anything as he turned and started leading me toward the exit. When we stepped outside, the cold midnight air whipped around me, making me shiver. Jamie immediately slipped his jacket around my shoulders, engulfing me in his smell again. I smiled gratefully.

There was a taxi stand at the corner in front of the club so we made our way over to it, standing there and waiting. Thankfully, we were the only ones there, so as soon as a cab pulled up we could jump in and get out of the wind.

"Can we go to your place?" he asked, pulling me close to him and starting to rub my arms to keep me warm.

Mine? No way that can happen, my parents would skin both of us alive! I shook my head. "Can't, I have a little sister," I said, desperately trying to think of somewhere we could go.

He looked thoughtful for a few seconds, then he cringed, cocking his head to the side. "We can go to mine, but it's really not a nice place. I mean, it's a rooming house, I've only been there for a week." He shrugged, looking embarrassed and uncomfortable.

"That's okay, whatever." In complete honesty, as long as I got to do some of the naughty things that were running through my head, I would probably go anywhere with him. I pulled him to me and kissed him. The kiss was getting hotter and hotter, but, annoyingly, a cab pulled up at that moment, interrupting the intense make-out session. Jamie stepped back, smiling as he opened the car door.

"Ladies first," he offered, motioning for me to climb inside. The gentlemanly gesture made my insides melt to a puddle. I slipped into the cab, scooting over to the middle but purposefully not allowing him too much space to sit down so I could still touch him.

He smiled that dimpled smile as he climbed in and leaned forward, telling the driver his address. When he settled back on the seat next to me I smiled, hoping I would look seductive and tempting. His perfectly straight teeth clamped down on his bottom lip, and I felt my tummy flutter as he shifted closer to me, his eyes locked on my mouth, his intention clear.

Before our lips connected, though, he abruptly pulled back, his eyes widening. "Oh, shit, I don't have anything, you have anything?"

"'Anything'? Like what, an STD or something?" I asked, a little shocked at his question.

"A condom," he clarified, grinning at me, obviously trying not to laugh.

I burst out laughing and blushed at my embarrassing stupidity. "Right, well no, I don't have *anything*," I replied, putting plenty of emphasis on the last word, giving it a double meaning. He laughed too and shook his head before leaning forward and relaying more instructions to the driver.

Shortly after, the cab stopped at a gas station, where Jamie jumped out and bought what I presumed to be condoms. When he was settled back at my side again, he rested his arm over my shoulder. "So, I haven't seen you at that club before. Do you go there a lot?" he asked, cocking his head to the side curiously, looking adorable.

I shook my head. "No, I'm not old enough. My friends dragged me there tonight because I'm mending a broken heart, apparently," I answered, rolling my eyes. I didn't realize at first, but he'd jumped away from me as if I'd just confessed to having the plague. He was looking at me with wide, horrified eyes. I had no idea what I'd said to warrant that reaction. "What's wrong? Don't worry, I don't really have a broken heart. Not that it matters to you anyway, but at least I get to have hot rebound sex, right?" I said, giggling at how slutty that made me sound. He was just staring at me, unmoving. "What?"

He pressed back against his door, running a shaky hand over the back of his short hair. "You're not old enough to get into the club? Please tell me you're not like thirteen or something."

I grinned wickedly, now catching on to his horror. He thought I was underage. "I'm seventeen; I'll be eighteen in three months."

He blew out a big breath, looking extremely relieved. "Thank Christ for that, I thought when you said . . . Oh, never mind."

"Well, how old are you?" He had to be over twenty-one to get into the club, but I wouldn't have thought he was much older than that at all. Maybe he'd even used a fake ID, like I had.

"I'm eighteen," he answered, grinning as he took my hand and pulled it into his lap.

"You are? You look older. I bet you get that a lot, huh?" I asked as he played with my fingers.

He shrugged. "Occasionally, but I've never heard it from someone as beautiful as you." He leaned in and peppered little kisses on the side of my neck.

I couldn't help but laugh at his effort. "Jamie, you've got me in the cab, we've just stopped to buy condoms, and you're still trying to impress me with corny one-liners? Trust me, they're really not necessary."

He laughed quietly. "Maybe I want to try out my best lines on you," he whispered against my overheated skin, making my heart melt and my stomach get butterflies.

"Wow, that was your best line? Jeez, stud, seriously? That was the corniest damn thing I've ever heard," I teased, laughing.

He faked hurt, pulling back and setting his hand over his heart. "Ouch, Ellie, that hurts. I'm really trying over here!"

I giggled and pressed myself tighter against his side. He laughed too, and that cute little dimple reappeared in his cheek.

When the cab came to a stop outside a run-down-looking building and Jamie leaned forward to pay the driver, I quickly pulled out my phone and sent a text to Stacey with his address. I might be being bold and daring tonight, but I wasn't stupid.

As he stepped out of the cab and held the door open for me, I tried not to react to where he lived. The building was a mess, and I knew this area wasn't exactly the best. Graffiti covered almost every surface, and the windows of his building were boarded up. I gulped and flicked my eyes around. Women were hanging out on the street corner, eyeing Jamie with seductive smiles. He was glancing around quickly, seeming cautious. His shoulders were tense as he strutted away from the cab, pulling me along quickly behind him, like he didn't want to be outside too long.

Once we stepped inside the building, it got even worse. There were cracks in the walls and more graffiti, saying things I wouldn't dare say in front of my mother. There was even a homeless guy asleep on the grimy, stained floor of the hallway.

I cringed into Jamie. This clearly wasn't my brightest idea ever. "I thought you said this wasn't a nice place," I joked, making him chuckle as he hurried me up the stairs. With each step I was becoming increasingly nervous. I was starting to feel a little stupid for coming to this part of town with a complete stranger for sex. This really wasn't me. I had never done anything remotely reckless in my life; I was always the sensible one.

He stopped outside a door and set to work on the lock. When the door opened, he ushered me in first. He didn't turn on the light, but to be honest he didn't really need to; there was a streetlight directly outside his window that bathed his room in a hazy, dull glow that was just about bright enough to see by. My eyes narrowed as I glanced around the place he called home. His room was totally bare, he literally had nothing except a chair, a bed, a small side table, and a chest of drawers. There was not a single photo or anything personal to say that this room was even being used. The door clicked shut behind me and I turned in time to watch him trap us in with three locks. I gulped and couldn't help the shiver that ran through me.

Yep, definitely stupid. I'm about to get murdered, beaten, and used…and probably not in that order.

He turned to me; I wasn't sure what my expression portrayed, but even in the dimly lit room, I could see the sadness and disappointment cross his features. "You want to go? We don't have to do this. I can call you a cab," he said softly, making no move to come anywhere near me as he withdrew a cell phone from his pocket.

I briefly considered my options. If he was saying I could go, then maybe he wasn't the bad guy my wild imagination was trying to make him out to be. This place itself, all dirty and scary-looking, seemed leagues away from the cute, cheeky guy I'd flirted with in the back of the cab. My eyes lingered over his face, wandered down his strong shoulders, over his chest and to his tanned, toned-looking arms. I definitely wanted him. To say that this guy didn't turn me on something chronic would be a complete lie.

Before I chickened out, I took a step toward him. He just watched me cautiously, not moving. Looking back at his face, I realized that he actually looked incredibly nervous, too. This gave me some confidence back, so I closed the distance and pressed my body to his.

"I don't want to go, just don't hurt me or anything." I said the words jokingly but was actually serious.

He smiled, moving his hand to cup my cheek. "I won't, I promise." He brought his lips down to mine softly.

As soon as he kissed me my body started longing for him again, worse than in the club. I wrapped my arms around his neck as he gently pushed me against the wall, running his hands down my body. My skin felt set alight as my scalp prickled with sensation. When he got to the bottom of my dress, I moaned into his mouth when he slowly inched it up. His fingers left a burning trail along my body as he pulled the dress up over my head. In the back of my mind I heard my phone clatter to the floor, but I was too excited to care. After he'd dropped my dress on the floor, he pressed his body back against mine and kissed me deeply, sliding his hands down over my skin slowly, making me burn with need and writhe against him. Where he was pressed against me so tightly, I could feel his body trembling.

While he was busying himself trailing kisses across my neck and groping my ass, I unbuttoned his shirt and pushed it off his shoulders, leaving him in a skintight white undershirt that highlighted the defined muscles of his shoulders and neck. His mouth claimed mine in a kiss that was so hot I was surprised we weren't both on fire. He moaned in the back of his throat as his arms encircled me, trapping me against the wall with his hard body. Alcohol was still sloshing around in my system, urging me to do something I'd never done before, something I wouldn't dare do if I weren't wasted. *Screw it, I'll never see this guy again anyway, so it doesn't matter if I make a complete fool of myself.*

"Do you have any music?" I asked as he licked the hollow at the base of my throat.

I felt him smile against my skin. "Not really; I have a radio." Without moving away from me, he grabbed the remote control from his chest of drawers and pressed a couple of buttons.

I grinned at the sound of the heavy bass in the song that started playing, and pushed him down roughly into his chair, immediately starting to dance in front of him, moving closer so I could grind against him. His bottom lip rolled up into his mouth as his eyes narrowed, looking at me appreciatively.

I'm actually giving a guy a lap dance! This is totally not me at all!

Surprisingly, I was enjoying it, and judging by the look on his face, so was he.

"Holy shit," he grunted as I bent over in front of him, putting my behind near his face, swaying seductively as I stood back up. He raised a hand and grabbed my ass, looking at me with a pained, needy expression.

I laughed and pushed his hand away, waggling my finger in reprimand. "No touching the dancers. House rule," I joked.

"Then don't put your sexy ass in my face," he growled huskily. I giggled as I straddled him and started grinding into him, trailing my fingers down his chest, feeling the toned muscles hidden beneath his undershirt. When my fingers found his belt buckle, I unfastened it slowly. He groaned and dipped his head, kissing the side of my neck as I slid his zipper down. Suddenly his hands gripped my hips, pinning me on his lap.

"I can't take any more," he whispered, kissing me passionately.

My will to tease him was gone as soon as his lips touched mine, so I wrapped my arms and legs around him, pressing into his chest as he stood up and started toward the bed.

"Are you not turning the light on?" I mumbled against his lips.

He grinned and shook his head. "Nah. It's more romantic like this, the streetlight glow is almost as good as candles. Don't ever say I don't do romance," he joked, dipping his head and kissing me again. I giggled, tightening my hold on him as he sat me on the bed and knelt in front of me on the mattress. Smiling excitedly, I reached for the bottom of his undershirt, easing the material up and over his head.

He seemed to flinch, his muscles bunching as if I'd somehow made the wrong move.

Even in the dim light my hungry eyes practically devoured his body. Getting to my knees too, I slid my hands over his chest and down to his stomach, noticing the outlines of his toned six-pack.

He stiffened and sucked in a sharp breath as my inquiring fingers found something else, several somethings, actually. Scars. They littered his abs and chest. I trailed my fingers over them, looking down but unable to really make them out in the semidarkness.

Jamie had grown very still, watching my face, seeming remarkably unsure for some reason.

I smiled reassuringly, wondering why he would be so tense. Gripping his shoulders, I pulled him closer to me, kissing him again. He immediately thawed from his frozen state and laid us down, settling himself on top of me.

His body covered mine, pressing me into the mattress, making the bedsprings squeak from the movement. His hands wandered over my body, seeming to take their time, as if trying to touch every part of me. Finally he fumbled at my back, unclasping my bra and pulling it off slowly. His eyes darted down to my breasts and then back to my face as he smiled that cute, boyish little dimpled grin at me. I smiled back and pressed myself to him tighter, raising my head so I could kiss him again. The way he seemed a little unsure and nervous was really endearing and sweet. I could already tell that this was going to be a good night.

Jamie's mouth trailed kisses down my neck before licking and sucking on my breasts. I gasped. My whole body felt like it was on fire at his touch. Miles had never made me feel like this. I pushed my hand into his jeans pocket and pulled out the box of condoms, tossing it to the side table where he could reach it when we needed it. The way he was making me feel made me wriggle under him with an unbearable need to be closer, to feel more of him against me, to be possessed by him completely.

Slipping my hands into the back of his jeans, I pushed them down over his hips until he took the hint and kicked them off. I was breathing heavily; my heart was beating out of my chest already. Jamie kissed farther down, nipping gently at my stomach as he pulled my panties off. My body was on a slow burn, waves of pleasure radiating from everywhere he touched me.

Seeming a little hesitant, he pushed two fingers into me. I arched my back and let out a breathy moan. I felt rather than saw him smile against my stomach, and then he moved, pressing his mouth between my legs while continuing to work his fingers. My moans were already bordering on obscene but got even louder when he started using his tongue. I squeezed my eyes shut and rubbed my hands over his short, silky hair. My body was pushing forward through the stages. I couldn't keep still; I was wriggling and moaning like crazy. Out of nowhere it felt like my body exploded as I climaxed, panting his name. He chuckled and kissed his way back up to my mouth. The taste of myself on his tongue made the kiss ten times more exciting and erotic. I eagerly pulled his boxers down and looked at him. I wanted him right now, I couldn't wait any longer, the anticipation was almost killing me. I reached over and grabbed the box of condoms from his side table and ripped the plastic off, opening the box. I got one out as quickly as I could and held it out to him.

"Is someone a little eager?" He breathed against my ear, nibbling on my earlobe.

"Jamie, come on now, please," I said with a gasp.

He just laughed and kissed down my neck. "Patience, Ellie," he mumbled against my skin.

"Jamie, please," I begged again, running my hands over his back. I could feel the same scars on his back as he had on his chest. My body was aching for him in an unpleasant, needy way.

He looked at me with obvious excitement dancing in his eyes as he pulled back, kneeling on the bed. With shaky hands he fumbled with the foil packet, trying to open it. After a few seconds he gave up and ripped it open with his teeth—which I found incredibly sexy. He slipped the condom onto his shaft, rolling it down achingly slowly. Once he was done, he lay back down on top of me, nudging my legs farther apart. I pushed my hips up in invitation.

"Fuck, you're so hot," he mumbled, dipping his head, his teeth grazing the base of my throat. When he pushed inside me, I cried out and dug my fingers into his shoulders as pleasure shot through my body. The feeling of fullness was incredible. I wrapped my legs around his waist, pulling him closer, taking him inside me completely. He groaned my name, burying his face into the side of my neck, his hands clenching into fists as he stayed perfectly still.

My eyes fluttered closed and I trailed my fingers up and down his back a couple of times, listening to his labored breathing. When he finally moved his hips, we both moaned. He pulled back, his eyes locked on mine as he stroked my hair away from my face before bending and kissing me softly as he started to build up a steady rhythm. As the kiss built in intensity, so did his thrusts. My body was a bundle of sensations; all of my nerve endings seemed to be alight and throbbing with pleasure. I raised my hips to meet his, matching his rhythm thrust for thrust. The look on his face as we moved together in perfect sync was totally adoring and exhilarated.

I moved my legs up higher across his torso, lifting my bottom from the mattress. The new position allowed him in deeper and caused my eyes to roll back in my head at the sheer luxury of it. He grunted, thrusting harder so that our bodies slammed together. The sound of the mattress squeaking with every movement just seemed to add to the whole sexiness of the moment. I could feel myself getting there, I would climax soon, it was building inside me.

When he went to pull out of the kiss, I captured his bottom lip between my teeth, biting down as my fingers dug into his back, clutching him closer to me. He moaned into my mouth and kissed me almost desperately. His movements were getting more frantic, jerkier, and his breath was coming out in pants, so I knew he was close, too.

When he slid one hand between our bodies and rubbed my clit gently, I just about lost my mind. My body was going crazy, I was tingling all over, I couldn't breathe properly. I moaned his name and my body convulsed as my climax hit me like a freight train. My legs clamped tight around him and my hips jerked up roughly to meet his. He groaned, his eyes narrowed, his jaw clenched tightly, and he bent forward, kissing me roughly. His shoulders hunched, and his fingers bit into my skin as he did a couple of last gentle thrusts before he stilled completely and slumped on top of me, pinning me down on the bed with his weight. I smiled tiredly as he kissed the side of my neck. Our sweaty bodies were slick against each other; the smell of sex lingered in the hot, stuffy room.

I wrapped my arms around him weakly, feeling totally and utterly exhausted. My muscles quivered from the small effort of moving. We both just stayed there, wrapped up in each other as we caught our breath.

He pulled back after a minute or so, kissing me softly before easing out of me and pulling the condom off, throwing it into the trash can next to his bed. He rolled onto his side, reaching out his hand and pulling me against him as he slowly ran his hands down my back.

"That was incredible, Ellie," he murmured, kissing my nose. He was grinning from ear to ear as he stroked his fingers across my cheekbone.

I smiled and sighed contentedly. "Yeah, it was." And it really had been. That was incredible; he had been soft and tender, his hands seeming to explore every part of me as he'd taken my body to heaven and back again. He wrapped his arms around me, pulling me tightly against him, tangling our legs together as he just looked at every inch of my face with a small, satisfied smile on his lips.

"You don't have much stuff," I stated after we'd been silently cuddling on his bed for a couple of minutes.

He frowned. "Uh, no, I haven't even been here a week."

"Where were you living before?" I probed, wanting to hear the sound of his sexy voice some more. He shifted uncomfortably, and I took the hint that he didn't want to talk about it. "That's okay, you don't have to say." I rolled so that I was on top of him and sat up, straddling him. He ran his hands up my thighs and rested them on my hips, just watching me with a satisfied smile on his face.

I sighed. It was time to go. This was where it got a little awkward. What was I supposed to say? Thanks and good-bye? "So, I guess I should get going. Would you mind calling me a cab?" I asked, climbing off him and looking around the room for my clothes.

The bed creaked behind me. "You're going? Why?" I didn't need to look to know he would be frowning—I could hear the shock in his tone.

I smiled at him over my shoulder. He was sitting up on the bed, a little pouty expression on his face as he watched my every move. "Well, I've never had a one-night stand before, but I thought that was how it worked: You have sex and then you leave," I joked as I pulled on my panties.

He shook his head. "No, I mean, why do you have to go now? You can stay the night; I'll drive you home in the morning."

"You want me to stay the night?" I asked disbelievingly.

He pushed himself up off the bed and walked to me in all his naked glory. I couldn't keep my eyes off his body. "Yeah, I want you to stay the night," he confirmed, smiling his sexy smile at me, making my stomach flutter.

Oh, I can definitely stay the night!

I nodded in agreement, hoping I didn't look too eager. I didn't want him to think I was the clingy stalker type. "Okay, I'll just text my friend and tell her. I'm supposed to be staying at her house." I grabbed my phone from the floor where it had been carelessly abandoned in a fit of passion, and then sent a quick message to Stacey, telling her that I'd go to her place in the morning and requesting that she leave the window unlocked for me so I didn't have to sneak through the front door and risk getting caught by her parents.

When I was done, I tossed my phone on the side table. Jamie was sitting on the edge of the bed, watching me with lustful eyes. I blushed when I realized I was wearing only a pair of panties. He patted the bed, and I grinned as I sauntered back over to him, swaying my hips seductively. A slow smile spread over his face as he gripped my waist and pulled me onto his lap, tickling me playfully and making me giggle and squirm. He pinned me to the bed before kissing me forcefully and starting over where we'd left off.

CHAPTER 5

I WOKE IN the morning with my head a little fuzzy from the alcohol and my body aching all over from our activities last night. Jamie was a lot of fun in bed and not like Miles at all. Miles was serious and dominant; he was a *"Lie on your back and spread your legs"* kind of guy. He never once wanted to change positions, and if I ever suggested that I be on top he refused adamantly, looking at me as if I had grown a second head.

Jamie, on the other hand, seemed up for anything, trying out different positions and angles. He wasn't serious at all; he was flirtatious and playful, chatting easily between sessions. After having sex for the third time we'd finally fallen asleep.

Jamie's arm was draped across the small of my back, pinning me to the mattress. It was a nice pressure. This was the first time I'd ever spent the night with a guy. Whenever Miles and I had been together it had been a quick fumble somewhere before we would go home. He never once stayed over, and since both of us lived with our parents that made real private time impossible.

I carefully rolled over to look at Jamie, hoping I hadn't had vodka goggles on last night. I breathed a sigh of relief when I saw him looking just as gloriously hot as I remembered.

Scooting closer to him, I felt his arm unconsciously wrap around me, holding me securely to his side. It was nice. When I glanced down his body, I drew in a shaky breath at what I saw. The scars that I had felt and vaguely seen last night in the dingy light after having too much to drink were really noticeable in the daylight. He had a lot of them, way too many to count. They were dotted over his torso. Most of them were small, but a couple were long, raised, and puckered and looked like they must have been deep. There were also a few little round marks that looked like old burns or something.

I trailed my fingers over them tenderly. When I got to a big scar that stretched all the way from his right hip to halfway across his stomach, I winced and tried not to imagine the pain that this must have caused him. Unable to stop myself, I bent my head and kissed it lightly as tears burned my eyes.

"Mmm, morning," he mumbled sleepily. I turned to look at him, willing myself not to cry about this. Suddenly he sighed deeply and rolled so he was on top of me. "Guess you're gonna ask me about that now, huh?" His tone was sad, resigned.

"I want to, but if you don't want to tell me, that's okay," I said quietly.

"You want the truth or the lie?"

"The lie," I whispered, running my hands up his back and pulling him closer to me, touching the scars there too, wondering how this beautiful boy could have been put through so much pain.

"I'm clumsy, I fall down a lot," he stated, kissing my neck.

"And now tell me the truth." I held my breath, not even sure I wanted to know.

He sighed and pulled back, looking at me with weary eyes.

"I didn't have a very enjoyable childhood, Ellie. The people who should have looked after me didn't," he said simply. I could hear the anger in his tone.

A single tear escaped my eye even though I was trying my hardest to keep them at bay and not make this harder on him. My heart broke for him, and I just didn't know what to say, so I pulled his face to mine and kissed him, wrapping my arms around him tightly, as if I could save him from the memory of it. He kissed me back fiercely and pulled away just as I was beginning to get breathless.

"Don't feel sorry for me. It was a long time ago. I don't need your sympathy, it's okay," he said quietly, kissing down my neck, heading lower, his intention clear.

When he planted an open-mouthed kiss just below my navel, I cupped his face in my hands and tilted his face so he had to look up at me. "There are no more condoms," I teased, smirking at him.

A devilish smile crept onto his face. "Yeah, I know, but that doesn't mean I can't make you scream." He raised one eyebrow playfully as he kissed back down my body again.

* * *

About an hour later I was dressed in my outfit from last night, staring into the mirror distastefully. The dress was way too short and way too tight. I cringed, trying to tug the bottom down and magically make it longer.

Jamie laughed quietly and pulled a T-shirt from a drawer, tossing it to me. "Here, you can put this on over it if you want."

"It's that obvious that I look like a dirty tramp, is it?" I asked, giggling awkwardly.

Before I could move, he grabbed my waist and pulled me flush against his body. "I think you look beautiful. Even more beautiful this morning with no makeup than you did last night, and that's saying something, because last night you took my breath away," he murmured before kissing me passionately.

Oh my God, this boy is too sweet! Corny, but sweet.

I pushed him away, laughing. "Again with the corny lines? You're out of condoms, being corny isn't gonna get you anywhere," I teased, slipping his T-shirt on over my skimpy dress.

"Well, will it get me your number?" he asked, seeming nervous.

My number? He didn't think this was a one-night stand? "Um, Jamie, look, you seem like a really great guy, and last night was awesome, but I've only just gotten out of a relationship. I'm not really interested in starting anything right now." My experience with him had been the best time I'd ever had with a boy, but I couldn't deal with anything heavy right now, not after Miles. I just wanted to be on my own for a while, do my own thing without having to worry or ask anyone's permission.

"Oh, right, yeah, okay, that's fine." He shifted on his feet, looking away from me as he grabbed another clean shirt from his drawer and pulled it over his head. "Come on then, I'll drive you home," he said quietly, ushering me out of his room. He led me a little down the street to a beat-up old pickup truck. "Sorry, bit pathetic, huh?" he said, looking embarrassed as he opened the passenger door for me. "Okay, where to?" he asked as he climbed in the driver's side.

I directed him to Stacey's because that was where I was supposed to have spent last night.

When we pulled up outside, I smiled nervously. "Well, thanks for the ride." I shifted in my seat, unsure what else to say. I'd just had a one-night stand. Me, Ellie Pearce.

"No problem. Here." He handed me a piece of paper with a

phone number written in extremely messy handwriting. I looked back at him, confused. He shrugged. "Just in case you ever need anything, I don't know, a ride in a crappy pickup or something, you can call me." He leaned over and pressed his lips against mine. I kissed him back immediately. Jamie's kissing was out of this world. If I could, I would live right in this moment and never move.

I pulled away after a minute or so and smiled. "I'd better go. Thanks for last night, it was fun."

"Bye, Ellie."

I closed the door and waved good-bye as I skipped off to the side of the house. Luckily for me, Stacey had a ground-floor bedroom, plus her on-again, off-again boyfriend used her window a lot, so he'd moved a boulder beneath it to make entry easier. I climbed through the window silently. Stacey was still asleep even though it was after ten in the morning, so I slipped into bed next to her and curled up for another hour of blissful slumber.

★ ★ ★

Something was poking my arm. "Wake up!"

"Ow, Stace, stop poking me, you know how easily I bruise," I grumbled. She laughed and poked me again repeatedly until I opened my eyes.

"Soooooo?" Her eyes twinkled with excited curiosity as she dragged the word out.

"So, what?" I asked innocently.

"So, that guy was so freaking hot! Was it good? Did you use protection? Where did you go? How did you get home? Are you seeing him again?" she asked, seemingly all in one breath. I sat up and stretched, yawning. "Oh, you're wearing his shirt!" she cooed, giving me the *that's so cute* face. "Come on, details! I want to know *everything*."

"Stace, jeez, slow down. Okay, yes, he was insanely hot. We went to his place. He was incredible. He drove me home, and no, I'm not seeing him again. Was there anything else?" I asked, smiling.

Her expression resembled that of a proud mother who'd just seen her child walk for the first time. "You had a one-night stand! Oh, your first, I am so proud of you! And wow, was he hot, I could climax just thinking about him." She laughed, fanning her face and making me laugh even harder.

Once we were dressed, we decided to go shopping for a while. It was nice to have the day to myself for once and do things I wanted to; usually I spent Sundays with Miles, either at his house or at mine. It was wonderful to be able to just do something regular, like shopping. After hitting a few stores, we stopped at a café for a bite to eat, ordering coffee and blueberry muffins.

"Hey, want to catch a movie tonight? You could stay at my house again; you already have your school stuff for tomorrow," she suggested.

I nodded. "Sure, I'll need to call my mom and tell her, though." I grabbed my purse, rummaging through, trying to find my phone, but it wasn't in there. I checked my jacket, but the pockets were empty.

"What's up?" Stacey asked.

"Can't find my phone, I must have left it at your house." I shrugged, carrying on eating.

She whipped out her phone and dialed. After a couple of seconds her eyes widened and a wicked smile spread across her face. "Well hi, who's this?"

I frowned at her in question, wondering who she was talking to.

"Right, no, this isn't Ellie. I'm Stacey. You obviously have Ellie's phone," she said. "I'm sure she'd love to meet you tonight for dinner to get her phone back, Jamie." Stacey grinned at me as she spoke. I gasped and reached to snatch the phone from her, shaking my head adamantly. I didn't want to go and meet him. Her smile grew larger as she held up one finger, signaling for me to stop. "Absolutely, she'll meet you there at eight then, okay." She laughed and disconnected the call, grinning with satisfaction.

I groaned and put my head in my hands. "Stace, I don't want to go out on a date. Can't I just be single for a little while without having to do stuff with a guy? What happened to girl time?"

"Oh, come on, it'll be fun. Plus, you said he was incredible in the sack." She waggled her eyebrows at me suggestively. I sighed in defeat. There was no way I could deny that fact—he *was* awesome. "You're going!" she insisted.

I groaned again. I guess I had to go; I needed my phone. "Fine, whatever."

Stacey clapped her hands excitedly. "We should buy you a new outfit," she chirped. I tried to ignore her enthusiasm, but as I sat there listening to her planning on doing my hair and makeup for me, I realized that I was strangely excited to see him again.

CHAPTER 6

JAMIE

WHEN I DISCONNECTED the call from Ellie's friend, I smiled to myself. I was secretly happy to discover Ellie had left her phone at my place. It meant I had an excuse to see her again. I almost couldn't wait for tonight.

But first I had something to do.

I'd been avoiding this all week, but I couldn't put it off any longer.

When I pulled into the churchyard, I stepped out of the truck, grabbing the flowers I'd purchased and looking around helplessly. I didn't even know where her grave was.

An old groundskeeper was raking the dead leaves at the front of the church, so I cleared my throat to get his attention. "Can you help me find out where someone is buried?" My voice shook as I spoke, and I hoped he didn't notice. I didn't like to show emotion. Emotions were a weakness, something that gave people power over you, and I never wanted anyone to have power over me again.

He looked up, pulling a red hankie from his pocket and wiping his brow with it. "Sure, let's go to the office and have a look at the records." He smiled kindly as he nodded over at the church.

I followed him through the church into the little back office. "What's the name you're looking for?" he asked, heading over to a file cabinet.

"Sophie Cole." Even saying her name hurt and made me feel so much guilt that my hands were shaking. He rummaged through the cabinet and came out with a book, flipping through the pages.

"Right, here we are. She's buried in section C, grave number 258. Want me to show you?"

"Um...yeah, that'd be great, thanks." I smiled gratefully.

We didn't speak as I followed him out to the other side of the cemetery. With every step, the pain in my heart grew. The wind whipped the dry leaves around us as we walked, swirling them over the gravestones as if they were dancing. I took deep breaths, trying to keep my grief at bay as I followed behind the old hobbling man.

After a few minutes he stopped in front of a little gray headstone. "Here you are. If you need anything, I'll be around the front."

"Thank you," I mumbled quietly. I waited until he walked off before looking back at the marble headstone. Placing the flowers down, I read the inscription. It was just her name, date of birth, and date of death. There was no quote or fond farewell like those that marked the neighboring headstones. My flowers sat there against the yellowing, patchy grass, looking lonely, just like I felt inside. I didn't know what to say.

I gulped, swallowing the lump that was rapidly forming in my throat. "I hope you're in a better place, Soph. I'm so sorry." My voice broke as I said the words that always formed in my head when I thought about my baby sister. When my eyes started to sting, I quickly turned on my heel and jogged back to my truck.

I hadn't been ready for this. This morning I thought I was, but I realized then that I wasn't even close to being ready to let her go.

After taking a few deep, calming breaths, I glanced at my watch. There was only a little while left before I had arranged to meet Ellie. I wouldn't even have time for a shower. My sadness over my sister was eating me up as I drove back to my place, heading to my room and digging in my drawer for a clean shirt.

As I stripped my old one off, I caught sight of myself in the mirror. My body disgusted me. I hated it, it made me loathe myself. I couldn't look at it, not without thinking about my past, and I refused to do that. The past was the past.

As I traced my finger over the biggest scar—the one that Ellie had kissed—I started to think about how it had happened. I suddenly got so angry that, before I knew what I was doing, I'd smashed my fist into the mirror, ignoring the pain in my knuckles.

"Shit!" I grumbled, looking down at my reddened knuckles, noticing one was oozing blood. Why had I done that? I was about to go on a date, for fuck's sake. Idiot! Still mentally cussing myself out, I stalked to the bathroom to rinse it.

Once satisfied the bleeding had stopped, I lifted the lid of the toilet tank. I reached in, pulling out the plastic bag that I was using to store my money. Once I'd fished out a hundred dollars, I wrapped the rest tightly in the bag, wedging it back in just above the water level. After grabbing my jacket and Ellie's phone, I headed out.

On the way, I stopped and bought a single red rose. She wouldn't really want a bunch of flowers to be worrying about all night, but I figured a single one should be okay. I hoped that would be romantic even though I had no clue how to even *be* romantic. This was my first actual date. I had no idea what to do or say.

As I stood outside the restaurant, which I'd chosen specifically because she'd mentioned last night while we were talking that Mexican food was her favorite, I silently cursed myself for not arranging to pick her up so she wouldn't have to walk anywhere alone in the dark.

A little while later a cab pulled up and out she stepped, looking like a goddess. The tight black pants she wore made her legs look long and perfect, and the belt made the white shirt she was wearing cling to her small waist. I groaned quietly and decided that it probably wasn't a good idea to meet her again; it was like torture wanting her and knowing she wasn't interested. She was so far out of my league that we were practically on different continents. And yet I'd never longed for anything as much as I longed for her. I wanted to be good enough for her; I wanted her to want me.

"Hey." She smiled nervously.

"Uh, hey, you look, um…you look…wow. I mean, you just look…yeah, just…wow," I stuttered. *Yep, you've just made yourself look like a first-class prick. Jamie, you are so smooth it's just unreal.*

She laughed and blushed, dropping her eyes to the ground. The red in her cheeks made her look even more beautiful. "Um, thanks, you look good, too."

I groaned internally again. I was wearing a plain gray T-shirt, and she looked like that. I was punching way above my weight here. My heart squeezed painfully.

"Here's your phone," I muttered.

"Thanks."

"I got you this, too." I held out the rose, feeling like a complete clueless idiot.

Her eyes widened. "You did? Thank you." She looked back at me, smiling gratefully as she traced her fingers over the petals.

Okay, I score one for that! She had the strangest-colored eyes I'd ever seen. They were a kind of gray but with a hint of blue around the iris, just indescribable and beautiful.

"I hope you're hungry," I said lamely, nodding to the door of the restaurant.

She grinned, nodding eagerly. "I'm starving. And I love Mexican."

"I remember," I replied smugly, loving the appreciative glint in her eye because I'd remembered something she'd said in the dead of the night. I pulled the door open and motioned for her to go in first. I couldn't help but discreetly look at her ass as she walked past.

As we were shown to our table and ordered drinks with the waitress, I started to calm down; the nerves were easing off as I remembered last night and how easy she was to talk to.

"You know what, I never asked what you did for a job," Ellie said while we looked over the menus.

Crap, now what? "Um...I work with cars. I'm currently fixing up cars for a junkyard, and then they sell them at auctions," I lied. Well, it wasn't a total lie—that *was* the plan, it just wasn't definite yet.

"You fix cars? That's handy to know. When my grandfather died a couple of years ago he left me his car. It's old and always breaking down, but it's my baby." She laughed. "I don't use it that often. It's easier to get cabs or the train."

"Lucky you have my number then, huh?" I was trying to flirt with her, but I wasn't entirely sure if it was working; I wasn't very good at it. "What about you? You're a senior, I guess. You wanna go to college?"

She nodded, shrugging nonchalantly. "Yeah, I'm a senior. I'm not sure what I want to do in college yet. I've never really had a specific thing I'm interested in. My mom is always hounding the crap out of me to pick a major, but I just don't care. I think I'd rather go traveling."

I laughed at her answer. "Well, who wouldn't rather go traveling than be in school?"

The waitress came over then and took our order. As she walked off, Ellie smiled. "So, Jamie, favorite TV show?" she questioned.

I racked my brains trying to think of something. There wasn't exactly much choice in juvie. "I don't watch much TV," I admitted, shrugging. "What's yours?"

She pursed her lips, thinking. "Either *Game of Thrones* or *Sons of Anarchy*. You like either of those?"

I shook my head. "I've read *Game of Thrones* but haven't seen it. The series is great." Juvie didn't have much in the way of TV but there was a pretty kickass library.

One of her eyebrows rose. "You like to read?" When I nodded in reply, she laughed, her eyes twinkling. "Hot guy reading. Nice. You know, there's this whole movement on social media dedicated to hot guys reading. I might have to take a picture of you and add it," she teased.

I chuckled and shook my head. Social media. I barely even knew what that meant, let alone anything about a movement happening on there. We certainly lived in different worlds. "Whatever," I mused, grinning. "Okay, to change the conversation from how hot I am," I started cockily, "tell me one random thing about you that no one else knows."

Ellie sat back in her chair, absentmindedly stirring her drink with her straw. After a full minute of thinking, she answered. "I used to love stargazing. My dad bought me a telescope for my eighth birthday and we'd spend hours on end outside trying to find constellations."

"Oh, so you're a nerd?" I joked, laughing as she dipped her finger in her drink and flicked a droplet of lemonade at me. "Sexy nerd, though," I added as we both laughed.

The arrival of our food meant we had to stop fooling around for a while, but we talked easily through the rest of dinner about places we wanted to go and why, books, and our favorite things. It was probably the easiest conversation I'd ever had in my life. I found myself acting normal around her, being me without the tough act I usually put on. Whenever the conversation turned to my past, I would deflect it to something else. I didn't want her asking about my past, where I lived, or my family. I didn't want to lie to her like I did to everyone else.

"It's only nine thirty, you want to catch a movie or something?" I suggested after we'd finished eating.

"Uh, yeah, sure."

I grinned and pulled out money to pay for dinner.

"I can pay," she protested, picking up her purse.

"I got it." I took her hand and led her away from the table, grabbing my jacket from the coat rack on the way past. As we stepped outside, I put it around her shoulders and discreetly left my arm there, too. She didn't protest at my lame move, so I grinned proudly as I led her to the movie theater.

The only thing due to start within the next hour was some crappy-sounding movie about a singer who lived in a trailer park, trying to make it big. When we went in we were literally the only ones in there.

After about ten minutes of the awful movie, I was totally bored, so I started making little jokes about the characters, which made her laugh. In the end, we gave up on watching it and started talking some more.

"How come you split up with your boyfriend?" I asked, taking her hand, hoping she wouldn't mind.

She smiled, but it didn't quite reach her eyes. "I don't know, he was kind of possessive. He didn't like me talking to other guys—not that I ever would have cheated on him or anything, but he just didn't trust me. It all got to be too much."

"When did you break up with him?"

"Friday night." She looked down at our hands as I played with her fingers.

I winced at the revelation. I'd slept with her on Saturday; no wonder it was too soon for her. "So you're definitely not looking to start anything right now then?" I asked, mentally crossing my fingers and hoping she would say she wasn't opposed to the idea of a relationship.

She shifted uncomfortably in her seat. "I just want to be on my own for a while, be my own person without having to worry about being part of a couple. I haven't really had that before. I got with Miles when I was fifteen, and that was it," she explained, shrugging.

Okay, well that was an *"I'm not interested, so please don't ask me out again, Jamie."* I couldn't help but feel disappointed. This girl truly was awesome.

I nodded and changed the subject to her friends; she was obviously uncomfortable talking about this Miles guy.

She was currently telling me about her friend Stacey, who Ellie thought was beautiful, and who modeled part-time. "Yeah, I would kill to look like her," she said enviously.

"Are you kidding? Why the hell would you want to look any different? You're the most beautiful girl I've ever seen." I shook my head at her absurdity.

"Again with the corny lines?" she teased, blushing.

"It's not a line, Ellie."

She moved in her seat and gently pressed her lips to mine. The kiss was sweet, soft, and just incredible. When she pulled away, I kissed her again, not wanting it to end. Her arms looped around my neck, pulling me closer to her as she kissed me back hungrily. This kiss wasn't sweet like the last one, it was hot and heavy. I loved it.

Needing to feel her body on mine, I pulled her onto my lap, kissing her desperately, savoring every last second in case I never got to kiss her again.

Seemingly out of nowhere, someone cleared their throat loudly. I pulled away from her quickly, opening my eyes and looking over her shoulder. An usher was shining a flashlight at us, frowning disapprovingly. Ellie buried her face in the side of my neck, so I put my hand on the back of her head, trying to hide her.

"Sorry. We're done," I said, grinning at the guy, who was shaking his head at us. Ellie quickly moved off my lap and back into her own seat, still looking the other way from the usher, and I couldn't stop laughing at her red, embarrassed face.

"Wanna go?" she whispered uncomfortably.

"Yeah, sure," I agreed, trying not to laugh again. She was so embarrassed that even her ears were a pale shade of pink, but it just made it all the more funny to me. Immediately, she stood up and headed down the aisle, stopping at the end to wait for me. When I caught up to her, I slipped my arm around her waist, and she hid her face against my shoulder as we walked out of the theater.

It wasn't until we stepped into the bright lights of the foyer that she finally raised her eyes from the floor. "Ugh, that was so embarrassing!" she grumbled, looking over my shoulder tentatively.

"It's okay, come on, it's funny. We were only making out," I replied, still chuckling to myself.

She slapped my chest, shaking her head disapprovingly, but a smile played at the edge of her lips. "You think that's funny?" she teased. I nodded. Suddenly her hand closed over mine tightly and she pulled me into the ladies' bathroom. "Let's see how funny you find it when you get caught in here." She leaned against the door, smirking at me.

"Hm, you know, maybe for our second date we could get caught making out in the park or something?" I suggested rather hopefully.

She stiffened. "Jamie, I can't, I'm sorry. You really are a great guy, but I just really want the freedom of being on my own for a while." Her apologetic look made my heart sink.

"Right, yeah, of course. I mean, you said earlier, and that's fine, it was just a thought," I said, quickly backtracking. I stepped closer to her and her breath caught in her throat; her eyes sparkled with excitement, making my breath catch, too.

She cocked her head to the side as she seemed to be thinking about something for a couple of seconds before she spoke. "Jamie, I don't want a relationship right now, but that doesn't mean I don't want you," she purred, her voice all sexy and husky, making me hard in an instant.

"What does that mean?" I asked, needing her to spell it out. I wasn't confident enough to make the first move in case I got shot down again.

She grinned and slowly licked her full bottom lip. "We could be friends who have fun together occasionally, like, friends with...benefits," she suggested, raising an eyebrow at me.

"I like the sound of the benefits," I admitted. There was no way I was passing up this opportunity; this girl was too incredible to say no to. I'd definitely take what I could get.

"I bet you do." She looked me over hungrily, biting her lip.

How the hell can she look at me like that, knowing what my body looks like? I wondered. But this was no time to question the how or why; she'd just given me an offer that I couldn't refuse.

I grinned and kissed her, pushing her against the wall lightly, running my hands down her body until I got to her ass, just marveling over her perfection. As the kiss deepened and turned into something passionate and animalistic, I lifted her off her feet. Her legs wrapped around my waist, clamping her to me tightly. I smiled against her lips and pressed her harder against the wall so I could free one of my hands to touch her. She pulled out of the kiss and started kissing my neck. As she tilted her head to the other side, it collided with the door frame.

"Ow!" she hissed, rubbing her head.

"Shit, you okay?"

She nodded and started giggling before pulling my mouth back to hers. I kissed her hungrily as I gripped her top and started to pull it off. But due to the limited space of the girls' bathroom, my elbow banged against the condom machine that was mounted on the wall, making a loud clang echo in the empty room.

She burst out laughing and shook her head. "This really isn't working."

I grinned. "No, it's not," I admitted, pushing her hair away from her face gently. "Want to stay at my place again tonight?" I would love to wake up with her again.

She looked a little torn. "I have school tomorrow."

I couldn't help but feel excited because she looked disappointed when she spoke, like she actually did want to stay with me but couldn't.

"That wasn't a no," I teased, dipping my head and kissing her neck. I slid my hand back down to her ass, moving her hips so we rubbed together intimately.

She let out a breathy little moan as her eyes locked on mine. I could see the want there. "You'll drive me to school in the morning?"

"Yep," I murmured, leaning in farther, pressing my lips to her neck and sucking gently, giving her a hickey. I wanted to leave my mark on her creamy skin; if this was the last time we did this, I wanted her to be reminded of me and how good it was. I wanted to leave her thinking about me, and no matter how much she said she didn't want to date me, I wanted it to be impossible for her to forget.

She moaned, her fingers digging into my shoulders. "Okay," she agreed. My insides clenched with excitement. "Come on then, stud, before the anticipation kills me." She unwrapped one of her legs from my waist. I kissed her lightly before quickly pumping the condom machine with all the change I had. She giggled and pressed her face into my back, her hands gripping my hips, obviously embarrassed again.

I held her hand as we walked to my truck; it was pretty cold so I wrapped my jacket around her shoulders again. She smiled at me gratefully as she called her friend to ask her to take her books and stuff to school for her in the morning.

* * *

When we pulled up outside my building, I checked everywhere for danger before opening her door. There was no one around tonight, not even the prostitutes who usually hung around out front.

When we got upstairs to my door, Ellie's arms slinked around my waist, pulling me closer to her, pressing her exquisite body against mine. I bent my head and kissed her, slipping my hands down to her hips as I lifted her and pressed her against the wall. Her long legs instantly wrapped around my waist, squeezing her to me tighter.

Lust was taking over, a primal urge creeping over me, making my muscles tighten and my dick ache, but I was acutely conscious that we were still standing in the crappy little hallway, and it wasn't really safe for her to be here. I knew I'd be able to protect her, but I didn't want her to have to witness that, so I reached to slip my key into the lock. I was so turned on already it was unreal. But as my hand brushed against the door, it creaked open a tiny bit. Frowning and confused because I'd definitely remembered locking it on my way out, I palmed the door and pushed it open, stepping over the threshold. I stopped and my eyes widened in shock. My stuff was everywhere, my clothes strewn all over the floor, the furniture upturned. Someone had broken into my room.

Ellie kissed back up to my mouth, but I needed to make sure no one was still in here. "Get down, now!" I ordered, supporting her weight with one arm while I unclamped her legs from my waist with the other.

"Huh?"

Grabbing her hand, I forced her behind me as I looked over the mess. I pushed her gently against the wall and strode over to my little bathroom to make sure whoever had been in my room had definitely left.

My eyes fell on the toilet tank, noticing the lid wasn't sitting properly. *Oh shit, please don't have taken my money!*

"Oh God, what happened? Have you been robbed?" Ellie asked breathlessly, obviously taking in the room for the first time. I didn't answer; instead, I headed straight to the toilet and lifted the lid of the cistern. There was nothing in there. The little plastic bag that I had put all of my money into was gone. "I'll call the police," Ellie said quickly.

I shook my head. The police couldn't come here, I'd probably get killed by someone in the building for bringing them. "No, Ellie, it's fine. Nothing's been taken; it's just a mess, that's all. I don't need the police to come," I replied quickly. My shoulders slumped in defeat. I had nothing now. There was twenty-five bucks and about forty cents in my pocket, and I was due to pay the next week's rent in two days.

"How do you know nothing's been taken?" Ellie asked.

I walked back into the bedroom; she was still pressed against the wall where I'd left her, her eyes wide and fearful.

"I don't have anything worth taking. All I have is clothes, and those are all over the floor." I shrugged, trying not to show her I was totally screwed. Come Tuesday morning, when I didn't have the rent money, I wouldn't even have this crappy little roof over my head. Now that was a depressing thought.

"Nothing's gone?" she asked, looking around slowly as if she could see something missing.

I shook my head and took her hand. "Come on, I'll drive you to Stacey's." I gave her a little tug toward the door. It obviously wasn't safe here, and I didn't want her anywhere near trouble.

She pulled her hand out of mine, frowning. "What? Don't be stupid." She bent down, scooping up an armful of my clothes off the floor and throwing them on the bed.

I watched her, confused by her actions. "Ellie, come on, I'll drive you to your friend's place. I don't want you here if it's not safe."

She just shook her head and carried on picking up my clothes, throwing them on the bed. When she had them all, she kicked off her shoes and sat on my bed cross-legged, starting to fold them, setting them in a pile. My heart melted at the sight of it and how thoughtful that was. She really was incredible. I'd honestly never met anyone like her in my life. She was so innocent in some ways, so oblivious to the danger of this place and the people who lived here. I sighed, watching her, in awe of her and her generous spirit.

"Well, don't just stand there watching me! If you don't need to call the police, then you need to fix your room," she ordered, nodding at the furniture on the floor. I snapped back to reality and lifted the drawers and dresser back up, putting them back in place. Ellie soon finished with my clothes, so she helped me put them in the drawers.

"Oh no, your photo got ripped," she said suddenly, stooping to retrieve something from the floor.

Photo? Oh, shit, not the one of Sophie! "What? No!" I cried angrily. She handed me two halves of a photo. I closed my eyes, so angry that I couldn't speak. This was the only photo I had of her; it was the only thing that mattered to me. I hadn't thought to take it out with me; I'd been too preoccupied with nerves about meeting Ellie to even think about it.

"Who is that little girl?" Ellie asked, setting her hand on my arm.

"That was my sister, Sophie. She died," I said quietly, not really wanting to talk about her.

Ellie gasped. "Oh, Jamie, I'm so sorry. How?"

I took a deep breath and put the ruined photo down on the side table. "She was murdered, four years ago," I replied, watching Ellie's face fall and her eyes widen in shock.

She wrapped her arms around me tightly and hugged me. "I'm so sorry, that's awful. What happened?"

I sighed heavily. "I don't want to talk about it, Ellie. Really, you should go; it's not safe for you here." I hugged her back, just enjoying being close to her. The last thing I wanted to do was endanger her, yet that was exactly what I'd already done by bringing her to this shitty little place. I wouldn't ask her here again; this just proved that she was too good to be in a place like this, with a guy like me.

"I don't want to go." She pulled back to look at me, her expression stern and confident.

"Ellie, really, I think—" I started, but she put her hand over my mouth to stop me speaking.

"Do you want me to go, and you're just saying you're worried as an excuse to make me leave?" she asked.

I smiled sadly and pulled her hand off my mouth. "I don't want you to leave. I just don't think a girl like you should be in a place like this. I shouldn't have brought you here, I should have known better." I was incredibly angry with myself for putting her in danger like this for my own benefit.

She pressed her lips to mine, silencing me. "I'm here now, so let's just stop talking, huh?" she whispered, running her hands down my chest, hooking her fingers into my belt loops.

I shivered at her light touch. I had no idea how she could do this to me when I'd never even been interested in dating a girl before. It was crazy how one girl could just blow apart everything I thought I knew in life.

She bit her lip, looking at me lustfully, sending shock waves through my whole body as she walked backward, pulling me with her by my belt loops. She stopped as her legs touched the side of the bed, obviously leaving the final decision to me.

With the easy decision made, I smiled and pushed her down onto the bed, climbing on top of her. I needed her so much. This girl had me completely under her spell already; I wouldn't have been able to stop even if I wanted to.

CHAPTER 7

I WOKE UP with Ellie's beautiful face inches from mine; she was lying on my arm. Smiling, I scooted closer to her, grabbing my cell phone from the side table and checking the time. It was only six thirty, which meant I had another couple of hours with her at least.

I sighed and let my eyes drag over her. Ellie made me forget all the things that had happened to me. She made me want to be good enough for her.

In her sleep, she stirred and pressed her face into my chest, moaning an unintelligible word before she sighed and snuggled even closer to me. Tangling my fingers in her hair, I kissed the top of her head. As I lay there, I couldn't stop thinking about what a pile of shit my life was. Today was going to be incredibly hard; I needed to find another twenty-five bucks somewhere so I'd have enough to pay my rent tomorrow morning. The car I'd fixed wasn't due to go to auction until Wednesday, *if* that even made a profit at all. I'd been foolish. I'd wasted all week on something that might not even work out, chasing a pipe dream when I should have been looking for a solid, guaranteed income.

I refused to go to Brett for the money; I refused to owe anyone anything. If I had learned anything from my shitty life, it was that the only one you could depend on was yourself. I needed to get the money, get a job, get the hell out of this hellhole, and be a better person. Maybe then I would deserve a shot at the beautiful thing lying in my arms, because I sure as hell didn't deserve her at the moment.

I brushed her hair off her face, pushing it over her shoulder so I could see the hickey on her neck. Grinning proudly, I dipped my head and kissed it, pulling back quickly when she stirred.

"Hey, what time is it?" she mumbled, planting a soft kiss on my chest.

I frowned distastefully, wondering how she could do that with all of my scars there. She didn't seem bothered by them at all. "It's about quarter to seven."

She smiled and pulled me closer, kissing me gently. "Good morning," she whispered against my lips.

"Good morning. Sleep all right?" I asked, hoping she hadn't heard the fight that had started outside at about three o'clock this morning.

She nodded and yawned. "Yep, you tired me out. I slept like the dead."

"Well, I slept like the dead, too," I lied. In all honesty, I had barely slept last night. I'd kept a vigil into the small hours of the morning, listening avidly in case someone broke back into my room so I could protect Ellie if needed. A little bit of tiredness to-day was nothing if it meant she was safe.

She pulled me closer to her, running her hands up my back, fingering the scars there. The curiosity was easy to see on her face, so I kissed her before she could ask me about them. I didn't want to talk about it, not with anyone.

* * *

An hour and a half later, we were dressed and ready to leave. I watched as she leaned over and began making my bed.

"Ellie, why are you making my bed?"

She shrugged and finished straightening the pillows. "Habit, I guess. It's one of my mom's rules at home, the bed has to be made, room tidy, blah blah blah," she mocked, waving her hand dismissively.

I laughed and grabbed her so we both fell onto the bed. "Well, I like an unmade bed. Want to help me mess it up again?" I smiled at her suggestively, loving the feel of her body under mine. Touching her and kissing her seemed to be *all* I could think about. I was almost turning into an addict.

She laughed and grabbed my wrist, looking at my watch before she shook her head. "I need to get to school, sorry. Maybe another time," she offered, arching one eyebrow. My insides danced with happiness because I would get to see her again. The agreement was: sex, no strings. What man would turn down an offer like that from a girl like her?

I sighed dramatically. "Come on then, little girl, let's get you to school," I mused, pulling her back up. She laughed and let me drag her from my room to my truck. This place didn't really wake up until midmorning, so there was no one around.

As we pulled into the parking lot of her school, she unclipped her seat belt and scooted closer to me. When she leaned in and kissed me, I put my hand on the back of her head so she couldn't pull away. Kissing Ellie was incredible and I would happily do it all day if she would let me.

I pulled away when we were both breathless and kissed the tip of her nose. "So, do I get your number this morning?" I asked hopefully. She nodded and held out her hand for my phone. As I passed it to her and watched her type her number in, I couldn't keep the smug grin off my face.

She pushed the phone back into my pocket, patting it teasingly. "There you go, stud. Now you can give me a booty call whenever you want." She winked at me as she climbed out of the truck and then sashayed off through the parking lot.

People immediately swarmed around her, begging for her attention. Boys and girls, they were all trying to talk to her. She didn't look too comfortable with the attention; the easy smile that she'd been wearing all morning was replaced by an obviously fake one. Judging by the way other students were crowding around her, she was some sort of queen bee at her school.

I frowned, more than a little surprised that she would want me to drive her to school in my crappy truck if she had some kind of image to uphold. As I pulled out, she waved good-bye. A smile slipped onto my face just because she'd acknowledged me in front of her friends.

My day was spent walking around trying to find a job. I went into every single store, bar, restaurant, and office, trying to find something, but there was literally nothing, not even cleaning toilets. As the day dragged on, the worry built.

I sat in the park and considered my limited options. There was no other solution I could come up with. I couldn't lose the place I was living. Sure it was dank and nasty, but it was better than sleeping in my truck. Gritting my teeth indignantly, I pulled out my phone and called Ray.

"Hey, Kid!"

I put my head in my hands and squeezed my eyes shut. This needed to be done. "Hey, Ray. Listen, I need some help."

"What's up?"

"I need money."

"Sure, how much you need?" he asked.

"I don't want to borrow money, Ray. I have no idea when I'd be able to pay it back. But I need to get my hands on some cash, quickly."

"I'll lend you some, you don't have to worry about paying me back, just spot me when you can," he offered.

I shook my head. I couldn't owe anyone; that wasn't going straight, in my eyes. Even owing Ray I would feel a debt. I needed to do this on my own.

"Ray, I don't want to borrow money. I was actually wondering if you could call Jensen and set me up for tonight?"

He gasped. "No fucking way, Kid. I'm not doing that! Those things have moved on a lot since you last saw one. No way. Nope!"

I'd known he would react like this. Ray's cousin Jensen ran an illegal fight club every night. People bet on the fights and the fighters got paid to enter. Just entering would be enough to pay my rent. I didn't even need to win, just get the shit kicked out of me for a few minutes.

"Ray, I need this. Does he still run it or not?"

"Kid, seriously, you know I've always hated those things. The fights now are brutal; it's not just a couple of guys wanting a bit of spare cash anymore. These guys that enter, they *really* want it, they want to win. I'll lend you what you need," he protested.

"Look, thanks for the offer, but please can you call Jensen for me? I need this to happen tonight if he still does it. If you won't do it, then I'll have to find him on my own. C'mon, Ray, do this for me?" I nervously ran my hand over my almost nonexistent hair. I had no idea how to find Jensen myself, so I prayed Ray would help get me in.

"Kid, you know you're gonna get fucked up, right?"

I frowned. "Yeah, I know, totally fubar. How much they pay

now? It still thirty bucks for weekday fights?" It was a shame it wasn't a weekend; weekend fights were higher profile and paid a lot more, but I'd take what I could get.

"It's fifty now, I think. The rules have changed, there are no rules," he said quietly.

I winced. That didn't sound good at all. There always used to be a "no hitting in the balls" rule—I quite liked that one.

"Okay, will you call him for me and get me in?" *Please say yes, please say yes.*

He sighed, and the line was quiet for a while before he answered, "Yeah, okay. I'll call you back."

I breathed a sigh of relief. "Thanks, man." He disconnected the call and I sat back on the bench, feeling my stressed muscles starting to relax.

By now it was almost four in the afternoon, so I decided to text Ellie.

Hey, have a good day at school?

A minute later she replied.

I did, other than having to see my ex. *groan* How was your day? Did you find out anything about who broke into your place? x

I smiled at the kiss at the end, loving that she actually cared enough to ask about my day. After sending back a quick lie that I'd had a good day, I headed to my place and flopped on the bed, waiting for the phone to ring and for Ray to tell me good news about the fight that night.

★ ★ ★

At a quarter to ten, Ray picked me up. He used the excuse of wanting to see his cousin as a reason to go with me, but in all honesty, it was probably so he could drive me home in case I was too messed up to drive myself. The whole journey there he tried to convince me not to do this, but I just ignored him, trying desperately to change the subject.

When we pulled up at the venue, an underground parking lot, I followed behind Ray, needing him to introduce me to his cousin. I'd met Jensen only once, so he probably wouldn't remember me. I'd grown up a lot since I last saw him.

I vaguely recognized Jensen when Ray stopped next to him and gave him a man hug. After they'd exchanged pleasantries, Jensen motioned toward me. "This your boy?" he asked.

Ray nodded, gripping my shoulder, looking like he was in pain for letting me do this. "Yeah, this is the kid, Jamie Cole."

A smirk crept onto Jensen's face. "I remember you. You were the only thirteen-year-old I ever let enter one of these. You made me a fortune that night. Every single person bet against you, so I raked it in when you kicked ass." He held out a hand for me to shake.

I nodded. I'd needed money then too, different reasons but still no other option, just like now. "Yeah, thanks for letting me in tonight, I appreciate it." This was short notice; fighters usually had to put their names down and wait to be chosen, so I knew Ray had called in a favor for me.

"No problem. So, you know there are no rules now, right? Anything goes. Fight ends when you tap out or are unconscious. Eight guys, four fights, the winners from each fight then enter a semifinal. You get a hundred bucks if you get to the semi. The two winners from that go on to the final round. If you lose the final it's two hundred, if you win then you get five. Feel free to bet on yourself, too," he explained, shrugging.

My heart leaped in my chest. "So just for entering I get fifty, but if I win the three fights, I get five hundred?" I clarified. If I won the final, I wouldn't have to worry about rent again for a while, even if the junkyard thing didn't pan out.

"Yep. You interested?"

Hell yeah, I'm interested! My earlier plan was to enter and lose, taking the fifty, but five hundred bucks sounded like a lifesaver right about now.

I nodded eagerly. "Yeah, definitely. So, who am I up against?" I asked, looking around at the guys standing around waiting for the fights to start. Most people were here to watch; you could tell which ones were competing because they were standing off to the side trying to focus.

Jensen pointed out a fairly well-built blond guy. He was sitting on a chair, his narrowed eyes totally focused and hard; he wanted to win. "That's Kurt; he's a regular, pretty tough. Think you can beat him?" Jensen inquired.

I studied Kurt again, assessing him, weighing my options. From the way he was sitting I could tell he was arrogant, cocky, and overconfident. He thought he would win, no problem; he was probably well trained in some sort of martial arts, judging by the dragon tattoo on his upper arm.

But I could take him.

"Yeah," I said confidently, watching a small smile spread across Jensen's face.

ELLIE

As I climbed out of Jamie's truck, the sweet taste of his tongue still lingered on mine. I actually didn't even want to leave him; I wanted more of his time.

Closing the car door, I took a deep breath and made my way

across the parking lot toward the school building, keeping my eyes peeled for Stacey so I could collect my books. People immediately swarmed around me, worse than usual. Today would be hard. This was the first school day since I'd broken up with Miles, and I wasn't looking forward to seeing him at all. Girls and guys immediately started talking to me, wanting to know if it was true, had we broken up, were we getting back together, did I want to go out tonight...it was never-ending. I plastered on a fake smile while silently wishing I were back in the truck with Jamie; he was so easy to be around. When his truck roared to life behind me, I turned and waved good-bye, watching as he drove up the street.

Stacey came bounding over, hugging me excitedly. "Have fun, young lady?" she teased, grinning knowingly as she handed me the books and schoolbag that I'd left at her house.

"Lots of fun, actually," I confirmed. She linked her arm through mine, directing me through the crowd of people who were still after the gossip about Miles. I smiled gratefully at her as we made our way to my locker, pretending not to see or hear the people whispering about me.

"So, are you seeing him again?" she asked once we were out of earshot of others.

I laughed and nodded. "Just casually, though. I told him I'm not interested in a relationship, which he was fine with."

"What do you mean, just casually?" Stacey probed.

"Casual, no dating, just booty calls." I grinned, chewing on my lip. I had always been the good girl, always done the expected—mundane, even—but this was something entirely new. The casual agreement with Jamie was thrilling and made me feel more alive than I had felt in ages.

Stacey squealed before bursting into a fit of laughter. "You? Seriously, that's too funny! Little Miss Innocent making booty calls?" she choked out around her giggles. I nodded, laughing too. It did sound a little weird when you put it that way. "No wonder he seemed to like the idea, what the hell kind of guy is going to turn down casual sex?" she teased. "So, when are you seeing him again?" she pushed, obviously not finished hearing about him yet.

"No idea. We've exchanged numbers; maybe he won't even call me…" I trailed off, frowning, disappointed at the thought.

"Are you kidding? Trust me, he'll call!" She scoffed. "On another note, give me your phone, I have a song for you that you'll love," she added, holding out her hand for it.

Obediently, I dug my phone from my pocket and put it in her hand.

Stacey was always sending music to my phone; we didn't really have the same taste so I just humored her most of the time. Suddenly a heavy arm draped across my shoulder. I jumped, looking up to see Miles just as he leaned in and kissed my cheek. I could feel all eyes on me again as the student body seemed to fall silent as one, eagerly watching to see what would happen.

Stacey shot me a sympathetic smile. "I'll see you in class. Give you two some time to talk."

I resisted the urge to groan as I watched her walk away, waving for everyone else to leave and go to class, too. Once we were alone, I discreetly shrugged his arm off and stepped back.

"I've missed you," he said softly. "And you didn't call me back all weekend." He cocked his head to the side as he reached out, brushing my hair away from my face. I suddenly got flashes of Jamie doing the exact same thing, and how soft and cute he'd been last night.

I raised one eyebrow. "Miles, I told you Friday night—we're done."

He shook his head and stepped closer, taking hold of my hips and pulling me against his body. "Don't be like that, baby. That was just a fight; we've had them before."

"Miles, seriously, I can't be in a relationship with someone who doesn't trust me." I put my hands on his chest, pushing myself back to get some personal space.

His eyebrows knitted together and his eyes hardened as I moved away from him. "Screw that, Ellie! I love you. You can't just call time on us because we have a damn fight!"

I shook my head. "This has been over for a long time, Miles, it's just that neither of us wanted to admit it. I'm done playing around now and putting up with your shit. We're over," I stated, turning to walk off. Our relationship was long since dead; it had fractured and turned into something destructive a long time ago—around the time that he'd begun prioritizing his image and status over me, and when he took it upon himself to assume I was one of his possessions instead of his partner. We were broken beyond repair, and now I was finally strong enough to admit that I deserved better.

His fingers closed around my wrist, thwarting my escape. "No fucking way! We've been together for two and a half years, Ellie. You can't just walk away." He looked at me pleadingly, so I quickly averted my eyes. This relationship wasn't good for either of us; he had to see that.

"I'm sorry, I really am," I whispered.

Suddenly he let go of my wrist, stepping back and shaking his head. "This isn't over. Not at all," he stated confidently, touching his hair, making sure it was in that perfect style he prided himself on. "I'm coming over for dinner tonight with my parents, remember? This will all blow over, I promise. I love you, baby." He kissed my cheek before turning and strutting off in the other direction, leaving me standing there utterly speechless.

I'd forgotten about him coming over for dinner tonight. Our

parents were friends, so they regularly got together for fancy dinner parties and boring conversation. My parents adored Miles, as did all of the school, probably because he didn't show them the dominant, angry side of his personality. He could certainly be charming when he wanted to be.

Groaning from frustration, I went to class. I'd just have to worry about dinner later. Maybe when I reminded my parents that we'd split up, they'd cancel their plans. In the back of my mind, though, I knew it wouldn't work out like that.

* * *

My day passed much as I thought it would. The girls were consoling me, asking if I was okay. The boys asked if I was now free to date. All I'd wanted to do was go home and curl into a ball. Of course, I couldn't do that, though; I had an image to uphold. People whispered wherever I went, but I kept my head held high. People looked up to me. I was the head cheerleader, and I needed to show people that I was still Ellie Pearce, with or without Miles Barrington.

Much to my surprise, there were no further incidents with Miles; in fact, I didn't even see him for the rest of the school day.

When I finally arrived home after school and cheer practice, I slinked straight up to my room, firing up my laptop and then digging in my bag to find the ripped photo that I'd stolen from Jamie's room while he was in the shower this morning. He hadn't said much about it, but I'd seen how upset he was about it last night. He'd been totally devastated seeing the ruined photo of his sister—and that was when I'd devised my plan.

Just as I was scanning the two halves of the picture and saving them to my laptop, my phone beeped with a message from Jamie asking about my day. A smile twitched at the corners of my mouth at his thoughtfulness. I sent him a quick text back and then clicked on my laptop, opening up Photoshop.

When I was finished with it, I smiled proudly at my efforts. I wasn't exactly a whiz at Photoshop, and the newly restored photo wasn't perfect by any means, but hopefully Jamie would like it. I printed off a copy and then saved the image to a spare flash drive I found in my drawer so he could make more copies if he wanted. After, I headed to the shower.

When I was out and dry, I pulled on a pair of ripped jeans and long-sleeve fitted black top, leaving my hair down to dry naturally. I didn't bother with makeup. There was no need to dress to impress tonight. Once I was ready, I headed downstairs to help my mother prepare dinner.

"Ellison, shouldn't you get changed?" Mom asked, her tone disapproving.

Of course, she would request that I change. For my mom, everything was about appearances, money, and status. She believed you had to look your best at all times; she wouldn't even do housework without a full face of makeup. It was one of the reasons she approved of Miles—his father was a big-time lawyer, and she liked that our relationship enabled her to associate with a different class of people. She was shallow, and I worked my hardest so that I would never end up like her.

My father, on the other hand, was incredible, and supported me wholeheartedly. I was a complete daddy's girl. I could do no wrong in his eyes. His attention made up for the years of disapproving looks I'd gotten from my mother when I climbed a tree or played football with the boys instead of holding tea parties with my dolls.

"No, I'm fine in this. Do you want help with dinner?" I asked politely, ignoring her disapproving glare.

"You could chop those." She sighed and motioned toward the

vegetables. "You do know the Barringtons will be here in an hour, don't you?" she asked coldly.

Bitch.

"Yeah, I know. You do know Miles and I have broken up, don't you?" I countered, trying to mimic her hard tone but failing miserably.

She waved her hand dismissively. "You two will get back together."

I didn't say anything; let her think what she wanted. Tonight was going to be extremely awkward. Miles always did know how to twist me around his finger and get me to do what he wanted; I just prayed I was strong enough to say no this time.

CHAPTER 8

WHEN THE DOORBELL rang an hour later, my heart sank. I'd been secretly hoping that Miles would cancel, but wishful thinking never really got you anywhere. My dad, who had arrived home only ten minutes before, was still changing his clothes in the bedroom, so my mother looked at me expectantly.

"I'll get it then, shall I?" I asked, rolling my eyes and heading for the door without waiting for her to answer.

I opened it to see the Barringtons standing there, smiling politely, holding an expensive-looking bottle of wine and a basket of fruit. Miles's parents were extremely wealthy, so it probably pained them to think that their son was dating a girl like me. Not that we were poor or anything; actually, my dad did really well for himself. He was a financial adviser, and we certainly weren't short on money, but compared to the Barringtons I would imagine that we looked like vagrants.

"Good evening, Ellie. How are you tonight?" Susan asked politely.

How am I? Uncomfortable, embarrassed, harassed, and annoyed.

"I'm fine, thank you, Mrs. Barrington. How are you?" I replied, smiling and ignoring the way she was looking me over in my casual clothes.

"We're very well," she replied, smiling awkwardly.

"That's great. Come on in, dinner's almost ready," I offered, opening the door wider, trying not to make eye contact with Miles. As the three of them stepped into the hallway, I regretted my choice of attire for tonight. They were dressed formally. Susan, Miles's mother, was in an immaculate red cocktail dress that probably cost thousands, and both Miles and his father were wearing tailored gray suits—though Miles had elected for no tie. They definitely made me feel underdressed. Thankfully, my mom appeared almost immediately and took them off my hands, showing them into the living room for drinks. I took their coats and headed to the closet to hang them up.

Miles followed me, as I knew he would, and wrapped his arms around me from behind as I hung the coats on the rack. "Hey, forgiven me yet?" he breathed down my neck.

I elbowed him in the stomach and pulled out of his arms. "Miles, seriously, stop it! I told you I don't want—" I started, but he caught my hips and turned me to face him. I didn't have time to think about what was about to happen before his head dipped and he forcefully pressed his lips against mine. I gasped, shocked that he would have the nerve to kiss me after I'd insisted we were over. Whipping my head back, I shoved my arms between us and pushed him away with as much force as I could muster.

"You are really starting to piss me off! Don't keep thinking that I'm going to change my mind; I won't!" I hissed quietly, not wanting our parents to hear.

Miles's face immediately turned pleading as he stepped closer to me again. "Ellie, please, I said I'm sorry, what more do you want? What can I do? I'll do anything. You want me to beg? I'll beg," he said, dropping down to his knees and taking my hands in his. "Please, Ellie?" he whispered, kissing the back of my hand.

My insides clenched and I squirmed on my feet with embarrassment and unease. If he were like this all the time, then things would certainly be different, but he wasn't.

"You like my shirt, Miles?" I asked, raising my eyebrows. He would hate it if I went out in this; it was just an ordinary black fitted top, but it had quite a low V-neck that exposed more cleavage than he usually tolerated.

His eyes dropped to my chest and a frown lined his forehead. "Yeah, it's nice," he answered immediately. The tiny twitch to his eye showed me he was lying, though.

"Yeah, I have it in white, too. I'm going to wear it to school tomorrow, with that denim skirt, you know, the short one that you don't like…" I trailed off, smiling sweetly.

That did it; he jumped to his feet, glaring at me. "Fuck that! You can't wear that to school, you'll look like a slut and all the guys will think you're easy. Don't you fucking dare!" he growled angrily.

Now there's the guy I broke up with! "Thanks, you just made this night a lot easier for me." I yanked my hands from his and walked off quickly before he could stop me.

All through dinner I ignored Miles playing with my hair and drawing a pattern on the back of my neck with his finger. I smiled when I was supposed to, and added my piece to the conversation when I was expected to. When the talk turned to Miles and me going to college, I gritted my teeth. Clearly he had neglected to mention to his parents that we'd broken up.

"So, obviously, what with you two applying to the same schools, you'll be spending quite a bit of time together. Do you think maybe you'll be considering living together?" Miles's dad asked, making me almost choke on my drink. He turned to my dad and smiled wickedly. "What do you think, Michael, are the kids going to live in sin for a while or will you be insisting on a proposal?" he joked, winking at him.

Miles laughed and answered before I could even open my mouth. "Maybe we could share a place; it would be easier if we rented together. And I'm not opposed to a proposal," he replied, smiling over at me, ignoring my attempts to kill him with my icy glare.

This had gone far enough now. As much as he was annoying me, though, I still couldn't bring myself to embarrass him in front of his parents.

Picking up my plate and my dad's, I stood. "Miles, how about you help me with the dessert?" I asked through my teeth, trying to keep my face neutral.

He stood and took the plates from my hand, smiling sweetly. "Sure thing, baby."

I stomped off to the kitchen, taking deep breaths, trying to calm my frayed nerves. As soon as he stepped through the kitchen door, I rounded on him. "What the hell was that? Are you not listening to me? It's over! This needs to stop; I want you to leave, right now. Tell your parents you're not feeling well or something and leave!" I hissed angrily.

He closed the door to the kitchen and shook his head. "You don't mean that, baby. I love you, and you love me." He wrapped his arms around me again, trapping me against his hard chest.

"If you don't get off me right now, I'm going to scream," I warned him.

He grinned, looking at me knowingly. "No you won't, you don't like to make a scene, you hate being the center of attention," he whispered, leaning in and kissing my neck. Suddenly he pulled back, his mouth popping open in shock. "What the fuck is that?" he spat through his teeth. He sounded so angry that I actually flinched.

"What?"

"*That!*" He pointed an accusing finger at the back of my neck. "You have a fucking hickey! I didn't do that! Where the hell did you get that from?" he growled. I had a hickey on my neck? I winced. Jamie must have done it and I hadn't even realized. "Well?" he demanded.

"We're broken up," I rebutted, as if that answered his question.

He slammed his hand down on the counter next to me. "No. We. Are. Not!" he spat, saying each word slowly. "I'm not letting you see someone else, Ellie; you're mine!"

"Screw you! I've had enough of your bullshit. What are you gonna do, Miles, huh? Nothing, that's what you're gonna do. Let's just go finish dinner, then you can leave. You're seriously pissing me off right now," I retorted, pulling my shoulders back, trying to appear more confident than I felt.

I turned to walk away, but he caught my wrist, forcibly yanking me to a stop. "Who was it? Who are you letting put their fucking hands on you?" His grip on my wrist tightened to the point of pain.

"You're hurting me!" I yelped, twisting my arm to get free. "It's none of your business who did it; we're over. Let me go."

He stepped closer, his nostrils flaring. His hard eyes latched onto mine as he leaned in so that our noses almost touched. "When I find out who it was, he's dead. You're mine; sooner or later you'll remember that." Without another word or an apology for hurting me, he marched out of the room. I blinked, shocked at his outburst. The skin on my wrist burned, but he hadn't squeezed enough to leave a mark. He'd never physically manhandled me before, or frightened me. I didn't quite know how to deal with what had just happened.

Thankfully, before I got too wrapped up in trying to process what had transpired, the kitchen door opened and my flustered-looking mother walked in.

"Are you getting the dessert or not? People are waiting!" she snapped, already headed to the refrigerator. I nodded, forcing a tight smile as I went to help her, praying for this night to just end already.

JAMIE

"Kid, seriously, you still have time to back out," Ray said, looking at me worriedly.

"Honestly, I'll be fine. I need to do this." I pulled out my last twenty-five bucks and handed the money to Jensen. "So, what are my odds?" I asked him.

He smiled and withdrew a little notebook from his pocket, scribbling my bet inside. "Kurt's pretty badass, so I'll give you four-to-one odds. People won't bet on you; he's won the last three competitions he's entered, and no offense, Kid, but you don't look that tough," he replied.

Ray dug in his pockets, pulling out a wad of cash. "I'll definitely take a piece of that; my money's firmly on the kid." He slapped me on the back, grinning.

My fight wasn't for another half hour, since I was third, so Ray and I went to stand on the sidelines and watch the first two fights. Ray was right, they were brutal, and nothing like what I'd seen here before. This really was going to hurt. I didn't care, though—in a way I welcomed the pain; it gave me something else to think about. I'd learned to think of it that way, and it had helped me out of many a situation.

From the corner of my eye, I watched Kurt. He was incredibly focused while warming up and stretching. The only thing I would have to my advantage was his overconfidence. He thought this would be an easy win. I wouldn't make it easy for him, though; I needed the money too damn badly.

Finally my fight was called. I smiled confidently at Ray, who looked like he was chewing off his already short nails. The fighting area wasn't cordoned off or anything, but there was a clear space where the action took place—marked out by the crowd standing in a large circle waiting to spend their money. Essentially, you could bet on anything, but I was only interested in betting on the outcome, not how fucked up I was going to get in the process.

The crowd parted as I walked forward. People blatantly sized me up, whispering to one another as they moved aside and let me enter the "ring." Suddenly the shouting began; people were screaming their bets at Jensen, waving cash in the air while he took their money and scribbled in his pad, giving them odds seemingly off the top of his head. I smiled as I heard one guy bet that I would be tapping out within a minute, and another bet that my nose would be the first thing to bleed.

Kurt smirked at me as he walked into the ring too, his green eyes shining with confidence. "I'm going to fuck you up so bad you're gonna wish you'd never woke up this morning," he growled, his voice low and threatening.

I shrugged off his threat. "Dude, look, we're both here for the money, we don't need to talk trash to each other," I replied, amused by how into it he was getting. He really did think he was Tyler Durden from *Fight Club*, judging by the look on his face.

"I'm going to tear you a new asshole," he spat.

I rolled my eyes. "Honestly? Can we stop with the small talk? Damn, you talk like a bitch."

"I'm going to hurt you so bad your grandkids are going to feel it!" he hissed angrily.

I burst out laughing at that. "Oh shit, stop making me laugh, this is a serious fight!"

I was still laughing when Jensen blew the whistle to start.

Kurt immediately came at me with a right jab. I jumped to the side. He rounded and came at me again. He looked like he wanted to kill me, and my body slipped into autopilot. As he brought his foot up to kick me, I dropped down onto one knee and punched him hard in the groin.

As soon as I did it, he let out a guttural groan and staggered back a couple of steps, his eyes watering.

"Shit, man, ouch! That hurt, right? I'm really sorry," I said, hissing through my teeth. I could see Ray and Jensen laughing wickedly in the corner.

"Motherfucker!" Kurt growled, righting himself and coming at me again. He was seriously pissed now, and I immediately regretted using the hitting-in-the-balls card too early.

He was actually a pretty good fighter and managed to land a few punches that would definitely hurt when the adrenaline wore off in a little while, but he wasn't too strong on defense. The next time he left his face unprotected, I elbowed him in the nose and then kicked him hard in the top of his thigh, making his leg give out. As he fell to his knees, I smashed my foot into his face, knocking him out cold.

I watched as he collapsed face-first onto the cold concrete floor. When he didn't move, I stared at his limp body in shock. Had I seriously just won? Relief washed over my body in waves. I now had money to pay my rent with.

Jensen strutted over and grabbed my arm, holding it in the air victoriously. "Let's hear it for Kid Cole!" he shouted enthusiastically. Some people clapped or cheered, but most of them were too busy scowling at Kurt's unconscious body on the floor. They had obviously bet against me. "Good job," Jensen congratulated me, grinning from ear to ear.

"Thanks." As I spoke, my jaw throbbed. While medics came

over to look at Kurt, who was now coming around, I walked over
to where Ray was standing. He pulled up a chair for me, and
I gratefully plopped into it. I moved my joints carefully, checking for damage. My stomach was hurting a little, but nothing I
couldn't cope with. Everything else was fine as far as I could see,
no permanent damage done ... yet.

Ray grinned down at me, holding out a bottle of water. "Kid,
that was too funny, I couldn't stop laughing when you apologized
to him for hitting him in the balls," he said, laughing his ass off
again, making me laugh, too.

Jensen came over a couple of minutes later. "Right, you're
fighting the winner of the next round." He nodded toward two
muscled guys as they walked into the middle.

"Oh, great. Well, I hope the smallest one wins," I joked. Jensen
handed me my $125 winnings. "So, what are my odds for the next
fight?"

He grinned. "After that little spectacle with Kurt, I'd say the
odds are certainly more in your favor now, so two to one." He
shrugged.

"Put that on me then," I requested, offering him the money.

He grinned and nodded, scribbling my bet in his notebook. "I'd
better go start the next fight. Good luck," he said, nodding at me.
I didn't need good luck; even if I lost the next fight I had already
earned $100 for getting to that round, which would pay my rent.
If I won then I'd have $200 for getting to the final plus $375 from
betting on myself, too.

Ray winced as we watched the two guys fighting; they were
both pretty strong and well built. "How much money do you
actually need? Why don't you call it a night on what you've got?"
he suggested almost pleadingly.

"I need as much as I can get." I didn't want to have to do anything like this again. Even though it was ten times better than

working for Brett, this wasn't exactly my idea of going straight. The more I earned tonight, the more pressure it took away, and the less chance there was of me getting caught in this situation again.

My phone beeped, so I pulled it open to see a text from Ellie:

Thanks for marking me Stud. You just got me in trouble! x

Marking her? Oh, the hickey! She'd finally seen it. I laughed unashamedly; I didn't feel guilty, I loved that mark on her skin. My next fight was due to start any minute, so I texted her back quickly:

Oops. I'll make it up to you. I promise x

"Who's that?" Ray asked.

"A friend." I smirked.

"Yeah? The redhead from the club?" he probed, his eyes wide.

"Yep," I stated proudly as he grinned and patted me on the shoulder in congratulations.

* * *

By the end of the three fights, I was exhausted. My entire body was sore and tender—but I'd won. I sat down in a spare chair cautiously, trying not to move too fast. I had undoubtedly broken a couple of ribs.

Jensen came over almost immediately. "That was awesome! Want a regular slot here? We could use someone like you to draw in the crowds. People are going to be talking about you now," he said, grinning. "Thanks for bringing him to me, Ray." He gripped Ray's shoulder, looking at him gratefully.

I shook my head, ignoring the pain that burned in my shoulder. "No thanks, Jensen. Tonight was a one-off."

He sighed sadly. "Yeah, okay. If you ever want to come back, you let me know; there's no waiting list for you." From his pocket he produced a folded stack of cash with an elastic band holding it together. "Right then, so all together, including your bet, I owe you... $1,625," he said, carefully counting it out before handing it to me.

Score! I shoved the money into my pocket and hissed through my teeth as my fingers brushed against the material. *Damn it, maybe I've broken a finger or two as well.*

"Right then, hospital, Kid?" Ray asked, looking me over slowly.

"Nah, it's not too bad, I've had worse. There's nothing serious." I shrugged and pushed myself out of the chair. Ray sighed before walking over to his car and opening the door for me. Smiling gratefully, I sank into the leather seat and closed my eyes as he drove me back to my apartment building.

"Please don't do this again. I don't want to see you hurt," Ray pleaded when we pulled up.

"I won't. Thanks for setting this up for me tonight, and driving me and stuff." I gave him a man hug, clenching my jaw tightly when he patted my back, making pain zip through my ribs.

I climbed out of the car and walked to my building, wearily climbing up the stairs and fumbling with my keys with my damaged fingers. As soon as I was inside, I leaned against the door and squeezed my eyes shut. My ribs were killing me; every time I took a breath they hurt. My hands were burning; I looked down at my swollen red knuckles and clenched them into fists, hissing as the pain worsened. I headed into the bathroom and ran the cold water, putting both of my hands under there, trying to cool them.

There was nothing seriously wrong with me, just plenty of bruising and a couple of broken ribs and fingers, but they'd heal on their own. After swallowing a couple of painkillers and washing my face with cold water, I headed back to my bedroom and stripped out of my clothes, trying to look in the broken mirror, but I couldn't see much. I had a split lip, and a wicked bruise was forming on the side of my jaw; I'd probably also have a black eye by the time I woke up tomorrow.

Despite the agony I was in, I smiled as I climbed into my bed. I'd done it, and without going to Brett.

I reached out to grab the photo of Sophie from the side table, but it wasn't there. It must have fallen on the floor, but I was just too exhausted to get up and find it. By the time the painkillers kicked in enough to let me fall asleep, it was almost two in the morning.

CHAPTER 9

PAIN. IT WAS everywhere at once. I groaned before even opening my eyes. My fingers were stiff; my chest and sides were throbbing. It felt as if I'd been hit by a freight train. I pushed myself up, hissing through my teeth as a white-hot pain shot up my back from where someone had kneed me in the kidneys last night. I'd have to keep an eye on it and make sure I didn't start passing blood when I peed.

I grabbed my cell phone to check the time; it was just past eight in the morning. There was nothing I needed to do today; the car I'd fixed at the junkyard was going to auction tomorrow night, so I wouldn't know until Thursday whether Connor and his dad were going to hire me to fix up their others.

I decided to call Ellie and see if she was still talking to me after I'd gotten her in trouble with the hickey on her neck.

The phone rang for a while on her end and when she answered she was laughing. "Hey, stud," she choked out around her giggles.

I smiled. "What's so funny?" I asked, licking my split lip gently.

"Stacey put a ringtone on my cell for you, I didn't realize. It made me laugh, that's all," she admitted, still chuckling.

"Yeah? What is it?" I settled myself back on the bed, loving the sound of her sexy voice.

"It's nothing, I'll take it off. It's embarrassing."

"It's embarrassing? Oh, now I definitely need to know what it is," I teased, imagining her pink cheeks.

"Nope, no way. I'm taking it off as soon as I get off the phone." She laughed.

I sighed, giving in. "Fine, don't tell me then. I was just calling to check in and make sure you're not pissed at me over the hickey thing."

"I'm not pissed, though it's going to take freaking ages to go away. You're a pain in the ass," she replied playfully. Thankfully, she didn't sound too mad at me over it, and it had the effect I'd desired—it had her thinking about me!

"Your parents give you shit over it?"

"It wasn't my parents. Miles, my ex-boyfriend, saw it and went off," she grumbled.

I frowned. "Went off? What does that mean? He didn't hurt you or anything, did he?" If he'd hurt her, then I'd have to hurt him back.

"No, nothing like that. He just got angry about it. He demanded I tell him who did it. Whatever, it's okay, it's none of his business anymore," she said dismissively.

I relaxed again. "Okay, well I said I'd make it up to you, so how about I take you out this weekend?" I mentally crossed my fingers for a yes.

"Actually, I was wondering if you wanted to meet me today. I have something for you."

I frowned. I couldn't see her today because I needed to give the bruises on my face a couple of days to settle down. "Uh...

Actually, Ellie, I'm not feeling too well today. It's probably best that we don't see each other for a few days, just in case I pass you my germs or something," I lied, praying she'd believe me.

"You're sick? What's wrong?" Concern colored her voice, and I smiled because of how adorable she was.

"I think I might have the flu or something coming on. My head is pounding," I lied. Well, actually, not a complete lie, my head *was* killing me.

"Oh, okay. Well, yeah, this weekend then. Listen, I'd better go get ready for school." Her voice sounded hurt, and immediately I was annoyed at myself for rejecting her offer.

"I'll call you later in the week. Have a good day, Ellie." I couldn't help but feel disappointed that I would have to wait all week to see her again; it certainly felt like a long time.

"Yeah, hope you feel better."

She disconnected the call, so I pushed myself up out of the bed and went for a long and fairly painful shower. Even the water hurt when it touched my skin.

Afterward, I proudly paid my rent, ignoring the sneer from the guy as he looked at me. I couldn't blame him, really; I mean, I *was* a crappy ex-con with a banged-up face. I didn't deserve much respect for that.

More cautious after the break-in, I rented a safe to keep my valuables in so I wouldn't get caught in this situation again. Ray called to make sure I was all right, trying again to convince me to go to the hospital, but I didn't want to spend all of my hard-earned cash on hospital bills for stuff that would heal itself anyway.

I didn't have the energy to go out all day, so I just stayed around my room, reading yesterday's newspaper. I decided that tomorrow, if I was okay to venture out, I'd buy myself a book to pass the time with.

At just after three o'clock there was a knock on my door. I pushed myself up and answered it. My eyes immediately fell on Ellie, who stood there looking toward the stairs, her whole body tense.

Panic washed over me because she could have been hurt coming here on her own. Those guys who sat at the front of my building would probably kill to get their hands on a girl like her. "What the hell are you doing here?" I scolded, grabbing her and pulling her into the room quickly. Did this girl have no sense of self-preservation at all?

She turned to look at me and gasped as her eyes filled with tears. "What the…? What happened? Are you okay?"

"I'm fine. Why are you crying?" I asked, moving her away from the door so I could go out after whoever had upset or hurt her.

"Your face! Christ, Jamie," she whispered, hesitantly reaching out to touch my lip.

She was crying because I was hurt? That realization made my heart ache a little. I caught her hand and interlaced our fingers. "I'm fine, honestly. It probably looks worse than it is," I assured her, shrugging and ignoring the blast of pain that roared through my shoulder.

"What happened?" Her lip trembled as she spoke.

I stepped forward and wiped her tears with my free hand. "Ellie, seriously, you don't come here again, you understand me? You shouldn't be here."

I was stupid and selfish for being in this girl's life. I tried desperately not to think of all the things the scumbags in this building would do to a beautiful thing like her.

"I just wanted to come and see if you were okay. I brought you some medicine and food, in case you couldn't go out to get it." She held out a brown bag as evidence.

My breathing faltered. "You did? That's really nice of you.

Thank you. But you shouldn't ever come here on your own; hell, I don't even want you here when I'm with you. This isn't a nice place," I said, softening my voice.

"What happened?" she asked again. She turned my hand over, looking at my sore and swollen knuckles.

"I was fighting," I admitted, not wanting to lie to her. Maybe I needed to scare this girl away from me, maybe I needed to show her who I was so that she wouldn't want to hang out with me again.

Her eyes widened. "Well, are you all right? What did the doctor say? And why did you tell me you were sick?" she asked, stroking my fingers softly.

"I didn't want you to see me like this, and yes, I'm fine, the doctor said I was fine. Just bruises and a couple of tiny fractures," I replied dismissively.

She winced. "Fractures? Like broken bones? Where? What the hell?"

"A couple of fingers and ribs, that's all. They'll heal on their own; it's no big deal."

She stepped forward and went up on her tiptoes to kiss me, but she still wasn't tall enough. I smiled and pressed my lips to hers lightly. She tasted delicious. It was like torture, and I wished with every bone in my body that I was different, that I deserved her attention and sympathy, but I didn't.

She pulled back after a second or two. "You're really okay?" she whispered. I nodded in confirmation. "Is there anything I can do?" she asked, trailing her fingers over my cheek and jaw softly.

"No, it's fine, I promise," I replied, closing my eyes, enjoying her touch.

"Oh, well, never mind then. I was going to offer to kiss it better, but if you're fine then I won't," she teased, smiling playfully.

"Well, it hurts a little," I admitted, playing along.

She grinned and led me over to the bed, guiding me to sit on the edge. Her hands went to the bottom of my T-shirt and carefully lifted it over my head, gasping as she caught sight of my body. Her eyes filled with tears again.

"Jamie, this looks awful! The doctor honestly said it was okay?" she asked, clearly horrified as she sat on the bed next to me. I glanced down at myself. The bruises had worsened since I dressed this morning, and almost my whole upper body was now shades of red and purple. She groaned as she moved to look at my back. "Jeez, Jamie, your back's even worse," she said quietly.

My eyes fluttered closed as she leaned in and planted a soft kiss on my back. The attention from her felt so nice that I forgot the pain. But as her fingers trailed tenderly across the healed scars, revulsion washed over me. When her lips pressed against one of them I pulled away from her and grabbed my T-shirt, disgusted with myself.

"Sorry. Did I hurt you?" she asked, wincing apologetically.

I shook my head quickly, frowning. "No, you didn't hurt me. I just don't want you to think you have to do that, it's not nice for you to do that." Her pretty mouth shouldn't be anywhere near my disgusting body.

She frowned and gripped my shirt just as I was about to pull it back over my head. "I don't understand, what's this about then? Your scars?" she asked quietly.

I groaned. I didn't want to have this conversation. "Ellie, look, just leave it, all right?"

She shook her head and pulled the shirt from my hands, throwing it on the chair. Her hand went to my shoulder and she pushed gently, her intention clear. I sighed and allowed her to push me down onto my back. She raised herself up onto her knees and straddled me, but she was obviously being careful not to touch me in case she hurt me. She leaned over me, resting her forearms on either side of my head, our faces inches apart.

"I know you don't want to talk about it, I can see that, and that's fine. But you shouldn't keep thinking that there's something wrong with your body, Jamie. Honestly, you are sexy as hell." She looked directly into my eyes as she spoke.

She can't really think that, though, no one in their right mind can look at that mess and find it sexy.

"Ellie, I know I'm not—" I started, but she put her hand over my mouth, stopping me from talking.

"You're not listening to me. These scars"—she sat up and trailed her fingers over my chest gently—"they make you who you are. I don't know what happened to you, or how you got these, but you're still here. You survived all of that, and it's made you the person who you are today. It didn't beat you; in fact, it probably made you stronger. These don't make you any less attractive. Believe me, stud, every single inch of your body makes my mouth water." She blushed, chewing on her lip.

As I looked into her eyes I could see the truth there: She actually wasn't bothered by my scars at all. My heart sped because of how incredible she was. I cupped her face in my hands and pulled her down to kiss me. After a gentle kiss, she pulled away and placed soft kisses down my neck before trailing them over my chest and stomach, running her tongue across my scars. I closed my eyes, soaking up her attention. My whole body was alight with sensation, and I had honestly never been this happy in my whole pathetic life.

I was so freaking hot for her it was unbelievable. She pulled away and lay next to me on the bed. "Better?" she asked, raising an eyebrow as her fingers tickled patterns across my chest.

I nodded. Heck yeah it was better; that acceptance from her had meant everything. "Yeah, thanks." I brushed her hair from her face, tucking it behind her ear, marveling over her flawless complexion and her compassion. Her bringing me food and medicine because she thought I was sick was easily the nicest thing anyone had ever done for me. I'd only known her for three days. "So, did you change the ringtone that Stacey put on your cell?"

She giggled and shook her head. "Not yet, but I will."

"Let's hear it," I suggested, laughing as I grabbed my phone from the side table and dialed her number quickly; she gasped and tried to snatch it from my hand. I gripped her wrist as her hand closed around my phone, trying to disconnect the call. She was giggling as I pressed my lips to hers, waiting for the song to start playing.

"I…I…I…I can make your bed rock" started blasting from her schoolbag.

I burst out laughing as she pulled the pillow from under her head and put it over her face, chuckling as the song continued to blast in the background.

"'I can make your bed rock'?" I asked, smirking. I'd only heard this song once before, I think it was by Young Money, or something like that anyway.

"The chorus is worse," she whined, lifting the pillow. Her face was an adorable shade of red and I couldn't resist bending my head and capturing her lips with mine while the song continued in the background—something about my room being a G-spot and "call me Mr. Flintstone."

We made out for about half an hour, and then she sighed and pouted. "I should go, my parents will be wondering where I am."

"So, you free Friday night?" I asked hopefully.

Her nose scrunched up. "I can't, Friday's game night."

"Huh?" I asked, wondering what sport she would play.

"I'm head cheerleader for the football team." She shrugged.

"Wait, back up a little...I'm screwing a cheerleader?" I groaned at the thousand lustful thoughts of her in a little cheer uniform. "You have a uniform?" I could feel myself getting excited at the thought alone.

She nodded, rolling her eyes. "What is it with guys and cheer uniforms?" she teased, trailing little kisses across my cheek.

"Seriously, Ellie, you wear those little gym shorts under your skirt?" I asked, my voice filled with lust.

She laughed against my neck. "Yeah, but they're called spankies, not gym shorts."

"What color are they?" I gripped her tighter, pinning her to me as she went to get up. I ignored the pain in my hands.

"Well, why don't you come to the game Friday? Maybe I'll let you see my spankies up close," she purred.

"Yeah? I'd love to watch you shake your...pom-poms," I answered immediately.

She giggled before pushing herself off me, bending to retrieve her schoolbag. "I need to go. So I'll see you Friday then. Game starts at seven on my school's field. I'll be on the sidelines if you want to come say hello."

"I'll walk you to your car."

Suddenly she gasped and her eyes widened in apparent excitement. "Oh wait, I almost forgot the reason I wanted to see you today!" she gushed. I watched, confused, as she dug around in her schoolbag. "I stole something from you yesterday when I left."

Stole something? Did I even have anything worth stealing? From her bag she produced my ripped photo.

"Why did you take that?" I asked, swallowing the lump in my throat at the sight of the ruined photo of my sister.

"I needed it so I could do this." She grinned, holding out a white envelope.

"What is it?"

"Open it and see." She shook the envelope at me, urging me to take it.

Taking it from her hand, I opened it, curious. When I saw what was inside my heart leaped into my throat. The photo of Sophie. My chest tightened as I struggled to breathe. This photo was the only thing in the world that mattered to me, the only thing of any value, and when I'd seen that it had been ripped I'd felt like I'd lost her all over again.

How the hell could this girl who I'd known for three days do something like this for me? She barely knew me, yet she went to all this trouble. She blew my mind and left me speechless.

Ellie pointed one slender finger at Sophie's face. "I couldn't get the line to go completely, and the hole at the bottom looks a little . . . strange," she said quietly.

I raked my eyes over it slowly; the photo looked almost perfect to me.

"How did you do this?" My voice was barely above a whisper.

"I used Photoshop." She shrugged dismissively, as if doing the nicest thing anyone had ever done for me was no big deal.

I'd never had anyone think of me like that before and, to be honest, I didn't know what to do or say. I wasn't used to being treated nicely.

"Thank you." The words just didn't seem to be enough. When my eyes started to prickle, I looked away from the photo. I never cried. I probably hadn't cried since I was about seven years old. Crying didn't get you anywhere; you just had to suck it up and deal with what life threw at you.

"You're welcome. I could tell you were upset about it. There's a flash drive in the envelope too, so you can get more copies if you want." She bit her lip as if unsure of herself. "Well, maybe I'll see you Friday then?" She turned, grabbing the door handle to leave.

My heart took off at the thought of her being outside here alone. "Hey, wait! Don't go out there on your own. I'll walk you." I reached out, holding the door closed.

She rolled her eyes and smiled. "My, aren't we a gentleman."

"I'm not a gentleman; I just don't want you to get hurt by the scum that live in this building." I pulled my T-shirt over my head quickly and slipped on my sneakers. After grabbing my keys, I pushed the photo into my pocket and took her hand.

As we walked out of the building, I glared warningly at the guy who immediately started checking Ellie out, and pulled her closer to me as a prostitute stood up, smiling at me seductively. "No thanks," I said, shaking my head quickly before she could proposition me. Ellie chuckled as she led us over to an old lime-green Volkswagen Beetle.

"This is the car your grandfather left you that's always breaking down?" I asked, smiling.

"Yeah. I love my car, but it's not too good when she refuses to start." She patted the roof affectionately.

"Well, it just so happens I'm pretty good with all things mechanical. I'm only a call away, and I take payment in kind," I said suggestively, pushing her against the side of the car gently and pressing my body against hers. A smile graced her lips as her hand slid around my waist and down to my ass, pulling me even closer. "Thank you for the photo."

"No problem."

She smiled, tilting her head up in clear invitation of a kiss. Smiling back, I obliged, slanting my mouth over hers and kissing her passionately. All I wanted to do was carry her back up to my room, lock the door, and never leave . . . but that couldn't happen because her parents would worry if she didn't get home soon. With a sigh, I pulled away and opened the car door for her.

"Ellie, promise me you won't ever come here again," I

instructed. She rolled her eyes in response, clearly not under-standing how bad this area was. "I'm serious. This is important, you don't come here again, I mean it!" I looked her right in the eyes, wanting to make sure she understood.

"Okay, Jamie, whatever you want," she replied, going up on tiptoes and pressing a kiss to my bruised jaw before climbing in the car.

Closing her door, I stepped back as she started the engine, ap-plying plenty of gas before it roared to life. While I watched her drive up the road and disappear from sight, I couldn't contain my smile. I had never been this happy before, and it was all down to this girl.

CHAPTER 10

WEDNESDAY PASSED THE same as Tuesday. I didn't really do much, just rested as much as possible so that if I was working on Thursday, I wouldn't be suffering too badly. Taping my two broken fingers together seemed to stop them from throbbing as much, which I was grateful for.

On Thursday morning I made my way to the junkyard, praying that this would work out. When I walked into the office, Connor turned to me, smiling. His face fell almost immediately once he caught sight of me, his mouth dropping open in shock as his eyes widened. "Whoa, what the fuck happened to you?"

I'd already decided to lie and try to play up that this wasn't my fault, in a bid to keep our agreement open. "I got mugged. I'm okay," I lied, shrugging.

"Damn. Did they catch the guy?" he asked, pulling a chair over for me to sit in.

I waved it off with a flick of my hand. "I'll stand, I'm all right. No, they didn't catch him."

"Well, that's bad luck. They get anything?" he asked, sounding concerned.

"Just my wallet," I lied.

"There are some real assholes around here now. This used to be a nice area." He sighed.

"So, how'd the auction go?" I asked eagerly, wanting to change the subject.

A smile crossed his face as he walked around the back of his desk and sat down. "It went great, actually. Car sold for almost eight hundred bucks. We only bought it for fifty, so..." He smiled, reaching into his desk drawer and pulling out a lockbox. He opened it and started to count out bills. "There's three hundred and fifty for you." He slid the pile of bills across the desk to me. "My dad loved the idea, he wanted to know when you can have another one done by."

I resisted the urge to jump up and whoop with excitement. "I could have one ready by next Wednesday, definitely," I told him, grinning ecstatically. Everything seemed to be working out perfectly.

"That's great. How about we have a monthlong trial? If it works out I'll put you on the books," he offered.

"Yeah, whatever you want," I agreed, still grinning wildly. If I worked hard, I should be able to get about two cars done a week. If I could get them to sell for the same price as this one, I would be earning decent money.

"Great. This was a really good idea, thanks for bringing it to us. Dad was thrilled with how it went."

I stood and nodded, shoving the cash into my pocket. "Guess I'd better get to work then, huh? Thanks for this, Connor, and thank your dad for me, too." My body finally seemed to relax. Maybe things would work out after all. "Hey, want to grab a drink tonight to celebrate?"

"I'm there," Connor answered immediately.

As I headed out to choose the next car from the line to work on, I couldn't keep the proud smile off my face.

* * *

On Friday night I pulled up in the parking lot of Ellie's school, excited to see her again. We'd exchanged a few texts over the last two days, but I hadn't spoken to her since Tuesday, when we'd arranged this date—well, technically it couldn't be classified as a date, considering she didn't actually want to date me.

Climbing out of my truck, I took a deep, calming breath. I looked a mess, I knew I did. Ellie would probably take one look at me, with my fading bruises, in my plain black T-shirt and jeans, and pretend she didn't know me in front of her friends. Part of me actually hoped she would because the more time I spent with this girl, the more I liked her, and that wouldn't end well because she wasn't interested in a relationship. Even if she were interested, I wasn't good enough for her anyway.

I sighed and followed the crowd around the back of her school to the large football field. The bleachers on both sides were filling up rapidly. It seemed like the whole school was here, with parents, too.

I headed to the fifty-yard line, trying to find a seat where I would have a clear view of Ellie shaking her perfect little behind.

After a few minutes the cheerleaders came jogging out, jumping around and shouting, exciting the crowd. My eyes found Ellie immediately in her little red skirt and red-and-white top, which clung to her breasts and showed off her flat stomach. Her hair was pulled up into a neat bun; in her hands were red and white pom-poms. My eyes widened. The uniform was hotter than I'd dared imagine it would be.

The cheerleaders huddled, talking for a moment before they broke apart and spread out, launching into their very well practiced dance routine. I watched in awe as she did all kinds of flips and leg kicks; they were dancing and throwing each other around.

I would like to say I watched her shake the pom-poms, but, to be honest, I wouldn't have noticed if she put them down halfway through. Those weren't what had my attention *at all*.

When the players finally graced the field, one of them slapped Ellie's ass on the way past. She glared after him, frowning angrily. While the game was played, I watched her. She wasn't interested in the football at all, she just kept an eye on the game so she knew when to cheer and shout. The cheerleaders did their little *go team go* bit whenever it was needed.

Just before halftime she turned and scanned the crowd. When her eyes settled on me, a smile slowly spread across her face. She was definitely pleased to see me.

"*Hi,*" I mouthed to her.

"*Hi,*" she mouthed back. Smiling seductively over her shoulder, she flicked the back of her skirt up, giving me a quick glance of the red cheerleading shorts she wore. I gulped and tried desperately not to think about them. I was getting so turned on I could barely sit still.

After the game, I watched the players all shaking hands and celebrating. Ellie's team had definitely won, I could tell by the smiles on their faces, but I couldn't tell you the score. I hadn't been able to take my eyes off the hot little redhead on the sideline long enough to actually watch the game.

Ellie made her way through the crowd and up to where I was in the bleachers. "Live up to your expectations?" she asked, doing a small twirl.

"Hell yeah it does. Damn, that's seriously going to be featuring in my fantasies from now on," I replied, trying to come off as joking even though I knew it undoubtedly would.

She raised an eyebrow. "Yeah? And would *I* be in any of those fantasies, or just the uniform?"

I smiled at that. "Little girl, I have a feeling you'll feature in my fantasies for a long time to come."

She grinned triumphantly. "Yeah, the spankies do it for you, huh?"

"Just a little," I replied, winking at her. "So, you want to go out and do something now, or..." I trailed off, looking at her hopefully.

"I can't. I've agreed to go to a party with Stacey. She's split up with her boyfriend again, and needs some support, apparently," she replied, rolling her eyes.

"You don't look too impressed about it."

She shrugged one shoulder. "Stacey and Paul are always breaking up. They'll get back together at the party, and I'll just be a third wheel." Suddenly her face lit up. "Hey, you want to come? When Stacey leaves me to go and get it back on with Paul, we can hang out. There'll be plenty of empty bedrooms, in case you wanted to see my spankies up close," she flirted, stepping closer to me.

Oh, fuck... "Yeah? You gonna leave them on?" My voice hardly sounded like mine because it was so husky and filled with lust.

Her eyes flashed with excitement. "If you want."

"Well, I'd love to get a closer look." I slid my hand down her side, across her hip, and onto her bare leg. She shivered, and I willed myself not to get too excited while standing in the bleachers, surrounded by people. Running my hand back up her leg, I traced one finger along the line of her spankies; she stiffened and stepped closer to me. I was so turned on I could barely even remember how to breathe.

Lost in her eyes, I didn't notice that one of the football players had run up the stairs until he grabbed her wrist and yanked her away from me. It was the same guy who'd slapped her ass at the start of the game. "What the fuck do you think you're doing?" he spat angrily.

My body jerked toward her. If he hurt her, I was ripping his head off. This was Miles, the ex-boyfriend; I could tell by the possessive way he tried to turn her and put his body between me and her. He was your typical jock stereotype; he was still wearing his muddy jersey. The guy was a little smaller than me, maybe five foot ten, and was quite well built, but he had nothing on me. He wasn't a threat at all. I took all of this in within a second. I was adept at reading people; I had to be, where I grew up.

Ellie jerked her arm from his grasp, glaring at him. "Go away, Miles!" she said firmly but quietly, as if she didn't want people to hear.

He made a scoffing noise in the back of his throat. "Screw that! Who the hell is he?" he growled, jerking his head in my direction.

"That's none of your business," she retorted, pulling away from him. I didn't want to get involved unless she asked me to. She already knew I'd gotten into a fight, but I didn't want her to think I was just a thug or something.

His shoulders stiffened as he fumed down at her. "Go get changed, we'll talk about it in the car," he ordered, stepping between us again.

I clenched my jaw. The anger was building inside me, but I couldn't blame the guy, really; he was clearly still in love with her and wanted her back. It must be hard for him to see her with someone else. I wouldn't ever want to let her go if she were mine.

Her expression was a little taken aback as she stared at him. "The car? Are you kidding? Miles, we broke up, for goodness' sake. I'm not going to the party with you!"

Confusion lined his forehead. "We always go to parties together."

"Yeah, because we were always dating then, but we're not now, so . . ." She trailed off, shrugging.

He wrapped his arms around her waist and pulled her closer to him, their chests pressed together. "Baby, enough is enough now. You've made your point. I need you. Let's just forget everything and start again, please? Give me another chance?" he asked, bending his knees to look into her eyes.

Jealousy simmered in my veins; I wanted to rip his arms off.

Thankfully, her face didn't soften at all as she shook her head. "You've had enough chances." She pulled his arms from around her waist and stormed off without another word.

The guy's eyes narrowed in warning as he turned his attention to me. "You had better not be making any fucking moves on my girl!" he growled, stepping closer. He looked like he wanted to kill me.

"She's not your girl anymore, asshole. Damn, you're not too good at listening, are you?" I mocked, raising my eyebrows.

A muscle in his jaw throbbed. "You stay away from Ellie. She's mine, and she's too good for a little shit like you. You come near her again and we're going to have a problem," he stated, sneering as he looked me over.

"Whatever you say, Miles." I smiled, trying not to laugh at his threat. He glared at me one final time before turning to walk off. Before he got more than two paces, I grabbed his arm, stopping him. Anger coiled in my stomach. "Hey, if I see you grab Ellie like that again, I'm going to break every fucking bone in your hand. You understand?" I growled menacingly.

"Screw you!" he retorted, jerking his arm out of my grip, causing my broken fingers to throb again.

While he strutted off, I took a deep breath, trying to rein in my anger as I sat back down on the bleachers, hoping Ellie would come out looking for me once she was changed. Less than a minute later my phone rang. I smiled and answered immediately, knowing it was her.

"Hey. Sorry I walked off like that, but he was driving me crazy," she apologized.

"It's fine, don't worry."

"So, do you want to go to the party with me?" she asked.

"Sure, if you want."

"Awesome. I'll just be ten or fifteen minutes then, okay?"

"Okay, I'll be sitting in the bleachers. See you in a bit," I agreed, grinning excitedly because I would get to spend some time with her again.

CHAPTER 11

WHEN ELLIE WAS finally ready, we hopped in my truck and she directed me out of the city and farther upstate. During the thirty-or-so-minute drive it was hard for me to keep my eyes on the road. She'd changed into a short denim skirt that showed off her long legs, a pale blue shirt that hugged her breasts, and a killer pair of black stiletto ankle boots. The smell of her perfume filled the car and made me so distracted I was surprised when we arrived at our destination fully intact. The whole time I'd been driving, my pervert brain had been half focused on her legs and wondering whether she was wearing the spankies under her skirt.

When we got there, I pulled in through towering wrought iron gates and headed up a long driveway. An enormous, grand building came into view. It looked more like a hotel than a house. "So, whose house is this?" I asked, swinging into a free space and cutting the engine.

"The guy's name is Sebastian. His parents have a lot of money, but they're hardly ever here so he hosts the postgame party almost every week." She led us to the front door. Inside, the music was banging already. "Um, Jamie, as head cheerleader I'm expected to take part in the games. Well, actually, I'm expected to *lead* most of the games."

"What sort of games?"

She waved her hand dismissively. "Drinking games mostly," she replied, turning her nose up. Drinking games? This party was getting better and better by the minute, and we weren't even inside yet.

She didn't knock on the door, just twisted the handle and let us in. Almost as soon as the door opened, a guy grabbed her hand, holding it in the air in a celebratory pose. "Yay, Ellie's here!" he sang.

She laughed and shook her head, pulling her arm from his grasp and pushing him away from her playfully. "Yep. The party can officially begin." She turned to me and smiled. "Come on, stud, let's get a drink." She nodded toward another room and her hand slipped into mine as she led us through the throng of bodies grinding on each other.

As I followed her into a huge kitchen, people immediately stopped talking, their expressions turning to looks of shock and intrigue.

"Hey, guys, this is Jamie. Jamie, my friends from school," Ellie said, waving her hand around the room.

Her blonde friend came over, smiling at me wickedly. "Boy, have I heard *a lot* about you."

I laughed awkwardly. "Let me guess, you're Stacey?"

"I am," she confirmed. "And ignore these douchebags staring at you; people are just looking at you like that because Ellie used to date the school's quarterback. They're not used to seeing her with someone else."

Ellie snagged a bottle of Smirnoff Ice from a bucket of ice that sat on the kitchen counter and looked at me expectantly. "What do you want, Jamie?" she asked, nodding at the array of drinks on offer.

"Just a Coke, thanks."

She smiled, pulling a can from the bucket before turning to the crowd of high schoolers milling around. "Where's the fun tonight? You're all standing there looking bored!"

Some of the guys smiled their game smiles at her. She was definitely popular with the males—not that I blamed them for looking. The funny thing was, her personality was probably even better than her looks, if that was possible. Maybe none of these guys had really taken the time to get to know the real her. They were missing out for sure.

"I thought *you* were the fun, Ellie," a guy answered immediately.

Smiling in response, she picked up a stack of plastic cups from the counter. "Someone get a Ping-Pong ball," she ordered.

I laughed and watched her setting up a game of beer pong. I noticed that Ellie started the game and had the first go, but then, smartly, she stood back to let everyone else get trashed. After beer pong, she started a game of "Where's the Water?" in the living room, hiding a shot of water among ten shots of vodka. Then, in the yard, she started a game she called Russian Beer Roulette, shaking up random cans of beer and hiding them among normal ones so people would get drenched opening them.

When everyone seemed busy, she pulled me over so we could dance for a bit. We had to stop every couple of minutes, though, because someone wanted her attention.

After a little while I excused myself to the bathroom and left her with a group of her friends. Once I'd done my business, I walked out of the bathroom and was immediately grabbed from behind and slammed into the wall, face-first. Instinctively, I went into self-preservation mode. Using the wall as leverage, I shoved myself backward, ramming whoever was holding me against the opposite wall. They let out a pain-filled groan but didn't loosen their arms, which were wrapped around my chest. My body throbbed with white-hot pain because of the pressure on my broken ribs. Raising my arms, I knocked the hands off me. I didn't even need to think about what I was doing; this kind of thing came naturally to me. Spinning around, I had my hand around the attacker's throat before I even saw who it was.

Miles. Ellie's ex.

"What the fuck are you doing?" I growled, putting my face inches from his, tightening my hand warningly but not enough to actually hurt him.

He struggled, thrashing, trying to squirm out of my choke hold. "Get the hell off me!" he shouted. I loosened my grip before shoving him away from me, watching as he stumbled and just managed to catch himself before he fell on his ass. "You little prick! You need to stay away from Ellie!" he demanded, raising himself to his full height, attempting to appear threatening as he glared at me.

"When she tells me to stay away, I will. Until then, you touch either me or her again, and you'll regret it." My words were full of acid and promise. From the barely concealed fear on his face I could tell he understood. He obviously knew I could kick his ass, so he wouldn't try to take me on his own. If he was going to do anything it would be with a couple of friends—and even then they'd lose. I had the edge in any fight, mainly because I just didn't care. It didn't matter if I died; it'd probably be better in the long run anyway. Not caring made me a better fighter; I didn't have any inhibitions or worries. When I was fighting I was like a machine; I didn't even feel pain at the time.

Miles snorted and turned, storming off. I glared after him,

shaking out my hands, wincing at the burning pain in my fingers and ribs.

After taking a couple of deep breaths to calm myself, I headed back down to Ellie, seeing her still chatting with her friends exactly where I'd left her. Weaving through the crowd, I stopped at her side. She smiled up at me and slipped one arm around my waist.

"Hey," she said.

Wrapping my own arm around her, I pulled her against my side, proud that I was getting affection from the prettiest and most popular girl in the room.

* * *

We spent another hour laughing and talking with Ellie's friends. They seemed like a nice group of people. Miles glared at her the whole time; she either didn't see him or ignored him, which made me smirk over in his direction. After a little while he came up to her. I stiffened, ready for more trouble.

"So this is it? I can fuck who I want. It's over?" he slurred, still looking at her hopefully, as if she was going to suddenly fall into his arms again.

"You can do whatever you want, Miles, or whoever you want. Go have some fun," she replied, shrugging.

"Fine, I will!" he snapped, walking off and grabbing a drunk-looking blonde girl and kissing her without even saying anything to her. She kissed him back immediately, wrapping her arms around his neck.

Ellie shook her head, crinkling her nose in distaste. "Ew... I hope he uses protection because Ruby is a real tramp." She giggled and turned to me, smiling. "Want to dance some more?"

I nodded and led her back to the living room, pulling her close, loving the fact that she didn't seem to see any other guy in the room.

Her friend Stacey was happily making out against the wall with a brown-haired guy. "Is that Stacey's boyfriend that you said she'd make up with?" I asked, pointing at them.

Ellie's mouth curved into a smile as she nodded. "Yep. Change of plan then. Upstairs, stud! You have some making up to do yourself," she flirted, biting her lip, looking so sexy that I couldn't help but groan.

Her fingers interlaced with mine as she wove through the throng of people, guiding me up the stairs. Once we were in a room at the back of the house, she locked the door and leaned against it, her eyes shining with excitement. My lust spiked immediately so I dipped my head and kissed her, running my hands down her body slowly, relishing the feel of her. My lips traveled down her neck as she gasped and tipped her head back.

"Jamie, be careful. I don't want you to hurt yourself," she murmured.

There she goes, being all thoughtful again!

"I won't hurt myself; stop worrying about me. I don't think I'll be up for sex, but I can definitely make you scream in other ways," I answered, taking her hand and tugging her toward the bed.

She giggled excitedly as I pushed her down onto the bed and hovered above her, ignoring the burning in my ribs due to the effort. I traced one hand up her leg, making her squirm under me.

"I have an idea," I said, my voice thick with lust.

"Oh yeah? What's that then?" She lifted my shirt slowly, trailing her fingers across my skin, leaving goose bumps in their wake.

"I never got to see the end of that dance last week. How about you finish it for me now?" Last week when she did it, I was so eager for her body that I couldn't take the teasing, but since I wasn't up for much tonight I would love for her to tease the life out of me.

"You want me to give you another lap dance?" She chuckled.

Hell yeah I do. "Mm-hmm," I mumbled against her neck, biting her gently.

She let out a breathless moan. "Okay, but take your clothes off first. If I have to be in my underwear, then so do you."

I pulled back immediately, stripping out of my clothes as quickly as possible. Ellie sat up, her eyes trained on my body. I didn't feel self-conscious around her now. She was definitely telling the truth; she really did like my body, scars and all. I could tell by her face and the honesty in her eyes as she looked me over.

When I was down to my boxers, she stood up. "Sit," she ordered, pointing to a chair. I sat down obediently, trying to rein in my excitement. She unbuttoned her skirt, pushing it down over her hips and letting it drop to the floor. "Shoes on or off?" she asked, putting one foot on the chair between my legs, lightly brushing across my overexcited crotch.

I wondered if she had done things like this for Miles. He was seriously lucky to have dated her for so long. I envied him, I really did. "Shoes on, definitely," I chose, looking down at the sexy little black ankle boots. "Those are seriously hot." I licked my lips as I imagined them digging into the small of my back while she wrapped herself around me.

She grinned teasingly. "Do you have a little shoe fetish, Jamie?"

My eyes raked up her body, taking in every inch of her long, toned legs. "I think I just have an Ellie fetish."

She smiled, brushing the toe of her shoe across my thigh before she put her leg down on the floor. My arousal spiked immediately. *Oh yeah, I'm definitely developing a slight shoe fetish!*

Her smile was seductive as she unbuttoned her long shirt

painfully slowly, making my breath catch. She turned her back, looking at me over her shoulder as she pushed her shirt down, exposing the creamy skin of her shoulders and back.

I groaned. Maybe this wasn't a good idea; this teasing was actually making my whole body ache and long to do things to her that would make her moan my name. She dropped her shirt to the floor and I gasped when I caught sight of the spankies she had on. They made her ass look edible. She unclasped her bra, dropping that to the floor, too. Turning back to face me, she sauntered over in just her little red cheer shorts and stiletto ankle boots. I had never seen anything more exquisite and perfect in my life. And based on the excitement that danced in her eyes, she was going to enjoy this as much as I was.

★ ★ ★

After an hour of making her breathe my name over and over upstairs, we finally headed downstairs to the raging party. We hadn't had sex because I just wouldn't be able to with my ribs, but I had certainly made up for getting in trouble with the hickey.

She had a few more drinks but still wasn't trashed. Apparently Miles had left with the blonde girl, which I was grateful for, since I didn't want him to be starting trouble and embarrassing Ellie tonight.

Ellie was so much fun. I watched her dance with her friends, play drinking games, and generally make the party more exciting for everyone. Not once did she look embarrassed that I was with her; she included me in everything that she did and every conversation she had.

At just after one in the morning, she stopped dancing. "Had enough?" she asked, looking at me hopefully.

I nodded. "Sure, if you have." Actually, I didn't think I would ever have enough of this night.

"Yeah, I'm all danced out." Her hand slipped into mine as we wove through the crowd until she spotted Stacey, who was still making out with the brown-haired guy. "Stace, we're leaving now. See you tomorrow, okay?" Ellie said, hugging her.

"Yeah, I'll be over around four," Stacey replied. She turned her attention to me. "Make sure you take my best friend home safely, you hear?" She hugged me, too. I could tell she was drunk by the way she swayed on her feet, leaning on me heavily—that and the fact that her breath was about eighty proof were dead giveaways

Ellie rolled her eyes. "Paul, don't let her drink any more."

Stacey smiled sweetly at her friend before slurring, "I'm not having any more. I'm just finishing this one, then moving to orange juice."

Ellie pointed to the cup Stacey was holding. "This one?" Stacey nodded. Ellie took it from her and downed the contents, wincing before handing back the empty cup. "There, you're all done. Juice from now on, yeah?" She threw a warning glance at Paul.

"Aww, Ellie Pearce, you're no fun." Stacey pouted.

"I know, so they tell me. See you tomorrow, Stace. Paul, you'd better look after her." The concern in her voice was easy to hear. Paul nodded, but he looked like he wasn't really paying attention. He was wasted too and wouldn't be able to protect his girl if there was trouble.

"Maybe we should take them both home?" I suggested, bending close to Ellie's ear.

Ellie's eyes widened in shock. "Really? You don't mind?"

"It's no problem." I would rather take them home than leave them here in the state they were in.

Ellie shot me a beaming smile as she looped one arm through Stacey's and the other through Paul's. "Come on, Jamie's going to take you two home." She led them to the door, ignoring Stacey's protests about one more dance.

We dropped off Paul first and then drove to Stacey's place. "So, Jamie, you gonna go make Ellie's bed rock?" Stacey asked, giggling in the backseat. "Friends with benefits, it's a great idea. Maybe I should do that with Paul. Then I could go out on dates with other people and still get to use him for his hot body," she slurred, looking like she was actually considering the thought.

Ellie laughed and rolled her eyes. "Yeah, but you love Paul, so for you two that wouldn't really work out."

"Yeah, but the feeling of first meeting someone, the first kiss, the first date, that's incredible. You two still get to do that with other people but have dirty, hot sex with each other whenever you want. Hmm...nice," she mused, closing her eyes and resting her head back, getting comfortable.

When we got to her house, Ellie walked her in, gaining a disapproving look from Stacey's father as he opened the door when Stacey struggled to get the key in the lock. I watched him give them both a lecture, and I was glad I'd waited in the truck.

"Oops, she's in deep shit," Ellie said as she climbed back in my truck.

She directed me to her house. Her street was really nice, the houses were large, and all the front yards were well kept. Her family definitely had some money. That surprised me a little, because she didn't act like the spoiled little girl that I thought would live in one of these types of houses.

"Stop here," she instructed, pointing to a big white house.

I pulled up at the curb and jumped out, going around to her side to open her door, still trying to behave like a gentleman. "This is your house?" I whistled appreciatively.

"No, I live next door." She shook her head and took my hand, leading me to an equally large house with a blue door.

"So why did I park there?" I asked, confused.

"I don't want my parents to see your car."

I stopped as we got to her door and leaned in to kiss her. She kissed me back immediately, wrapping her arms around my neck as I pressed her against the door, savoring every last second so I could picture it until I saw her again.

"I'll call you tomorrow; maybe we could meet up next week?" I asked hopefully.

A frown lined her forehead. "You don't want to come in?"

"Uh, do you want me to?" I asked incredulously. She smiled and nodded, slipping her key in the door. "But what about your parents? Won't they be up?" I winced as I imagined her dad coming downstairs and seeing me looking the way I did, covered in fading bruises. That really wasn't the type of first impression I would want him to have of me.

"They'll be in bed; so will my sister, Kelsey. It's fine. If we're really quiet, I can sneak you in. They leave every Saturday morning at nine to go and visit my nana, so you can just leave after they've gone."

She wants me to stay the night at her house? "Really? You sure?"

"Yeah, but only if you want to. I mean, you don't have to...I just thought that—" she stuttered, but I cut her off by kissing her fiercely. She giggled against my lips and pulled back. "I'll take that as a yes." She turned, unlocking the door and stepping inside, immediately looking around. "All clear. You want a drink or something to eat?" she whispered.

I shook my head and stepped in, closing the door quietly behind me. "I'm fine."

She grinned and then headed to the stairs, stopping at the bottom to remove her shoes. Following suit, I kicked off my sneakers, grabbing them before silently following her upstairs.

Her bedroom wasn't how I thought it would be. I'd imagined it to be girlie and pink. Instead, three walls were painted white, and one had black wallpaper. There was a large black leather sleigh bed with black sheets, and even the furniture was black. There *was* some pink in the room, but it wasn't the cute baby pink that I'd imagined, it was a hot pink, bright and in your face. On the walls were framed black-and-white prints of Paris and Milan. This room was Ellie all over—surprising, sophisticated, and sexy as hell.

"This wasn't what I was expecting," I admitted quietly, taking in all of her room, from her fancy dark wood dressing table with a sewing machine on top, to the thigh-high pile of shopping catalogs piled in the corner, to the hot-pink chair that was covered in sketchbooks and colored fabric swatches.

She smiled and locked her door before switching on her bedside light and closing the drapes. "No? What were you expecting?"

I wrapped my arms around her waist and walked her over to the bed. "I'm not sure, not this, though," I replied, kissing her softly.

She moaned quietly and kissed me back. I immediately got to work on her clothes, tugging them off, as she did mine. She moved onto the bed and lowered her naked body, looking at me expectantly as she pulled the sheets to the side in invitation. I climbed in eagerly, immediately kissing down her neck and across her breasts and stomach, tracing my fingers over the contours of her body.

"Hmm, I wonder how quiet you can be," I teased, grinning wickedly as I kissed lower down. She giggled and pulled a pillow over her face as I trailed my tongue over her tummy, dipping it into her bellybutton. The pillow was probably a smart idea; she was a bit of a screamer.

CHAPTER 12

THE FOLLOWING MONTH was easily the best one of my life. Ellie and I continued to see each other casually. We texted back and forth every day and I saw her at least twice a week.

My job was going well at the junkyard, too. The money was more than I had hoped and Connor's dad even put me on the books so I was legitimate and paying taxes. The best thing was that they didn't ask for references or anything about my past, just accepted me at face value, so I didn't even need to lie.

Because I now had a steady income, Ellie and I were going to look around at a few apartments today, so I could finally move out of the craphole I lived in.

When I pulled up outside her house I noticed that her parents' car was still parked in the driveway; they hadn't left to visit her nana yet.

I grabbed my phone, dialing her number. "Good morning!" she answered after a couple of rings. The sound of her voice brought a smile to my face.

"Hey, little girl. I'm outside, are you ready or . . ."

"Oh, you're early; I just need like ten minutes or something. I'm still eating breakfast."

"Okay, I'll wait in the truck then."

"Don't be silly, come on in," she scoffed, as if I'd said something stupid.

I chewed on my lip. I'd never met a girl's parents before, and although we weren't technically dating, I *wanted* to date her, so I still needed to make a favorable impression.

"It's okay, I'll wait outside until you're done," I protested.

She disconnected the call, and I frowned, thinking I'd annoyed her or something by rejecting her offer. Movement from the corner of my eye caught my attention, and I looked up in time to see her open the front door. She stood there smiling, leaning against the door frame, looking smokin' hot in skinny jeans and a gray knit sweater that hung off one shoulder and made her look mouthwatering. Her red hair was loose and fell around her flawless face in messy waves. One of her hands rose and she beckoned with one finger for me to go to her.

"Shit," I mumbled, climbing out of the truck and heading to her, trying to think of a few subjects I could talk about to charm her parents with. I wasn't exactly prepared for this moment.

"Hey. Come in, silly boy," she scolded, taking my hand and practically dragging me inside the house. "I'm hungry, I won't be long."

I nodded, and she pulled me through the house toward the kitchen. I knew my way around. We kind of had free rein here on Saturday mornings after her parents left. Over the past month, we'd done many naughty things around her house.

As we walked into the kitchen, I stopped. Her family was sitting around the round wooden table that was nestled in the corner, and all stopped talking to look at me as I walked in. Ellie's sister's eyes widened. From what I'd been told, she was ten. She resembled Ellie, but her hair was the same brown as her father's.

"Guys, this is my friend Jamie Cole. Jamie, these are my parents, Michael and Ruth, and my little sister, Kelsey," Ellie said, gesturing around the table.

I smiled uncomfortably. "Uh...good morning."

Her dad stood, holding out a hand to me, smiling warmly. "Hi, Jamie. How's it going?"

As I shook his offered hand, my shoulders relaxed slightly. He seemed like a nice guy, and from what Ellie had told me, she worshipped her father. Her mother, on the other hand, she wasn't so fond of. I could see why too; she was looking me over slowly, as if trying to make up her mind whether she wanted to talk to me or not. She had the same red hair as Ellie, and some of her features were also the same, but she was nowhere near as beautiful as her daughter. Her face was hardened, not open and friendly the way Ellie's always was. She was dressed impeccably, her makeup perfectly applied even though it was barely past nine in the morning.

"Good, thank you, sir. I'm sorry I'm early, I said I'd wait in the car, but..." I flicked my eyes to Ellie in explanation.

"Don't be silly. And you can call me Michael. You hungry?" he asked, turning to Ellie's sister without waiting for me to answer. "Kels, get another plate for Jamie."

Ellie smiled and sat down at the table as the little girl got up and trotted over to the cupboard, coming back with a plate.

I swallowed awkwardly. "Are you sure this is okay? I mean, I could wait—" I started, but her dad cut me off, waving his hand dismissively.

"It's fine. There's plenty, right, Ruth?" he assured me, smiling at his wife.

She nodded stiffly in response. "Sure, it's fine," she replied politely, her face hard and clearly annoyed.

Ellie patted the seat next to hers, and Kelsey passed me a plate as I sat down. Ellie nodded to the huge pile of bacon and scrambled eggs in the middle of the table. I didn't really want anything; I was actually too nervous to eat, the food would probably get stuck halfway down and I'd make a complete dick of myself.

"Eat, Jamie!" Ellie instructed, rolling her eyes playfully as she scooped food onto my plate.

"So, where are you kids off to so early?" Michael asked. I noticed he had a big smile for Ellie. If I didn't already know she was a daddy's girl, I'd be able to see that just from meeting him now. This guy adored his wife and two girls, that much was obvious.

"Ellie's going to come and help me scout out a new apartment. Mine's coming to the end of its lease, and I wanted a second opinion," I lied smoothly.

He recoiled slightly. "You live on your own? Ellie never mentioned that."

Ellie squirmed in her seat and I nodded. "Yes, sir, I've lived on my own for a while now."

"Really? Well, how old are you, Jamie?" he asked, his concern clear.

"I'm eighteen, sir." I smiled reassuringly, showing him that I wasn't some older guy coming to take advantage of his daughter.

"Oh. It's a little strange for an eighteen-year-old to live on their own. What do your parents think about it?" he asked, his forehead creasing with a frown as his eyes flicked to Ruth and back to me again.

I shrugged awkwardly, wondering how to reply. Ellie shifted in her chair next to me; she didn't know the full story, but I'd told her I hadn't exactly had a happy childhood. I assumed she would draw her own correct conclusions from that. "My father died when I was young, and my mom and I never saw eye to eye," I replied, watching Michael's reaction to make sure he wasn't going to demand I stop seeing his daughter. "I've been emancipated for a couple of years now. It's not ideal, but what can you do?"

He nodded, his eyes still showing caution. "Oh, I'm sorry about that. I'm sure it's not easy."

I drew in a deep breath and shrugged. "I just get on with it. You can't help the hand you get dealt."

Michael's face seemed to soften at that, and he looked at me almost appreciatively. "Very true," he agreed. "Life is there to try us," he added before picking up his knife and fork again and scooping up some eggs.

We were quiet for a minute or so as we ate, but it wasn't too uncomfortable because Ellie kept smiling at me, her eyes telling me I was doing fine with her parents.

Ruth cleared her throat as she set down her knife and fork on her now empty plate. "So, Michael, I was thinking of inviting the Barringtons over for dinner one night this week. What do you think?" Her smile was calculating.

Ellie gasped, her head snapping around to look at her mother. "What? Why would you do that?"

"We're still friends with the Barringtons, Ellison. I can invite them for dinner if I want to," Ruth replied coldly.

Ellison. Was that Ellie's full name? It was pretty, but Ellie suited her better.

"For goodness' sake, Mom, can't you just leave it?" Ellie asked, frowning angrily.

Okay, what is this about?

"Ellison, you two need to work it out sooner or later. Susan said that he's missing you. You two make such an adorable couple, and you need to think of your future," Ruth stated, her eyes darting to me at that last phrase.

Wait, "adorable couple"... Is she talking about Miles?

"Well, Miles isn't part of my future; he's part of my past. Invite them to dinner if you want, but leave me out of it. Tell me what day they're coming and I can guarantee I'll be busy," Ellie retorted, glaring at her mother.

"Ellison, you *will* attend a family dinner, and you *will* behave properly," Ruth said, looking at her daughter warningly.

"You know, Mom, you can push this and push it as far as you want, but Miles and I aren't getting back together, no matter what you, or his mom, or even he thinks. It's over and has been for five weeks. You really need to move on," Ellie snapped.

"You should think about it, Ellison. Miles's family is so proper and well established. Miles is going to college to be a doctor. You'd be set for life," Ruth said, looking at her pleadingly. "Think of what he can give you. You'll never want for anything."

Ellie closed her eyes. "Mom, you honestly think I want to be with someone because of what they can give me? You got together with Dad because of the money his parents had or because you knew he'd be a successful financial adviser, did you?" Ellie challenged.

"No, I got together with your father because I loved him, and it just so happened to work out perfectly. Most people aren't that lucky. For example, what do you do plan on doing, Jamie? I'm assuming you're in college?" Ruth asked, addressing me directly for the first time since I came in.

Wow, this woman is nasty.

I opened my mouth to tell them I was a mechanic, but Ellie cut me off. "It doesn't matter what he does for a living. Stop being like this! If you're trying to make him jealous or start an argument over Miles, then it's not going to work. Life doesn't revolve around money and possessions, you know." She stood up and turned to me. "Are you done eating? Because I'm ready to go."

I nodded and stood. "Thanks for breakfast. It was nice to meet you," I said to Michael uncomfortably.

Michael chucked. "You can come back another time and witness another family feud, okay?" he teased, smiling broadly and holding out a hand to me.

I shook his hand and laughed. "Yeah, this was fun," I joked.

He patted my shoulder, grinning.

Wordlessly, Ellie grabbed her purse from the counter before signaling to me that she was ready to go. I looked her over; she would be cold without a jacket or something. "You might want a jacket, Ellie. It's gonna be cold today, apparently," I said, nodding at the window in evidence of the lack of sunshine.

"Oh, okay, well I'll just grab one then." She turned and stalked off to the stairs, leaving me standing there with her parents. Michael snickered and picked up the empty plates from the table, heading over to the sink.

Ruth stood. "Come on, Kelsey, let's go style your hair," she instructed, heading out of the room without looking at me again. The little girl followed behind her, smiling at me shyly on the way past.

"Don't take anything that Ruth says personally. She wanted Ellie to get back with her ex-boyfriend. It won't happen, though, she likes you too much," Michael said once we were alone.

Shit. He thinks Ellie likes me? "Yeah? Did she tell you that?" I asked hopefully as I grabbed another couple of plates and put them on the counter near the sink.

"No, but she doesn't have to; I can tell."

I smiled proudly, silently praying he was right. Moments later, Ellie wandered into the kitchen with a black jacket on over her sweater and a beautiful smile on her face.

"I'm ready. Let's go find you a place," she said to me before walking over and hugging her dad. "Bye, Daddy."

"Bye, pumpkin. Have fun," he replied, kissing her forehead. He turned to me and smiled. "Take care of my girl, Jamie."

"Will do," I promised, nodding. He'd never need to worry about that while she was with me.

Ellie rolled her eyes and gripped my shirt, pulling me from the kitchen out to the front door. When we were a safe distance from the house, I slung my arm around her shoulder as we walked to my truck. "Right then, little girl. Now that we've both sat through an embarrassing family feud, how about we go get bored looking at apartments? Once we find one, I'll be able to take advantage of your perfect little ass in a bed more than once a week," I suggested, winking as I opened the passenger door for her.

"Who said I would let you do that anyway?" she challenged, pursing her lips and narrowing her eyes teasingly.

"You would," I replied confidently.

She smiled and looked me over slowly. "Yeah, maybe you're right. After all, you are incredibly sexy," she agreed, chewing on her bottom lip.

A smug smile slipped onto my face. "Yeah, I knew you wouldn't be able to resist me." She laughed and I shut her door, walking around to the driver's side.

"I'm sorry my mom was saying that in front of you. She really wants me to be with Miles; she's still going on about it now. She's all about status and money, she always has been," Ellie said, looking at me apologetically as we made our way to the real estate office.

"It's fine, don't worry." I shrugged, trying to appear unconcerned.

"It's *not* fine," she protested, frowning. "What she said was wrong. I don't care about money and stuff like that. I think you should be with someone who makes you happy. My mom had no right to look at you like she did."

"Ellison, it's fine," I teased.

She glared at me. "Don't you dare start calling me that, or trust me, you'll be having a booty call for one."

"Okay," I agreed, laughing. "But that's a damn sexy name."

"Yeah, well, *Ellison* doesn't do booty calls, so be careful," she warned playfully.

I wanted to ask her if Ellison did boyfriends. What her dad had said about her liking me was spinning around and around my head.

When we pulled up outside the real estate office I walked to the door, then waited for her to catch up. We walked in together with her hand casually slipped into my back pocket.

* * *

Two hours and six apartments later, we finally found one that we both liked and I could afford. It was a small but tidy furnished one-bedroom with a fairly nice bathroom and kitchen, and the area was pretty decent, too. I settled with the agent and followed him back to his office to sign the lease. I could move in on Monday.

Ellie grinned as we got back into my truck after completing all the paperwork. "That was a nice place," she enthused. "So do I get an invite?"

I raised one eyebrow. "Hell, Ellie, you can move your cute little behind in there with me if it means I get to see you naked more often."

She snickered as she buckled her seat belt. "Yeah, but then you'd get fed up with me."

"Yeah, you're probably right, you do look like a bit of a mess in the mornings," I joked.

"I'll remember that! Next time my cell beeps with a text begging for my company, I'll say no." She waved her hand, faking offense.

I pulled the truck over by the side of the deserted street and unbuckled her seat belt. She looked a little confused until I gripped her waist and pulled her onto my lap, claiming her mouth with mine. She kissed me back immediately, her delicious taste exploding onto my tongue, making my arms tighten around her, clamping her to me possessively.

As the kiss broke, I rested my forehead against hers. "Thank you for coming with me today. I really appreciate your help."

She smiled, tracing her hands down my chest, hooking her fingers in my belt loops. "Yeah? How much did you appreciate it?"

"Oh, I appreciated it a lot. If there's ever anything I can do to thank you, then you only need to say." My voice was so husky and thick with lust that it was almost embarrassing.

She pressed herself to me tighter, her beautiful gray eyes locked on mine. "There is actually something that I want you to do for me," she whispered before kissing down my neck, sucking on the skin gently.

Tipping my head back, I closed my eyes, loving the feel of her mouth on me. "And what can I do for you, little girl?"

"You can say no if you want to..." She trailed off, looking up at me worriedly.

"I won't say no," I promised. Whatever the hell it was that she wanted, I'd do it, even if I had to cut off my arm. The thought of just how far I would go for her scared the life out of me, but I couldn't help it; I'd fallen for her so hard it was unreal.

"I have prom coming up at my school," she said, pressing her forehead to mine. "Take me?"

"Take you, like...be your date?" I clarified.

"Yeah. But you don't have to if you don't want to." She bent her head to kiss me again. I moved one of my hands from her ass and cupped it around the back of her head, holding her there as I deepened the kiss.

Her arms looped around my neck, her fingers running through my hair. I smiled against her lips at the feel of it. My hair was actually starting to get fairly long and messy now; for the first time in almost five years I would have to go for a proper haircut.

She broke the kiss, her eyes shining. "When you go to prom it's pretty much a given that you have to have sex at the end of the night, and there's no one else I'd rather have sex with than you," she whispered, brushing her nose against mine.

I swallowed around the lump in my throat. "I'd love to take you to your dance, Ellie, but not just so we can sleep together at the end of the night."

"Oh really, you don't want to get laid?" she teased.

"Of course I do, but..."

"But what?"

I took a deep breath. "Ellie, I'd just love to take you as a date. Like a proper date, as a couple. Like, as your boyfriend."

A smile pulled at the corners of her mouth. "Seriously?"

Yes, seriously! She was the first person I thought of when I had good news, the person I always thought of last thing at night or when I woke up in the morning. I needed her in my life.

"I don't want to ruin what we've got going on, and I know that I'm not good enough for you—you deserve so much better than me—but I just can't stop myself from wanting you."

She smiled, her cheeks turning the cute shade of pink that I adored and her eyes shining with happiness. "That was so damn sweet."

"Yeah? I thought it sucked big time," I admitted.

She shook her head, pressing herself to me tighter. "It didn't suck," she protested, "but maybe you could just go with, 'Hey, want to be exclusive with me?' or something along those lines."

My eyes widened in shock as I realized she was about to say yes. My insides were doing a little happy dance. I wanted to shout a celebration, rip my shirt off and run around swinging it above my head, singing the national anthem.

I grinned, fighting to contain my excitement. "Ellie?"

"Yes, Jamie?" she replied, pulling back from me, pretending she didn't know what I was going to ask.

"Want to be exclusive with me?" I asked hopefully.

She grinned. "Hell yeah I do," she replied quickly, crashing her lips into mine.

CHAPTER 13

ELLIE

EXCLUSIVE, EXCLUSIVE, EXCLUSIVE. The word kept buzzing around in my brain, causing me to fidget excitedly in my seat. Biting my lip to try to quell my ridiculously happy grin, I glanced over at Jamie as he drove us back to my house.

My boyfriend. My heart thumped erratically at the title.

My gaze raked over him, taking in every delicious inch as another wave of happiness hit me, making me sag in my seat with contentment.

When we started out, I'd meant what I'd said about it being a casual hookup and nothing more. Jamie was just supposed to have been my brush with the wild side, something I never thought I would have the courage to do; he was *meant* to be a one-night stand. I really hadn't been looking for a relationship, not after Miles. I'd just wanted to be my own person without being restricted or having to ask anyone's permission.

But the thing I hadn't realized was that I could have that with Jamie—in fact, I *did* have that with Jamie. He allowed me to be my own person, allowed me to make my own decisions, and was there to support me and back me up. He never restricted me in any way.

I'd never had that before; Miles had been my only real boyfriend, and I guess I'd sort of based my ideas of what a relationship was on what we'd had and how he'd behaved toward me.

But with Jamie it was so different, so much more. There was trust, support, and mutual respect that I'd never been afforded by Miles. Jamie just seemed to like spending time with me and like me for me, and he didn't treat me like some sort of trophy on his arm. I loved that.

Although I'd tried to keep it casual, my feelings for him had been building over the last couple of weeks, piling up, swelling and morphing into something I didn't have control over. Without my permission, the boy had wormed his way into my heart and carved out a little place for himself there.

Thank God I left my phone at his place and Stacey was such an interfering little witch! I grinned. *I must remember to thank her again for that.*

Probably sensing me watching him, Jamie half turned his head in my direction, his eyes flicking to me for a second before turning back to the road. As his hand reached across the seats and rested lazily on my knee, he smiled that dimpled smile that I loved. His warmth radiated through my whole body, heating me in more ways than one as my mind turned to other places I'd like him to put his hands.

"You okay?" he asked, squeezing my knee gently.

"I'm great." I nodded, placing my hand over his and sighing contentedly as his smile grew more pronounced.

When we pulled up outside my house, Jamie cut the engine and looked over at my parents' car, which was still parked in the drive. "Looks like your parents didn't go to your nana's today," he observed.

I nodded, reaching for the door handle. "Want to come in for a drink or something?" I asked. He'd seemed a little hesitant to meet them this morning, but now that he'd gotten the intros out of the way and charmed my dad, the way he seemed to be able to charm everyone, it would be easier the second time around.

One of Jamie's eyebrows rose. "I'm not sure your mom would want me to."

I shrugged one shoulder nonchalantly. "She'll just have to get over it then, won't she?" I replied.

My mom would need to get used to Jamie now that we were dating. Her superiority complex was way out of control. The only way she would stop looking down her nose at Jamie was if I showed her I wasn't going to back down. I could be just as stubborn as her when I wanted to be. Eventually he would charm her too; I was confident in his skills.

He sighed but nodded and climbed out of his truck, stopping at the curb and waiting for me to reach his side. As we walked up the path, his hand slid into mine, our fingers interlacing as I pushed open the door and led him inside.

My parents were sitting on the couch, my dad watching some documentary about sea turtles that he'd recorded the other day while my mom read one of her crime novels. "Hey," I said, tugging Jamie into the living room and stepping over my sister, who was lying on the floor, her drawing materials and scraps of paper spread out all over the place.

My parents both looked up, and Dad smiled. "Hey, guys. Didn't hear you come in," he replied.

My mom didn't smile. Her gaze was firmly on our entwined hands, her jaw tightening as her lips pressed into a thin line. She didn't like this new development.

"Afternoon." Jamie gave a curt nod as his hand tightened on mine, as if asking me not to go anywhere. I wasn't surprised, really; the look my mother was giving him was probably enough to draw his balls back up into his body.

"How'd the apartment hunting go? Any luck?" Dad asked.

Jamie nodded. "Yeah, it was good. I found a nice one. I get the keys on Monday."

"That's great. You know, I have some boxes in the garage. If you need any, I can dig them out for you," Dad offered.

Jamie was smiling now, his shoulders loosening a little. "I think I'm good. I don't have that much stuff to move. But thanks."

"Does anyone want a drink, coffee or anything like that?" I interjected before throwing Kels a quick wink because her wide eyes were firmly latched onto my boyfriend.

"No, thanks," Dad answered, turning his attention back to the TV.

"I'll take a coffee, thank you, Ellison," Mom answered.

From the corner of my eye I saw Jamie's mouth twitch at my full name but, luckily for him, he chose not to remark on it.

★ ★ ★

Jamie stayed a little over an hour. It had been so nice just to spend time with him in normal surroundings and with my family. He'd chatted easily with my dad about sports and cars, ignoring snide comments my mother made about Miles and his family. After complimenting Kelsey on her drawings and making her blush, he'd won her over too, and she sat at his feet casting sly glances up at him. Even she was a Jamie Cole fan, not that I blamed her in the slightest. Everything was so different with him, I felt so at ease, our relationship was very uncomplicated and effortless.

As I was seeing him out the front door, he leaned down and pressed his lips against mine, kissing me forcefully, his arm slipping around me and clamping me against his sculpted body.

I sagged against him as the kiss deepened, my hormones going wild as his mouth claimed mine in a scorching-hot kiss that ignited a spark of passion inside me so ferocious in its intensity that I was surprised it didn't burn us both. I'd had my way with him only last night, after the usual postgame party, but it felt like ages ago, and my body was craving his. As he looked down at me with those dark, brooding, lust-filled eyes, I knew he was thinking the same thing.

"I can't wait until I get my place and we can have some real alone time without having to rush things or be quiet," he whispered, his eyes wandering over my body as his hand slid to my ass.

My muscles clenched all over and I briefly wondered what my chances were of sneaking him up to my room for a little alone time right now without my parents noticing. Pretty slim, I would bet.

"Me too," I replied breathily.

He pulled back, looking like it hurt him to do so, and smiled. "I'd better go. Hey, want to come help me decorate my new place on Monday after school? I can pick you up and we can order take-out for dinner," he offered hopefully.

"Sure!"

"Okay, it's a date then. I guess that'll be our first official date as a couple, huh?" he mused.

"Guess it will. I get to choose the takeout, seeing as you're just using me for my decorating skills," I bargained.

"Oh, I'll be using you for a lot more than that." He dipped his head and bit the side of my neck playfully.

I squealed and squirmed away from him, setting my hand on his chest and giving him a little push. "Get out of here, flirt, I have stuff to do." I laughed, kind of wishing he'd never leave.

"Whatever. I'll call you later." He grinned and shot me a cocky wink before turning and strutting back to his truck.

Sighing happily, I watched him climb in and drive off before I closed the door and looked back into the living room, seeing my family still sitting around. My smile faded. I didn't want to go back in there and face the barrage of questions or disapproval from my mother at my choice of boyfriend. I wouldn't allow her to kill my euphoric mood. So instead, I headed upstairs and firmly closed my bedroom door. Putting on my music to play softly in the background, I walked to the bed and flopped back onto it, my thoughts already returning to Jamie and our new official status.

A wave of contentment washed over me and I let my eyes close, just thinking about our moment in the truck and how sweet he'd been when he stumbled over his words and asked me to be exclusive. He might not have liked it and thought it sucked, but to me it was perfection. And now we were going to prom together! I hadn't really been looking forward to it before; I probably would've preferred to skip the whole thing, but Stacey would never have allowed me to. I'd been building up to asking Jamie for the last couple of weeks, knowing that if he was there the dance would be more bearable, but I hadn't quite worked up the nerve in case he told me no.

My breathing hitched when my brain wandered to Jamie in a tux and how hot he would look. At the thought of it, excitement bubbled in my veins and my teeth sank into my bottom lip. Now I just needed to figure out my dress…

Sitting up quickly, I leaned over and pulled my sketch pad from my bedside table, flicking it open and thumbing through the pages until I got to the one I wanted. My design for my prom dress. I'd been working on it for weeks, changing little bits until I finally got the perfect design. I traced my fingers over the sketch, imagining the feel of the silky material between my fingers and how it would sit against my body. Making clothes was a passion of mine, something I loved to do but which I had always been told by my mother and Miles would never amount to anything more than a hobby. Looking at the dress, I worried my lip with my teeth. I'd never made anything so extravagant and was a little concerned about how it would turn out. Until now, I hadn't felt like making a start on it because there was still six weeks or so to go, but with Jamie's agreement to accompany me swirling in my brain, I couldn't think of anything I would rather do.

Grinning, I jumped up and headed to my desk, unlocking my sewing machine and plugging it in and then digging in my closet for my stash of fabric samples, deciding a trial run was in order before I attempted to make the real thing. I wanted to get it right and make it absolutely perfect. I wanted Jamie to be wowed by me on the night and unable to take his eyes off me, because I was pretty sure I wouldn't be able to pry my eyes from him all night.

CHAPTER 14

JAMIE

EVERYTHING WAS JUST about perfect. I'd moved into my new place that Monday, and Ellie had come over in her little denim booty shorts and a T-shirt that she'd tied up in the back, exposing her flat stomach, and we'd painted the walls. That day was a lot of fun; though I was pretty sure we ended up with more paint on us than on the walls. I was actually having the time of my life. Not that it was hard to top anything that had ever happened to me before, but my girlfriend just made life a whole lot more interesting.

Ellie was beautiful, smart, kind, and caring, not to mention thoughtful. I'd never had anyone treat me the way that she treated me all the time. It was little things that she did—like sneaking out of bed early in the morning when she stayed over so that she could make me a sandwich to take to work with me. Or she would randomly buy me my favorite candy, or rent movies that I'd said I wanted to watch, or show up with a car magazine or an article she'd clipped from a newspaper just because she saw it and thought I'd like it.

We'd now been officially dating for a month. That month

had passed in a blur of laughing, flirting, and talking about everything—well, everything apart from my past. I tried to keep that as far away from Ellie as possible, because I couldn't take the risk of her not wanting to be with me if she knew the real me. I couldn't risk losing that look that she had for me all the time, that soft, tender look. I needed that look; I loved that look; that one look from her made my life worth living.

Just as things were working out for me and I thought that I might have a chance at a happy life, just as I started to believe that, maybe, somewhere up there, someone had decided to give me a break...karma had to come and knock me on my ass again.

I woke up on Sunday morning to my cell phone ringing. I winced and quickly grabbed it before it woke up the beautiful girl who was using my stomach for a pillow as she snored lightly.

Blinking a couple of times to try to clear the sleepy fog that clouded my brain, I pressed the phone to my ear. "Hello?" I croaked, subtly covering Ellie's exposed ear so that she wouldn't wake up. Luckily for me she was an extremely deep sleeper.

I was greeted by Ray's voice. "Hey, Kid."

"Hey. What's up?" I asked, yawning and trying to move so I could get out of the bed—but Ellie had other ideas about that. She groaned in her sleep, throwing her other arm over my chest, her hand slapping the side of my face by accident. I laughed quietly to myself; she was such a freaking menace when she was unconscious. She talked in her sleep sometimes too; it was extremely cute. We'd had whole conversations about baking cookies and Rollerblading that she had no recollection of in the morning. I loved it when she stayed over. Her parents didn't know, of course; they wouldn't allow it according to Ellie. Instead, she usually lied and told them she was staying with Stacey. Either way worked with me—as long as I got to wake up with her on occasion I was happy.

Ray cleared his throat. "Look, Kid, I'll get straight to the point because there's no use in beating around the bush with this. Your mom's in a bad way. I bumped into her just now at the store. She's banged up. Her arm is broken, and her face is pretty bruised. I asked her what happened, and she just shrugged it off and tried to tell me she fell down the stairs."

I gulped, clenching my fist at the thought of her being hurt and what that could possibly mean. Unconsciously, my body tensed up. I didn't have a relationship with my mother at all—in fact, the last time she saw me she told me that I had ruined her life and she wished I was dead—but she was the only family I had, I didn't want anyone hurting her. "She fell down the stairs?" I repeated sarcastically.

"That's what I was thinking. Anyway, I know you don't see her, but I just thought you should know," Ray said almost apologetically.

I closed my eyes and nodded. "Thanks, Ray." I disconnected the call and pressed the phone against my forehead.

If she was getting battered again, did that mean she was back to her usual habits? I'd sacrificed so much to get her out of it, and she was back in trouble again? It almost made me wonder why I even bothered in the first place. But I knew why: She was my mother. She was a sorry excuse for one, definitely, but the woman had given birth to me; I owed her.

Sighing heavily, I set my phone on the bedside table and looked down at Ellie's flawless face, trying not to let my anger consume me. She moved slightly, snuggling against me, pressing her face into my stomach, so I froze, hoping she'd sleep a little while longer just so I could marvel over her some more. She sighed deeply in her sleep.

"Jamie, will you buy me some ice cream? Not the mint one, though, I don't want to have to clear up the chocolate chips," she muttered, frowning.

I grinned and tried not to laugh. "Sure, Ellie. What flavor should I get?" I asked, playing along with her in a bid to keep her sleep-talking.

She sighed again. "Whatever you want, I only want to throw it at the cats anyway."

I burst out laughing at her randomness and she jerked up, looking around with wide, frightened eyes. "What?" she asked. Her voice was husky and thick with sleep as she put her hand over her heart, sporting a bewildered expression.

I smiled and rolled to my side, pulling her close to me again. "You're so cute sometimes."

She rolled her eyes and snuggled into the crook of my arm.

"Hey, you know, before we go to the movie later, you think maybe we could stop and get some ice cream? There're some cats down the road that piss me off to high heaven," I joked, laughing again as she looked at me like I was crazy.

"What? Are you on something I don't know about?" she asked, her nose scrunching up in confusion.

I grinned and maneuvered on top of her, pinning her down to the bed. "Yeah, I'm *on* you."

She immediately blushed, as usual, a smile blooming on her lips. "Well, while you're there..." She trailed off suggestively, hooking one leg around my waist. My whole body rejoiced as I pressed my mouth against hers.

★ ★ ★

Three hours later I was sitting in McDonald's with Ellie, Stacey, and Stacey's currently on boyfriend, Paul. I couldn't stop thinking about my mom. I could tell Ellie was getting worried, and probably slightly annoyed with me, because she kept having to repeat herself when I wasn't really listening to her. My mind just kept wandering off, wondering what sort of trouble Mom had gotten herself into this time. I tried my best not to care, but I couldn't help it.

When Ellie's foot collided with mine, I jerked out of my worry again to look up at her. She was sitting across the table, a concerned look on her face. Glancing around, I smiled apologetically at Stacey and Paul, who were also both looking at me, waiting for something. Clearly they'd been talking to me and were expecting an answer.

"Sorry," I muttered sheepishly.

Ellie's hand stretched across the table and covered mine, squeezing gently. "Is everything okay? You've been distant all morning. What's up?" Her gray eyes bored into mine as if she were trying to pull the answer she wanted from them.

I smiled apologetically. "Yeah, I just..." I trailed off, not really wanting to elaborate, especially not in front of her friends. It was then that I realized that I wasn't going to be able to get this out of my mind until I saw for myself what was going on with my mother. "Actually, I have a couple of things I need to sort out. I don't think I'm going to be able to make the movie." I winced, waiting for her reaction to my just canceling our plans without so much as a proper explanation.

She nodded, her expression nothing but concerned. "Okay. Want me to help you with whatever it is?"

I was struck by another wave of love for her. Just the way that she looked at me made me feel different. I loved the Jamie Cole that she saw. I wanted to be the guy she thought I was, the one she saw in me.

I smiled gratefully. "No, thanks, though. Sorry I have to skip out on the movie."

Ellie waved her hand dismissively. "No worries, I'll let you make it up to me another time." She smirked at me, and I couldn't help but laugh at the suggestion on her face. I knew exactly how I'd be making it up to her, and I would imagine it involved me and her ... watching *Pitch Perfect* again.

I got up out of the booth and pushed my tray in Paul's direction, motioning for him to finish off my untouched fries. Stepping to Ellie's side, I bent down and kissed her fiercely, showing her how grateful I was that she was such an amazing girlfriend. I pulled away after a few more seconds and kissed her forehead lightly, letting my lips linger on her skin, hoping that her taste and her smell would overpower the bitterness that I would feel from the visit to my mother.

"I'll call you later," I said before winking at her and walking away.

When I slid into my truck I took a deep breath, trying to calm down the turmoil of anger, hurt, and misery that was churning in my stomach. I really didn't want to go and do this. I didn't want my mother to drag me back into the life that I fought so hard against every day. I was finally free of it all, and I desperately wanted to stay that way. I was no longer Jamie Cole, expert car thief and all-around badass. I was Jamie Cole, guy who worked his butt off at a junkyard every day just to earn the money to treat his sweet little girlfriend to things she'd like. But it was more than that: I also wanted to build a normal, stable life for myself. I'd never had that before and I was getting so close to it, I could almost taste it.

The drive seemed to take forever, and my heart sank with each passing second. When I pulled up outside the familiar house, I couldn't get out of the car. I tried to force myself to get out and walk up the broken path and knock on the door, but I just couldn't move. I could barely even breathe through the emotions that this one brick building was stirring in me.

I raked my eyes over the place that I should have known as

"home," but I'd never seen it that way. This two-story house looked more like a prison to me. Everything about it screamed unloved, abandoned, and abused, which summed up my whole life.

Dragging my eyes over the cracked bricks, I noticed that the gray slate roof was missing a couple of tiles, causing a black patch on the wall where the water was just running down the side of the house instead of going down the broken guttering. All of these things seemed to make this place even more daunting to me, even scarier, and I felt like a kid again. The memories that I knew were inside were taunting me, laughing at me even. I had no idea how my mother still lived in this house after everything that had happened here.

I tried my hardest not to remember that day. It was the worst day of my life, the day that the one thing that was important to me was lost. That was the day that I ceased to matter. The day that made my whole existence no longer necessary. That was the day that my little sister died.

I looked down at my hands and was a little shocked to see that they weren't still covered in blood, that my knuckles weren't still raw and bleeding. It felt so real coming back here. All the loss and grief seemed to be flooding back, and I wasn't sure if I could cope with it.

It was worse than when I went to her grave; this place was where she died, this was her home. It was the place where she would kiss me good night, and jump on me in the morning because she wanted me to make her breakfast.

What hurt me the most was that this shitty, derelict little place was the last thing she'd seen before she died. She never got the chance to experience life, she never got to travel or have her first kiss, never got to go to a party or fall in love. She missed out on so much, and it was entirely my fault.

CHAPTER 15

MY HAND CLOSED over my cell phone. I really needed to speak to Ellie right now, just to hear her voice for a second. It scared me how much I was starting to need her. I didn't like to need anyone; that way I'd never have to be disappointed. Huffing out a deep breath, I pushed the phone back into my pocket and looked at the house. I needed to face my demons instead of pretending that all that bad stuff had never happened.

My jaw tightened as I pushed the car door open, and fierce determination settled over me. I'd get this done, sort my mom out, and then leave, and that would be it.

I couldn't help but wonder what her reaction to me would be. Maybe she wouldn't even recognize me after all this time. She hadn't seen me since I got sent down; she visited me once while I was waiting for my trial, just to tell me she wished I were dead, but she didn't once visit me in juvie. The last time I saw her I was in court, where I pleaded guilty to murder and was led off in a pair of handcuffs while she watched, not even crying for me.

The door opened a minute after I knocked, and my heart

was in my throat at the sight of her. She looked a lot older than I remembered. The years hadn't been kind to her. Her cheek was bruised, her lip split, and there was a little cut in her eyebrow.

Fell down the stairs my ass; I can practically see the fist print on the side of her face.

Her brown eyes, the exact same shade as mine, settled on me; they were curious for a split second before recognition washed over her face and her mouth dropped open in shock. Her whole posture changed in an instant. Instead of the relaxed woman who'd opened the door, leaning against the frame in her overly tight, short skirt and revealing shirt, she seemed to stiffen all over, her shoulders squaring as her eyes turned hard.

"What the fuck do you want?" she growled. Her eyes flicked up and down the street, obviously checking to see if anyone saw me standing there.

I sighed. The way she was looking at me made me angry and sad at the same time; I didn't know which emotion to feel first because they were both so strong. She actually didn't deserve my help at all; I should just turn around, climb into my truck, and go back to the life that I was building for myself. But I couldn't. Loyalty was always one of my more prominent traits, even when it wasn't warranted.

"I heard through the grapevine that you fell down the stairs. I came to see if you wanted anything. You know, bread, milk… wayward son to beat the shit out of the abusive pimp you obviously have?" I offered sarcastically.

She sneered at me hatefully. "I have no son!"

I flinched internally at her words but didn't let anything show on my face as I put my hand on her shoulder and pushed her out of the way so I could step into the house. Slamming the door behind me, I turned to face her. She was glaring at me with so much hate that I was surprised I hadn't burst into flames from the intensity of it.

"Look, I'm here to sort out whatever shit you've gotten yourself into this time. You might not want my help, but you're getting it. Now tell me who this guy is, and I'll go fix it!" I said, looking her right in the eyes, ignoring how her hands clenched into fists at my words.

"You can't just come in here! Get the hell out and don't come back! You stupid little shit, Jamie. I don't need you and the way you 'sort things out'; I've never needed you to sort anything out for me. You did everything on your own and look where it got us! You go to jail, and I lose everything! Just get the fuck out!" she cried, grabbing the door handle, yanking the door open angrily and gesturing for me to leave.

Without answering, I turned around and walked deeper into the house, down the short hallway, trying not to look at anything on my way through to the living room. I tried not to notice that the peeling wallpaper was the same as when I lived here, or the drawing that I had done on the wall by the stairs. I tried not to notice that the threadbare carpet hadn't been replaced, and still had the little burn mark where I had dropped a lit cigarette after being made to smoke a whole pack one after the other, apparently to teach me not to steal my mother's from her purse. I tried not to notice these things, but I just couldn't help it.

The thing that got to me most was the smell of the place. It still smelled exactly the same. The acrid smells of burnt weed, alcohol, mold, and general uncleanness hung in the air, bringing back memories that I just didn't want to have. That pungent, unpleasant smell made a cold shiver trickle down my spine and the hair rise on the back of my neck.

Behind me, my mother was screaming hateful things, telling

me what a useless waste of space I was, how I'd ruined her life, how I'd screwed her over and left her with nothing. I ignored it all and stepped up to the last door on the left. My hand hesitated, hovering over the knob. This room was where my worst nightmare happened. I was scared that I would walk in there and see Sophie lying on the floor, blood seeping from her head, her eyes open and vacant. I was scared I would see a young me crouched over her body, crying and sobbing like I had never done before or after that moment.

I bit the inside of my cheek and grabbed the cold brass knob, pushing the door open in one quick movement. My eyes automatically flicked to the right, to the wall that had been covered in blood the last time I had seen it, the plaster cracked from the force with which her head had been smashed against it. I honestly was expecting it to be the same, for the stain to be there still, but it wasn't. The room had been painted a pale yellow, the carpet had been changed to a dark brown—obviously they couldn't salvage it with the massive amounts of blood that had seeped into it that day.

Thankfully, I didn't have a long time to dwell on my memories, though, because before I knew it, my mom was in the room behind me, screaming profanities at me at the top of her lungs, slapping angrily against my back.

I closed my eyes and tried to force everything else away. I needed to focus on what I came here for; I couldn't keep thinking about Sophie. Twisting on my heel, I grabbed my mother by the tops of her arms to stop her hitting me, shaking her to get her to shut up and listen to what I had to say.

"Stop it!" I demanded.

"I hate you!" she screamed. Her face was red and blotchy, and the veins in her neck stood out, she was so angry and tense. She pursed her lips and then actually spat in my face. I closed my eyes and let her go, using the bottom of my shirt to wipe her saliva from my cheek.

"I hate you, too," I admitted. It actually felt quite nice to say those words to her. I'd never said that out loud before—I'd thought it since I was about seven years old, but I had never spoken it. I was a little shocked at myself, at how much feeling I had put into the words as they left my mouth.

Her face crumpled, and for a couple of seconds she actually looked hurt, but then her hands dropped down to her sides and all traces of emotion were gone. Her face was hard as stone. "Then leave. We're nothing to each other; I don't need your help."

"I won't let people hurt you. You're still my mother. Now tell me what happened," I barked, folding my arms over my chest, waiting.

Her eyes dropped down to the floor as she touched the plaster cast on her arm, frowning. "It's nothing."

I sighed and sat down in the armchair, keeping my eyes on her, not allowing myself to look around the room and see if there were any photos of Sophie that I could take with me when I left. "If it's nothing, then you won't mind telling me," I countered, my tone firm and hard, letting her know I wasn't leaving here until she told me the name of the guy who did that to her. It was pretty obvious from the clothes she was wearing—or hardly wearing— that she was back on the game. Her pose as she opened the door had clearly signaled that she thought I was a john come for a little afternoon delight.

Instead of getting angry again and shouting, like I was expecting, she did something I never thought I would see her do. She sat down on the sofa opposite me, put her head in her hands, and cried. I gulped at the sight of it. She hadn't ever showed any emotion when I was a kid; usually she was too intoxicated on either booze or drugs to actually "feel" anything. I didn't know what to do. I knew I should comfort her, put my arm around her and tell her it was okay. But I couldn't summon any compassion for her at all. She didn't deserve it. But that didn't mean I would stand by and let some guy hurt her because he thought he owned her.

"Just spit it out, Sharon!" I demanded, using her name because I couldn't bring myself to call her Mom. I needed to stay detached.

She sniffed and wiped at her face, her eyes not meeting mine. "I...I don't have a pimp, not anymore, not since..." She trailed off, shaking her head, wincing slightly.

She didn't appear to be lying to me; her eyes actually looked scared, terrified even. "So who did this?" I asked, waving my hand at her face and then her arm.

"I...I...borrowed some money. I had a little trouble keeping up with the repayments," she whispered, breaking into another round of sobs.

It was worse than I thought. "Please tell me you borrowed from a bank," I begged, knowing the answer to that before I even asked. What type of bank would take payment in the form of violence? No respectable bank, that's for sure.

She shook her head in answer. My heart sank. Loan sharks. I really didn't want to be getting involved in this at all. I mentally added up how much money I could get my hands on. I probably had just over $1,000 in the bank; I got paid weekly, so if I worked extra hours I could probably get three cars done for next week instead of two. If I didn't eat properly or go out for a couple of weeks, then I could scrape about $1,800 together, maybe a little more.

"Who did you borrow from?" I asked, not even wanting to know the answer.

She sniffed loudly. "Tony Grier."

My back stiffened at his name. I needed to get the hell out of this house. Tony Grier would take everything she owned, chew her up, and spit her out before selling her to the highest bidder and then doing the same with every member of her family and friends until there was nothing left to take.

Ironically, it would have been much simpler if she just had a new pimp who was bashing her around. I could deal with that so easily, but this, this was different.

"How much did you borrow?" I asked, closing my eyes, dreading the answer.

"Two thousand," she replied. Her tone had changed now; it was softer, more pleading, as if she suddenly thought she needed to be courteous to me so that I'd help her.

I nodded, my body relaxing fractionally because it was a fairly achievable target. "I can get it for you within two weeks."

She sniffed loudly. "That's…that's just what I actually borrowed," she stuttered.

I opened my eyes and looked at her; she was leaning forward on the sofa, her hand half outstretched, reaching out for me. I flinched, pulling my hands back quickly. I didn't want her to touch me; the woman repulsed me and if I had any choice I would never see her again.

"Interest," I guessed. I should have known it wouldn't be that easy. "So how much do you need to pay it off?"

She swallowed and ran her hand over her hair, trying to smooth her ponytail as she looked away from me. "Thirteen."

I gasped. "Holy shit." There was no way I could get that money, and if she didn't pay it off then it'd go up more every day. "Why would you borrow from him? Why didn't you go to Brett?" I snapped. He would have given her the money; he wouldn't have charged interest like Tony Grier had, either. Brett always looked after the families of his boys; he would have just let her borrow the money, no questions.

She shrugged, her lip trembling. "I wasn't thinking. I needed a hit, I was desperate, and no one would give me credit. I'd borrowed a couple hundred from Tony in the past and paid it back with no problems. I thought everything would be fine, but then I missed a payment and he just went crazy, smashing everything up and shouting threats. Then the interest was added, and now I'm even paying interest on the interest! Business was really slow last week because I was ill, so I couldn't afford the latest payment," she explained, looking down at her arm and wincing.

I bit back my angry retort. This all started over drugs? She had borrowed money from a loan shark to buy drugs. How idiotic could one person get?

"I don't know what to do," she whispered, not even bothering to wipe the tears and snot from her face. She looked so helpless, vulnerable, and weak. But she wasn't helpless; she had me, she always had.

I took a deep breath and shook my head, pushing myself up from the armchair. "I'll sort it out. Just don't pull this shit again. This is the last time I'm fixing anything for you." I glared at her warningly. I was trying to go straight, and this wasn't what I needed. I wanted to be free of this life, and just like I'd thought she would, she was pulling me back into it again.

She gasped and jumped to her feet. "You have the money to pay it off?"

I nodded. "Yeah," I lied.

"Thank you," she whispered. Her eyes bored into mine, showing a compassion and gratitude that I had never seen from her before. But it was too late now, we were done, I was cutting all ties.

"Don't mention it." I turned and strode toward the door. Thoughts of what I was going to do were running through my head. Now I had to go see Tony Grier and see what could be done about my drugged-up hooker of a mother's debt.

* * *

Twenty minutes later, I pulled up to his lavish office. From outside, the place looked respectable. The sign above the door read YOU NEED IT, WE LEND IT, NO QUESTIONS ASKED.

Tony Grier actually ran a legitimate money-lending service too, structured loans with payment plans—that was his official business. If the tax man or cops came along and looked into it, they would find a guy who did well for himself and loaned money to people for a fast payback, everything legal through the books. Of course, there were borrowers like my mother who went off the books, and that was where the real money lay for him. People borrowed small amounts, and after interest and charges were added, they ended up signing over their houses and possessions.

I headed inside and over to the receptionist's desk. "I need to speak to Mr. Grier," I told her.

She tapped on her keyboard, looking at the screen. "He's in with someone at the moment. I'll just take your name and you can wait here."

"My name's Jamie Cole. Tell him that he knows my mother, Sharon Cole."

As the minutes passed, I could feel myself getting angrier and angrier. Either this guy had hurt my mother, or he'd had one of his goons do it. I took a deep breath. As much as I wanted to smash his face in, I knew that this was how it worked in his line of business. I needed to stay detached.

I looked up just as Tony Grier opened his office door. He was probably in his early fifties, average height, a little overweight, slightly balding, his body encased in an expensive-looking charcoal suit. He smiled at me before heading over with his hand extended. I stood and tried to keep the hatred and anger from my face as I played the polite role of person begging for more time.

"Jamie Cole. I hardly recognized you."

"It's been a long time," I said. All I wanted to do was knock his teeth out and shove them down his throat.

He led me into the office, shutting the door behind us, and motioned for me to sit while he headed behind his desk. "So then, Kid, what can I do for you on this fine Sunday?"

"I'm here to talk about my mother's debt."

A slow smile crept onto his face. "Ah, I thought it would be something like that." His eyes were calculating now; he looked a little more alert, like maybe he thought I was going to grab the gold-plated letter opener from his desk and shove it deep into the side of his neck. I was actually considering it.

I nodded. "Yeah. She owes you thirteen thou, right?" I asked, cocking my head to the side, still trying to keep this conversation light and casual.

He opened one of his desk drawers and pulled out a binder, dropping it on the desk and opening it slowly. Whether he was doing it slowly just to piss me off I couldn't be sure, but if he was, it was certainly working. "Let me check." He sucked his teeth with his tongue, coming to rest on a page fairly near the front. He sighed exaggeratedly. "I'm afraid that thirteen was last week's total."

I bit back my groan. "And this week's total?" I pressed, not even wanting to know the answer.

He closed the file and pushed it back into his drawer before speaking, "You know how these things work, Kid. Interest, late payment charges, callout fees—I have to pay guys to go and chase up the money."

Answer the fucking question, asshole! "I know how it works. So what's this week's total?"

"Fourteen and a half," he answered, touching his fingertips together and sitting back in his chair, watching me closely.

It went up by $1,500 in a week? I was in serious trouble here. I tried my best not to show any reaction. Standing, I dug in my pocket, pulling out the seven hundred bucks that I had managed to get from the ATM down the street. I threw it on his desk and sat back down.

His eyes were alight with amusement as he looked at it. "I may not be Rain Man, but even I can see that doesn't quite cover it."

"I know. Call it a down payment or something. I want you to leave my mother alone. I'll be taking over her debt, so from now on, you deal with me." I looked at him sternly. That wasn't a request; if he touched my mother again, then I was cutting him to pieces and mailing his wedding ring back to his wife in a clear plastic bag.

He smiled and leaned forward in his chair. "Oh, really? Brett Reyes's little protégé owes me money? Well, call this my lucky day," he said, his tone joyful.

I ignored the little glint in his eye when he thought about me being in his debt; maybe he was thinking I still had links to Brett and his organization or something. "I can get you about a thousand a month," I offered.

He laughed right in my face, a big booming laugh that echoed in the room, reverberating from the walls. "The interest alone is five thousand a month."

My heart sank. I didn't even earn five thousand a month. "Right, like you'd get that much from my broke mother. You know you'll get more from me than you ever would her, so let's just cut the bullshit and work something out."

He shrugged nonchalantly. "Nothing to work out, debt needs paying. I don't do payment plans, you know this, Kid." He sat back in his chair with his fingers together under his chin, his eyes scanning my face. "However, if you were to come and work for me, I could forget this debt ever existed."

"No thanks." I shook my head fiercely; my loyalty was and would always be to Brett, I wouldn't ever jump ship like that. "Look, I'll figure something out, just transfer the debt into my name and forget you ever heard the name Sharon Cole. I'll get you your money as soon as I can. In the meantime, if I find out that one of your boys has even looked at my mother the wrong way, I'm killing them." I stood, signaling the end of the meeting.

He laughed wickedly. "You always were a scrappy little shit."

"So they tell me," I muttered, strutting out of the office without looking back.

When I got back to my truck I swallowed my pride and just did what needed to be done. There was no way around it; it was either this, or I'd wind up dead. I pulled out my phone and dialed. When he answered, his greeting warm and cheerful, I felt empty, emotionless, and resigned to the fact that a loser like me might never be able to escape a life of crime.

I cleared my throat. "Hey, Brett. I'm, uh…I'm in a bit of trouble, and I need a couple of jobs."

CHAPTER 16

SO, THEN, KID. What kind of trouble are we talking here?" Brett asked as I sat in his office.

I sighed deeply. "My crackhead mother borrowed from a loan shark and has gotten herself in a little debt," I stated. I looked up to see him frowning angrily, and I knew what he was going to say before he even said it. "I told her she should have come to you," I chimed in before he could blow up about it.

He shook his head angrily and raked a hand through his hair. "I always look after my boys' families, she knows that! Why would she go to someone else?"

I shrugged. "It's done now, there's no point in stressing about it. Anyway, I just need a couple of boosts or something to pay it off." I looked at him hopefully. If he refused to let me back in, then I was done for. It was usually really hard to get out of an organization like Brett's—usually people stayed for life, but if they did want out they had to work their way out. If you did get out, though, you didn't come back. This was highly irregular, and I just prayed that he accepted it. The alternative—working for Tony Grier—really didn't appeal to me.

He sighed and sat back in his chair. "How much you need?"

"Three jobs should cover it." I'd already worked it out, and based on my old nightly boost fee, that would clear the debt.

He nodded thoughtfully. "I have a small job lined up for Friday night that you could run for me. Give me a chance to spread word you're back in the game, and I'm sure we'll have more soon."

"I just want three jobs, Brett," I said quickly, wanting him to know that I wasn't back for good.

He laughed and shook his head. "It doesn't work like that, Kid, and you know it. If you want to come back then you come back, but I don't just hand out jobs freelance. You want back on the team, then you're back on the team. Take it or leave it," he offered, shrugging easily.

I swallowed awkwardly. I really didn't have another choice. I needed the money badly. Now that I'd taken over the debt, if I couldn't pay, then Tony would come after me. If I still couldn't pay after that, then he'd look for other ways to hurt me—Ellie would be the prime target because of how much I cared about her. I couldn't let that happen.

"How about a deal?" I offered.

"What kind of a deal?"

I ran my hand through my hair, trying to think of something he would go for, something that would be to his advantage but that wouldn't tie me in to his organization too much. Time. I could give him a certain amount of time.

"I'll give you a month. I'll do as many boosts as you want within that month, but after that, I'm gone," I said.

He frowned. "It'll take me more than a month to spread the word that you're back. I won't get that many lined up for a month." He steepled his fingers. "Six months."

I shook my head forcefully. I would be sucked back in by then.

Six months of boosting cars and I would be addicted to the rush again. I couldn't do that. "Three," I countered.

Silence hung in the air before he finally nodded. "Deal. But I want you completely back on the team. You'll be at my beck and call, not just for boosts but for anything else that I need a good man for."

I groaned at the thought of what that would entail. Protection. Violence. Drug running. Robberies. Basically, everything that I hated about my old life. The only other choice I had was to go to Jensen, Ray's cousin, and see if I could fight every night at his club. I would get pretty bashed up, though, and after a few nights I would be too messed up to win. There was just no other way out of this for me.

Resigned, I nodded. "Fine. Three months and then I'm done. No matter what, I'm out after three months."

"Excellent. Good to have you back, Kid." A slow smile spread across his face. "Speak to Ed about the boost on Friday night," he said, motioning toward the door, signaling that the meeting was over.

Friday night. Why did that ring alarm bells in my head? Suddenly I realized. Ellie's prom was Friday night. "Um, Brett, I can't do Friday."

"Tough shit. Make it happen, or our deal is off. The cars are to be in the container, bound for Germany, by five a.m. on Saturday."

The first damn job and it was already interfering with my relationship. Agreeing to do this for three months had to be the worst idea in the history of bad ideas. But there was no other way I could get my hands on enough cash to clear the debt.

What if I went to the dance and did the boost after? I could bail out early and tell Ellie I wasn't feeling well. "How many cars?" I asked, mentally calculating how much time would be required and whether it was feasible.

"Three. All within an hour's drive of here," he answered.

I nodded, standing. "I'll get it done."

CHAPTER 17

I WOKE WITH a headache. Three days had passed since I'd spoken to Brett, and for some reason, I hadn't slept right since. Depression was sinking in because of the situation I was stuck in. The only thing that seemed to be able to boost my mood was Ellie.

Trying not to wake her, I quietly pushed myself up from the bed and headed into the shower, trying to let the spray alleviate some of the tension from my body.

"Jamie, your cell's ringing, want me to answer it?" Ellie called from the other room a few minutes later.

"No! I'm coming," I replied quickly. I didn't mind her answering my phone, but I didn't want Brett or anyone like that anywhere near her.

Sighing, I switched off the water, wrapping a towel around my waist as I stalked back to the bedroom. Ellie was lying on the bed, her arm over her eyes as the phone vibrated on the nightstand next to her head. I grabbed it and answered without looking at the name on the screen.

"Hey, Kid."

I groaned inwardly. Brett. This call could mean only one thing—my first task. "Hey, Brett. How's it going?"

"Good. Listen, I need you to do a job for me today. Just accompany me to a deal and show your face a little. I'm slowly spreading the word that you're back on my team, but it'll be a lot quicker if people see you for themselves. We'll get more orders that way."

Ellie moved her arm from her face and smiled up at me, her sleepy eyes still half-closed. I smiled back, and her hand reached out, hooking in the knot at the front of the towel I had at my waist, pulling me closer to her with a wicked glint in her eye.

I caught her hand, holding the towel closed as I answered Brett. "What time? I have work today."

"Be here in an hour," Brett answered casually.

I frowned but reluctantly agreed; I couldn't exactly say no to him. Now I'd have to call in sick to work.

Ellie got to her knees on the bed; the sheets fell away from her naked body, making the muscles in my stomach tighten as my eyes raked over every inch of her. I honestly didn't think I'd ever get used to her perfection, even if I had a million years to worship it.

"Come to the warehouse. Don't be late, Kid."

"I won't be late," I agreed. He disconnected the call, and I looked at Ellie sternly, which made her giggle and chew on her lip. "You're a bad girl," I scolded playfully.

She shrugged unashamedly as she slid her hands up my chest, wrapping her arms around my neck. "Maybe you should try to tone down the sexiness a little and then I'll be able to leave you alone."

Sexiness, yeah, right. "Ellie, I have no idea how I got a girl like you," I admitted.

She grinned and pulled me down on top of her, her legs wrapping around my waist. "I know. You deserve much better than me. It must have been my lucky day when you looked in my direction," she purred, guiding my mouth to hers. I smiled against her lips, knowing that statement was the total opposite of the truth. She would always be the one who deserved better than me, but while she was passing out the attention, I'd take what I could get.

★ ★ ★

By the time I got to the warehouse, I was in a foul mood. The reason for that was the guy who was following me around; he wasn't even bothering to be discreet about it, either. As I'd walked out of my apartment with Ellie, I'd spotted him immediately. He was leaning on his car outside my place. I'd then watched as he followed two cars behind me, pulling up at the curb outside Ellie's school as I dropped her off. I recognized him as one of the guys that used to work for Tony Grier. Which meant Tony was keeping tabs on me already.

The guy pulled up into the parking space next to mine at Brett's warehouse and smiled at me. I growled in frustration and pushed open the door of my truck. I made a show of locking the truck before I walked around to the driver's side of his car, knocking on the window. He smiled at me wickedly as his window slid down.

"What the fuck are you following me for?" I snapped.

He tipped his head to the side. "Just learning a little more about you. Your first payment is due in a couple of days. I was just scoping out to see your day-to-day life. Pretty little girlfriend you have there. And she's still in school, huh? She's probably a bit young for me, but if you step out of line maybe I'll take your payment from her ass," he rasped, shrugging nonchalantly.

My body stiffened, and before I knew what I was doing, I'd

reached in through his window and wrapped my hand around his throat. "If you even look at her again I'm going to kill you," I growled. I couldn't rein in my anger; I already wanted to kill him for even mentioning Ellie in front of me. He laughed—until my hand tightened on his throat, which made the laugh turn into a strangled yelp as his eyes widened. I leaned in close to him, my face inches from his. "I'm warning you right now that if you so much as breathe too heavily in her direction I'm going to bring down so much shit on you that you'll wish your whore of a mother had aborted you when she found out she was pregnant," I hissed. "You tell Tony that she's off-limits. Better yet, don't even tell him I have a girlfriend, because if anything happens to her, then I'm hunting you down first." I let go and pulled back, straightening up. His hand went to his throat as he gasped for breath. "You tell Tony that I'll have his payment on time, so he should stop sending his goons to watch me." I spun on my heel, not waiting for an answer as I strutted into the warehouse like I owned the place, nodding at the couple of people hanging around.

My whole body was tight with stress. Deep down, I knew I should break it off with Ellie now that she'd been noticed by them. I had no right to drag her into this seedy world with me; she deserved better. But the selfish part of me couldn't let her go; I needed her to keep me sane, otherwise what would be the point of me fighting so hard? There was no freedom without her.

My jaw ached with tension as I rapped on Brett's door.

"Morning," I grunted when he opened it

"Perfect timing, Kid. Let's head out then," he replied, pushing his gun into the holster that hung from one shoulder. His jacket slid into place over the top so the holster was out of sight. Brett never left his office without a gun.

"So, where we going?" I probed as we climbed into the backseat of his Bentley.

"I'm meeting with Carlos and Greg about them taking over more of the block for me. A couple of my suppliers have been letting me down lately. I had to let one of them go because he was skimming my profits," he replied. I tried not to react to the "let one go" comment—that meant he'd killed one of his drug dealers. "So I want Carlos and Greg to expand their territories to cover more pushers in the area. Carlos's brother is into cars, you know that. I want him to see you and pass the information on to his brother that you're back. So far I've only managed to set up two boosts for the month. People have found someone else to fill their requests. There's another guy that people are claiming is the new you." He shrugged, looking a little bored by it all.

"The new me?" I repeated, frowning.

He nodded. "Yep, they call him Dodger. Original name, I know," he said sarcastically, rolling his eyes distastefully. "He's twenty-one and apparently can boost pretty well. He's very in demand at the moment. He took advantage of the situation and got popular when you got sent down."

"Why didn't you recruit him then, if he's that good?" I asked. Brett always snapped up fresh talent, and he was obviously lacking in the car-stealing area since I got sent to juvie.

He smiled and patted my knee, rolling his eyes. "What did I need him for? I wanted to wait for you to get out. Kid Cole is worth waiting for." He winked at me, and I couldn't help but laugh proudly. He could have gotten that guy on his team years ago, when I was sent down, but out of loyalty he would rather lose his customers and wait for me. That said a lot about our relationship.

"Bet you were pissed when I said I wanted to go straight when

I came out then," I mused, wincing as I remembered him putting a gun to my head.

He smiled sadly. "Of course I was pissed that I lost you off my team, but I'm happy that you look happy, Kid. I've never seen you like this before. It suits you."

We rode the rest of the way in silence. I watched the streets pass, just wishing that I hadn't woken up this morning.

* * *

The meeting went well, as expected. I didn't have to do much, just shake hands with a couple of people and then stand back with my arms folded over my chest, looking like I was one of Brett's heavies.

Instead of dismissing me when we were done with the meeting, Brett asked me to go with him to his "new venture." Apparently he had just worked out a deal to run a legit security firm that would be placed in a string of strip clubs across the city. By the sound of what he was telling me, this was the only legal part of the business he had going.

So that's where we were heading right now. A strip club.

I looked around hesitantly as I got out of the car outside the club. I didn't really like places like this, and I certainly didn't want it getting back to Ellie that I was in strip club.

It was midday, so there were a few patrons in for lunchtime drinks. A few half-naked girls walked around, but they didn't interest me in the slightest. A blonde wearing nothing but a tiny silver bikini caught my eye and gave me a seductive smile. The only thought that ran through my head was *My girlfriend is a lot prettier and has longer legs*. Ellie had ruined me as a man. I laughed at myself quietly and shook my head as Brett exchanged pleasantries with the owner of the club, Matthew Torrent.

"Kid, this is Mr. Torrent," Brett said.

I nodded, respectfully shaking his offered hand. "Nice to meet you."

Mr. Torrent smiled. "You too. I've heard a lot about you," he replied. His eyes raked over me from my head to my toes. "From the things I've heard about you over the years, I always thought you'd be bigger," he added.

I laughed at that. "Everybody does. I like to keep an air of mystery about me. It works to my advantage when people under-estimate me."

He grinned. "I'm sure it does."

"You two will be getting to know each other a lot better from now on," Brett said.

I frowned, confused. "How's that then?"

"I'm putting you in charge of the security detail across the clubs," Brett replied nonchalantly.

My muscles bunched up with stress at his words. I didn't want to do that at all. "I'm not the best person for that. Someone like Shaun or Wayne will do better here than me. I'm sure Mr. Torrent wants the best person looking after his staff," I countered.

Mr. Torrent shook his head. "I asked for you as soon as I heard you were back in Brett's employment. I've heard a lot about you—everyone has—and I'm sure just the name Kid Cole will pretty much guarantee no trouble at my clubs," he rebutted confidently.

"I'm only here for three months," I protested.

Brett snorted and rolled his eyes. I knew right then and there that he was assuming I would get addicted to the rush and the money, and I wouldn't want to leave at the end of the agreed time. "Let's just get things sorted out for now, and we'll cross that bridge if we come to it."

I wanted to correct him and say *"when* we come to it," but instead I just nodded in agreement. I just needed to get through the three months, and then I could leave all this behind me.

We spent another hour in the club, going through the basics. I would have five guys in each of Matthew's seven clubs. Those guys would work security at the door, inside the club, and in the back rooms where some of the girls provided "extra services." Basically I was just on call and would need to show my face on the weekends so that people would see me. I had no idea why both Matthew and Brett seemed to think that my being here was a good idea and that it would help stop trouble. It seemed like stories about me had been blown wildly out of proportion when I was sent down. In reality, I wasn't even legal to drink; I was a few months shy of nineteen. But I did as I was told and agreed to come here on Saturday night for a few hours.

I was starting to resent my mother more and more. This new security detail was going to significantly limit my time with my girlfriend.

When we got back to the warehouse, I lingered in Brett's office with him.

He took off his suit jacket, hanging it on his coatrack, eyeing me suspiciously. "What's up? You don't usually hang around after being dismissed. Something wrong?"

I shook my head and decided to just ask what I'd been thinking all morning. He could only say no, it was no big deal. "I was wondering if I could get an advance on my wages. Not the fee for the boost, just the weekly rate. My first payment to Tony Grier is due soon, and I want to have the money ready," I said hopefully. Having that money early would take off some of the pressure, and stop me stressing so much about it—and about Ellie.

Brett sighed and immediately headed over to his safe, which sat behind a picture on the wall. I watched as he pulled out two bundles of money. Each had a band around it with $1,000 written on it. He slammed the safe door shut and tossed the cash into my lap. "Just don't be telling the other boys I did that, I don't want them all in here asking. That was the only exception, and only because it was you. Understand?"

I smiled gratefully and some of the tension in my shoulders loosened as I shoved the money into the inside pocket of my leather jacket. "Thanks, Brett. I'll see you tomorrow night before the boost." He waved me off with a flick of his fingers, so I walked out quickly before he thought of anything else he wanted me to do for him.

CHAPTER 18

ELLIE

HE'S GOING TO do it tonight, I just know it," I moaned, putting my head in my hands.

Stacey sighed and rubbed her hand across my shoulder supportively. "Jesus, El, he's not going to dump you! Get a hold of yourself. You're ruining your makeup and we're going to prom in an hour!" she scolded, prying my hands away from my face with her other hand.

I looked up at her and willed myself to believe her, to listen to the words that she'd been repeating over and over for the last week—but I couldn't make myself believe them. Jamie was going to break up with me soon, I just knew it. He'd been incredibly distant lately. Everything was changing between us.

"Stace, seriously, we've barely even spoken lately. He just goes off daydreaming all the time and gets this look on his face that tells me he doesn't want to talk about stuff when I ask what's wrong. He jumps every time his phone rings. He told me last night that I can't stay at his place tomorrow night because he has, and I quote, 'plans with Connor,' yet I'm sure he mentioned last week that his boss, Connor, was going away with his family for a few days and wasn't back until next week!"

Stacey shook her head and plopped down onto the bed next to me. "Ellie, just stop thinking about it. Whenever I see you two together you're laughing and flirting. You're constantly talking on the phone. Do you know how rare that is, for people to be able to just talk on the phone to their boyfriends for ten minutes without losing their interest? Yet you and Jamie can talk for an hour and still have more to say to each other. I can't do that with Paul, not even close. You've probably just got your weekends mixed up. This Connor guy is probably going away some other time and you're just reading too much into things because you're getting scared."

No. Something was wrong. I knew it. What possible reason could there be for Jamie being so distracted and distant lately?

"I'm not getting scared," I countered, frowning.

She rolled her eyes. "Yes, you are. I know for a fact that you're crazy about that boy and that it scares the life out of you because of how Miles turned out. You're scared to let yourself fall for him, so you're making up excuses so that you don't get too close. You're hoping to convince yourself that it's going nowhere so you don't end up getting hurt in the long run."

I closed my eyes and shook my head. I wasn't just being scared—sure, I *was* scared to fall for him because Miles had started out great too in the beginning, but that wasn't what this was at all. Jamie was acting different at the moment. Not like the usual, attentive, loving Jamie that I was indeed falling for.

"I'm not scared." I opened my eyes and looked at Stacey again, forcing a smile so that she wouldn't see how upset this was making me. "I guess we'll see who's right eventually. Either he'll break up with me, or I'm being stupid and this is all nothing. There's nothing I can do about it either way." My own words hurt.

She smiled and raised one perfectly plucked eyebrow. "Actually, there is something we can do about it. We can make you look drop-dead gorgeous tonight, and maybe he'll cancel his plans with Connor and chain you to his bed for the weekend instead," she suggested, grinning wickedly.

I laughed and rolled my eyes at her crudeness. "I do have a pair of killer heels that he's going to love," I admitted, smiling at the thought.

*   *   *

I stood in front of my full-length bedroom mirror and gulped. Stacey had spent almost an hour curling my hair for me, then scooping one side up off my face severely so I had a mass of curls going over one shoulder. My makeup had been reapplied after my freak-out, and the eye shadow and mascara that she'd plastered on me made my gray eyes look wide and excited. My skin appeared soft and buffed; my nails were perfectly polished.

My eyes headed farther down and skimmed the bluish-gray satin dress I was wearing. It looked like something straight out of a magazine. It had turned out even better than I'd imagined.

My eyes flicked to Stacey in the mirror as she spoke. "It's beautiful. The neckline, the little mesh bit at the top, so beautiful. You did such an amazing job, El," she gushed, shaking her head in awe. Her arm linked through mine as she smiled happily, smoothing the formfitting bodice of her red satin dress. "We're gonna own that prom."

The doorbell rang, and my mom immediately shouted for my dad to answer it. As we bustled out of my room, I heard dad stomp into the hallway, grumbling something under his breath.

He stopped as he spotted us standing at the top of the stairs, his eyes widened, and his mouth twitched with a smile.

"Wow, you two look beautiful," he said, looking at us both in turn.

Stacey laughed and nodded, while I frowned and tried not to squirm because he was seeing a dress that I'd made myself—not that he knew that, of course. "Thank you, Michael," Stacey purred.

I sighed and shook my head, squeezing her arm a little tighter. She had always had an old-man crush on my dad, it was gross.

My dad smiled up at me, and I couldn't help but smile back because of how proud he looked. "I need to find my camera," he stated, heading over to the sideboard and rummaging through the top drawer.

The doorbell rang again. "Maybe you should get the door first, Dad?" I suggested, laughing as we headed down the stairs to him.

He nodded and walked to the door. From the hallway, I heard both Paul and Jamie's voices greeting my dad. My stomach immediately tingled in anticipation of seeing my boyfriend in his tux. I was going to be the envy of every girl in school tonight when I walked in on his arm. Jamie was incredibly handsome, all the girls agreed on that from meeting him at parties and such, but he had something even better than his looks—he was just a beautiful person inside. So thoughtful and selfless; he was incredible. I was going to have serious heartache when he broke it off with me tonight.

"You'll have her home by midnight, are we clear?" my dad said sternly from behind me.

"Absolutely. You can trust me with Ellie, you know that," Jamie answered.

A smile crept onto my face as their voices approached. I turned and waited. As soon as Jamie stepped around the corner I fought my urge to swoon. The rented black tux fit him perfectly, showing off his strong, broad shoulders and tapering in at his toned waist. His gaze settled on me and his eyes widened as his lips popped open in what seemed like shock. I tried not to squirm as his big brown eyes slowly glided down my body, seeming to take in every inch of me before his eyes met mine again and a beautiful smile stretched across his face.

"Shit . . . wow," he breathed.

My dad punched him in the arm playfully. "No cussing," he scolded, while Jamie just laughed sheepishly, his eyes not leaving me for a second.

"Hi," I whispered nervously.

He stepped closer to me; his gaze seemed to trap me as he grinned happily. I couldn't look away from him as I prayed with every bone in my body that he wouldn't break up with me. I was totally crazy about this boy, and Stacey was right, he *did* scare me. He scared me because I didn't want our relationship to end up like mine and Miles's had, I didn't want him to change like Miles had. I was definitely falling for Jamie, and falling hard.

He reached out, catching one of my curls and rubbing it between his thumb and forefinger gently before stroking the back of one finger across my cheek. There was an almost awed expression on his face. I memorized him as he looked right now. I wanted to be able to capture this moment perfectly so that when it ended and he never looked at me like that again, I could still picture it.

His smell enveloped me, that scent that made the hair on my arms stand up. It was indescribable, it was just purely Jamie, and I loved it. "Ellie, you look . . . *so* beautiful," he said quietly, so that no one else would be able to hear him. His smile showed me the truth to his words, and my face instantly warmed up because of the intense way he was looking at me. "This dress, it's incredible. You just look…" He gulped. "Wow," he finished.

I chewed on my lip as I raised one hand and stroked the lapel of his jacket. "You look wow, too," I admitted.

"This old thing?" he joked, winking at me. I laughed and he brought his hand from his side, holding out a little plastic box containing a white-and-green corsage. "Got you this."

"Aww, Jamie, that's adorable," I murmured. The thing was beautiful. I smiled at him gratefully as I took the box, popping it open and gingerly taking out the delicate flower bracelet.

He smiled and took it from my hand, helping me put it on. As I looked back up at him, he bent down and captured my lips in a sweet kiss that made me sigh in contentment. I'd never had a boy treat me with so much kindness and adoration before. Miles was never romantic like this; if I had been going to prom with him tonight he would have turned up and grunted a "Hey, you ready to go?" before nodding at the door. He wouldn't have looked at me the soft and gentle way that Jamie was.

"Any time this week would be great, guys."

Startled out of the moment, I suddenly remembered that we weren't on our own in the hallway. I nodded sheepishly. "I'm ready."

Jamie's arm slipped around my waist, pulling me closer to him as he turned for the door. "You have your dancing shoes on?" he asked, grinning at me.

I raised one eyebrow as I tugged up the hem of my dress slightly and lifted one foot from the floor so he could see the three-inch open-toed black stilettos I was wearing tonight. "Yep," I confirmed, smirking at him as his eyes widened and his fingers dug into my waist a little. Jamie definitely had a thing for heels.

"Oh yeah, those are nice," he growled.

I smiled and let the dress drop back down again, pulling out of his arms and heading over to my dad, kissing his cheek. "Bye, Daddy. Don't wait up for me, I have a key," I stated. *Then I can sneak Jamie in with me tonight and you won't even know...*

"Let me get a photo before you go," he said quickly, plucking the camera from the drawer and fiddling with it.

I stepped back to Jamie's side, leaning into him, both of us smiling as the camera clicked and clicked. Finally my dad seemed to be satisfied that he'd taken enough, so we were allowed to leave.

Paul was driving tonight and had borrowed his dad's Jaguar, so we were riding in style to prom. I sat in the back with Jamie; he held my hand the whole time as we chatted about the dance. I already knew that he was nervous about coming with me tonight; I was pretty sure he'd gotten it into his head that this would be a posh party with an old-fashioned string quartet or something. He was going to be pleasantly surprised.

When we pulled up and headed into the school gym, he laughed. The place had been decorated with streamers and balloons, with food laid out. The normal lights were off and white fairy lights covered the ceiling instead. A local band was already set up and playing warm-up songs.

I turned to Jamie and grinned, pulling him into the gym. "Drink?" I offered, nodding toward the drinks table. "The punch will already be spiked, I would imagine, so if you want alcohol then I'd go for that."

A small frown lined his forehead. "I don't want an alcoholic drink tonight. You can if you want, though" he offered, following me over to the table.

I shook my head and grabbed two cans of Pepsi and two plastic cups. "Nah, I don't want to be too drunk to take you out of your tux," I teased, raising one eyebrow suggestively.

His frown was back as he smiled apologetically. "I actually

won't be staying at your house tonight," he replied, taking my can and opening it for me, pouring it into the cup.

I resisted the urge to pout as I took in what he'd said. I couldn't stay at his place tonight because my parents would know I was there; it would be too obvious if I went to the dance with Jamie and then didn't come home. So instead I had been hoping to be able to sneak him in with me tonight. He could just leave after my parents went to visit my nana, like he used to in the old days before he moved into his new place.

"Why not?" I pressed.

I already knew the answer to that question. He wasn't planning on staying at my house because he was planning on breaking up with me instead. I had a feeling it would happen as soon as prom finished. No doubt he was being the gentleman and waiting until after the dance so that I would still have someone to go with. It really wasn't Jamie's style to leave a girl stranded, and since he'd committed to coming with me, he probably didn't want to break his promise. I gulped a few times, trying desperately not to cry about it.

He shrugged. "I can't sneak into your place, your dad will know. He likes me, and I don't want to ruin that by betraying his trust," he answered, not looking at me.

I decided not to push it; I needed to have some dignity. I'd had a fantastic couple of months with him, and I wouldn't have changed that time for the world. I decided then and there not to dwell on it and ruin our last night together. I'd just forget that my time with him was limited and make this night fun for us both.

"Well, in that case, I'm having the punch," I stated, not taking the cup of Pepsi that he offered me. Instead, I ladled a spoonful of the punch into an empty cup, downing the contents before pouring another. The alcohol burned my throat a little, but I welcomed it so that I would have something else to think about other than the fact that I was probably going to wake up single.

Jamie smiled and bent forward, kissing my cheek softly. "Let's get this party started then," he whispered, smiling and tugging me toward the dance floor.

* * *

Two hours later I was already overly tipsy. Jamie steered me toward an empty table and pulled out a chair for me to sit on, but I wasn't having any of that. Instead, I pushed him into the chair and plopped myself into his lap, wrapping my arms around his neck.

"You know, you look mighty fine in your tux. Kinda like James Bond," I flirted, playing with the collar of his shirt.

He laughed. "But without the British accent?" he teased, shifting me on his lap and getting more comfortable as I tucked my face into the side of his neck, breathing him in.

"If you had a British accent I would have to jump you right now in front of the teachers, so it's pretty lucky you don't," I countered, giggling.

He laughed and kissed the top of my head. "I could totally pull off the accent," he joked. "Well, 'ello there, miss. Would you like some crisps and biscuits?" he asked, sounding like the guy from *Mary Poppins* instead of James Bond.

I burst out laughing and pulled back to look at him. "Sexy," I confirmed, still laughing.

His cell phone rang for what had to be the millionth time and he sighed as he pulled it out of his pocket, disconnecting the call and tapping in a text instead. Frowning, I moved into my own chair, downing the last of my drink, trying not to glare at his phone, which seemed to be getting more attention than I was tonight. So much for making the most of my last night with him! I was seriously contemplating stealing his phone and "accidentally" dropping it so the damn thing would stop going off. It beeped again and he ground his teeth before sending another message, frowning angrily at his screen.

"I'm going to dance," I mumbled, pushing myself to my feet.

He looked at me and smiled apologetically. "Sorry. I'll be right there, okay?"

I nodded and tried not to huff as I headed across the room to where a group of my friends were dancing. I joined in with them, discreetly keeping my eyes on Jamie. He was talking on the phone now, and he looked a little angry. He kept glancing at his watch and waving his hand around as he spoke, like he was having an argument with someone.

"Ellie?"

I turned back around only to find Miles standing next to me, grinning. I bit back my groan. Things between us were still beyond awkward. It had been ten weeks since the night we'd broken up, yet he still hadn't given up on us. He'd been sleeping around—from what I could make out, it seemed like he went home with a different girl every week after the game—but he still asked me all the time for another chance. I was bored of it already.

"Hi, where's your date?" I asked, looking around for whoever he was with tonight.

He frowned. "I came on my own. I didn't want to bring someone to prom if it wasn't you," he replied, shrugging.

I winced and silently hoped that Jamie didn't come over right now; I didn't want trouble between them. The atmosphere when they were near each other at the postgame parties was so tense that you could almost cut it with a knife. "Oh" was the only thing that I could think of to respond to that remark.

He smiled sadly. "Want to dance?"

I laughed and waved down at myself and the group of people I was dancing with. "I'm already dancing."

He nodded off to one side, suggesting that we would be dancing together instead of just part of a group. "On our own?" he clarified.

My eyes jumped to Jamie again. He was still on the phone, running a hand through his hair. He looked stressed. "Um…"

Miles sighed and took my hand. "You're allowed to dance with another guy, I'm sure," he scoffed.

I shook my head and looked at him disbelievingly. If we were still dating there would be no way he would allow me to dance with another guy, so that statement was just ludicrous. I had no clue why he hadn't given up already. Ten weeks was a long time to pine after someone. Before I had time to reject the dance offer, an arm snaked around my shoulders. I jumped and looked up to see Jamie; he was frowning in Miles's direction.

"Thanks for looking after *my* girlfriend for me," he said.

Miles's jaw tightened. "No problem, she was looking a little neglected. Important phone call, was it?"

Jamie seemed to stiffen as he nodded. "It was, but I'm done now." He turned to me and smiled apologetically. "Sorry, little girl. I'm all yours now, I promise."

He cupped my face in his hands and kissed me. I knew this was for show, for Miles's benefit more than mine, but I kissed him back regardless. Everything else faded away when Jamie kissed me. My eyes fluttered closed. I literally could have been anywhere, and it wouldn't matter so long as his lips didn't leave mine. I crushed myself to him, wrapping my arms around his waist, wanting to melt into him and stay there forever. But as with all good things, it had to end sometime. He pulled out of the kiss and smiled, stroking my face with his thumb. Glancing to the side, I saw that Miles had already walked off, probably so he didn't witness us kissing. No doubt that had been Jamie's intention.

His nose trailed up the side of mine. "Sorry," he whispered.

I shook my head dismissively. "Don't worry about it. Is everything okay?"

He sighed and nodded, his smile fake. "Yeah, fine. Want to get some fresh air or something? I have a headache," he replied, motioning toward the gym doors.

I smiled sympathetically. It was probably the music that was giving him a headache; it was pretty loud in here. "Sure."

As I followed him outside, he slipped off his jacket, wrapping it around my shoulders. He walked over to the little brick wall and sat down, taking my hand and pulling me toward him gently so I was standing between his legs, our faces level. He gripped the edges of his jacket, pulling it closed around my body as he pressed himself closer to me, keeping me warm. My eyes locked on his and I seemed to get caught in his gaze. We didn't speak, I just looked at his handsome face and memorized every inch of it. The music playing in the background, the stars shining down on us, the solitude, all of it was perfect and almost magical.

"How are you feeling now?" I asked after a couple of minutes, stroking his cheek with one finger.

He blew out a big breath and shook his head, rubbing his forehead. "It's pretty bad actually. Right above my eyes," he replied. "You don't have any pills for it, do you?"

I shook my head apologetically. I usually carried painkillers on me, but I only had that silly little clutch purse with me tonight. "No, sorry, I don't. Maybe we could try to get you something from the first aid room?"

He sighed deeply. "Ellie, I'm gonna have to go home, I'm sorry. My head feels like it's gonna explode," he moaned.

I nodded quickly; I didn't mind leaving now, actually. I would rather just leave if he wasn't feeling well anyway. "Okay, let me just find Stacey and tell her we're leaving, and then we can call a cab," I replied, turning back for the door we'd come out of.

Jamie's hand covered mine, squeezing gently as he pulled me to a stop. "I'd rather leave you here with Stacey. That way you can enjoy the rest of the night." He stroked the side of my face, looking at me apologetically. "I really wish I didn't have to go. I'm so sorry. I'll make it up to you, I promise," he whispered, kissing me again.

I smiled against his lips. "Stop apologizing. You're not feeling good, that's nothing that can be helped. Go get some sleep," I instructed.

He smiled and pulled the jacket tighter around me. "You keep this; it'll be cold later, when you leave. Stay inside, and don't go wandering off in this hot little dress, it's way too tempting for guys not to ravage you when you look like this," he teased, winking at me. I laughed and he kissed my forehead. "Want to meet me for lunch or something tomorrow?"

I frowned. "You still going out with Connor tomorrow night?"

He nodded, his gaze dropping to the ground, shifting on his feet. Jamie was a terrible liar. I refused to allow myself to think about what he'd really be doing tomorrow night—maybe meeting another girl, or maybe he just didn't want to see me and he was going to break it off with me tomorrow at lunch instead…

"Okay, yeah, lunchtime then. Call me in the morning," I agreed, swallowing the lump in my throat.

"I will. See ya," he replied, squeezing my hand gently before he turned and walked across the parking lot. My eyes stung with tears as I caught the lapel of his jacket, stroking the material. Jamie had basically confirmed my suspicions, it really was over.

"You okay?"

I turned to see a smug-looking Miles. I nodded in response, forcing a smile so he wouldn't know I was upset. "Yep," I lied, turning and heading inside. Miles kept pace with me as I walked straight over to the drinks table and downed another glass of punch.

"Think maybe he's gonna go meet that chick he's been texting all night?" Miles asked at my side.

Oh God. Why had it never even entered my head that it might have been a girl who was distracting him all night? I swallowed and poured myself another drink. "No. He's gone home to bed. He's not feeling well." Even I could hear the doubt in my voice.

Miles laughed. "Yeah, sure," he agreed sarcastically. "Want to dance?"

I shook my head. I just needed to go home now too; I didn't want to be here without Jamie. There was no point in waiting for Stacey and Paul; my night was ruined already so why stretch it out for another hour?

I pushed myself away from the table and headed over to Paul, gripping his sleeve. He smiled down at me. "Hey, I think I'm just gonna get a cab home. Tell Stacey I said bye, okay?"

He frowned and shook his head adamantly. "Jamie will have my balls if I let you leave here on your own. I'm supposed to be driving you home. You know what he's like," he rebutted.

I shrugged nonchalantly. "He won't know if we don't tell him. I'll be fine. See you Monday. Tell Stacey that I'll call her tomorrow." I headed off quickly before he had a chance to stop me. He was right, Jamie would be seriously pissed if he found out I was leaving on my own. He was very protective like that.

As I walked through the crowd I tugged his jacket around me tighter, cloaking myself in his scent.

Once outside, I leaned against the wall and dialed the local cab company, but the lady told me they didn't have anything for an hour. I debated calling my dad and asking him to pick me up, but it was now past eleven and he was probably in bed already.

Pushing myself away from the wall, I started walking toward my house. Thank goodness my heels were comfortable. I figured it'd only take me twenty minutes—thirty, tops.

After about three minutes, car headlights lit the road next to me. The car slowed, keeping pace with me. I swallowed my unease, walking a little faster, trying not to look, silently wishing I hadn't decided to walk. This was a decent area, but it was late, and dark, and I was in a stupid little dress. I should have put a sign over my head saying DEFENSELESS, SLIGHTLY DRUNK TEENAGER, PLEASE FEEL FREE TO ATTACK ME. My stomach clenched as I began to think of all the things that could happen to me. When the car's horn blasted, I yelped, startled, and flicked my eyes up to it without slowing my pace. It was too dark for me to see properly, plus the headlights were on full, hurting my eyes.

Gritting my teeth, I pulled out my phone, getting Jamie's number up on the screen, ready to call him. I knew he would help me; even while sick he would race here and pick me up if I called him and told him I was frightened. I snuck a glance at the car to see that it was still following me, just about three feet behind me, slowly creeping along.

"Shit," I muttered, stopping for a split second to rip off my heels in case I needed to run. In my mind I planned out where I would go. The school was the closest place; if I darted down the next street I could double back and run there.

In my hand, my phone buzzed and started ringing. I frowned, seeing Miles's picture flash in the darkness. "Miles?" I answered. Maybe he could come and meet me if I told him I needed him.

"Yeah. Ellie, will you stop walking? Why are you ignoring me?" he asked incredulously.

"Huh?" I mumbled, sneaking another look at the car, but it

hadn't started up again; it was just stopped where I had stopped seconds before to take off my shoes.

"Ellie, just get in the car and stop behaving like a drama queen. You shouldn't be walking home in the dark."

"Car?" Without easing up on my run-walk, I looked at the car again and squinted through the glare of the lights to see that it was black, sleek, and expensive looking. The air whooshed out of my lungs in one gust as I realized that it wasn't some deranged ax murderer who was following and honking at me, it was Miles! Laughing with relief, I disconnected the call and sprinted toward his car with my shoes knocking together in my hand. As I threw open the door, I had never been happier to see Miles in my life. "Oh God, you scared me," I scolded, climbing in and punching him in the arm.

He laughed and rubbed his arm, looking at me like I was crazy. "I honked at you. You forget what my car looks like already?"

I sighed and rested my head back on the headrest. "I couldn't see, it's dark!" I protested, smiling because my heart rate was starting to slow down to a normal pace again.

He laughed and put the car in drive. "Put on your seat belt," he instructed, pulling out again and heading in the direction of my house. We didn't speak during the ten-minute drive. I sat there uncomfortably, hugging Jamie's jacket around myself. When Miles pulled into my driveway, he smiled at me. "Think I could use your bathroom? I need to pee. Drank too much soda, I think," he said, already taking off his seat belt and killing the engine.

I frowned but nodded anyway. I didn't really want him to come in, but after he'd just driven me home I couldn't exactly say no. He quietly followed me inside the darkened house. He headed to the downstairs bathroom while I went to the kitchen to see if there was any food for me to eat.

Finding some leftover pizza in the fridge, I pulled out the plate and sat at the kitchen table to snack on it. Miles came in after a couple of minutes and smiled. "That looks good. Can I have some?" he asked, nodding at the plate.

I shrugged and pushed the plate in his direction as he sat down next to me. "Thanks for the ride home. Even though you did scare the crap out of me," I said, grinning and blushing at my stupidity.

He smiled and bit into his pizza. It was a little awkward. Conversation had never flowed easily between us, and talking hadn't been one of the key points of our relationship—then again, there weren't actually many key points to our relationship at all. I'd loved him in the beginning, but then it just kind of fizzled out, but by that time we'd been together too long to just give up on it, so we stayed together and the relationship turned a little sour.

"So, what are your plans for the weekend?" I asked politely.

He shrugged. "Not sure. My dad wants me to go into his office tomorrow and help him prepare for a big case he has coming up; nothing interesting really. What about you?"

"I'm seeing Jamie tomorrow afternoon. Got nothing else planned, though."

"Want to catch a movie or something tomorrow night? That actor that you like has a movie out, I think." The hopeful tone to his voice was obvious.

I squirmed in my seat. "Um...Jamie took me to see it last week."

"Oh. Well, maybe we could see something else? Or have dinner?" he asked, giving me the little-lost-boy look.

I smiled sadly. When Miles wanted to, he could be sweet...but this nice-guy act never lasted long. He would be nice right up until I wore something he didn't like, or spoke to someone without his being there, or even accepted a drink from someone at a party.

He was crazy possessive. If he was thinking I'd forgotten the reasons that we broke up just because he suggested we go see a chick flick together, then he was very much mistaken. Even if Jamie did break up with me, there would be no chance that I would ever go back to Miles.

"Miles, I'm with Jamie."

A frown lined his forehead as his eyes hardened. "Ellie, it's not right that we're not together! We were a great couple. Just give me another chance, please?" He hopped off his stool, stepping closer to me.

"You should go. Thanks for the ride home, I appreciate it." I eyed the door as I stood too, signaling the end of the conversation.

He obviously didn't get my signal, though, because he gripped the tops of my arms, pulling me against his body as his lips crashed against mine, kissing me fiercely. I whimpered and squirmed, turning my head to the side to break the kiss, but his grip tightened on my arms, his fingers digging into my skin as he kissed me again.

Somehow, I got my arms between our bodies and shoved him as hard as I could, causing him to stumble back a couple of steps. Swiping at my mouth with the back of my hand, I glared at him. "Just get the hell out," I growled quietly, not wanting to wake my parents or sister.

"Ellie—" he started, but I held up a hand to cut him off.

"Leave. Now," I ordered, marching out into the hall and wrenching the front door open.

He did follow me out there, but he didn't look happy at all. His jaw was tight; his eyes were piercing into mine as he stomped over to the open door. "I love you, Ellie. Sooner or later you'll realize that you're dating a loser, and you'll come begging me to take you back."

I snorted and shook my head, not looking at him as I opened the door wider to prompt him. He sighed, and before I could stop him, he bent forward and kissed me again for a second before heading out. I growled in frustration and closed the door, wanting nothing more than to scream and kick the wood in frustration.

After locking up and throwing the rest of the pizza back into the fridge, I headed upstairs. Just as I got to the top, my mom came out of the bathroom, crossing the hallway, heading back toward her bedroom. She smiled at me; the little glint in her eye told me that she'd witnessed at least some of that little exchange between me and Miles.

"Hello, Ellison. How was the dance?"

I sighed and shrugged. "It was okay, I guess," I replied. "I'm going to bed. G'night, Mom."

"Good night, honey."

I ignored the smug smile on her face and headed into my room, practically ripping the dress off over my head and flopping down on the bed in my underwear. I buried my face in the pillow and tried my hardest not to cry. I refused to think about Miles kissing me. If I started thinking about him, then I'd end up getting angry about it and then I'd never get to sleep. My thoughts turned to Jamie. I silently wondered if he'd made it home okay or if he needed me to go there and play nurse for him. I longed for him to be here with me, to fold me into his arms and kiss me good night. I missed him like crazy. I was both excited to see him tomorrow and scared at the same time because I was dreading the moment that he would say what I knew he was going to say—that it was over. How was I going to cope with that when he said it? My best guess was that I wouldn't handle it very well at all.

CHAPTER 19

JAMIE

EARLIER IN THE DAY, I'd parked my truck near Ellie's school so I could drive myself to the warehouse when the time came. As I pulled my keys out and walked to it, anger and resentment boiled in my chest. The resentment was firmly directed toward my mother for dragging me into this situation in the first place. The anger—and it was a lot of anger—was directed toward the douchebag who had been calling me constantly all night, asking when I was getting there and panicking about the boost being late.

I felt like shit. I hated everything about my life at the moment: the pressure, the illegality, but mostly the fact that I'd left Ellie stranded at her prom. It wouldn't surprise me in the slightest when she dumped me for it. I truly was a worthless boyfriend right now, and she deserved better than me.

I sighed as I approached my beat-up old truck, unlocking it and slipping inside. Ellie's concerned face was all I could see as I started up the car. I'd never had anyone worry about me like she did. I loved it.

It had almost killed me to walk away from her tonight. She

looked beautiful, almost too good for my sanity. The urge to tell her that I loved her had been so strong tonight that I had no idea how I'd managed to keep the words at bay.

Driving straight to the warehouse, I swung my car into an empty space and slammed the door with way too much force as the anger built even more. Stepping into the warehouse, I unconsciously tightened my hands into fists, my fingers immediately aching because of the force of the movement as I spotted his smug face. Shaun. The bastard who'd been calling and texting for the last three hours, ruining the limited time I got to spend with my girl.

I didn't focus on anyone else; I ignored the greetings of the rest of the team, who were standing around. Instead, I walked up to Shaun, smiling politely as I approached.

"Fina-fucking-ly!" he cried, throwing his hands up in exasperation.

I didn't answer; simply put both hands on his chest and shoved, hard, making him stumble back against the wall. Gripping a fistful of his shirt, I smashed my fist into his stunned face. He grunted as his lip split, gushing blood down his chin. I didn't stop at that, though; I wasn't satisfied with just a split lip. Drawing my fist back again, I punched him in the stomach, taking out all of my frustrations on him.

"I said eleven, asshole! Why keep calling me? I told you I was busy, you prick!" I shouted as I punched him in the ribs. He was trying to fight me off, struggling against my hold, but that didn't matter, I knew his efforts were futile. He was a good few inches taller than me, and probably outweighed me by about thirty pounds, but I knew I could put him down easily.

Arms wrapped around me from behind. "Kid, calm the hell down," Ray hissed, dragging me back a couple of steps.

I could barely hear him through my rage as Shaun reached into his pocket, bringing out a silver switchblade. As the blade snapped out, I elbowed Ray harshly in the ribs so that he'd let go.

"I'm gonna fucking kill you," Shaun spat angrily. I smiled at that threat. A couple of months ago, that probably wouldn't have bothered me in the slightest. Now I had Ellie.

I stepped closer to him, watching as rage, and maybe a little fear, crossed his broken face. He was definitely wary of me, and with good reason, too.

"Calm down, both of you. Shaun, put that shit away," Ray ordered, his voice tight and controlled. No one else moved or said anything.

I smiled wickedly. "Yeah, Shaun, put that shit away before you hurt yourself. You really shouldn't play with knives," I mocked, raising one eyebrow.

His lip curled up, exposing his bloodstained teeth. "You talk a big game for a street-rat, son-of-a-whore murderer!" Shaun mused.

I knew he was trying to goad me into making the first move, but it wasn't going to work. I'd been called a lot worse in my time. Truth be told, I *was* the murdering son of a whore, so I couldn't exactly disagree.

He moved quickly, lunging with the knife. Stepping to the side, I grabbed his wrist, roughly slamming it against the wall to get him to drop the weapon. He didn't drop it, though; instead, he twisted his body, smashing his knee into my side. I hissed through my teeth as pain radiated up my chest from my almost healed ribs. I gripped one hand around his throat, putting my leg behind his, and stepped to the side, twisting his body so he lost his balance and stumbled over my foot. As he fell to the floor I let myself go with him, landing on top of him as I slammed his wrist against the cold concrete floor this time. The knife finally left his hand, skidding across the floor, going underneath a red convertible that was sitting ready for collection.

Shaun made a strangled gurgle as my hand tightened on his throat. At the same time I pushed myself up to my knees and straddled him, my other hand colliding with his face in a hard punch. I knew I needed to show him that he wasn't in charge here; I wasn't going to be putting up with this nonsense all the time, and he needed to learn that quickly. I punched him over and over in the face and chest. I hadn't lost control, though; I knew what I was doing. If I had lost it, then I wouldn't have been able to hear the people shouting at us to break it up, and I wouldn't be able to feel someone tugging at the back of my shirt, trying to get me up. I had lost control of myself only once before, and I never wanted to do that again.

When I was satisfied he'd suffered enough, I gripped his shirt and leaned over him, my face inches from his. I looked into his watery eyes as I spoke. "You ever pull a knife on me again, and I'll run it through your heart." I let my eyes stay on his for a few seconds, allowing my words to sink in so he'd know I was serious.

Ray was pulling at my upper arms as he shouted orders at me. Finally I let him lift me to my feet. I ran a hand through my hair, dimly aware that my hands were shaking from the adrenaline coursing through my system. Turning to look at Ray, I smiled reassuringly, showing him I was in control of myself. He was frowning angrily, but that anger was clearly directed at Shaun as he glared at him.

"So, are we ready to get this show on the road, or what?" I asked, choosing to ignore the past few minutes and move on. I had a job to do, and the sooner I got it done, the sooner I could go home to bed. I didn't look at Shaun as he struggled to get to his feet.

Ray sighed, turning back to me again. "You okay, Kid?"

I nodded, shrugging nonchalantly. *Of course I'm okay, I'm always okay.* "Yep. Where's my pack?" I asked, looking around for the

details of the boost tonight. Ray motioned toward the brown envelope on the desk. As I headed over to get it, something rammed
into me from behind, making me crash against the hot little red
sports car.

"No! Careful of the car!" Ray screamed like a little girl.

I didn't have time to laugh like I wanted to; Shaun was obviously back for more. He pinned me against the car, so I thrust my
head back, connecting with his face. He grunted in pain and his
hold on me loosened. Pushing myself back, I threw him off me
before turning to look at him warningly.

Shaun's eyes dropped to the floor off to my right. Following his
gaze I saw the handle of the knife lying about three feet away, just
under the car. I looked back at him and shook my head. I didn't
want to have to go that far, but if he came at me with a knife again
I wouldn't be lenient. Before I could open my mouth to discour-
age him, he dived for the knife, his eyes a little crazy.

I stepped to the side, and as his hand closed around it, I raised
my foot and stamped on his hand as hard as I could. The sicken-
ing crack of his fingers breaking rang in my ears for just a split
second before he let out an involuntary scream. He pushed himself back up using his elbow and looked at me angrily. His eyes
told me he still wasn't ready to give up. I sighed as I raised my
foot again and slammed it into his face, making him fall onto his
back. The room had gone quiet again now; the only sound was
Shaun's ragged breathing as I stalked toward him. When I moved
my hand, he flinched, thinking I was going to hit him. Instead, I
pulled open the door of the sports car, hearing Ray's little whimper behind me because I was touching one of his babies.

Smiling wickedly, I looked down at Shaun, who was painfully
scooting backward, trying to move away from me. "Did you
know that if you break the bones in your hand enough times,
you'll never be able to use it properly?" I asked, keeping my tone

light and friendly. He didn't answer, just sneered at me angrily, glaring through his rapidly swelling eyes. "So, for example, when I slam this car door on your hand repeatedly, you'll probably never be able to use it to jack off again," I continued.

"Kid, don't..." Ray said behind me.

I raised one eyebrow at Shaun. "I did say that if you pulled a knife on me again I'd kill you with it, but this tux is rented; if I get blood on it I won't get my deposit back," I mused, waving my free hand down at my white shirt and rented black pants.

He shook his head, gulping loudly.

Smiling, I reached out, gripping his injured hand, moving it quickly toward the opening of the car door. That was when the pleading started. He whimpered and begged as he tried to wrench his hand from my grasp, struggling and thrashing.

"No, please? Don't, please!" he begged, shaking his head fiercely, his eyes scared now as I pinned him to the ground and held his hand in place. He was finally admitting defeat.

I grinned and shrugged, moving my other hand on the car door, swinging it inward. Shaun's deafening, high-pitched scream reverberated off the walls as the door swung toward the hand that I was pinning against the metal, where it would connect in less than a second or two.

I stopped it just a couple of inches before it made contact, though. I looked down at Shaun to see that he was lying there with his eyes squeezed shut, the scream still coming out of his mouth. I laughed and shook my head at the pathetic sight before me.

And he accused me of talking a big game?

"You scream like a bitch," I teased, pushing myself off him, standing up, looking down at him. He slowly opened his eyes, the piercing scream stopping as he looked first at me, then at his hand, which was untouched by the door. "Are we done?" I growled. I had no problem going through with the plan if he was still insisting on trying to prove himself.

He took a couple of ragged breaths before he nodded. "Done," he agreed.

Nodding back, I offered my hand to help him up. He looked at it hesitantly for a few seconds before putting his good hand in mine, whimpering as I pulled him to his feet. "Just so you know, next time I won't stop," I told him, cocking my head to the side, meeting his eyes so he'd know I was serious.

He shook his head. "No next time."

Before I could answer, someone applauded from behind me. "Bravo, bravo, what an awesome show of dominance," Brett mocked. I turned to see him smiling a fake and clearly annoyed smile at us as he stood at the bottom of the stairs, leaning there with one leg crossed over the other. "Trouble is, now I'm down one team member, and I have an order to fill. If that's late, then I'm going to hold you personally responsible, Kid."

I smiled reassuringly. "It won't be late, don't worry."

He grinned, seeming satisfied with my answer as he walked forward, patting my shoulder affectionately. "I know." He turned and looked toward Shaun, who was cradling his hand to his chest, one of his eyes swollen, his lip split, his jaw bruised. He was favoring one side slightly, so obviously his ribs were painful, too. "Didn't I already tell you not to mess with the kid? Next time maybe you'll listen, huh?"

Shaun nodded, dropping his eyes to the floor as he shuffled on his feet. "Sorry, boss."

Brett looked away from him distastefully. "Someone take him to see Marlon," he instructed. Marlon was Brett's brother-in-law. He was a doctor at the local hospital, and he and Brett had an agreement of treatment, no questions. Shaun immediately limped toward the exit of the warehouse with Ian following behind him. Brett turned back to me. "I don't want to know what that's about, and frankly I don't care, but don't think you can come waltzing in here and start shit with my employees, Kid. Talent or not, if you start messing with my business, our friendship will cease to exist, you get what I'm saying?"

I smiled and nodded, laughing quietly. That threat wasn't exactly subtle. "Sure. You're saying, screw up again and go for the long walk."

He laughed and slung his arm around my shoulder. "Exactly." He looked down at his watch and frowned. "You gonna get this order done?"

"Don't I always?"

"Yeah, Kid, you do. That's why you're the best." He winked at me before turning for the stairs. "I'll be upstairs in the office. Someone tell me when it's done."

Ray was busy running his hand over the car that I'd fallen into, a worried expression on his face. I grinned. "No, careful of the car!" I mocked in a high-pitched girlie voice.

Ray sighed and turned around, looking at me exasperatedly. "Do you have any idea how long it took me to polish this angel up? Beauty like this needs to be respected," he gushed, tracing his hand on the roof.

"Thanks for being concerned about me, man. I'm touched," I joked, putting my hand over my heart.

He grinned and shook his head. "You can handle yourself. This little baby, on the other hand"—he bent down and kissed the expensive paint job—"she needs loving."

I laughed and picked up the pack from the desk, ripping it open, excitement building in my chest at what was about to happen. I couldn't help but love the rush that coursed through my veins at the mere thought of boosting cars.

"What the hell do you look like anyway?" Ray asked, coming

over and sitting next to me, flicking the black tie that hung loose around my neck.

I grinned over at him. "An American James Bond, apparently."

* * *

As usual, when I woke in the morning, my first thought was of Ellie. Rolling to the side, I stretched my hand out for her but met nothing but air. A long groan escaped my lips when I remembered she hadn't stayed over last night—instead, I'd left her at her prom to go and steal more than a million dollars' worth of cars and one motorcycle.

I finally cracked my eyes open, looking at my alarm clock. It was just after eleven o'clock. I sat up quickly and gasped. I'd told her that I'd call her this morning, but I knew I wasn't going to be able to. I'd dropped my phone last night in the scuffle with Shaun and the stupid screen had cracked beyond repair. She was going to be even more annoyed with me that I hadn't called her like I'd promised.

"Damn it," I mumbled, pushing myself up from the bed. I was still tired, my body refusing to wake up after a mere four hours of sleep. Today was going to be another crummy day. I was seeing Ellie for lunch, which was great, but tonight was my first shift at the strip club, which I wasn't looking forward to in the slightest. I'd much rather be cuddled up with my girlfriend on the sofa, talking about random stuff and joking around with her like usual. I stretched my sleep-deprived muscles and then headed to the shower, setting the water to cold so that it'd wake me up a little.

Half an hour later, I pulled up outside Ellie's house unannounced, hoping she was already awake. If she wasn't, then I'd use the spare key that I knew the Pearces kept hidden under a stone and sneak into her bed to surprise her. I smiled at the thought. But the smile faded when I saw the Pearce family car still in their driveway. They had usually left by this time of the morning to make the hour-and-a-half drive over to see Ellie's grandmother.

Pushing myself out of the truck, I strutted up to the door and knocked. I took a deep breath as I ran through the apologetic speech that I was going to make about bailing on Ellie last night. But she didn't answer the door; her mother did.

I winced as the polite smile that she answered the door with faded when she realized it was me. She frowned and looked me over distastefully, and immediately I was wishing I'd put on a nice shirt instead of the faded band tee I had thrown on. The woman never failed to make me feel like a scumbag.

"Good morning, Mrs. Pearce. Is Ellie around?" I asked, forcing a polite smile.

She raised one eyebrow at that and pulled the door closer to her body, closing the gap in a *you're not welcome in my house* gesture. "And what are you doing here, Jamie? I was under the impression that you two had broken up," she replied, her voice cold and emotionless.

I frowned and shook my head. "We didn't break up," I corrected her, wondering why on earth she would think that.

She frowned and cocked her head to the side, the way Ellie did when she thought hard about something. However, when Ellie did it, she looked cute, like a curious little puppy, whereas when her mother did it, she resembled a cobra waiting to attack.

"Well, you definitely weren't the one who brought her home from the dance last night," she countered.

I sighed and shook my head. "No, I wasn't feeling well, so I left early. Paul and Stacey drove Ellie home for me," I said, trying not to show my lie in my voice.

She laughed quietly and rolled her eyes. "I think I can recognize Miles when I see him; my daughter dated him for long enough."

Miles? Miles drove Ellie home last night?

I hated the thought of that guy anywhere near her. I didn't begrudge her male friends, I would never tell her that she couldn't talk to another guy, but Miles just rubbed me the wrong way. I think it was the fact that he was so much better suited for her and was the complete opposite of me. He was respectable, ambitious, talented, smart, and he wanted to be a doctor—every mother's dream date for her daughter. I hated him because I knew that, at some point—and it seemed like that point might be now—I would lose her to him, or someone like him without the possessive edge.

"Miles drove her home?" I checked, swallowing my unease.

She smiled smugly and nodded. "Mm-hmm. I just assumed that you two had broken up because Ellison and Miles were kissing...maybe she just hasn't told you?"

Kissing? What the fuck!

Disappointment and sadness settled in the pit of my stomach as my blood seemed to turn to ice in my veins. It was over. Ellie had finally come to her senses and wised up to the fact that I was a waste of space and she was better off with someone else. I wasn't even angry about it because I just wanted her to be happy.

I tightened my jaw as Ruth continued to speak while looking at me like I was something nasty on the bottom of her shoe. "So maybe you should run along and corrupt someone else's daughter. Clearly your time with the rich little cheerleader is over."

"Is Ellie home? I'd like to hear it from her," I replied tersely. If it was truly over, then I could accept that, but not from this hateful witch. If Ellie told me that we were done, then so be it, but I wasn't walking away from here without asking her for one last chance—even just a chance to be friends would suffice. I just needed to keep her in my life.

Ruth shifted on her feet, stepping out through the door and then pulling it closed behind her. Her gray eyes, which were the same as Ellie's, just harder and less forgiving, locked onto mine as she turned her nose up at me. "She's sleeping," she answered. "Look, Jamie, let's be honest here, we both knew this was coming. All girls go through a bad-boy stage at some point in their lives, and it looks like you were my daughter's. But it's done now. I'm not letting you ruin her future. She deserves better than you."

I gulped. I couldn't even disagree with her words because they mirrored my opinion exactly.

"So just leave. You're neither wanted nor welcome here," she finished. Before I could answer or even think of what I wanted to say, she turned her back on me and headed inside, closing the door in my face.

I squeezed my eyes shut as my heart ached at the thought of not being with Ellie. Part of me wanted to walk away with my tail between my legs. Ruth was right, I *had* known this was coming, but that didn't ease the pain one little bit. The more selfish part of me wanted Ellie so badly that I would literally do anything to keep her with me so I wasn't facing the world on my own with no reason to keep trying to be the person I wanted to be.

Instead of walking away, I bent down and picked up a couple of small pebbles from the ground and strutted around to the side of their property, scaling the six-foot gate and dropping down on the other side. I walked into the backyard, looking up at Ellie's window on the second floor.

I took a deep breath and threw the first little pebble. It hit its target, tapping on her window gently. When nothing happened, I threw the next one and then the next. I bent and picked up a couple more, throwing them, too.

The last one had already left my hand as the window slid open. Ellie squealed before laughing and sticking her head out. "What the heck are you throwing stones at me for?" she asked, giggling and rubbing her forehead. She leaned out the window, and I noticed that she was fully dressed, her hair brushed and pulled back into a little bun.

Sleeping my ass, her stupid mother lied!

I smiled apologetically. Movement from inside the house caught my eye and I looked over to see her mother walking through the kitchen toward the back door, an angry expression on her face. I turned my attention back to Ellie. "Sorry. I just wanted to talk to you," I said quickly.

Ellie frowned, doing that little cocking-the-head move, and I smiled at how different it was from her mother's look. "Well, why didn't you just knock, silly?" she asked, laughing.

I did. "Can you come down?" I asked hopefully. She nodded and disappeared inside, sliding the window shut after her.

"What on earth do you think you're doing?" Ruth hissed, wrenching the back door open, glaring at me.

I opened my mouth to answer, but Ellie's dad walked up behind her, pushing the door farther open, smiling at me happily. "Hey, Jamie. How's it going?"

I smiled in return. It was actually going pretty crappy right now, but I didn't want to say that to him. "Good, thanks, Michael. I thought you guys were heading out this morning?"

He blew out a big breath and raked his hand through his hair. "Stupid car won't start. Got someone coming out on Monday morning to look at it."

Ellie skipped up behind him, smiling broadly at me. Confusion consumed me. Why was she smiling at me like that if she was going to break up with me? She was still looking at me softly and affectionately.

"Morning! You feeling better?" she chirped, weaving past her parents and walking to my side.

I nodded and gulped. I couldn't lose her; I didn't think I would survive losing another girl from my life. She reached up, stroking my forehead with her fingertips. "Poor baby. Glad you're feeling better," she whispered, smiling, taking my hand.

"I need to talk to you," I said. My eyes flicked back to her mother. I tried not to react to the hateful look she was shooting me.

"Okay, come on in," Ellie replied, tugging me toward the door. As she turned in her mother's direction Ruth's face immediately righted itself to a polite smile, like she always put on when someone else was around. "Want a drink?" Ellie offered, heading to the fridge.

I nodded in response, wondering why she was being so casual about this. Was the thought of breaking up with me really so unimportant that it didn't even warrant a sad, wistful smile?

Her parents left the room and Ellie sat down at the counter, pushing a can of soda toward me.

"So, you okay this morning? Was Paul all right on the way home?" I asked, trying to think about how to start, or at least prompt her into saying the words I knew were coming.

Her eyes widened before she looked down at her drink, clearly flustered. "Yeah, fine."

I gulped and sat down next to her, trying not to let the scent of her hair affect me. She always used the most mouthwatering vanilla-scented shampoo. "Did he walk you to the door?" I asked, watching her reactions.

She shifted on her stool, tracing her finger on the edge of her can, avoiding my gaze. "Um...yep," she lied, nodding, taking a swig of her drink.

I sighed deeply, deciding to get it over with. "Miles drove you home, Ellie."

She gasped, her eyes shooting up to meet mine. "Don't be angry with Paul. I didn't give him a choice."

I rolled my eyes. Paul was the least of my worries right now. "Okay."

She frowned, turning in her seat, her knees pressing against my thigh as she leaned closer to me. "You're angry with me for letting Miles drive me home?" Her expression was apologetic. I didn't answer; she still hadn't said anything about kissing him. She sighed and frowned. "I didn't want to stay there without you, so I started walking home. A car started following me," she explained. My muscles tensed up; I thought she was going to tell me that Tony Grier or one of his men had laid his hands on her. Gritting my teeth, I waited for her to say the words that would make me kill another person. "I got scared. I was going to call you, I had your number up and everything. But it turned out to be Miles. I didn't want to walk home after that because I was already frightened, so I let him drive me," she continued.

It wasn't Tony? "It was Miles in the car? No one…hurt you, right?" I asked, eyeing her cautiously.

"No one hurt me." A confused frown creased her forehead. "Please don't be angry with me, Jamie. I know you're probably annoyed that I left the dance on my own after you told me not to. On top of that you're probably pissed that I let Miles drive me. But I just didn't want to walk home."

My body relaxed now that I knew she hadn't been touched by Tony or his men. "It's cool. I knew it would happen eventually. Maybe we could still be friends, though? I'd like that. Maybe we could hang out occasionally?"

She frowned, her mouth dropping open in shock. "You're going to use the Miles thing as an excuse to break up with me?" she snapped, shaking her head. "I didn't think you were a coward, Jamie. Just man up and say what this is really about, that

I'm not good enough and that you want someone prettier or nicer!"

Dumbstruck, I almost choked on air at her words. *Someone prettier than her?* "Ellie, what?"

She groaned and pushed her drink away from her, looking extremely frustrated. "I'd like for us to be friends, too. You don't have to say it, it's fine, I get it."

"You think that I'm breaking up with you?" I asked. She nodded as she swiped at her face, wiping a tear away, but she looked like she was trying not to show any emotion. "Ellie, you seriously think that *I'm*"—I pointed to myself to clarify what I was saying—"breaking up . . . with *you?*" I asked incredulously, pointing at her.

Her breath seemed to catch in her throat as another tear fell down her face. "Yeah?" she replied, suddenly looking unsure.

I need to get her booked for a CT scan quickly, because something must be seriously wrong with this girl for her to even entertain the thought that I would break up with her. I cupped her face in my hands, wiping another tear away with my thumb as I looked into her watery eyes. "I'm not breaking up with you. I thought you were ditching me," I whispered.

She frowned and shook her head. "No."

Smiling, I bent forward, kissing her lips, reveling in how perfect they felt against mine. Her arms looped around my waist, crushing her body against mine as she returned the kiss. I pulled back after a few seconds, setting my forehead against hers. Happiness was burning in my veins, my feet itching to do a happy dance in the middle of her kitchen because she wasn't ditching my worthless ass.

"Why would you think that I didn't want to be with you?" I asked.

She sighed, closing her eyes. "You've been distant and quiet lately. I thought maybe you were just waiting until after prom so I wouldn't have to go on my own."

I stepped even closer to her. "Ellie, I'm so totally crazy about you. I'm hooked; you have me for as long as you want me," I assured her, brushing a loose strand of her hair behind her ear.

The corners of her mouth pulled into a smile. "Corny line." She pressed against me, her face nuzzling into the side of my neck. I grinned and stroked her back, feeling totally and utterly happy...but then she spoke and my happiness wavered for a second. "Miles kissed me last night when he drove me home," she whispered, her breath blowing down the side of my neck. "I didn't kiss him back, I promise. He caught me by surprise and then I told him to leave. Seeing as we're putting stuff out there, I thought I should tell you that."

I nodded, kissing the side of her head, deciding not to tell her that I already knew because her mother had told me. "Thanks for telling me."

She pulled back to look at me worriedly. "I didn't kiss him back. I promise I didn't."

I smiled reassuringly, seeing the truth in her eyes. "I know. Don't worry about it. But if at any point you decide that you've had enough of me and want to go back to him, or someone else who makes you happy, then just know that I won't stand in your way."

She frowned and shook her head. "I don't want anyone else. I'm so totally crazy about you, too," she replied, using my words, smirking at me.

I grinned. "Corny."

She laughed her tinkling little laugh and nodded. "My boyfriend is the king of corny. I guess it's rubbing off on me a little."

I laughed and pressed my lips against hers, kissing her passionately, trying to convey that I loved her without actually saying the three little words. I broke the kiss just as it was getting a little too heavy for the middle of her parents' kitchen. "Stay at my place tonight?" I asked hopefully.

She frowned. "I thought you were out with Connor."

Another lie I'd told her to cover up the fact that I was going to be working tonight. Maybe I should tell her the truth; she'd been honest with me about Miles. "While we're giving out confessions, I should probably tell you that I'm not going out with Connor tonight. I never was." A hurt look crossed her face that I never wanted to see there again. "I have a second job that I'm starting tonight. I'm gonna be working at a bar," I continued, omitting a little bit of the truth—she didn't need to know it was a strip club.

Understanding flashed across her face. "You are? How come?"

"You're expensive," I joked, kissing the tip of her nose. She rolled her eyes and playfully pinched my stomach. "My rent is a little more than I thought, I just need a second job for a while, that's all. Everything should be okay in a few weeks," I lied.

"Okay. But if you're working, then how am I supposed to stay at your apartment? Are you gonna pick me up after or something?"

I shook my head. "No. Stay while I'm not there. Treat the place like your own, eat all my food, make a mess, and let me come home to you. I'd love to come home and have you waiting there for me."

She grinned. Clearly she liked the idea of that, too. "Okay."

I tightened my arms around her, lifting her off her feet, spinning in a little circle, making her squeal and grip me tighter as she pressed her lips to mine again. When I set her down, I took her hand, nodding toward the hallway. "Let's go fix your dad's car," I suggested, grinning happily.

* * *

I spent the afternoon at her place working on the car. Her dad was helping, leaning over the engine, watching intently, asking questions as I worked. Ellie just sat on the wall on the edge of her driveway, watching me, making cold drinks every now and again. I felt totally at ease here with both of them. Michael was a great person; he was definitely where 99 percent of Ellie's personality came from. Even Kelsey, Ellie's little sister, was playing on the grass, singing along to the radio and passing us tools from the box. I'd never felt so included in anything. I loved it. Ruth didn't show her face for the whole afternoon, and I couldn't help but be glad about it. That woman didn't deserve a great family like this one, it was wasted on her.

When the car was in full working order, Ellie and I went to buy a new phone for me, then went for dinner after. Once she'd filled her stomach with as much cheesecake as she could eat without hurling, we headed to my place so I could get changed and go to my new job.

She settled herself on my sofa, flipping through the shows I had recorded for her during the week, the girlie crap that she liked to watch on weekends. When I was ready to go, I leaned against the door frame and just looked at her stretched out on the sofa in my apartment, looking completely at home. I smiled as she laughed at the movie she was watching. *Mean Girls*. She'd seen it probably five times in the last month, yet she still watched it over and over. It was an adorable sight.

I knew I needed to go, so I pushed myself off the door frame and headed over to her, crouching down next to her head. "So, I'll see you in a couple of hours. I'll be home by midnight," I promised. I wasn't staying there late tonight, I was just going to show my face, get the staff organized, and then leave. I planned on doing the same thing at each of the clubs over the next few weeks, just show up occasionally and be at the end of the phone.

She smiled and sat up, gripping the back of my head, guiding my lips to hers for a second. "See you later then," she whispered. "Good luck at your new job."

I smiled and kissed her forehead. *I love you* was right on the tip of my tongue, but I swallowed the words. I'd never used the L-word before. I wanted to make sure it was special when I finally said it, not just randomly thrown out before I went to work. "Thanks."

I left before I wouldn't be able to and drove to the club. When I got there, I stopped to talk to the guy who was working the door, telling him not to let anyone in who was already drunk, giving him instructions on what to do if there was trouble. As soon as I walked into the club, I immediately wanted to leave. The music was loud and made the floor vibrate, the air was smoky, and the place was packed with perverted men who were eyeing the half-naked girls like they were their next meal.

During my stay, there wasn't much trouble at all. A couple of drunken people who thought they could touch the girls—they were removed quickly. Someone couldn't pay their tab, so the cops were called. Nothing exciting happened. Mostly I just sat at the bar, drinking a bottle of water because the smoke machine was making my throat feel like it had been raped by a hedgehog. I spoke politely to anyone who wanted to talk to me, showing my face like I was supposed to.

The girls who wandered around didn't interest me in the slightest. When one of them—Candice, she'd said her name was—offered me a free session out back, I declined and told her that I was hopelessly in love with the foxy little redhead who was waiting for me at home. She'd called me adorable and walked off gushing to one of the other girls about how some guys were too good to be true.

Knowing that Ellie was at my place waiting for me, that I was going to get to hold her in my arms tonight, made the time pass more quickly and kept the smile on my face all night long. When midnight came, I left and sped home, eager to see her.

As I stepped into my apartment, the first thing I noticed was that the title screen for *Mean Girls* was playing over and over. I frowned, wondering why she hadn't turned it off. I saw why as soon as I got closer—she was asleep. She was curled up on the sofa, snuggled in my hoodie. A moronic grin stretched across my face as I locked the doors, turned off the TV, and then slipped my arms under her body, lifting her up carefully.

She groaned in her sleep, her face snuggling into the side of my neck as I held her against me tightly, trying not to wake her as I walked toward my bedroom. "So, which do you like better, Jamie, Tom or Jerry?" she asked tiredly.

I grinned, knowing she was still sleeping. "Gotta be the mouse, he always outsmarts the cat in the end."

Her arms looped around my neck. "Mice are cute, but I wouldn't want one living in my place. They poop on stuff," she replied.

I laughed quietly and settled her carefully on the bed, smiling when she immediately snuggled into the sheets. Kicking off my shoes, I climbed in bed with her, wrapping her tightly in my arms, listening to her ramble some more about mouse poo and why it couldn't possibly be confused with raisins. My girl was seriously crazy at times, but I loved her more than anything.

CHAPTER 20

IT HAD BEEN a month since the dance. A whole perfect month of being with Ellie. The month hadn't been perfect workwise, though. Things had been getting more...*involved* recently. I'd been doing more of the things that I'd hated doing when I was younger. I was essentially one of Brett's hired thugs and had to hand out more than my fair share of beatings to people who were taking liberties or trying to muscle in on Brett's turf. The strip club stuff was getting easier; I didn't need to go there too much because there wasn't that much trouble. I'd had to sort out a few problems with people who used to run the security firm before Brett took it over; they weren't too happy that they'd lost the contract, but they were over that now. Also, there was a dealer issue that I dealt with pretty quickly. One of the girls had trouble with an ex-boyfriend who wouldn't leave her alone. All in all, it had gone pretty smoothly. People knew that I was there, so lately there was no trouble at all.

Thankfully, somehow I'd managed to keep my job at the junk-yard too, though that meant I was getting by on about five hours' sleep a night because I'd be out doing boosts about three times a week and then other stuff on the nights off. I was exhausted, which made me irritable and snappy.

The only good thing about working so much, as far as I could see, was that I earned a bucketload of cash. Word had spread quickly that I was back with Brett, and deals were rolling in and orders piling up quickly. I was earning, on average, about $18,000 a week. Last week I had gained immense pleasure in taking a wad of cash and throwing it down on Tony Grier's desk in full payment of my mother's debt.

Even Shaun and I had been getting along better since our little indiscretion with the knife after Ellie's prom. We were on friendly enough terms. He worked security in one of the strip clubs for me.

I'd even managed to set myself up with a bank account, which I'd never had before. There was less than two months left and then I'd be able to say good-bye to this life forever. Maybe then I could start being the man Ellie thought I was.

I sat in Brett's chair, swiveling it back and forth, desperately trying to keep my eyes open as I focused on his ceiling. Tonight was a big deal, a huge boost, and it was certainly going to be a long one. There would be ten guys out with me, and we were stealing a total of twenty-five cars. On paper, it sounded impossible, but in reality, ten of those cars were in one place—a warehouse just outside the city. We were killing two birds with one stone tonight. The owner of the Jaguar garage whose warehouse it was wanted to pull an insurance job, so we were stealing his cars, and then Brett had lined up a buyer for all of them, meaning we'd get double payment. The other fifteen cars, however, were scattered around all over the place, so I knew I'd be here until the early hours of the morning. That was going to be a pain, considering I had places to be tomorrow. It would be

Ellie's eighteenth birthday, and I refused to let a little tiredness ruin the day that I had planned for her.

My crew was already assembled downstairs, but I had needed just a couple of minutes to collect my thoughts. I had a bad feeling about tonight. Something wasn't sitting right in my stomach. I think it was the fact that five of the guys who were helping with tonight's boost weren't even used to stealing cars. They had no experience whatsoever and were used to working another part of Brett's business for him. Inexperience and a high-profile boost just didn't mix well, but with the number of cars that we were talking about, I couldn't exactly refuse the help. There just weren't enough hours of darkness for the usual crew to complete this task on our own.

"Your father used to get that look on his face when he was concentrating hard on something."

I jumped and looked up to see Brett walking into his office. I frowned as I took in what he'd said. "You knew my father?" I asked. He'd never said anything about him before; I wasn't aware they even knew each other.

Brett nodded, shrugging out of his suit jacket and throwing it over the empty chair opposite me. "Yep. It was a long time ago, but you just reminded me of him for a second there."

"How did you know him?" I probed, sitting forward, interested now. I'd never really spoken to anyone about my father before. The only one who'd ever talked about him was my mother, and that was usually to rant about what an inconsiderate asshole he was.

Brett smiled and motioned with his hand for me to move. "Out of my chair. You don't run this place yet, you know."

I laughed and pushed myself out of his leather chair so that he could sit down. "Sorry."

He grinned and rolled his eyes. "I worked with your dad a long time ago, years before you were born, when he was just a kid like you are now." I stood watching him intently, waiting for him to continue and tell me something I didn't know about the man who had made me. All I knew about him was that he was twenty-three when he died and that he had brown hair and brown eyes, the same as mine. I was only two at the time of his death, so I had no memories of him at all, all I knew was just what my drunk, drugged-up, and saddened mother had told me.

"He was good with cars, too," Brett continued.

I smiled at that. "Really?"

"Yep, I worked with him for about a year. I saw him steal cars without leaving a trace; he was like you in that respect, a ghost. You have his talent. Quick, nimble fingers and an eye for detail." He smiled and pulled out a cigar from the little wooden box on his desk, nodding down to them in offering. I waved it off politely. "He was a good guy. It was a shame he was killed. I liked him."

I chewed on my lip thoughtfully. "How did he die, exactly?"

Brett sucked on his cigar as the flame from his silver lighter licked at the tip of it. "He'd moved on and was working for a guy named Tommy Harris—he's long dead now too—but Jason, your dad, he was on an arms deal with a new supplier. Apparently something went wrong, a double cross or something, and he got shot. Damn shame, such talent."

I chewed on the inside of my cheek as I imagined how that had gone down. Things went sour so quickly at deals like that, there was a lot of room for error when a group of highly charged alpha males got together and tried to make a deal. I tried not to imagine how different my life would have been if he hadn't gone to the deal that day. Would I still be where I was today, or would he have not wanted his boy to go into the business like him? I sighed and nodded, not knowing what to say.

"You should go get started, the guys are beginning to get antsy down there," Brett suggested, nodding at the door in encouragement.

"Yeah. See you in the morning," I muttered, heading out of his office. Trudging down the stairs, I stopped when I saw the unorganized rabble standing around waiting. Another of those uneasy feelings washed over me because I recognized hardly any of them.

I cleared my throat loudly, staying on the bottom step so I was a little higher. The murmur slowly died down as people turned to look at me with interest. "Right then, we're ready to go. You've all been given your packs, so you know which cars you're going for. For the five that have never done this before, you guys have each been paired with an experienced booster. We'll all go together for the first one, the warehouse job, then after that we'll split up and go get the rest of them. Don't take risks. Don't get cocky, or speed, or run lights. Someone will boost the car for you, so all you need to do is drive it safely back to the warehouse. There'll be transporters outside ready for you. Just stay focused and do your job," I said sternly.

There was a nod of approval from the group, signaling that they understood, so I waved my hand toward the blacked-out minibus that was waiting to drive us all to the warehouse where we could get the Jags. Immediately the crowd started moving toward the bus.

One guy caught my eye, so I smiled and headed over to where he was leaning against the desk, a cocky smile on his face. Dodger—the new me. I'd suggested that Brett hire him for the night to help with the boost; we certainly needed the extra set of hands, and this guy was supposed to be good. Apparently he was at loose ends because he'd lost a lot of his trade when I came back to work for Brett. I was secretly surprised the guy didn't hate me.

"Hey. I'm Jamie, by the way," I said politely, holding out my hand. We'd spoken on the phone a lot this week, but this was the first actual face-to-face meeting.

"The kid, yeah, it's nice to meet you in person," he replied, putting his hand in mine. "Dodger."

I winced. I really didn't want to call the guy that; it had to be the worst nickname ever, a total rip-off of *Oliver Twist*. "Yeah, uh, what's your real name? I'm not calling you that," I said, laughing and shaking my head.

His eyes tightened. "It's Vincent, but I prefer Dodger when I'm working."

"Vincent it is then," I stated, dropping his hand.

He frowned. "You don't want me here, that much is obvious. Am I encroaching on your territory?" he mocked. A sarcastic smile played at the edge of his lips as he raised himself to his full height. I would imagine that he was trying to be intimidating, and he would totally have pulled it off too, with his muscles that could be clearly seen through his black T-shirt. The dark brown skin of his arms was covered with tattoos of quotes about cars and his nickname inked up the inside of one forearm. On the other biceps was a big cross with a quote from the Bible underneath. He would have been intimidating to others, I have no doubt in my mind about that, but he didn't scare me in the least.

I shrugged nonchalantly. "Dude, you can have my territory, I don't want it. I'm only here for another two months, then I'm out." I ran a hand through my hair. "And I'm glad you're here, actually. I wouldn't be able to keep these guys organized on my own. Once we're done with the warehouse job, I'll assign two of the newbies to you, you'll boost the cars, and they'll drive them back for you; that's how we usually roll."

Dodger nodded, slipping his black jacket on and picking up his carryall from the table. "I'm excited to work with you. They say you're the best."

I laughed incredulously. "*They say* a lot of things; you should know not to believe half of the shit that floats around." I grabbed my bag too, and we both headed toward the minibus.

"How come you're only doing this for two months then?" he asked as we climbed on.

"Personal issues. I agreed I'd do it for three months; I have just under two left, then I'm going straight. I have a girl who would hate it if she knew I was into this kind of thing," I explained, skirting around the issue.

I sat down at the front of the minibus and was just about to put my bag on the seat next to me when he plopped down in it instead, his expression incredulous. "You're going straight for a girl?"

I laughed at the disbelief that colored his tone. He obviously loved his work and wouldn't be giving it up anytime soon, especially for a girl, by the looks of it. I could understand that; the rush from boosting was definitely addicting. "I wanted to go straight before I met her, but yeah, basically."

He pursed his lips and ran a hand over his short, wiry hair, his dark brown eyes locked onto mine. "She hot?"

A proud but semi-smug smile crept onto my face. "Smokin' hot," I confirmed.

He nodded thoughtfully. "You share her?" he asked. I raised one eyebrow and looked at him warningly because he was extremely close to disrespecting my girlfriend. He recoiled slightly, holding his hands up innocently as he shifted in his seat. "I'll take that look as a no," he muttered.

Closing my eyes, I decided to get half an hour of sleep on the way to the warehouse. Unfortunately, Dodger had other ideas about that. He talked the whole damn way there. I'd never met a guy who talked as much as him. It was as if he had a gossipy teenage girl trapped inside his butch masculine exterior. My eyes were stinging by the time we got to our destination.

As soon as we pulled up a little way down the road, though, I was wide awake. I stood up as best I could in the confined space of the minibus, zipping up my black hoodie and pulling the ski mask from my bag. Usually for a job like this we would disable the cameras first, but the guy was paying extra for us to leave them rolling to capture the action. Apparently it would help his insurance claim. As a precaution, I'd instructed that everyone wear plain clothing, nothing identifiable, plain sneakers. Clothes were to be burned tomorrow, as per Brett's orders.

Turning back to the rabble that were pulling this boost with me tonight, I smiled reassuringly. Now that we were here, the adrenaline was rushing through my veins, creating that high that I got off on.

"Masks and gloves on, boys. I'm disabling the sound system in there, but the cameras will still be rolling. Once Vincent—" I started, but "the new me" cleared his throat loudly next to me, so I rolled my eyes and corrected myself. "Sorry. Once *Dodger* and I have made sure the coast is clear, then I'll call Shaun and he'll open the front gates. No one moves in without my say-so. Do exactly as you've been told. No hero shit in there or I'll personally kick your ass," I said sternly, looking around slowly to make sure they got it. There was no way I was getting in trouble because some dipshit wanted to be a big shot and do something he shouldn't. "Wait on the bus then. No one takes off their mask until they're at least two blocks away."

I looked down at Dodger and raised one eyebrow. A devilish grin slipped onto his face as he cracked his knuckles and then plucked his ski mask from his pocket. "This had better not mess up my hair," he joked, winking at me as he pulled it down over his face.

I laughed and pulled mine on too, grabbing my bag and slipping on some latex gloves so we didn't leave fingerprints. "Let's go then, hotshot," I teased, nodding at the open minibus door, and we both stepped out into the blackness of the night.

The warehouse was about fifty yards ahead, the gates a little beyond that. We didn't speak as we walked quickly to the darkest part of the perimeter and stopped by the chain-link fence. I slung my bag over my shoulder and grabbed the cold metal, immediately starting to climb it. We'd spoken about this a lot on the phone, and both of us had been over the plans, but it was slightly different having a guy I didn't know do it with me. Usually, at this point, I'd be flying solo. Two people were a necessity, though, since two guards patrolled the inside of the building.

I dropped down to the concrete on the other side just seconds before Dodger landed gracefully next to me. "Silent as a ninja," he whispered, laughing quietly.

I grinned but punched him in the arm at the same time to tell him to shut up. The guards were stationed on the other side of the warehouse, watching the grounds on little monitors. We'd purposefully chosen this spot to climb because Mr. Randall, the owner, had moved one of the cameras by a couple of inches to allow a blind spot. I put my finger to my lips and then nodded to the side of the building. Apparently if we stayed as close as we could to the wall and moved quickly, then we could outsmart the cameras, which rotated on a continuous sweep, taking in the whole area. It just meant getting the timing right and not screwing up.

It took a good ten minutes of stopping, starting, and crouching behind stuff to avoid the cameras before we finally made it to the security door of the warehouse with no alarms going off. Dodger pulled out a lock-pick kit, sticking in two metal pins and fiddling with them until the sound of the click filled the air. The door sprang open with a slight creak.

We moved quickly. As we stepped in I pulled out the gun Brett had given me. I didn't usually carry guns, but this was all for show on the cameras. The guy was paying extra for little details. I pointed down the hallway to where the sound of quiet talking could be heard. Dodger nodded, and we both made our way there slowly. I kept my eyes peeled for signs of movement, but there was nothing at all.

"I see your three, and I'll raise you…another three," someone said from the last room on the left. I already knew this was the monitoring station because of the building plans that I'd been meticulously studying for the last week.

"Ooh, confidence. All right. Call," someone else answered.

I smiled because that meant that they were both in there, just like they were supposed to be. Stopping outside the door, I risked a quick glance around the frame. Two middle-aged, overweight, and bored-looking security guards were sitting opposite each other at a table. Playing cards and matches littered the desk in front of them. Neither of them was even facing the monitors. I felt a pang of annoyance that Dodger and I had just done our *Mission: Impossible* impression for nothing if they weren't even looking.

I could see the cards of the guy sitting on the left; he had two pair. A pretty strong hand. I nodded to Dodger and stepped around the corner, raising my gun. "I'd save my matches if I were you. He's got two pair, tens over eights," I deadpanned, pointing my gun at the one on the right. He gasped, his eyes widening as he dropped his cards on the floor. His half-eaten doughnut froze on its way to his mouth.

The one on the left lunged for a red button mounted under the monitors. Preempting his move, I smashed the gun on the side of his temple, knocking him out cold before he could touch it. He slumped forward, his face connecting heavily with the wooden desk.

"Right, then, we can do this the easy way or the hard way,

which would you prefer?" Dodger asked the remaining guard, dramatically pulling out a long strip of duct tape and grinning wickedly.

"What do you want?" the guy croaked in response.

I laughed and pointed to the middle monitor. It was making a sweep of the inside of warehouse 3, which housed ten perfect, brand-spanking-new Jaguars. "Those little babies."

The guard gulped when Dodger stepped forward. As Dodger taped the guy to the chair, securing his arms and legs with plenty of duct tape, I got to work on the security. I grabbed the guy I'd knocked out and pushed him into a chair, wheeling him away from me so I had more room to work. Sitting on the floor, I leaned under the desk and yanked off the plastic covering for the security wires. It took a while to find the right one, but I finally located the audio feed, cutting the wire quickly. I made a show of cussing for good measure, slamming my hand on the desk in apparent frustration. This was all for show, I needed the guy to think I couldn't disable the cameras, otherwise they'd wonder why I'd disconnected the audio and not the visual feed.

When I was satisfied, I pushed myself out from under the desk and turned to the crying security guard, who was all taped up like a Christmas present. "You know how to disable the visual?" I asked him.

He shook his head quickly, his eyes tight.

I turned back to Dodger. "I can't do it. We're gonna have to leave it on. The audio's gone, but..." I trailed off, acting as best I could. The guard would have a pretty little tale to tell the police in the morning, which was exactly what Brett's client wanted.

Dodger shrugged. "Let's just get this done. No one will know it's us anyway. Let's get the cars and get out," he replied, securing the unconscious guy to his chair, too. "I'm done here."

Nodding, I picked up my bag from the floor before turning to the conscious guard. I smiled apologetically and raised the gun, bringing the butt of it down on the side of his head just hard enough to send him off into slumber but not cause any long-term damage.

As we stepped out of the room, Dodger held up his hand for a high five. I grinned and slapped my palm against his victoriously. The rest was the fun part—the boosting.

Once we got to the room where the ten cars were parked, I stopped and just let my eyes rake over the beautiful sight before me. My gaze settled on the C-X75; these things weren't even for sale yet. I staked my claim on it quickly. "That's mine."

Dodger shrugged, immediately walking up to the side of a XKR-S convertible. "Whatever. You can keep your eco car, I want this!" he rebutted, running his hand over the hood in awe.

I grinned and pulled out my phone, dialing Shaun to inform him that the coast was clear. The guys were cutting the lock on the front gates and coming in that way. That would be the way we would leave too, driving straight out the front.

"Let's get to work then," I suggested excitedly, unzipping my bag and reaching inside for my tools. Dodger saluted playfully and followed suit.

By the time the others entered the warehouse, seven of the cars were already sitting there, engines running, ready to go. Jaguars were easy pickings if you knew what you were doing and had the correct tools; we'd be home free in less than five minutes.

Dodger and I were the only ones boosting tonight. Because the cars were being immediately shipped off, there was no margin for error. No scratches would be tolerated because someone had been too forceful. Everything had to go perfectly, which meant I had a busy night ahead.

After starting the final car, I pushed myself out of the seat and walked up to the group, who were talking in hushed whispers.

They all quieted as I approached, looking at me with expectant eyes.

I nodded. "All ready to go. No one touches that." I pointed to my car of choice. "That's mine. You know your routes. Stick to the plan and keep it legal. Straight back to the meeting point using the route you've been assigned," I instructed. All of us were headed in different directions to get back to Brett's tonight; it would look slightly obvious if ten brand-new Jaguars drove down the street in a neat little line. "Go. See you all back there." Immediately, they all ran to their chosen cars. Dodger was sitting in his, appreciatively running his hands over the wheel.

I walked to the sliding garage door and grabbed the bolt cutters, positioning them around the lock and clamping down tight. When the lock and chain clanked to the floor, I raised the door and stepped back as the cars filed out of the warehouse in turn.

I let everyone else go first and just sat in my car, taking in the expensive smell of the new leather. The mileage counter only read 2, and that was probably just the test run in the factory when the car was made. It was beautiful.

Dodger leaned out of his window as he inched forward so he was level with me. I wound down the window and looked at him expectantly. "You seriously think you'll be able to give up the buzz that you get from this shit? You look like you're having a cargasm. Don't jizz on the seats," he joked, winking at me before pulling out.

Laughing, I followed behind him, turning left at the gates like I was supposed to. He flashed his hazard lights at me as a good-bye as we went in different directions.

* * *

The hours passed quickly. Dodger was proving to be a valuable asset. He was a total pro. The only fault I could see was that the dude couldn't stop talking, but at least he was funny with it.

Almost done with the boost, Dodger drove to the next location. Shaun sat in the back, still gushing about the Harley-Davidson he'd just driven back to the warehouse. We were down to our last two cars now. Shaun was taking the sleek little red BMW that we were stopped next to, and then Dodger was driving me on to the last boost of the night, the Aston Martin Vanquish.

I hopped out when he stopped the car, heading over to the BMW, sliding in the bar and popping the lock quickly. Yanking the door open, I leaned in, disabling the alarm and immobilizer before climbing in and sparking the wires to start it up. I pulled out, closing the door as I drove down the road, and stopped a few streets away to swap with Shaun. He skipped to the car, slapping me on the shoulder on the way past, grinning happily.

As I slid back into the seat of Dodger's Porsche Boxster, he grinned. "I'm hungry. After I drop you off I think I might stop for a burger or something. Want me to get you anything?" he offered, fiddling with the radio to find some rap station.

"It's three thirty in the morning," I countered, looking at him to see if he'd lost his mind.

He shrugged unashamedly and rubbed his stomach. "When a boy's gotta eat, he's gotta eat."

I laughed and shook my head. "Nah, I'm all good, thanks." He didn't reply, just mouthed the words to the Missy Elliott song and bobbed his head to the beat.

Ten minutes later we pulled up at the last car of the night. "Can't believe we pulled off this boost. This was awesome, and most certainly one for my memoirs," he joked.

"Yeah, we make a pretty wicked team," I agreed, stepping

out of the car and into the cold night air. "See you at the warehouse."

He nodded. "I'm gonna stop and get food. You sure I can't tempt you with some grease and animal flesh?" he offered, waggling his eyebrows.

I grinned and shook my head. "No thanks, man. See ya in a bit." I strutted off to the car, excited to get the job done. As much as I loved the high, I was tired now. This had been a seriously long night, and all I wanted to do was curl up in my bed and not get up until Monday. That wouldn't happen, though; I had Ellie's birthday tomorrow. The thought of her brought an instant smile to my face as I set to work on my last car. Dodger waited until I had it started, then he turned and headed in the direction of the main street, probably to find the nearest open takeout place.

As I drove down the road, heading toward the warehouse, my cell phone started ringing. I dug it out of my pocket and answered, immediately switching it to speakerphone. "What?" I asked, not really in the mood for pleasantries. I just wanted to get this job done and get home to my bed now.

"Kid, what time is Shaun back with the beamer? I need to get it loaded onto container three, then it's good to go," Ray asked.

I frowned. I'd given the car to Shaun more than half an hour ago; he should definitely be done by now. "He's not back?"

"Back? No. I assumed you two were still picking it up."

My hands tightened on the steering wheel. Shaun left before I went to go pick up this car; he should have been back ages ago! "I'll call him and see what the holdup is," I suggested, disconnecting the call without waiting for his answer. Dialing Shaun's cell, I waited. After several rings, it cut to voice mail. I frowned and dialed again.

When he didn't answer, I disconnected and threw my phone onto the passenger seat. I pulled over and turned the wheel hard, doing a U-turn and heading back the way I came. It had been a while since I'd left him, but I knew which route he would have taken back to the warehouse.

After about ten minutes of fast driving, flashing lights appeared up ahead and the breath caught in my throat. I pulled up about a hundred yards away from them and groaned as I took in the scene before me. The beautiful car that I'd boosted less than an hour ago was a total wreck. Another car had hit it from behind, practically lifting the little red sports car up off the ground so that its rear end was perched up on the hood of the other car.

There was glass everywhere, metal twisted at odd angles. Emergency vehicles were parked around, lights flashing. A fireman was busy cutting the doors off the other car—obviously someone was trapped inside. There was no sign of Shaun.

FUCK!

My eyes flitted around quickly, trying to see where he was. He needed to get the hell out of there; it wouldn't be long before someone ran the plates on the car and realized that the freaking thing was stolen!

A deliberate tap on my window made me jump. I gulped as I turned toward the window, seeing a Highway Patrol officer standing there, smiling. I silently wondered if I should just floor the accelerator and drive off. But the smile on the guy's face was friendly. He didn't look like he knew I was sitting there in over 3,000 pounds of stolen sports car. Forcing myself to remain calm, I pressed the button to roll down the window.

He leaned on the frame, his eyes scanning over the car appreciatively. "Hi there. Sorry, I can't let you through; there's been an accident up ahead. We're diverting traffic off down another street."

I nodded, trying to keep my heart under control when all I wanted to do was scream Shaun's name so I could find him and get him the hell out of here before they started running plates and stuff on the cars. If Shaun got arrested, then they could look into who he worked for, who he worked with. We would all be screwed tonight if he didn't keep his mouth shut.

"Yeah, it looks bad. Are the drivers okay?" I probed, nodding at the wreck. My hands tightened on the wheel as I hoped he would say that Shaun was missing or something. *Hit and run. Hit and run. Hit and run.* I chanted it over and over in my head, praying for the words to leave his mouth. They didn't.

He nodded grimly. "The driver of the front vehicle isn't too bad, concussion and seat belt damage, I would imagine. He's with the EMTs on the way to the hospital. The other driver is okay, I think, they just can't get him out because the doorjambs are bent. They should both be all right, though," he replied.

Shaun is with EMTs, injured, on his way to the hospital, and then he'll be questioned by police…

My heart sank. "Is there anything I can do?" I asked, noticing how my voice wavered as I spoke. The cop seemed too preoccupied with watching the firemen work to notice my shaky voice, though.

"No, thank you, sir. We've got everything under control," he assured me.

My mind was whirling with what needed to happen now. I needed to get the hell away from here, call Brett, and tell him of this new development. He'd call around until he found Shaun in the hospital; then, depending on how much he liked him, he'd either order a hit on him so that he couldn't incriminate everyone else, or he'd get him a damn good lawyer and have him out of there within a couple of days. It depended on how much Brett trusted Shaun to go down without taking everyone else down with him.

"Well, I'd better let you get back to it," I suggested, forcing a smile.

He stepped back, patting the frame of the door. "You have a good night, sir."

Wordlessly, I put the car into drive, turning slowly, not wanting to draw attention to myself. I drove down the road, knowing that Brett was going to go crazy when he found out. I didn't stop as I pulled out my phone, calling Brett's number, my eyes flicking in my rearview mirror every couple of seconds to make sure I wasn't being followed. Brett answered almost immediately.

"What's up, Kid? Nearly back?"

I took a deep breath before I spoke. "Slight problem," I admitted. "Shaun's been in a wreck. The car's totaled, and he's on his way to the hospital in an ambulance."

I winced as the string of expletives that he let rip rang in my ears. After a full thirty seconds of him shouting words that would make Ellie blush that adorable shade of red, he finally calmed down enough to talk to me. "Where are you?"

"On my way back. I have the Aston, do you want me to come to the warehouse with it, or are you gonna have the transporter meet me somewhere else?" I asked, not wanting to lead the police back to Brett in case they were following me.

"I'll have them come to you. Go to the secondary location and someone will be there to meet you and take the car off your hands." He sighed. "Kid, you think Shaun will keep his mouth shut?"

I honestly didn't know the answer. "You know him better than I do, Brett."

He was silent for a minute, obviously thinking through his two options. I kept my eyes on the road, turning off and heading out of the city to our prearranged secondary exchange point. The streets were still deserted; it was almost four in the morning.

"All right, look, just go to the second drop-off point. Call me when you get there," Brett instructed, disconnecting the call. He probably had more important people to talk to than me—either his lawyer or the hit man.

At the location, I pulled into the field we had prearranged as the secondary spot in case things went bad. Turning off the engine, I sat there in the dark, praying that this didn't come back on me. This was just my luck; I was going straight, and now Shaun was probably going to drop me in it again.

I called Brett. "Hey, I'm here."

"Good. They'll be there soon. Ray's bringing your truck." He took a deep breath. "I'm gonna get Shaun a lawyer and everything will be fine. He's a loyal worker, I have complete faith that it'll go smoothly. I have people inside, and he'll be out quickly. But just in case, you need to get yourself an alibi. Something strong. Make sure it's not connected to work, or me, in any way. Call that hot little girl of yours that you're always bragging about."

Dread settled in my stomach. Ellie. I was going to have to bring Ellie into this? "Seriously? Can't you set me up with an alibi or something?"

He sighed. "You know how this works, Kid. Just get yourself an alibi and lie low for a couple of days. I'll sort everything out, but the further you stay away from everyone here, the better for you. You need to think of your parole right now, okay?"

My jaw tightened. I hated the thought of Ellie being anywhere near anything illegal . . . but I had no one else to ask.

I slammed my forehead down on the steering wheel and closed my eyes, running through everyone I knew to see if they could give me an alibi instead of Ellie. I even debated going to my mother for help, but she wouldn't help me anyway, she had no compassion or sense of loyalty. Ten minutes later, a transporter truck pulled into the field. When a guy jumped out and let down the tail ramp, I drove my stolen vehicle in. Once it was settled inside, I hopped out. As I trudged out of the transporter, I was kind of hoping for a meteor to fall from the sky and blast me into oblivion. That would certainly be preferable to having to tell Ellie the truth and beg for her help.

Ray had pulled up in my truck and was standing against the hood with his arms crossed, a hard expression on his face. The other car in the field was Dodger's sleek-looking dark blue Boxster.

I headed toward Ray and shook my head. "This is all shit!" I grunted.

He nodded and held out a manila envelope, probably full of my fee for the night, plus extra cash because of the size of the job. "Yep, it is. You gonna be okay? Who you calling?" he asked, regarding me curiously.

I sighed and closed my eyes, not wanting to say it out loud. "Ellie, I guess."

He smiled sadly. "If she's as awesome as you always claim she is, then everything will be fine."

Behind me, the transporter pulled away.

Ray squeezed my shoulder supportively. "If for whatever reason she doesn't want to do it, then call me. I have a slutty cousin, you could probably pay her to say that you spent the night with her," he suggested.

I laughed humorlessly. It would be so much easier to do that, just pretend I'd hooked up with some random girl for the night, but I didn't want to risk that. Knowing my luck it'd somehow get back to Ellie and she'd think I cheated on her. I didn't know which was worse, but at least if I went with the truth then I'd have a chance of keeping her.

"Thanks, Ray. I'd better get going," I muttered, shoving the envelope into my hoodie pocket. I turned to Dodger and smiled. "It was good to work with you; you did a great job tonight."

He smiled and stuck his hand through his open car window. "You too. Kid Cole is just as badass as I'd heard. Looks like the rumors were true. Maybe we could work together again some-time."

I shook his hand and laughed. "Maybe. We'll see what Brett lines up." Once I'd said good-bye to Ray, I climbed into my truck, twisting the key and making it roar to life. I hated the thought of what I had to do now. Now I had to risk everything, put myself out there, and tell Ellie exactly what type of person she'd been as-sociating with. Not only that, but after I'd told her that I'd been lying to her for the last three months, I'd then need to ask her to help me out of trouble. I looked upward, praying for the meteor, but there was not even a cloud in the sky. Just my fucking luck.

CHAPTER 21

I DROVE TO Ellie's house quickly, parking down the road a little way. Luckily, the street was deserted. My heart was racing as I climbed out of my truck and walked swiftly to the house, stopping off to the side so I could call her. I felt sick doing this. This was the last thing I wanted, I never wanted her anywhere near trouble, yet here I was, bringing it right to her front door.

Pulling out my phone, I closed my eyes and pressed Call. It rang for a while, and my nerves seemed to double as I chewed on my lip.

"Jamie?" she croaked groggily.

I winced. "Uh, yeah, hi," I mumbled, rubbing my forehead to try to relieve some of the tension headache that was building up.

She yawned before she spoke again, "Everything okay?"

Taking a deep breath, I mentally crossed my fingers that someone was watching over me and I wasn't about to lose the best thing that had ever happened to me. "Actually...no, it's not. I need to talk to you."

"What's up?" She sounded more awake now.

I flicked my eyes over to her house. "I need to see you. Can you come down?"

"Down? You're outside?" she asked, her voice filled with shock.

"Yeah."

The line disconnected and a minute later the downstairs light turned on before the front door opened. Ellie stepped out, immediately hugging herself against the cold. She was wearing only a tank top and what looked like a pair of my boxer shorts. Her hair was whipping about as she looked around, an adorable little confused expression on her face.

I stepped out of the shadows and waved her over, wanting a little distance from the house in case her parents heard us talking. She shivered but immediately stepped onto the path, flipping the latch on the door before closing it silently, wincing as the gravel crunched under her bare feet. I shrugged out of my hoodie quickly as she stopped in front of me.

"What happened?" she asked, smiling gratefully as I slipped the hoodie around her shoulders.

"I'm in some trouble," I admitted.

Her eyes tightened. Even in the dim glow of the streetlight I saw the worry that was etched across her face. "What kind of trouble?"

I raised one hand and stroked her cheek, memorizing the feel of her soft skin under my fingertips, savoring it in case this was the last time I got to touch her. "There are some things about me that you don't know."

Her eyes darted back to the house as she shifted on her feet nervously. "Come inside, it's cold out here," she suggested, pulling the hoodie tighter around her body. She turned to walk away, so I grabbed her hand, making her stop. I couldn't go inside. Once she found out the truth about me, she might not want to be near me or something. That, and the fact that when she started screaming at me that I was a worthless liar, it might wake her parents up, and they'd probably call the cops for her. I knew Ruth would for sure.

"It's better if we do this outside, Ellie. You're not going to like what I tell you." Even I could hear the hopelessness in my voice.

Her hand tightened on mine as she flinched. "Did you cheat on me? Is that where this conversation is going?" Her voice wavered as she spoke.

I laughed humorlessly. Clearly she had no idea how crazy I was about her. "No, Ellie. Never."

Her eyes fluttered closed as she huffed a sigh of relief. She was probably going to wish that I had cheated on her when I told her what this was really about, that I'd been lying to her for the last three months. "Just tell me, Jamie, you're scaring me."

Fuck. "I just stole a car, and now the cops are probably looking for me. I need an alibi that puts me somewhere else when it all went down," I whispered, looking at my feet, not wanting to see her expression when she realized what a lowlife I was.

"You...You stole a car?" she croaked.

I nodded. "Twenty-five of them, actually," I added nonchalantly.

"Jamie, what the fucking hell?!"

I looked up at her then and saw the expression that I'd never wanted to see on her face. Disappointment, shock, confusion, and horror.

"I'm not the person you think I am."

"Not the...I don't...It's...What?" she sputtered.

"Please don't freak out," I begged, even though I knew it was too late to ask that of her. The panic had already started; I could see it building like a storm on her face.

She ran both her hands over her hair, smoothing it down unconsciously as the wind continued to whip it in all directions. Her mouth was agape; she shook her head as if struggling with her thoughts. "'Don't freak out'? Of course I'm going to freak out, for goodness' sake; you've just told me that you stole twenty-five cars and that the police are looking for you. A normal person's reaction is to freak the hell out!" she cried.

I winced as her voice echoed in the nothingness of the night. I stepped closer to her, quickly covering her mouth with my hand. "Shush, please, shush," I pleaded, glancing around for any signs of movement on her expensive-looking street.

Her hand covered mine as she looked at me with wide eyes, taking deep breaths through her nose. When her rant seemed to have died down and some of the tension had left her shoulders, I removed my hand and stepped back to give her some personal space. She probably needed it after my revelations.

"Who are you?" she asked, shaking her head, her eyes filling with tears.

I smiled weakly, knowing that there was no chance of her wanting to be with me after this. "I'm the same guy that you've been hanging around with for the last three months. I'm still the same guy that holds you when you sleep, and who kisses you good night. I'm still the same guy that values you above everything else. It's just…my past, it came back to haunt me. I didn't have a choice, Ellie," I replied, trying to explain everything. My knees felt a little weak, so I sat on the half wall that ran the length of the driveway.

"Your past?" she whispered.

I nodded and closed my eyes. "Yeah. When I was eleven I started working for a guy, doing small jobs for money, illegal jobs. Things got heavier; I started stealing cars to order."

She whimpered and sat down on the wall next to me, playing with her hands as I continued to explain.

"I stopped. I was out of it. I'd given it all up before we met; I was going straight, but..." I trailed off, not knowing how to convey that I didn't want to be this person anymore, that I wanted better for myself than this life I was sinking into.

She swiped at her face quickly with the back of her hand. I couldn't bring myself to look at the tears that I knew I had put there. I hated myself for making her cry; I would never forgive myself for it.

"What happened?" she asked. "You said you didn't have a choice."

I shook my head fiercely. "I *didn't* have a choice. My stupid mother, she borrowed some money from some bad people and couldn't pay it back. I had to help her out," I explained. "But I couldn't afford it either, it was so much money, and I didn't have it. I had to go back to my old boss and ask him for a job or two so that I could help my mom. The people my mother borrowed from, they're not exactly a normal lending bank. If I hadn't done this, then they would have killed her eventually, for sure."

She gulped; her breathing quickened the more I spoke. "So you had to do this to get money for your mom?"

I nodded. "I've just finished paying off her debt now, but Brett, my boss, he wouldn't let me just do a couple of jobs, I had to agree to work for him for a certain amount of time. I agreed to do it for three months. I have just under two left."

"Three months of stealing cars?"

"Among other things."

"Like what other things? What else have you been doing?" she asked, frowning.

I took it as a good sign that she was still sitting next to me, asking questions. Wouldn't she have run by now if she was going to? "Lots of things that I don't want to tell you about. It's best if you don't know in case anything bad happens because of it."

She snorted at my answer. "Anything bad, like being wanted for grand theft auto?" she snapped. She groaned and put her head in her hands. "I knew you had a bad past but that you didn't want to talk about it. I knew that something awful had happened to you, but I never suspected that you were in a damn car-stealing gang."

"Ellie, I'm so sorry. I—" I started, but she cut me off.

"What do you want me to do?" she interjected.

My mouth popped open in shock as my pulse quickened. *Is she being serious right now? She's accepting my past, just like that?* "Brett said we needed to get alibis. One of my crew got in an accident tonight while we were on a boost, and the police will be asking questions about the car soon. Everything should be fine. Brett will take care of him and get him out, but just in case one of us gets linked to him, we need a backup plan that's not connected to anything illegal. You're the only one I have," I replied, hating to put this pressure on her.

She nodded, picking up a stone and rolling it around in her hands as I spoke. "So you want me to say I was with you tonight?"

I nodded silently, having no words.

"My parents were with me tonight. They went to bed just after ten. I could say that I snuck you in after they went to bed so that you could wake up with me on my birthday. They'll see you in the morning too which will strengthen the story. Is that good enough?" she asked.

"Ellie, why would you do that? You're going to get in trouble with your parents in the morning when they see me. Why would you do that for me?"

She stood, dropping the stone at her bare feet, turning to face me. Her eyes locked onto mine, and I felt the hair on the back of my neck prickle because of the intensity of the look she gave me.

"Because I love you, Jamie," she replied simply.

Air rushed out of my lungs in one large burst. Until then, I hadn't even realized that I was holding my breath. She loved me. Ellie Pearce was in love with me. I had never heard sweeter words in my life.

I forced myself to stand even though my legs felt weak. She didn't move as I stepped closer to her, so close that I could feel her breath as it blew across my chin. Her eyes didn't leave mine for a second.

One of my hands cupped the side of her face as I just marveled over her perfection. I needed to say it back quickly before she thought that I didn't feel the same. This wasn't how I'd pictured this moment happening at all. I'd planned on telling her that I loved her on her eighteenth birthday. I guess, technically, it *was* her birthday right now anyway—but I had planned to make it romantic and special, complete with picnic, cheesy music, and flowers.

Standing with her in that second, though, with her beautiful gray eyes burning into mine and my hoodie wrapped around her body, I realized that we didn't need music and flowers or candles and expensive food, all we needed was us.

"I love you, too," I whispered, bending slightly so I could lose myself in her gaze.

A beautiful smile stretched across her face as her arms looped around my waist. I didn't move, not wanting to ruin the moment. I wanted to live in this perfect moment forever. The sound of her soft laughter brought me out of my happy daze.

"Usually now's the part where the guy kisses the girl," she teased, squeezing my waist in a prompt. "I thought you were the king of corny stuff."

Chuckling, I stepped closer to her, pressing my body against hers. "I guess I'm not as corny as you always make me out to be," I joked. "I love you, Ellie." I repeated the words for good measure and then bent my head and captured her lips in a kiss that showed her exactly how true those words were.

By the time I pulled back we were both a little breathless. "Let's get inside then." She nodded over her shoulder toward the house.

"You sure? You don't have to do this. I hate that I've asked you to. You deserve better than this."

She smiled and trailed one hand up my body, setting it against my chest, hovering above my heart, which was still hammering wildly from the confession that she'd made.

"Jamie, I know you. I know who you are, in here." She tapped on my chest with one finger. "If you tell me that you only went back into this stuff to help out your mom, then I believe you. You said you wanted to go straight; well, in two months, when your agreement is up with this Brett guy, you'll be able to. I wouldn't love you any less for this. Your past is the past. Hopefully, after this, it'll stay there, and you'll get a second chance. Everyone deserves a second chance," she replied. "Besides, who else would put up with my sleep-talking that you claim happens?" she asked sarcastically.

I laughed and kissed her again, clamping her against me tightly. The heavens must have been smiling down on me after all. "I love your sleep-talking."

She pulled away from me, taking my hand. "Come on, let's go to bed," she suggested. "And, by the way, my mother is going to hate you even more when she finds out that you snuck in last night." She nodded knowingly.

I groaned. Her mother was going to throw a fit tomorrow when she saw me, but I guess it needed to be done because people would need to think I stayed the night for the alibi to hold. I pulled Ellie to me, bending and sweeping her into my arms so that she wouldn't hurt her feet again on the gravel driveway. She smiled up at me and pressed her lips to mine as I carried her into the house, wondering just how I'd gotten so damn lucky.

CHAPTER 22

WRIGGLING. SHE WAS wriggling against me, her body brushing against mine in ways that made the male part of me jump for joy. I smiled and pressed my face into her hair, breathing in the vanilla scent that made my skin prickle. Tightening my arms around her, I tried to keep her still so I could go back to sleep...but she was squirming, trying to get away.

"Jamie, I need to pee!" she whined.

I laughed and released my death grip, rolling onto my back and untangling our legs. My eyes cracked open just in time to see her spring from the bed and hotfoot it out of the room. I was still tired, so I settled back against her pillows, deciding on more sleep.

A minute later her bedroom door opened and she padded across the room. The bed dipped and then suddenly a heavy weight plopped onto my stomach, making me let out a soft groan because I wasn't expecting it. She giggled, resting her hands on my chest.

Forcing my stinging eyes open, I looked up at the girl who made my whole body ache. She was straddling me, sitting on my stomach, smiling down at me. Her red hair hung loose around her face, tangles and snarls everywhere, her bangs flicking out the way she hated. In the sunlight that was streaming in through her window, she looked beautiful.

"You need to wake up, sleepyhead. I'm hungry," she chirped. "Besides, it's time you gave me my birthday present."

FUUUUUUUUCK! Her present! "Oh shit, Ellie, I left it at my place. I didn't know I was going to be coming over. I'm sorry."

She rolled her eyes and bent forward, pressing her chest against mine, her face hovering close enough that I could taste her minty breath as it blew across my lips. She'd obviously taken the opportunity to brush her teeth while she was in the bathroom.

"Not that present, silly. This one," she whispered. Her mouth claimed mine in a soft kiss that took my breath away. I kissed her back immediately, running my hand up her back and twisting it into her hair as the kiss deepened. She moaned into my mouth, so I rolled her underneath me and broke the kiss, tracing my nose up the side of hers.

"Happy birthday, little girl."

She grinned and nodded, looping her arms around my neck. "Yep, it totally is."

I laughed at her happy expression. "So, I get you for the whole day, and the night, that's what we agreed, right?" I asked, taking a quick glance at the alarm clock. It was almost half past ten; we'd already wasted most of the morning.

"Right," she agreed.

I sighed contentedly, just looking at her face. I didn't need anything else in the world other than for that smile to always stay stretched across her full lips. "I love you, Ellie." I loved finally saying those words.

She closed her eyes and snuggled closer to me, her finger tracing one of the scars on my chest. "Love you, too." We made out for a couple of minutes before she pulled back and sighed.

"Maybe we should go and get that parent bit out of the way now?"

I groaned and nodded, reluctantly releasing her from my embrace. She kissed my lips softly before pushing herself out of the bed and picking up my hoodie, which she'd thrown on the chair when we came to bed last night. As she put it on and zipped it up, I climbed out of the bed too, stretching before pulling on my jeans and T-shirt.

"Um . . . Jamie?"

I turned, concerned by the tightness to her tone. I realized what had caused it as soon as I looked in her direction. In her hands was my envelope from the boost last night. It wasn't sealed, so you could easily see the bundled cash inside it. She was staring down at it with wide eyes.

"Uh, yeah," I mumbled, rubbing the back of my neck nervously.

She gulped. "That's not real money, is it? I mean, it looks like real money, but . . ." She shook her head and looked up at me with the cutest little bewildered expression I'd ever seen.

"It's real," I confirmed. "Doing what I did last night pays really well." At my words she drew in a ragged breath, nodding absentmindedly as she held the envelope out to me. I sighed deeply. "Don't freak out," I pleaded.

She smiled weakly. "I'm not. It's just . . . that's a lot of money. I've never seen so much cash."

"You can have it if you want. Buy yourself something with it? A new car, maybe, so I can stop spending my weekends fixing up your decrepit old one?" I suggested, laughing. I didn't need the money at all; I already had almost forty thousand dollars sitting in the bank from the last few weeks. "I owe you anyway, for the alibi," I added as an afterthought. She deserved that for helping me out last night.

Her forehead creased with a scowl as she closed the distance between us and slapped the envelope against my chest. "You think I want to be paid for that?" she snapped. "I don't want your money. I just want you safe and not in trouble. Money's not important, you are!" Her eyes flashed with passion as she spoke, showing me the truth of her words.

I didn't have an answer for that, so I just wrapped an arm around her waist and pulled her to me roughly, making her squeal. Smiling, I dipped my head and kissed her passionately. I had no words to describe how that little speech had made me feel inside. She was just too incredible for me, but I selfishly hoped she never realized it.

She pulled away from me and grinned, taking my hand and tugging me toward her bedroom door, obviously eager for her birthday breakfast, which she said was always her dad's famous deep-stacked pancakes. As we stepped out, I shoved the envelope into my jeans pocket. Ellie stopped almost immediately, making me walk into her back when I wasn't paying attention.

Looking up to see what the problem was, I spotted it immediately. The problem was just walking out of the family bathroom across the hallway. Ruth seemed to be frozen, half out of the door, her eyes wide as she looked at the pair of us exiting Ellie's room. Suddenly her posture changed, her shoulders pulled back, and her expression turned from disbelief to anger in a heartbeat.

"What on earth is this?" she snapped. Her voice was tight and accusatory as her death glare turned on Ellie.

Ellie's grip tightened on my hand, almost crushing the bones in my fingers. "Um…I asked Jamie to stay over last night so that I could wake up with him on my birthday," she lied.

Ruth's eyes flicked to me, a disgusted expression on her face. "He stayed here…all night?" she pressed, her eyes wide.

Ellie nodded, and I hated myself for putting her in this position.

I needed to say something, something that would make this better. "Nothing happened, I swear," I assured her. That was the truth; we'd done no more than cuddle and sleep last night.

Ruth made a little whimpering sound as she closed her eyes, recoiling as if she'd just encountered something horrific. "I should hope not!" she barked, shaking her head fiercely.

I gulped, not knowing how to make this situation better. Ellie spoke first. "Sorry. I knew that if I asked you you'd say no, and I really just wanted to wake up in bed with my boyfriend to make my birthday more special. It is my eighteenth."

Ruth snorted at the word *boyfriend*. "Of course I would say no! You can't have boys over in your bed, especially not *that* boy," she hissed, nodding her head at me distastefully.

Ellie's back stiffened. "'*That* boy'?" she repeated sarcastically. "Are you kidding me right now, Mom? Jamie's not just some random guy, he's incredible, and if you can't see that then that's your problem, not mine," she retorted. "I'm not having this 'he's not good enough for you' conversation again. You have no idea what you're talking about as far as he's concerned. You've never even tried to give him a chance; you're just being judgmental, as always. We're going to get breakfast!" She stepped away from me and tugged on my hand while her mom just stood there with wide eyes and her hands clenched into fists, looking like she wanted to skin both of us alive.

Oh shit. Damn, my girlfriend is feisty! I loved that she would defend me like that, even after what I'd told her in the early hours of the morning.

I followed her down the stairs with Ruth silently marching along behind us. I hated myself for causing this friction, especially since it was Ellie's birthday. I'd wanted to make this day special, not cause a family argument. Her eighteenth was probably going to be memorable for a different reason than what I'd intended.

As we stepped into the kitchen, I smiled weakly at Michael when he looked up from his newspaper with a huge grin on his face. "Ah, the birthday girl's finally up!" he greeted Ellie.

She laughed and nodded. "Yep! Do I get pancakes this morning?"

Michael bobbed his head in confirmation, his eyes settling on me. "Morning, Jamie. Didn't hear you come in," he said, pushing himself up from the chair and walking over, pulling Ellie into a hug.

"Of course you didn't hear it. He snuck in last night!" Ruth bit out nastily.

Slowly, the smile fell from Michael's face, and I knew that I should have just taken the risk of getting put back inside. I'd broken his trust, which was something that I never wanted to do. I loved that he trusted me with his daughter, was happy for us even, but right now he looked seriously pissed off.

"Last night?" he repeated, his tone hard and accusatory.

I smiled apologetically and nodded. "Yeah. Sorry." I winced, waiting for his reaction. He was perfectly within his rights to throw me out of his house for taking advantage of his hospitality.

His eyes flitted between me and Ellie, a shocked expression on his face like he was only just now realizing that we were "together." The look clearly told me that he thought his daughter was some sweet, innocent young child in a woman's body. "You stayed with Ellie, in her bed?" His voice was tight and controlled.

Ellie stepped forward. "Daddy, nothing happened. I just wanted to wake up with him this morning. I asked him to come over. Stop looking at him like it's his fault, it's not. I practically had to beg him to stay because he didn't want to go against your wishes."

He frowned, running a hand through his hair. "You shouldn't have had him over last night, Ellie. You have to be responsible and think of Kelsey. She wanted to come in and wake you up this morning. Thank goodness I stopped her! She's only ten. Can you imagine what she would have thought if she'd gone into your room to find Jamie in your bed?" he scolded, shaking his head in frustration.

Ellie sighed and gave him the puppy-dog face; right then and there, the guy was done for; he stood no chance against that look. "Sorry, I didn't think about Kels, I just wanted to have Jamie over for my birthday. I should have asked you, I'm sorry," she pouted.

He sighed and rolled his eyes. "Just don't let it happen again, all right? I'm not up for this staying-over thing, not with Kelsey in the house. I don't expect this to be repeated."

Ellie and I shook our heads in unison, confirming it wouldn't.

Ruth was watching the exchange with wide eyes and an even wider mouth. "What? That's it? She just gets to sneak boys into her bed, and you're not even going to punish her for it? Wow, you really are a soft touch, Michael! I didn't know you were so spineless," she cried, throwing her hands up in exasperation.

Michael frowned. "It's not like she does it all the time, and besides, it's not boys, plural, it's just Jamie. I don't want it to happen again, but surely there can be a little lenience this time considering it's her birthday," he countered.

"Oh, we'll see how lenient you want to be when he knocks her up and ruins her life!" Ruth snapped, slamming her hand on the table.

Michael's eyes tightened at her words, and he looked up at me. I shook my head quickly. "Nothing happened, I promise. Ellie's not getting pregnant," I assured him, holding my hands up innocently.

He sucked his teeth with his tongue, seeming to think about it before he relaxed. He definitely wanted to believe that his daughter was still his little baby girl. Denial was a powerful thing.

Finally he sighed. "Just don't do it again, all right? This was a one-time thing, a birthday thing, but I'm pretty annoyed that it happened." He looked at Ellie. "Pumpkin, you know I like Jamie, but just... You need to respect that this is my and your mother's house and, therefore, our rules."

Ellie smiled innocently, batting her eyelashes to perfection, and I practically saw him turn into putty in her hands. "Okay, Daddy. Sorry. It won't happen again," she promised.

He rolled his eyes and stepped back, seeming to ignore the hard glare that was aimed in his direction by Ruth as he shoved the sleeves of his sweater up and grinned. "Who's up for birthday pancakes?"

Ellie squealed and clapped her hands excitedly. "Yes! Me!"

Breakfast was beyond awkward. Ruth's face was hard and angry the whole time, and she barely spoke except to throw some bitchy comment in my direction or answer a direct question when Michael tried to include her in the conversation. I honestly had no idea what a great guy like Michael could see in her. She was nothing like the rest of them.

After breakfast and watching Ellie open her presents from her family and friends, I headed home. I needed to get her gifts from me, and the day that I'd planned for us needed to start soon, too. We had a pretty packed day to get through.

CHAPTER 23

WHEN I PICKED her up an hour later, she skipped to my truck before I even had time to cut the engine. Grinning, she threw her overnight bag into the backseat. As usual, her parents didn't know she was staying at my place; they thought that she was spending the day with me and the night with Stacey. After their reaction to me staying last night, it was more important than ever that the lie remain in place.

"Ready to start celebrating?" I asked. My eyes wandered over her body appreciatively. She was wearing black skinny jeans that showed off her long legs and a pretty little midnight-blue silk V-neck top. It showed just enough cleavage to make my heart speed up. She was obviously dressed to impress. "I thought I told you to wear older clothes and that you might get dirty?" I mumbled, my mouth watering at the sight of her. It had been days since I'd had my way with her—something I would rectify tonight.

She frowned down at herself. "This is kinda old. What's wrong with it?"

"Ellie, that's like a designer shirt, it must have cost a fortune." I laughed, shaking my head.

She smiled as she played with the soft material. "It's not designer; it didn't cost me anything, actually," she replied. "You like it?"

I grinned and leaned in closer to her. "It's beautiful, just like you." She giggled and kissed me quickly. She didn't have to say the word *corny* for me to know she was thinking it. I smiled against her lips and pulled back. "I have your present, but I'd rather give it to you later, if that's okay?"

She grinned, buckling up her seat belt. "Sure," she chirped. "So, where we going?"

"It's a surprise."

When I pulled into the parking lot of the Bronx Zoo, Ellie's eyes lit up. "We're going to the zoo?" she asked excitedly.

I smiled. "Kinda. You're gonna be a zookeeper for the afternoon."

Her mouth dropped open in shock. She definitely wasn't expecting that, judging by the look on her face. "Seriously?"

I nodded. "Yep. You wanna?" Ellie loved animals; in one of her sleep rambles she'd said that she had always wanted to be a zookeeper. I was just praying that was one of the more serious unconscious conversations we'd had, as opposed to when she told me that she wanted to be the first woman to walk on the moon.

Her eyes widened. "Hell yeah! Really? Oh my God, thank you!" The loudness of her voice echoed in the cab of my truck and made my ears ring. Without waiting for me, she sprang out of the door, jumping on the spot excitedly. "Come on, slowpoke!" she cried, waving me out of the truck. I laughed and grabbed the paperwork for her visit before climbing out and slinging my arm around her shoulder. She was beaming up at me. "I love you so much, Jamie. Oh God, thank you! This is gonna be awesome!" she squealed, gripping the front of my shirt and kissing me fiercely, giggling against my lips.

I pulled back and grinned. "First stop, gift shop. Let's buy you a zoo T-shirt to cover up that hot little outfit you're wearing so it doesn't get ruined." Her smile widened as I led her toward the entrance.

★ ★ ★

The day was incredible. Ellie got a tour with one of the keepers while I trailed behind, watching her go inside some of the enclosures. She got to feed the tigers and cheetahs. She had to bathe and play ball with an elephant. The best part for me by a clear mile was watching her go into the zoo's nursery and feed an orphaned chimp with a baby bottle. She cried the whole time. It was adorable.

The only damper on my afternoon was a phone call from Brett. Apparently Shaun had been arrested, and as soon as he was discharged from the hospital he'd been taken in for questioning in connection with the stolen vehicle he was driving.

Brett instructed me not to worry, assuring me that he would take care of the situation. Although it dimmed my mood a little at the time, as soon as Ellie was back at my side again, my spirits lifted. She'd finished her tour, so we bought a sandwich and sat on the grass outside the lion enclosure. I sat there just listening to her gush about it and how this was easily the best birthday she'd ever had.

"So, should I give you your gift now?" I offered.

Her eyebrows rose. "This isn't my gift?" she asked, waving her hand around at the zoo.

I laughed and shook my head, pulling out the palm-sized gift box from my pocket. "No. This is your present." *Well, part of it anyway.*

She gulped as I held the box out to her. "Jamie, I don't need you to spend your money on me."

"I'll remember that for next year, when I'm broke again," I joked, waving the little box at her. "Come on, take it. And if you don't like it, then we'll change it, all right?"

She chewed on her lip as she looked at me gratefully, her hand hesitating for a couple of seconds before she ripped off the silver gift wrap and lifted the lid of the box to reveal what was inside. Almost immediately her eyes filled with tears as her free hand covered her mouth. "Oh, Jamie, it's…" She shook her head, and I started to panic that she didn't like it.

"You can exchange it," I offered.

She made a little whimper. "Exchange it, are you crazy? It's beautiful. Thank you so much, this must have cost you a fortune," she whispered, tracing her finger along the line of the silver Pandora bracelet I'd bought her. Ellie liked silver, she never wore anything gold.

"You sure?" I searched her eyes for signs that she was lying and trying to spare my feelings. "I don't mind if you want to—" Her mouth pressed against mine, stopping my insecure ramble.

She broke the kiss, her eyes still glazed over with what I was hoping were happy tears. "Put it on for me?" she asked, holding out the box. I smiled and took the bracelet from its pillow, clasping it around her slender wrist. The bracelet was one of those ones with the beads that you collected and added on to it. Hers had only four beads so far, one of them inlaid with a little diamond. I planned on collecting them for her and filling it up as the years passed. "Oh, Jamie, I love it, thank you," she gushed.

"Welcome." I grinned.

After the zoo, we headed back to my place, losing ourselves in each other's bodies for a couple of hours before showering and getting ready to go to her favorite restaurant.

Before going to the restaurant I'd booked, I drove a fair way out of the city and stopped next to a deserted field.

"What are we doing here?" she asked, looking at the nothingness around us.

"Last gift." I pulled an envelope from the glove compartment and held it out to her. She frowned and took it, opening it with that curious-puppy expression on her face.

I watched her as she read it over. "I don't understand, what is this?" she asked.

"I had a star named after you. I wanted to get you something you could keep, and I remember you once told me that you liked stargazing when you were a kid, so..." I frowned. "It's actually pretty lame," I added, wincing and now wishing I hadn't done it. I really was turning into one of those romantic saps that the boys all ribbed on at the warehouse.

She gasped, looking down at the sheet again. "Are you kidding me? Jamie, oh God, I love this! I can't believe you remembered..." She looked up at me in awe and it suddenly didn't feel so lame anymore. "I seriously have my own star?"

I nodded, prying my phone out of my pocket. "Want to see it?"

She turned to me with wide, excited, tear-filled eyes. "Heck yeah!"

"Come on then, I'll find it for you." I pushed myself out of the truck, grabbing the spare jacket that I'd brought for her so that she wouldn't get cold. She climbed out too, and walked to the front of the truck, looking up at the clear night sky. I slipped the jacket around her shoulders before gripping her waist and lifting her quickly, setting her on the hood of my truck before climbing up, settling myself behind her, and pulling her close to my chest. I fiddled with my phone, finding the star map app that I'd downloaded for tonight, then pointed it in the general direction of her star.

It took a few minutes to find it, but finally we had it. Ellie was raving and gushing about how incredible it was and how it was the most thoughtful and special gift she'd ever received.

We just cuddled on the hood of my truck, looking at the constellations for a while before talk turned to her school and the fact that she only had just over two months left of her senior year. Coincidently, she would finish high school a week after my last day of working for Brett.

We spoke about colleges and where she was going to attend. She already had her acceptance letters, and the time was approaching where she'd have to make her decision. But Ellie didn't seem too happy about the thought of college at all; she'd told me several times that she had nothing specific in mind for a career and that she didn't even really want to go to college. She'd just applied because that's what people always expected of her.

"So there's actually nothing that you want to do? If you could do absolutely anything, what would it be?" I asked. Everyone had a dream, didn't they?

She shifted sheepishly, shaking her head. "There's nothing."

I frowned. She was lying to me. "That's not true, Ellie. What is it you want to do?"

"You'll laugh and say it's stupid," she protested.

I sighed. Clearly she didn't know me as well as she thought she did if she thought I would be anything other than supportive. "I won't, I promise," I assured her.

Closing her eyes, she seemed to gather her courage before finally speaking. "I want to have my own label."

Label? "Huh? What kind of label?"

"A clothing line," she explained.

I raised one eyebrow at that. "Really? Have you ever designed anything before?" I asked. She nodded sheepishly in response. "Something I've seen?" I pressed.

She nodded again, clearly uncomfortable with this conversation. "Yeah, I designed and made that dress that I wore to my prom."

My mouth dropped open at her words. "Holy fuck, really?" I was shocked. That dress was incredible; I had been sure it was an expensive little number.

"Yep," she replied, looking like she was bracing herself for something bad.

"Wow, shit, that dress was amazing, Ellie. I had no idea you were so talented!" I gushed excitedly.

A smile crept onto her face; her shoulders seemed to relax a little. "Seriously, you liked it?"

I nodded eagerly. "Liked it? I did more than like it, I loved it. Damn, that dress was beautiful; I can't believe you made that."

She blushed furiously. "I made that shirt that I wore today, too," she admitted quietly, as if she was ashamed of it or something.

"The blue one? Wow, that was incredible too, Ellie. You should definitely go to design school or something," I encouraged her.

A frown lined her forehead. "I just do it in my free time for a hobby. I don't really show people my designs."

Is she crazy? If I had a real talent like that, I would be showing it off to everyone! "Why not?"

She shrugged, scrunching her nose. "I don't know. The only people I've ever spoken to about going into fashion are Miles and Stacey."

"And what did they say about it? That you should be going to design school and not wasting your talent by hiding it away?" I guessed.

She nodded weakly, playing with her fingers. "Stacey did."

"And Miles?" I prompted.

She sighed, shrugging, looking even more uncomfortable as she squirmed on the spot. "He didn't think much of the idea. He didn't like my designs, said most of them were trashy and classless. He said I'd be wasting my time studying fashion and that I should just keep it as a hobby," she finished.

Trashy and classless? The prick had clearly knocked her confidence with that remark. "Ellie, for fuck's sake, the guy was a jerk, a controlling asshole who probably didn't want you to make anything of yourself because then you might leave him for someone better!"

She smiled at that. "Someone better, like you?"

I couldn't help but laugh. "Someone much better than me. Someone who could give you the world."

She smiled and pointed up at the sky. "Who needs the world when I have my own star?"

"Now who's corny?" I joked. She pressed her lips to mine, kissing me fiercely. When she pulled away we were both a little breathless. "Just think about it for me, okay? I'd love for you to do something that makes you happy. I'll always support you, no matter what it is, and you need to know that."

She sighed wistfully, looking at me like I was the sweetest guy in the world. "I'd settle for just traveling around for a while. I've always wanted to see the world. Paris, Rome, Egypt, England..." She sighed again and snuggled against my chest, pulling my arms tighter around her.

Traveling? I'm definitely up for traveling if she's serious. "Really? You want to travel?"

She nodded vigorously. "Yeah. It's a dream of mine to take a boat trip up the Nile, climb to the top of the Eiffel Tower, swim with dolphins in a crystal-clear ocean, shop in Milan. I'd love to do that."

I gulped, about to make an offer that could shape our lives together. "I'll make you a deal."

She raised a curious eyebrow. "What kind of deal?"

"Take a gap year. Travel with me when you finish high school. We'll go do everything you've just said and more. Then, after about six months, we come back and you apply to study fashion in college in the fall. Deal?"

"You want to go traveling with me? You're serious?" Her eyes were wide with excitement. I nodded in confirmation. "Really? Really, really?"

Laughing, I nodded. "Yeah, really, really."

"We can't, though." She said the words, but the excited smile remained on her face. "We can't, can we? Not really."

I shrugged easily. "I have nothing tying me here. If you want to climb some crappy metal tower in France, then I want to, too," I joked, laughing as she slapped my arm, giggling. "I'm being serious, though. Think about it: you and me, traveling the world. That sounds like a great idea to me."

She was chewing on her lip so hard that I was frightened she was going to bite it in half. Her eyes searched mine; indecision and wonder were both clear on her face. "Oh God, I'd love that," she whispered.

"Then we'll do it. But when we come home, you have to apply to design school, or fashion school, or whatever it's called. Deal?" I bargained. Excitement was building in my chest, thoughts of waking up in a different country with her, taking cheesy tourist photos of some of the world's most famous landmarks. I would actually give anything for that. A new start, away from here, with her. Perfection.

Her smile fell, replaced by a worried frown. "Jamie, I'm not good enough to go to fashion school. I'd get laughed right out of there!"

I scoffed. "Ellie, I've seen two things that you've made—unless you've worn something else you designed?" She shook her head in response. "Right, well those two things are incredible. *So* beautiful. You need to do something with your talent. Have confidence and believe in yourself. I believe in you."

"Can't we just do the traveling and not add school into the deal?"

I smiled and shook my head slowly, brushing my nose up the side of hers. "No."

She kissed me then, a serious kiss; the force of it made me practically fall back against my windshield as she crushed herself to me. After a minute of kissing so fiercely that my lips were tingling, she pulled back to look at me; her eyes danced with excitement. "You're being serious? Traveling for six months?"

I nodded in confirmation. "Then school."

She chewed on her lip thoughtfully; I could practically see her mind whirling, thinking it through, weighing out the pros and cons. "Okay, I'll apply, but if I don't get in, then that's the end of it. Agreed?" she bartered.

I suddenly got so excited that I could barely keep still. Images flashed in my mind of her standing next to the Eiffel Tower, or her sunning herself in a bikini on some beach somewhere, and us wandering through little market towns together. "Agreed." My hand tangled into the back of her hair, guiding her mouth to mine as she gave an excited squeal.

* * *

My phone rang just as we were getting out of the truck to go into the restaurant. Frowning, I looked at the caller ID. Brett.

"Sorry, I gotta take this." I smiled apologetically at Ellie. She nodded, leaning against the wall, waiting patiently. "Hey, Brett," I answered as I put the phone to my ear, pacing away a few steps so that Ellie couldn't hear the conversation.

"Hey, Kid. How you doing? Get stuff sorted out with your girlfriend like I told you to?"

"Uh, yeah," I confirmed, knowing he was referring to my alibi.

"That's great; it shouldn't be necessary, but it doesn't hurt to be cautious. Everything's going according to plan. The situation should be resolved soon. Shaun hasn't talked about anything and Arthur, my lawyer, said that he should have him home by tonight. Apparently they have enough evidence to charge him, which is a pain, but we'll deal with it. I'm confident that, with my resources, it won't go to trial."

I breathed a sigh of relief that Shaun hadn't squealed and fingered me in anything. "Awesome."

"Yeah. There is something you need to be aware of, though. Apparently they pulled Shaun's phone log and your number came up as calling him around the time of the crash. Delete all your shit and ditch your phone, okay? You didn't call Shaun at all, you were tucked up in bed with your girlfriend all night, understand?" he coached.

Sweat coated my palms as I gripped the phone tighter. There was something, however small, connecting me and Shaun. Now that I had Ellie in on it, willing to lie for me, I needed to make sure nothing went wrong.

"How do you know that?"

"My lawyer keeps me informed about stuff."

"Right, well, thanks for letting me know. I'll get rid of my cell right after this call," I agreed.

"I've already had a new one sent over to your place so we can keep in touch. It should be there now waiting for you. Take a few days off. Lie low and chill. I'll keep you informed."

The phone felt like it weighed a hundred pounds in my hand as he disconnected. Quickly turning it off, I slipped off the case and pulled out the memory card, pushing it carefully into my pocket. It contained lots of photos of Ellie that I didn't want to lose. After fiddling with the back for a few seconds, I managed to get the SIM card free—and then immediately snapped it in half. I'd owned the phone for only a month, but I didn't hesitate in dropping it on the ground and stomping on it as hard as I could.

"Jamie, what the heck are you doing?" Ellie gasped, rushing to my side.

"I called Shaun on the boost last night, so I need a new phone and number," I replied. Her eyes widened as I stamped on the pile of broken plastic and glass again for good measure. "Everything's fine, I promise," I assured her.

She frowned. "Really?"

I nodded. "Yep. He should be out tonight," I replied, bending and picking up the mess before throwing it in the nearest trash can.

She rubbed at her forehead and closed her eyes. "I'll be glad when this is all over, and I can stop worrying so hard about you."

I forced a smile, wrapping my arms around her tightly, crushing her against my chest. "Stop worrying about me; you have more important things to worry about."

She winced. "My finals?"

I shook my head. "You have nothing to worry about there, you'll ace them all. I have every confidence in you."

"Aww," she murmured, looking at me like I was the cutest puppy in the world. "Well, what then?"

I kissed the tip of her nose. "Like what clothes you're gonna pack for our trek around the world," I teased.

She made a little squealing sound and bounced on the spot.

"Oh God, don't even get me started on that. I'm already way too excited, and we have to wait two whole months. Plus, we have to break it to my mom first, too. I have a feeling she's gonna freak out and tell me I can't go or something." She frowned. "I can see big fights happening in our near future."

CHAPTER 24

ELLIE

Fighting to Be Free 279

HIS HAND WAS too tight in mine; my fingers were starting to lose feeling. Squeezing back gently, I winced in his direction, nodding toward our intertwined hands, silently telling him to relax. Jamie smiled apologetically and loosened his death grip, moving my hand into his lap, tracing my knuckles with his thumb.

My gaze flicked up to my parents, who were sitting opposite us on the other sofa. Both of them looked shocked. My mom's shock was mingled with horror, my dad's with worry.

"So, let me get this straight. When you finish high school, you two are planning on traveling the world. That's what you just said, correct?" Mom asked incredulously.

I nodded, trying to appear confident even though her hard eyes were burning into me. "Yeah, for six months," I confirmed. "Or, well, until we've had enough and want to come home, but that will be the maximum, so that I can go to college next year."

At my answer, my mother made an angry scoffing noise in the back of her throat, and my dad sat back, running a hand through his hair. "I've always wanted to travel," he mused.

My mom gasped and slapped his chest with the back of her

hand, her eyes flashing with anger. "Michael, we're *not* allowing this!"

My dad cocked his head to the side, looking at her. An amused smile played at the corners of his mouth as he said, "Ellie has your spirit and fight, Ruth; you honestly think that we'd be able to stop her from going? She's an adult now; she can do what she wants."

I almost choked on air. *I'm nothing like her, she's a bitch!*

"Michael, seriously? Don't you think it's about time you stepped up and behaved more like a father should?" she snapped.

His shoulders stiffened at that remark. "Don't even think about questioning my parenting skills. You know I love my girls, all three of you. Just because I don't rule with an iron fist like you do doesn't mean I'm not a good father!" he practically growled. "You of all people should know what it feels like to be repressed by a parent, yet you're doing the same thing now."

Whoa. Go, Dad! Dad one, Mom zero.

Hurt flitted across her features. The anger immediately dissipated from his face as he reached out, placing a hand on her knee, squeezing gently. "I know you want the best for her, but what you need to realize is that sometimes the best things come from unexpected places," he continued. "Happiness was all that mattered to us at their age, so you can't begrudge Ellie the same thing."

Mom pouted some more, and I watched her curiously, wondering what he meant about having a repressive parent. My maternal grandparents lived on the other side of the country; we didn't see them often. Thinking about it now, my mother never truly relaxed when we visited them. She always had to check and recheck her makeup, fussing over me and Kelsey to make sure we looked respectable enough before she knocked on their front door. My maternal grandfather was a little strict, quiet, reserved even. Had he been controlling of her when she was younger? Maybe it was a learned behavior, and she was the way she was because of him and her upbringing.

My dad turned back to me and Jamie as we silently watched the exchange between them with interest. "So, how are you planning on paying for this trip?" he inquired.

"Granddad's inheritance money," I answered at the same time that Jamie said, "I have enough money saved up."

My dad nodded, pursing his lips. "Okay, so Jamie can pay for himself, and you're planning on using the money my dad left for you in his will, Ellie?" he clarified. I nodded, hoping he'd go for it. "What about when the money runs out?"

"We'll get jobs or something," I replied quickly. Jamie made a little strangled noise from next to me, like he was going to speak. I squeezed his hand, urging him to remain quiet. I knew what he was thinking: He had enough money to pay for us both for six months without jobs.

My dad nodded thoughtfully, turning his full attention to Jamie. The silence became uncomfortable as he seemed to be assessing Jamie's aura or something. "I can trust you to look after her, can't I?" he finally said.

Jamie's hand left mine, his arm snaking around my shoulder possessively. "Absolutely. No worries there at all," he confirmed confidently.

My dad stroked his chin, seeming to ponder it for a few seconds more. All three of us watched him—my mother included. "Okay, we'll allow it," he agreed.

At his words, my mom gasped, her eyes widening. "Oh no! No chance, it's not—"

My dad cut her off quickly, his voice resonating with that firm tone that he'd used earlier. "I said we'll allow it, Ruth."

Make that Dad two, Mom zero!

Her mouth snapped shut, her teeth clicking together from the force of it. When no more protests left her lips, Dad smiled and bent forward, kissing her softly. "She'll be fine with Jamie," he whispered as he pulled back, cupping the side of her face with one hand. "You need to let go of her sometime."

I knew I should respect their soft and tender moment, but I was just too damned excited to sit still for a second longer. I sprang from the sofa, literally doing a little happy dance as I fist-pumped the air. My years of being a cheerleader wanted to surface in me as I struggled not to do a full-fledged cheer routine in the middle of my living room, including backflips and the splits.

"This is gonna be awesome!" I practically screamed.

Jamie laughed and gripped my hips, pulling me into his lap. I squealed excitedly and looked up at his face. He was grinning ecstatically, his eyes sparkling with happiness as he bent forward and kissed the tip of my nose. Telling them had gone a lot smoother than anticipated. We'd both been dreading this conversation with my parents for the last two weeks, since we'd first come up with the idea.

"Now all we have to do is plan out where you want to go," he said, stroking the side of my face.

"England."

We both looked up, shocked because that answer had come from my mom. She smiled weakly, gripping my dad's hand tightly, seeming to need the support.

"England is somewhere I've always wanted to go. Maybe you could go there and send me some photos?" she continued.

I gulped. Us traveling was obviously a big thing for her to concede on, and I needed to appreciate the gesture appropriately. "Sure. Maybe we could look on Google later, and you could show me some of the things that you wanted to see," I suggested, not quite knowing how to connect with the woman after all this time of her being a standoffish parent.

. Her smile was pained as she nodded. I could see how much effort it took for her to let me go. Maybe all the time that I'd resented her controlling, bitchy nature, she'd actually been struggling to show me how she felt. Maybe control was how she showed affection. I didn't know, but either way I was getting to go traveling with Jamie, so I didn't really care how that came about.

* * *

As I stretched out on my bed, combing through my books, trying to study for my biology final, Kelsey sat next to me cutting out pictures of places that I wanted to go.

"Tag ma hall? What's that?" she asked, frowning at my list of things I needed to see.

I laughed at her pronunciation. I was actually really going to miss her. "Taj Mahal," I corrected. "It's one of the seven wonders of the world. It's a mausoleum an emperor had built in memory of his late wife," I explained.

Her nose crinkled in confusion. "What's a mausoleum?"

"It's like a resting place for the dead. Her body is inside the Taj Mahal," I replied, flicking through one of the travel brochures and finding a picture to show her.

"So it's basically like a grave?"

"Kind of. But it's also a symbol of the love that the emperor had for his wife. It took over twenty years to build. I would love for a guy to be so devoted to me that he would do that," I gushed, raking my eyes over the picture of it.

Kelsey nudged her shoulder against mine. "Jamie loves you that much."

Heat flooded my cheeks and my stomach fluttered at the mere mention of his name. "Maybe," I allowed.

She nodded confidently. "He does. He's taking you to all of these places, so he must love you a lot."

Kelsey adored Jamie. He was great with her too, playing games with her, buying her candy and magazines, listening to her ramble on about school and never once showing he was bored.

"He does," I agreed. I still had no idea *why* he loved me, but I knew he did.

"I'm gonna miss you both. I really can't come? Not even for a week?" she begged, shooting me the Puss in Boots eyes.

Kelsey had been hanging around me constantly since I told her I was leaving. She was like my new shadow, wanting to be in my room all the time. Sometimes, like now, I didn't mind because I could keep her distracted by getting her to do little menial things for my plans. Kelsey clipped out pictures to perfection, and she spent ages pinning them on the huge world map that I had stuck on my wall. The three of us had covered it with clippings, Post-it notes, and colored pins. It was a mess, but it made my heart race every time I looked at it. Even my mom had helped search for a few pictures to go on there.

Other times, like when I wanted some alone time with my boyfriend, Kelsey was like a thorn in my side.

As a result of her clinginess, I only really got peace and quiet when I was at Jamie's place—but even then I used the time to study. I missed Jamie. I saw him every day, but what with everything going on and my finals approaching, I didn't get to hang out with him and enjoy his company like I wanted to. Plus, he worked a lot. Weekends, nights, days; he was so busy that he was practically exhausting himself, too.

Studying, planning our trip, sleeping, and eating. That was literally all my life consisted of right now.

* * *

The two months passed. Slowly, but they passed. It wasn't smooth sailing by any means—there was a lot of stress, sleepless nights, and studying involved—but I finally made it through all of my exams and graduated.

To celebrate our graduation there was a huge party at Sebastian's house for seniors only. I hadn't planned on going at all, but Stacey convinced me to go for a little while. Apparently this was my last duty as head cheerleader, and then I would hand the title off to Marie, my successor. I was actually pretty happy to give it away, to be honest.

My plan had been to stay at the party for only an hour, but I'd already been there for almost two. It seemed like everybody wanted to talk to me about my trip, which started tomorrow. There were just way too many people to say good-bye to. It didn't help that Stacey was hanging all over me, blubbering about how much she was going to miss me.

I was flying solo tonight too; I had no boyfriend to get me through the night and keep me sane. Jamie and I were spending the night apart. If I finally managed to escape Stacey's clutches, I was going to head home and spend some time with my family and call it an early night. But Jamie, well…Jamie was doing something more…risky.

Last week he'd finished his agreed time with Brett, but somehow he'd been roped—or maybe forced, because he didn't look happy about it—into doing one last job. He was going out around eleven o'clock to meet with his boss.

Since he planned on working into the early hours of the morning, he would be seriously tired tomorrow and no doubt would sleep through the entire flight to Rome. That meant I wouldn't be joining the mile-high club. Well, not tomorrow anyway, but there would be plenty of opportunities for that; we had lots of flights planned.

A sloppy kiss on my cheek and a squeeze to my shoulder brought me out of my reverie. "Not fair. I hate it, I tell you," Stacey slurred, nuzzling her face against the side of mine.

I smiled, supporting most of her weight as she swayed unsteadily. It was only seven thirty, but due to the fact that she'd started drinking at five, she was wasted already. "I'll email all the time, and send postcards, lots and lots of postcards," I assured her for the hundredth time.

She pouted. "But what am I gonna do without my bestie? You're gonna forget all about little ol' Stacey Gordon." She hiccupped as she spoke, her watery blue eyes locked on mine.

I cupped her face in my hands, looking at her sternly. "Stace, I couldn't forget about you even if I tried," I promised.

She seemed to breathe a sigh of relief. While she was temporarily placated, I decided it was time to go. I'd already said good-bye to everyone and done my duty, passing the cheerleading torch to Marie. Now I wanted egg rolls and family time. "I'm going. I'll see you tomorrow, okay?" I kissed her forehead before stepping back and nodding to Paul, who was watching the scene. Stacey sniffed and turned to him, immediately crying into his chest, wailing that her "bestest friend in the world" was abandoning her.

I winced, wondering if I should take her home.

As if answering my question, Paul motioned toward the door, smiling as he patted Stacey's back, soothing her as if she were a hysterical child.

I took a deep breath, taking one last glance at the people around me. Most of them were fake friends and popularity seekers; to be honest, I wasn't going to miss this scene much at all. My high school career was over, but I was moving on to more exciting things, so there was no nostalgia at all.

Making a swift exit through the front door before anyone else could approach me, I finally stepped out into the fresh air. A happy smile crept onto my lips. Tonight was the start of the rest of my life. I practically skipped toward my beloved Beetle.

However, about thirty steps from freedom, someone called my name. I looked over my shoulder to see Miles. Suppressing a groan, I waved, trying to be friendly. "Can't stop, I was due home thirty minutes ago," I called as I continued my escape.

"Ellie, I need to talk to you."

I shook my head, turning to face him but walking backward toward my car as I held my hands up in protest. I knew what this would be about, and I didn't want to hear it. I'd had plenty of lectures from him over the last two months about the huge mistake I was making by traveling instead of attending school in the fall.

"Gotta go. Go have a drink and enjoy your night," I suggested. I reached the car then and jammed my key into the driver's side, opening the door and preparing to get in.

"Ellie, can you just stop for a minute?" Miles asked, frowning as I continued to try to escape.

I sighed and turned to face him, already expecting this to be something along the lines of a last-ditch attempt to get me back with him. He knew I was going away tomorrow with Jamie, so this was probably the last big push to put a stop to that. "What is it, Miles?" I threw my purse into the car.

He stopped in front of me, his eyes searching mine. "I know you're gonna think I'm making this up in an effort to get you to stay," he started. *Bull's-eye!* I put my hands on my hips, waiting. "Well, I'm not, honestly. I'm just telling you this because it needs to be said. I'm actually not allowed to tell you; my dad made me promise because, technically, I'm breaking some sort of law right now."

"Huh?"

He blew out a big breath and ran a hand through his hair, leaning against my car. "Your boyfriend isn't as great as you think he is. In fact, you don't even know him at all."

This conversation was starting to make me feel a little nervous. I didn't know Jamie at all? What on earth did that mean? "Miles, just spit it out, you're making no sense!"

He nodded. "I've been helping my dad a lot at the law office recently. Last week, he needed me to research a couple of things for a high-profile client of his," he explained.

"Okay," I mumbled, waiting for him to continue.

"At first I wondered what was so special about this case. It was just a grand theft auto, nothing major. But my dad seems to be working so hard on it, putting much more effort in than normal."

I gulped, slowly understanding what this was about. *Shaun. Miles's dad is Brett's hotshot lawyer for Shaun?*

"So I start helping with the case, right? It turns out that the cops are trying to pin a load of other stuff on this guy, too. They're trying to link him to other known criminals and turn up other illegal things that he's into, arrest more people and stuff. My dad has a friend inside the police department who told him all about this case they're trying to build," he said, looking at me intently, as if checking whether I was following what he was saying.

Was I following? I still didn't understand why he was telling me all this. "Miles, this is a great story and all, but..." I shrugged, looking at my watch obviously.

He nodded. "I'm getting to the point," he confirmed. "Yesterday I stumbled upon a stack of files my dad had in his office. I'm not sure he was supposed to have them because they looked like police surveillance stuff to me." He reached into his pocket, pulling out a couple of folded-up sheets of paper. "Inside one of the files was all sorts of information about my dad's client, him meeting up with known criminals and things like that. They have photos, times, dates, all that stuff. One of the guys in the photo, well, it was Jamie." He held out the pieces of paper to me, keeping one back to himself.

My heart clenched with worry, but I knew I needed to play dumb. I couldn't let Miles know that I knew Jamie was stealing cars and working for this Brett guy. "My Jamie? Don't be so stupid!" I retorted, willing my voice to come out strong and not show the total panic that was brewing inside me.

Miles nodded. "Yeah. I'm pretty sure it's him; it says his name, too. Jamie Cole. Look at the photo, it's him, right?" He motioned to the paper he was still holding out to me.

I gulped and took it, opening it up. Immediately I was confronted by a black-and-white photo of Jamie laughing with three other guys.

Miles pointed to the younger one. "That's my dad's client, the car thief. And that's Jamie with him, right?"

I nodded, unsure what I should say that wouldn't incriminate Jamie further.

"Ellie, he's not who you think he is. There was lots of information about him in the file my dad had. Jamie's not a good guy," he whispered, producing another piece of paper from his pocket.

I opened my mouth to defend Jamie and rebut that statement, but Miles cut me off before I could protest.

"He's been to jail, Ellie. I looked it up. I have his rap sheet here," he said, unfolding it slowly.

I recoiled. *Jail? What the hell, no way!* "No," I muttered, shaking my head fiercely. Jamie would have told me if he had. Sure, he had secrets and his past was bad, but he would have told me something serious like that, definitely!

Miles nodded, frowning. "Yeah, Ellie. He…He killed someone. He was let out of juvie a few months ago, around the time you two met, actually."

I couldn't breathe.

Killed someone.

Jamie had killed someone? Did Miles seriously just say that?

"No," I muttered again, trying not to let myself even entertain that thought. He was wrong. My Jamie couldn't kill anyone; he was too adorable and sweet.

Miles held out the last piece of paper to me. "Yeah," he stated. "I don't have any details, but it says he was sentenced to five years in juvenile detention for murder. He was only fourteen."

Murder. The word made my blood go cold.

I snatched the sheet out of his hands, not believing him, but the words were clearly printed there. Jamie's name, date of birth, known affiliates, dates of his sentence. He was released from juvie just under a week before I met him and is currently on parole for the remainder of his sentence.

Suddenly it felt like a fog had been lifted off me and I could suddenly hear words that Jamie had spoken to me all those months ago. *"That's my little sister, Sophie. She died. She was murdered, four years ago."*

"Oh God." My eyes filled with tears as the reality of it all sank in. Jamie had murdered his little sister when he was fourteen?

"You okay? You look a bit pale. Want to sit down?" Miles offered, taking hold of my elbow and guiding me to sit back into my car.

My heartbeat was so loud that it almost deafened me as I pictured the little girl from the ruined photo, the one with the lovely smile. She had been murdered...by her brother? My boyfriend?

There had to be some mistake, there had to be some explanation for it. Maybe it was an accident but he was charged with murder? I needed to see him. I needed to look him in the eye and ask him. I needed him to tell me that the person who I'd fallen hopelessly in love with wasn't in fact an act, that the Jamie Cole who had stolen my heart actually existed and wasn't just some illusion.

Had I really let myself fall in love with a murderer?

CHAPTER 25

THE DRIVE TO Jamie's apartment seemed to take forever. Questions were forming in my head, so many questions. And anger, a lot of anger, was settling in the pit of my stomach because the guy I was in love with hadn't told me any of this. I'd asked him to be honest with me, and he'd told me about the cars. He'd also told me he did other stuff for this Brett guy, but he wouldn't tell me what. I knew it was bad, though; I knew he hated doing it; I knew that he didn't sleep properly on the nights when his knuckles were bruised. But I never pushed the subject because he didn't want me involved. Murder was different. And this was his past; he'd lied to me by keeping this from me, allowing me to fall in love with a person who didn't actually exist!

When I pulled up outside, I wasn't sure if I wanted to go in. What if he told me it was true? What if he had murdered his little sister? How was I supposed to feel about him then? Would I look at him differently? Would I no longer want his hand to take mine because subconsciously I'd be thinking about the fact that that hand belonged to a convicted murderer?

I groaned in frustration. The anger was still there, but sadness was taking over as the dominant emotion in my body. I loved him so much—maybe too much. What was I going to do?

After taking a few deep breaths, I forced myself out of the car. His truck was parked in his allocated space, so I knew he'd be here. He'd told me he wasn't starting his "job" until eleven, so I had time to speak to him before that.

Zombielike, my legs carried me up the two flights of stairs, and I stopped outside his door. My whole body felt cold. I didn't want to know, but I had to. Why did Miles have to tell me? I had been perfectly happy not knowing this little piece of earth-shattering information, but now my life was threatening to fall to pieces around me.

"Please let this be a mistake," I whispered as I knocked on the door. As I waited, I imagined all sorts of scenarios, accidents that could have resulted in her dying and him being wrongfully charged with her death. After a few seconds, the door swung open and there stood the love of my life.

"Hey!" he greeted me, his expression shocked.

The sound of his voice made my stomach ache; the tone was so rich and welcoming. His voice alone made me swoon. I dragged my eyes over his handsome face, biting my lip so that I didn't just burst into tears. A smile was stretched across his face, his eyes soft and tender as he looked back at me.

"What are you doing here?" he asked, grinning, reaching for my hand.

I gulped, unsure what I should say. My eyes searched his face as his fingers linked through mine and he stepped a little closer to me. Could this beautiful, thoughtful, adorable boy standing in front of me *really* be a killer? Was it even possible?

A sob rose in my throat and I opened my mouth to speak, but no words came out.

"Ellie, you okay?" He cocked his head to the side, regarding me worriedly. "I thought we weren't seeing each other tonight." He tugged on my hand, making me step into his familiar apartment.

I had no words, so the only thing I could do was reach into my pocket and pull out the crumpled piece of paper that Miles had given me. Jamie's "rap sheet," as he'd called it. I held it out to him, and he frowned, looking confused as he took it from my hand and straightened it out so he could read it.

I watched his face as he scanned it. His eyes twitched, his jaw tightened, his shoulders seemed to stiffen. He blew out a big breath and his eyes flicked up to meet mine. I was praying for some emotion to cross his face, any emotion: anger, shock, disbelief, just *something* to disprove the words on that piece of paper. But what I saw instead broke my heart even more. I saw guilt, plain and simple. His sad brown eyes said it all—the truth was printed on that sheet.

"Ellie, where...where did you get this?" His normally smooth and silky voice was tight with stress and emotion.

"Miles," I croaked.

"Miles...What? How?"

I sniffed, wiping the tear that escaped even though I was trying to hold it back. Was he seriously not going to tell me? Was he stalling for time so that he could come up with a lie? "Shaun's lawyer is Arthur Barrington, Miles's dad. Miles has been helping with his case. He told me that the police are trying to link Shaun to other crimes and criminals," I muttered. I needed to sit down; my legs were becoming weak as we stood there assessing each other.

Jamie nodded, his face hard and emotionless as he closed the door, shutting us both in the apartment. "Miles's dad? Well, that sucks," he grumbled, balling up the paper again and throwing the crumpled ball onto the end table. "I already knew about the association thing, Brett told me."

I looked at him incredulously, waiting.

His eyes met mine, and he gulped loudly. "I should have told you," he mumbled.

A humorless laugh escaped me. "Really, ya think?" I snapped. He grimaced, stepping closer to me and stretching out his hand toward me, his expression pleading. Instinct and anger made me slap his hand away just before he touched my cheek. "Don't touch me," I growled.

His hand immediately dropped down to his side again as he looked at me so remorsefully, so softly, that it made my heart ache. "Ellie, please, I love you," he whispered.

His words were painful. Emotion was washing over me as my eyes stung with tears that I refused to let fall. "You went to jail for murder?" I questioned, my voice barely above a whisper.

He nodded slowly, his eyes locked on my face as he raised his hands innocently. He was doing everything so slowly, almost like I was a frightened animal and he was trying not to scare me off. "I didn't want to tell you. I didn't want you to look at me the way you are right now. I didn't want you to know that side of me. That's not the person I want to be."

My chin wobbled as he stepped closer to me. Too close. So close that I could feel the heat coming from his body. I couldn't let him that close to me, I couldn't concentrate when Jamie was in such close proximity, so I stepped back and shook my head. I was fighting a losing battle to hold on to my anger as it was, and I didn't need him stepping into my personal space and getting behind the barriers I was trying so hard to keep up. His shoulders slumped as he hung his head almost shamefully. He looked so defeated that it broke my heart.

"I had a right to know. That's not something you can keep from someone. You should have told me!" I cried angrily.

Again he nodded. "I know, but I didn't want to lose you. Then, as time went on, it became more like I *couldn't* lose you. It got harder and harder to tell you, then it was impossible because I'd left it too long," he explained, still looking at the floor.

"Jamie, you killed someone! You didn't even tell me. You let me fall in love with you knowing that the person I was falling for didn't exist!" I accused. He shuffled on his feet, his eyes firmly fixed on the floor, and I hated that he wouldn't look at me. "Oh, just give up the lost-little-boy look, for Christ's sake, that's not helping your case, so man the fuck up and look at me!" I slapped his shoulder as hard as I could, resulting only in making my hand sting from the blow. "Ouch," I muttered.

"You okay?"

I laughed incredulously and rolled my eyes. "Screw you," I snapped. He needed to give up the kind-and-caring-boyfriend routine. The stupid boy was a murdering car thief who worked as part of a gang. *This* was the real Jamie Cole, not the illusion that he'd shown me for the last six months.

"I'm sorry," he whispered, his face a mask of sorrow.

"Sorry just doesn't cut it," I retorted.

He sighed deeply. "This is exactly why I didn't want you to know. I can't stand this, this hardness, this revulsion, not from you," he said quietly.

"This hardness is because you lied to me about who you were!" I practically screamed as I slapped his shoulder again for emphasis, this time ignoring the pain in my hand.

"I was scared of how you'd react, Ellie! I guess now I know, and I was right to have been scared." He ground his teeth and shook his head.

I snorted. "You don't know how I would have reacted. You should have told me and let me decide if I could deal with it; it wasn't your choice, that wasn't fair."

He raised one eyebrow. "And how would you have reacted to

being told that I was a convicted murderer? Would you have given me the time of day? Would you still have fallen in love with me? No, you wouldn't!" he replied, throwing his hands up in exasperation.

"Well, it's too damn late to find out now, huh?" I glared at him for a few minutes while he just stood there, looking at me apologetically, seeming to be choosing his words, or maybe he was just waiting for me to bitch him out some more. I sighed. I just needed to know once and for all; this was killing me slowly. I thought I knew who he was as a person, I thought I knew all of him, but I was so totally wrong, and that was what hurt the most. *Betrayal* was probably the word that best described my emotions; it was almost like he didn't trust me with his secrets.

"Jamie, just…just tell me what happened. Was it an accident? If it was, then that's different. If you didn't mean to kill her, then it's something different entirely. Please, just tell me what happened," I begged, hanging blindly on to the small hope that it had been an accident.

Jamie took a step back, his eyes tightening as he looked at me with a bewildered expression on his face. "Her? What do you mean, her? Why are you assuming it was a girl?"

I frowned. "I thought…You said she was murdered." I stumbled over my words and suddenly his whole posture seemed to tighten as he practically glared at me.

"Sophie? You're talking about Sophie? You think I killed my little sister?" His voice was full of acid as he straightened his shoulders, raising himself to his full height so that he towered above me.

I flinched from the abrupt change in tone. "Yeah?" I confirmed weakly, but it came out as more of a question because of his disbelieving expression.

He made a strangled growling sound as his eyes burned into

mine. "Seriously, even after all the time that we've spent together, you really think that I'm capable of murdering my own sister?" His tone was truly menacing, and for the first time, I could see the "hard Jamie" that he said he turned into when he was working.

I didn't know what to think now; confusion was settling over me. He looked so angry with me for suggesting it that I actually felt terrible for even entertaining that thought. Obviously this wasn't about his sister, I should have known that. I'd jumped to the wrong conclusion, I could see that now.

"I just put two and two together," I replied quietly.

"And came up with thirty-fucking-five," he barked, sneering at me. An involuntary whimper left my lips as he stepped forward. His whole body language was menacing and intimidating.

"I thought it was an accident or something. I was hoping it was an accident," I explained, trying to look away from his accusing eyes as he advanced on me.

His teeth ground together as he stepped even closer, so close that I stepped back to get some personal space and bumped into the wall behind me. He bent down so our faces were on the same level, our noses almost touching as his hard brown eyes met mine.

"So that's the type of person that you think you fell in love with? If you think I'm capable of murdering a little girl, then what's to stop me from killing you, too? I could do it, you know. I could put my hands around your neck and snap it like *that*," he growled, snapping his fingers on the last word. "I could cover it up too, have someone bury you somewhere your parents would never find your body. Easy, I could get away with it this time."

I raised my chin, keeping eye contact with him, knowing he was angry and just trying to push my buttons and scare me. But the thing was, I wasn't scared of him. "You wouldn't hurt me. You love me," I said confidently.

His hands traced up my sides, making my skin prickle like it always did when he touched me. They came to rest on my throat. His fingers wrapped around my neck, his thumbs applying the softest pressure against my larynx.

"I loved her too, but I still killed her." His grip tightened just enough to let me know where his hands were, but he applied no pressure at all.

Somehow I knew it wasn't true. From how he'd reacted, how angry he'd gotten when I said the words, I knew he hadn't done it. He was clearly outraged and hurt that I had even suggested it in the first place.

I didn't break eye contact as I shook my head awkwardly because of the placement of his hands. "Jamie, just cut the act. You wouldn't hurt me, so stop acting like you would. I'm not scared of you."

His jaw tightened as he moved even closer, pressing me into the wall with his hard body. "You should be, Ellie. The information that Miles gave you was right; I *am* a convicted murderer, and not the accidental kind, either. I *did* kill my baby sister. I also beat someone to death with my bare hands, the same hands that are currently wrapped around your throat. Don't think I'm not dangerous, Ellie. I don't regret what I did; I'd do it again in a heartbeat."

My brain struggled to comprehend what he was saying; everything was so jumbled in my head that it was making my ears ring. Looking at Jamie as he pinned me against the wall, I knew only one thing: He would never hurt me.

Behind the tough, scary act, his eyes were begging me to stay and love him unconditionally.

I raised my hand and gripped his wrist, pulling his hand away from my throat as I shook my head. "Stop it. It's not gonna work. Now just tell me what you should have told me six months ago, and stop trying to scare me away from you so that you don't have to deal with it," I ordered.

His face softened as he looked at me, shocked. He'd truly expected me to run out of here screaming. He closed his eyes as I slid my hand down his arm to take his hand, squeezing gently to prompt him. It didn't really matter what he said next, I'd already made up my mind; his past was his past, and it had no bearing on the future I still envisioned for us. Yes, I wanted to know the truth, but only so that nothing could ever come between us again.

"I love you, Jamie, but no more secrets. Stop shutting me out, please," I begged.

He groaned, resting his forehead against mine, his shallow breath blowing across my lips. His other hand, the one that was still wrapped around my throat, moved to the side, cupping my neck instead, his thumb stroking my cheek softly.

"It's bad, Ellie," he whispered.

I nodded, trying to prepare myself once and for all to hear about his past. I was confident in the knowledge that no matter what came out of his mouth, I was doomed to be in love with him.

I wrapped my free arm around his waist, holding him tightly as he spoke. "Ralf Montague. He was my mom's pimp, and the prick who killed my little sister right in front of me. That's who I murdered."

CHAPTER 26

I HELD MY breath as I digested his words. First off, his mom was a prostitute? And secondly, her pimp had killed Jamie's sister right in front of him? He had been a fourteen-year-old boy and watched his sister get murdered? I didn't know what to feel more, horror at the whole situation, or pity because no one should have to see anything like that. I tightened my arm on his waist, clamping him to me as his uneven breath blew across my face.

"Oh God, Jamie, I'm so sorry." My chin trembled as I struggled not to burst into tears for him.

He nodded, pulling back, his eyes dropping to the floor. I'd never seen anyone look so sad and defeated in my life. It was gut-wrenching to see such a strong and beautiful person have so much pain etched across his face. "So there you go. Happy to be included now?" he asked acidly.

My mouth dropped open in shock as he pulled away quickly and turned away from me, his back stiff as he fisted both hands into his hair. I didn't know how to answer. Yes, I was happy to be included because I wanted to be included in every part of his life, but in another way, hell no; I wished I didn't know that information. I had a feeling that what he was going to tell me about his childhood was going to make me cry myself to sleep for days when I thought about what he'd been through.

Because I had no words, I did the only thing I could think of. I stepped closer to him and pressed my face into his shoulder blades, breathing him in, circling my arms around his waist. His stomach muscles tightened under my hands as he drew in a sharp breath.

"Will you tell me what happened?" I asked quietly, my voice muffled because my face was still pressed against his back.

"Ellie, what difference does it make? He killed her, so I killed him, that's all there is to it."

I shook my head and moved in front of him, not letting him out of the cage that I'd made with my arms. "That's not all there is to it; there's more, much more, I can tell. Please? I love you, Jamie, I want to help you. It's not good for you to keep all that stuff bottled up inside you, you'll go crazy," I whispered, gripping the back of his shirt. "You can talk to me. You can tell me anything," I encouraged him.

He gulped and closed his eyes. There was a tightness to his mouth that I longed to kiss away so he would smile again. "Fine," he finally said with a sigh, his arms dropping to his sides as he gripped my wrists and unwrapped my arms from his waist. "Let's go sit down then or something." He didn't wait for me but let go of my hands and stalked away into the living room.

I took a couple of deep breaths and looked at the ceiling, fighting my building horror. When my fried nerves seemed to be under control, I turned and followed after him. I just about had time to notice that the room was bare apart from a few things scattered here and there. He'd already put most of his stuff into storage; all he had left out were his clothes and what had come with the apartment when he rented it.

Jamie was sitting on the sofa, his shoulders slumped, his head in his hands. My weary legs carried me over to him and I plopped down in the space next to him. I didn't know what to say or do to make him feel better, so I remained silent. It wasn't long before he started talking.

"My dad died when I was two, so it was always just me and my mom on our own. Things were hard on her; she had no qualifications and couldn't find a job, so she started sleeping with men for money. She'd bring them back to the house, and I'd get locked in my room so that I couldn't interrupt or anything. I didn't really know what was going on at the time, it was only as I got older that I realized what she was doing." He cringed, fisting his hands in his hair. "She got pregnant. I don't know who Sophie's dad was; no one ever stuck around, so I assume it was one of her clients."

His gaze flicked to me, so I tried to keep my expression neutral even though I was crying on the inside. His voice was so full of pain already that it hurt me to listen to it. I nodded encouragingly. I wanted to take his hand, but my body was frozen in place, just waiting for the rest of it. My eyes shot to one of the scars on his neck; you could only just see it under the collar of his T-shirt. Silently I wondered how it got there, and how he'd gotten all the marks that were on his body.

"I was seven when she was born, and from that day, I had to grow up quickly. My mom, she never bonded with Soph, she never held her for longer than necessary, never smiled at her. Even at the age of seven I knew something was wrong, so I tried to be the best brother in the world to make up for the fact that my mom never seemed to want to be in the same room as her."

I gulped and tried not to hate his mom, but the more he spoke, the more I wondered how a person such as her could birth an amazing person like Jamie.

"I used to play with her all the time, feed her and change her and stuff. I made it into a kind of game, and we got through it. When Soph was about one, things got worse. My mom started taking drugs." He blew out a big breath and shook his head. "That was about the time that she forgot she even had two kids. She was barely home at night or on weekends. I was eight, and I'd be left home alone with Sophie. My mom would forget to buy food, or she wouldn't have the money for it because she'd wasted the food money on drugs. During the week I used to get Sophie dressed and give her breakfast, then I'd put her in her crib and go to school. When I'd come home she'd still be in there, her diaper dirty because I hadn't been there to change it. Sometimes she'd get such bad diaper rash that it'd bleed. Know what, though? She didn't even cry when she was left in there all day. It was kind of like she knew that no one would come and get her, so she never bothered. The whole time my mom would just be passed out on the sofa or working."

"Oh God, Jamie," I mumbled. My eyes prickled with tears as I imagined an eight-year-old boy trying to be a dad to a one-year-old baby while his mom spent their money on drugs. It was horrifying.

He smiled weakly, still not meeting my eyes. "I was eight and a half when I first broke the law," he stated. "I went to the local store, and I stole a loaf of bread and a pack of ham so I could feed my baby sister." He hung his head as if he was ashamed to admit that.

The lump in my throat seemed to get bigger as I struggled to swallow. Suddenly my body seemed to thaw out, and I could move. I scooted closer to him on the sofa and put my hand on the back of his head, resting my chin on his shoulder, looking at the ceiling so that the tears wouldn't fall. His body was trembling against mine, and I realized that I'd never hated anyone as much as I hated his mother for letting him go through all of that. He'd never even had a childhood. Most eight-year-olds would probably pitch a fit because they wanted the latest G.I. Joe, but the starving eight-year-old Jamie was stealing food to feed himself and his sister.

"Sophie was an amazing kid. She was so happy, so loving and adorable. I did everything I could to keep her safe and smiling. I'd steal practically everything she needed: food, clothes, medicine. My mom was barely around, so it was just us, really." His voice broke and I could hear the agony in his tone.

"Why didn't you tell someone? A teacher or something?" I asked quietly.

He snorted and shook his head. "I couldn't. I knew that we'd be taken and put into foster care or something, and I didn't want to lose my sister. They would have split us up and I never would have seen her. I couldn't have that. I was scared to be alone; I guess I was selfish in that respect. I should have thought about what was best for her in the long run, but I selfishly thought that *I* was what was best for her. Now I wish I'd told someone, though. Maybe if I had, then she'd be alive. Hindsight can sometimes give you nightmares," he replied sadly.

I gripped the back of his head and pressed myself to him tighter. "You aren't selfish, Jamie. Jeez, don't ever think that!" I said fiercely as a lone tear escaped down my cheek.

He turned his head, and his eyes finally met mine for the first time since this whole revelation began. "Ellie, don't try to make me feel better. I don't need your pity looks."

My fingers twisted in the back of his hair as I pressed my forehead to his and squeezed my eyes shut. "Jamie, you can't stop me from feeling these things. I love you, so of course it's going to upset me that you went through all that. If I told you these things about my childhood, would you be able to stop yourself from feeling sorry for me?" I asked incredulously.

He sighed, his warm breath caressing my cheek and ruffling the hair at my neck. "I guess not."

I sniffed and nodded, pulling back and resting my chin on his shoulder again. We were almost at the worst part now; I just needed to brace myself for the impact. "Who was the guy who killed her?"

His body tightened when I asked that; his jaw snapped shut with an audible click as his hands clenched into fists where they rested on his knees. "My mom got with Ralf when I was ten. They kind of dated, but he used to pimp her out, too. She loved him more than anything, more than me and Soph. He moved in with us and things got better in some ways and worse in others."

"What do you mean?" I asked, not entirely sure I wanted to know the answer.

He shrugged. "At least there was food in the house once he moved in."

I narrowed my eyes at his detached tone. "What got worse?" I asked. He groaned and looked at me pleadingly, as if he didn't want to talk about this anymore. "Jamie, please? What got worse?" I repeated.

"Ralf was a sick asshole. He...he got off on hurting people. Me especially," he answered.

"He was the one that—" I couldn't say it, so I traced my finger on a small round burn mark at the base of his neck.

He nodded, seeming to look anywhere but at me. "Yeah. He used to like it. You understand what I mean by that?" he asked.

Like it...

"Oh God," I muttered as I realized what he was talking about.

Jamie nodded again, shrugging me off him as he stood, rubbing one hand on his arm as if he were cold. "Yeah, he'd get drunk, and she'd be off earning him cash, so he'd have a little fun by kicking the shit out of me. Afterward, he'd tell me to clean up my wounds and stuff. He'd watch me do it and... touch himself."

Images of that seemed to flood my brain. I had been right earlier; this information was definitely going to make me cry myself to sleep for weeks.

"Did he ever"—I took a deep breath—"touch you?" My voice came out too high pitched as horror and anger seemed to build up inside. Bile rose in my throat as I wondered how much worse this conversation was going to get.

Jamie shook his head quickly, and I breathed a sigh of relief. "No. He was a sadist, so he just used to like it when I was in pain. Thankfully, he never paid much attention to Sophie. Well, not until the day she died anyway." He practically growled the last part. "I hated him so fucking much, Ellie. I used to dream about fighting back, about taking the knife that he always had clipped on his belt and ramming it through his heart. But I couldn't because things were better for Sophie with him there, so I just let it go on."

"You let it happen so that your sister could eat? That's, that's—" I shook my head, not having the words.

He shrugged as if it were nothing. "She was the most important thing, and when he was there things were better for her. I coped with it."

"Jamie, I'm sorry," I whispered.

"Sorry you ever met me, huh? Yeah, you probably should be. You don't need someone like me in your life," he stated flatly.

I stood up and walked the four paces to him, gripping his hand, pulling gently to try to get him to look at me. He turned, but his eyes were firmly fixed on the floor again now. I'd never realized how insecure he was; he was like some sort of little lost boy thinking that everything was above him and he didn't deserve things.

"You're wrong. I *do* need you in my life," I corrected him. I went up on tiptoes and pressed a kiss on the edge of his jaw. He made a sort of whimpering noise as his hands went to my hips, pulling me to him so tightly that my body was almost crushed against his. He bent and buried his face in my hair as I snaked my arms around his waist, hugging him fiercely.

"I need you, too. I love you, Ellie, so, so much," he mumbled into my hair.

We stood there holding each other until I could stand the silence no longer. "What happened?" I asked, meaning with Sophie.

He sighed and guided me over to the sofa again. He sat and pulled me close to his side. My ribs were starting to ache because he'd clamped me to him so tightly, but I didn't say anything about it. He obviously felt like he needed to keep hold of me, so I wasn't going to ruin that feeling of security for him.

"I decided to leave. I came up with a plan for me and Sophie to leave, and for me to take care of her on my own. I was already doing that anyway, but I thought that if we left it'd be better for both of us. Trouble was, I had no money. I started asking around to see if anyone wanted to give me a job, but I was only eleven, and no one wanted a schoolkid working for them. Then one day this guy came to the house and had this huge blowout with Ralf about something. I'd hidden at the top of the stairs and listened to them argue. Apparently Ralf had promised to do some robbery job for this guy, but he'd backed out last minute. I followed the guy out and asked if I could do the job instead. He said no because I was a kid, but he did offer me something else. A delivery job. I didn't ask what I was delivering, I didn't need to know. All I needed to know was that he paid me a hundred bucks for it. I went back the next day and did another delivery after school and got more money, and then the guy asked if I wanted to do more jobs," he explained.

Understanding washed over me. "This was how you got tangled up with Brett."

"Mm-hmm." He nodded. "It started out easy; a delivery job here and there. Then things got more involved, and I got paid more. Money seemed to be all I could think about. The more jobs I did, the more money I got and the closer I came to having enough for me and Soph to start over on our own. I started skipping school all the time, and I'd hang out at Brett's workshop with the guys who worked for him. I started training with them all too, doing weights and fighting and stuff, so I learned a lot about self-defense, but I continued to let Ralf do what he wanted so that he wouldn't know that I was planning on leaving with Sophie. Ray, the head mechanic, he would let me help him with the cars, showing me how to fix them and stuff. By the time I'd been there for six months, I could strip an engine and put it back together again. Ray also showed me how to steal them. Turns out I was pretty good at it," he said, laughing quietly.

"I was saving up. I decided to wait until I was sixteen so that I could rent a place legally. A couple of years passed that way, then one day I spent too long at the warehouse. Ray and I got caught up cooing over some sports car. Funny how I can't even remember what the car looked like now." He frowned, obviously trying to recall that insignificant detail. "I was fourteen, and Sophie was seven. I was late getting home. Ralf had been drinking, and I guess because I wasn't there to—" He stopped talking and squeezed his eyes shut as he shook his head.

"Jamie?" I prompted when he didn't carry on.

"It was my fault," he whispered suddenly.

"What? No." I shook my head fiercely.

He nodded. "Yeah. I should have gone home right away; if I had then he wouldn't have laid his dirty pervert hands on her." He choked on a sob. "He...hurt her. When I walked in the living room she was sobbing in the corner while he sat there and—" He groaned, and I dug my fingers into his thigh as I finished his sentence in my head. I'd never heard of anything so sick in my life. What kind of despicable person got off on seeing a child in pain? I felt dirty even thinking about it.

"Where was your mom?" I asked, the tears flowing down my face freely now.

He gulped. "Just sitting there," he said disbelievingly. "She didn't care. She loved Ralf, he gave her what she needed, she let him do what he wanted." His chin trembled, and I saw a tear fall down his face and drop onto his jeans.

I covered my mouth as I whimpered. She'd done nothing while her boyfriend had physically abused her daughter and was getting himself off because of it? That made her just as guilty as if she'd done it herself.

"Sophie was cowering in the corner, crying, her nose bleeding, her lip split. He'd used the knife that he always used to use on me, and sliced a big gash on her forearm. She was so little, and he was sitting there, jacking off while he watched her cry. I totally lost it. I knew we couldn't stay there anymore, so I told them we were leaving. I shouted at Sophie to get up and pack a bag, but he got between us. He said we weren't going anywhere, that he owned us all and that Sophie was going to earn him money too, when she was old enough." Jamie's face was red from anger.

"Ralf and I started fighting. The whole time my mom just sat there, watching with her glassy eyes, like she wasn't even aware of what was going on," he ranted. "Sophie got in the way, she was trying to stop us from fighting, I think. He...he grabbed her, and he slammed her head against the wall." His voice broke and his fingers dug into my forearm unconsciously as he squeezed his eyes shut. "I can still see it, Ellie. When I close my eyes I can see it, clear as day. I can still hear the crack that her skull made as it smashed against the plaster. I can still picture the smear of blood on the wall as Soph crumpled to the floor."

I whimpered as I looped my arms around his neck, probably squeezing too tightly to be comforting, trying to save him from the memory of it. I prayed with every bone in my body that I could erase it, that I could somehow make it better or take it away. But there was nothing I could do.

"I shoved him off me, and he crashed into the sideboard and was drunkenly trying to get himself up from the floor. I ran to Sophie, screaming at my mom to call for help, but she didn't. She just fucking sat there!" he cried, wrapping his arm around me tightly. "I tried to help her, but it was no good. There was blood everywhere, the smell of it made me gag. Sophie was so still, so still…"

I gulped, desperately trying not to picture it because I was attempting to be strong, but my mind was wandering there, grieving for the little girl I'd never met, the little girl from the photo. I pictured a young Jamie holding her in his arms, screaming at his spaced-out, drugged-up mother for help that never came.

"When she stopped breathing, I just lost it. I totally lost it. My reason for living was gone, and it was all his fault. I…I killed him with my bare hands, but I just couldn't stop. I have no idea how long I was hitting him for, but apparently one of the neighbors heard screaming and shouting and called the police. They busted the door down and dragged me off. I was arrested for murder, but I didn't care. All I could think about was that there was no point to my life anymore. The entire reason for me being alive was to be a big brother, but he took that away from me." His voice broke with emotion as he buried his face into the side of my neck, his body trembling against mine.

I tightened my arms when I felt his warm tears wetting my

shoulder. Chewing on the inside of my cheek, I stroked his back soothingly while he cried. My chest was tight with grief, my stomach was churning and twisting because the love of my life was in pieces in my arms, and I had no idea how to help him, or even if I could.

CHAPTER 27

IT'S OKAY, EVERYTHING'S OKAY," I whispered, stroking the back of his head.

He'd stilled, his body no longer shook, but he was still clinging to me as if he was frightened to let go. "If I hadn't spent too long at the warehouse drooling over that fucking car, if I had just told a teacher or someone what was happening, or maybe if we'd left earlier instead of me stupidly deciding to wait until I was sixteen, she would be here now. She didn't deserve that, Ellie, she didn't deserve to die," he said softly, looking at his hands in his lap, a heartbroken expression on his face.

"Jamie, you can't blame yourself for something that someone else did," I countered, shaking my head as I stroked the side of his face, wiping one of the tears away. "She was lucky to have a brother like you who looked out for her all the time."

"My mom said it was my fault," he whispered.

If I didn't hate her before, I certainly hated her in that moment. What the hell kind of person wrongly blames a child for the death of his sister like that? It was despicable. "Why?" I asked disbelievingly.

He licked his lips and gulped. "She said that I started the fight, that Sophie got in the middle of something that I started, and that's why she got killed, and that I'd as good as murdered her myself."

My teeth ground together as I fought the urge to go find this woman who I'd never met and smack her in her sorry face for putting Jamie through that guilt. "Jamie, she sat there and let him hurt her yet blames you for killing her? *She's* the one who did wrong! *She's* the one who didn't protect either of her children from a sicko! *She's* the one who deserved to go to jail, not you!" I ranted angrily.

Jamie smiled weakly. "She didn't kill anyone, though; I did."

I didn't know what to say to that. Anger was still surging through my system, making my hands shake as my jaw started to ache where I was clenching my teeth together so tightly. "You went to jail for killing Ralf?" I clarified. Jamie nodded. "But why? If he killed your sister, then surely it was self-defense," I countered, confused.

Jamie laughed humorlessly. "Wasn't self-defense, Ellie. They had to have a closed casket at his funeral, apparently, because of the mess I'd made of him. Brett told me that the only way the coroner could identify him was from his fingerprints because his face and dental records were unrecognizable," he stated casually.

I cringed, thinking about Jamie doing that to another human being, but I didn't think badly of him for it like he was probably expecting. He'd killed a sick person who had probably hurt hundreds of people in his life. I wasn't going to condemn Jamie for taking a sadistic pedophile off the streets, even in that brutal manner.

"But the courts must have known the reasons for you killing him. Didn't you tell them what he used to do to you? What he'd done to Sophie? Surely they could have been lenient on you because of extenuating circumstances," I protested.

He frowned and shrugged. "I didn't tell them anything about Ralf. I actually didn't tell them anything. I was distraught with grief and guilt, and I didn't talk to anyone about it. But the investigation established that he'd abused Sophie and then killed her first, and that I'd killed him after. I pleaded guilty to murder, but I didn't tell them anything else. I didn't want anyone to know. I guess I was ashamed of everything that happened. The judge was lenient because of the circumstances and Sophie being killed, so I didn't get as long as I could have," he explained.

"What about your mom? Didn't she tell them what happened?" Anger leaked into my voice as I mentioned his mother. I'd never hated anyone like I hated her, and I'd never even met the woman.

He smiled sadly and shook his head. "No. She sat there in the courtroom and watched me get sent down for it," he replied. "She came to visit me once when I was waiting to be sentenced. She told me that she hated me for killing Ralf, that I'd made her life unbearable because she loved him and I'd taken him away."

I almost growled with fury when he said that. She was angry with Jamie for killing Ralf, even though her abusive pimp had killed her daughter? That was disgraceful.

"She told me that she had no son. I never saw her again. Well, not until she got involved with the loan shark anyway," he stated, shrugging.

The loan shark. He'd told me that she'd gotten in trouble and that he'd gone back to work for Brett to help her out. "Jamie, why did you help her? Why did you start working for Brett again, just to help her? I...I wouldn't have done that, I would have told her to go screw herself, and I would have left her to it," I admitted. Clearly Jamie was a better person than me; I wouldn't have been able to help someone who let me go through that as a child. Someone who cared more about scoring drugs from her pedophile boyfriend than she did about her children.

He sat back on the sofa and shrugged, looking at me with sad eyes. "She's still my mom," he said simply, as if that explained everything.

Closing my eyes, I shook my head. "You're an incredibly forgiving person."

"She's not forgiven." He snorted. "But I guess maybe I owed her for leaving her on her own. Sophie and Ralf both died, I went to juvie, and she had to deal with all of that alone. She's an addict, Ellie. Addicts just can't control or look after themselves."

Scooting closer to him, I pressed against his side and rested my head on his shoulder. "Jamie, I'm so sorry that you went through all of that. Sophie was a lucky little girl to have you as a brother and have you love her so much. You can't blame yourself for anything, it wasn't your fault," I promised, absentmindedly fingering the bottom of his T-shirt.

He shifted and wrapped his arm around my shoulder, managing to pull me even closer to him as he traced his nose on the side of my face. "Why do you never react the way I think you will? You confuse me so much," he whispered.

I smiled sadly as he ran his fingers through my hair, just looking back at me softly. "Maybe you should stop second-guessing me and just trust me a little more with your secrets."

A smile twitched at the corners of his mouth. "Maybe I should."

My hand unconsciously moved to his stomach, slipping under his T-shirt as my fingers found the biggest scar he had. I'd often wondered how he got it, but now that I knew the reason why he had it, I wasn't sure I was strong enough to hear the finer details of his abuse at the hands of that sicko.

"Do you want to talk about these?" I asked, following the line of the jagged scar that ran across his hip and over most of his stomach.

His jaw tightened as he shook his head fiercely. "No. You don't need to know that; it's in the past, it needs to stay there."

"It's not good for you to bottle it up," I countered, looking at him sympathetically. "Maybe you should talk about it. It might make you feel better."

He shook his head again, his eyes hard and determined as he said, "Ellie, I don't want you to know those things because you'll look at me differently. You won't see *me* anymore; you'll just see the knife wounds, the belt marks, and the burns. I don't want you to view me differently. I love the way you look at me," he whispered, stroking the side of my face with the back of one finger.

My chin trembled as I looked into his pleading eyes. He was silently begging me to let it go and not keep asking. Maybe it was too painful for him to talk about; he couldn't seriously be worried about me looking at him differently, surely. He should know me better by now.

"I love every part of you, and if you want to talk about it, then I'll listen and be here for you," I replied.

His answering smile was beautiful. "I know that, thank you."

We lapsed into silence, just sitting there looking at each other. His eyes told me everything I needed to know; I could practically see the love shining there. His fingers combed through my hair as he pressed his forehead to mine, his breath blowing across my face, making my heart race.

I tilted my head up and softly brushed my lips against his. He made a little moan in the back of his throat as he returned the kiss just as gently, before pulling back and looking at me in awe. My love for him was a little overwhelming as tears prickled in my eyes. He smiled at me, that beautiful smile that made me go weak at the knees, and I couldn't help but smile back.

As his mouth inched toward mine again, everything seemed to fall into place. This boy in my arms was my whole world, my future.

He made love to me there on the couch, but it was unlike anything I'd ever felt before in my life. We'd had sex before, I would swear on the Bible that he'd "made love" to me before, but this, this was so very, very different. It was magical. Every caress and kiss was different, like he was touching my very soul. The whispered words of love seemed to fill the room as the passion built to impossible heights. He literally gave me everything in that moment, everything of himself, all of his love and passion. It was the most breathtaking thing that had ever happened to me, and I'd never felt closer to anyone. It was almost as if, in that moment, we were one person. It made my heart swell and ache in my chest. It was so special that a tear escaped my eyes, and he simply kissed it away as he whispered how much he loved me.

Afterward, he just lay on top of me and pressed his face into the side of my neck, his hands continuing to trace the contours of my body as we both caught our breath. I didn't want to move, didn't want to shatter this moment and take away the magic of what had passed between us. So instead I closed my eyes and held his sweaty body close to mine, letting his safety and protectiveness cover me as I drifted to sleep with a small smile on my face.

* * *

I felt him move, his warm body shifting away from mine, instantly making me feel cold. I was just about to complain when something soft and fluffy was placed over me, tucking up under my chin. I wriggled to get more comfortable and forced my tired eyes open to see him pulling on his jeans, moving stealthily as if trying not to wake me. He'd put a blanket over me, so I snuggled under it.

I smiled to myself as I watched the muscles in his back tense and relax as he moved. When he bent over to grab his T-shirt from the floor, I chewed on my lip as my eyes practically devoured his ass.

"Walk of shame?" I teased.

He jumped, turning and looking at me over his shoulder with a shocked expression. "Sorry, did I wake you? I was trying to be quiet," he apologized.

I smiled and shrugged, rolling onto my side and putting my hand under my head. His sofa wasn't exactly comfortable, especially now that I was on it alone. "S'okay. Where you sneaking off to anyway?" I asked, raking my eyes over his chest before he covered up his hotness with the stupid T-shirt. Clothes really should be outlawed where Jamie was concerned.

He smiled and knelt down next to the sofa. "I have to go do this job. I'll be back before morning, though. Why don't you go get some sleep in the bed and I'll try not to wake you when I get in," he suggested, bending and pressing a soft kiss to my forehead.

"I thought you didn't have to be there until eleven," I countered, pouting because I could spend another couple of hours with him if he didn't leave early.

He smiled, tapping the tip of my nose with one finger. "I don't, sleepyhead, but it's almost ten thirty now."

Ten thirty? Shit! I should have been home hours ago! I gasped, throwing off the blanket and jumping up, almost knocking him on his butt, I moved so quickly. "I'm so late! My mom's gonna kill me!" I cried, panicking as I looked around for where we'd tossed my clothes.

"I take it you're not staying here then," he said, laughing quietly, stooping to pick up my panties, and then swinging them around one finger with a smirk on his face. I went to grab them so I could hurry and get home, but he moved them out of my reach and grinned wickedly as he pushed them into his pocket. "I'm taking those with me, so you'll have to go without. It'll make you think of me, and it'll definitely make me think of you," he teased.

I gasped and felt heat flood my face because that was a little kinky. "You're a pervert," I scolded, laughing as I wriggled my way into my skinny jeans.

He shrugged unashamedly, holding out my shirt to me. "What time were you supposed to be home?"

I winced. "Seven."

He hissed through his teeth, cringing. "Ouch. She's gonna chew your ear off. You sure you don't want to stay here?"

I sighed. I would actually love to stay here—I loved waking up with Jamie wrapped around me—but I couldn't. "I can't. I have to finish packing and spend some time with my family before tomorrow."

He nodded in agreement.

Smiling, I wrapped my arms around him, craning my neck to look up at him as his arms wrapped around me, too. His eyes locked on mine, and I suddenly remembered how hurt he'd looked when I assumed he'd killed his sister. "Jamie, I'm sorry I jumped to the wrong conclusion about Sophie. I shouldn't have even considered the possibility that you would hurt her. I'm so sorry. I wasn't thinking straight," I apologized.

He frowned, a muscle in his jaw twitching. "I wish you hadn't thought that of me, that hurt a lot." His hand traced up my back and cupped the back of my neck gently.

I nodded, wishing I could rewind time so that I hadn't hurt him with my ludicrous assumptions. "I know. I'm sorry."

"Don't worry about it." He dipped his head, kissing me softly for a second. "So, I'll pick you up tomorrow at twelve," he stated, obviously wanting to change the subject.

I smiled, excitement building inside me because there was just one more night. I felt like I was a kid again; I'd been counting down the days since we booked our trip. "So we're really going?" I checked.

He grinned and kissed my forehead. "First stop Rome," he agreed. I couldn't help the little squeal that escaped my lips, and he chuckled as he pushed me away from him gently. "Get out of my place, little girl. I have work to do."

Taking my purse from his outstretched hand, I stepped closer and smiled as he bent and kissed my lips softly, just once. The kiss was so sweet and tender that it made me wish it would never end—but, unfortunately, everything had to end at some point.

I took a deep breath as I turned and walked out the door, trying not to look back because it would make it harder for me to leave for the night if I saw him standing there again. Come tomorrow night, I wouldn't ever have to say good-bye to him for the night again. That thought made my heart squeeze in my chest and a goofy smile stretch across my face as I headed to my car.

By the time I got home my smile had faded because I'd already seen that I had eight missed calls and four text messages, all from my mom asking where I was and if I was okay. I was in some serious trouble. I gulped as I turned off my beloved car and looked up at the house. The downstairs lights were all still on, so I knew my parents were waiting up for me.

I winced as I got out of the car and headed into the house. My mom had obviously heard my car pull up because she was standing in the hallway with her arms folded and an angry look on her face—or maybe she'd just been standing there for three and a half hours waiting to bitch me out; I wouldn't put that past her, to be honest.

I smiled sheepishly. "Hi. Sorry I'm late."

She raised one accusing eyebrow. "Your excuse?"

I knew I couldn't mention Jamie. She already had enough reservations about us going away together, and she'd be even more annoyed if she thought he'd made me late. "I really did mean to be on time, I wanted to spend time with you guys and have our last dinner together, but there were so many people to say good-bye to and I just lost track of time. I'm really sorry, Mom."

"Your dinner's ruined," she stated haughtily.

I nodded, trying to ignore how the smell of the takeout made my stomach ache with hunger. "I figured that. Sorry."

She sighed deeply, her shoulders loosening as her arms unfolded. "I guess I can see if I can salvage anything from it. Maybe the noodles will heat up nicely," she suggested, offering me a small smile.

I grinned. "Yeah? That'd be great, thanks," I chirped. I had no idea what had changed to make her so laid back lately; maybe it was the fact that I wouldn't see her for six months. Whatever it was, I was grateful for the change.

As she rolled her eyes and headed into the kitchen, I peeked into the living room to see my dad sitting on the sofa, watching TV. Kelsey was nowhere in sight, but because of the late hour, she was most likely already in bed. "Hey," I said, walking over and plopping down next to my dad.

"You're in trouble," he whispered, leaning in and flicking his eyes to the hallway. "Mom's maaaaad," he added, drawing out the word for dramatic effect, chuckling quietly.

I cringed and nodded. "Yeah, I know. Sorry."

He smiled and shifted in his seat so I could settle myself against him while my mom banged around in the kitchen. "Have a good night, pumpkin?"

I didn't really know what to say to that. Parts of my night had been fantastic, but some of it had been a nightmare that I would probably relive once I was in bed alone. "Yeah, I guess."

My mom came in then, carrying a plate that had steam swirling up from it. The smell made my mouth water. "Not sure what it'll taste like reheated, but you should have come home on time if you wanted it to taste good," she stated, shrugging.

"Thanks, Mom." I smiled gratefully, already loading my fork with egg fried rice and kung pao chicken. She smiled back tentatively, and I started shoveling in my food like it was my last meal.

I hung out with my parents for a little over half an hour, making small talk about the party and stuff. No one mentioned tomorrow because every time I talked about going away, my mom would go quiet and look in the other direction. I had the distinct impression that she was going to miss me a lot more than I'd first thought she would.

"I guess I'd better go finish packing," I muttered when I couldn't leave it any later. I had everything sorted into piles, but I hadn't even started putting anything into a suitcase yet.

My mom frowned and nodded at the same time. "Want me to help? You know you're not too good at packing."

I smiled at that. I actually sucked at packing and could never manage to fit everything in that I wanted. I was praying that Jamie was better than me because he'd have to sort out my luggage for me in each new place we went to. "Thanks, that'd be great."

I smiled and stood, noticing how my dad winked at my mom and squeezed her hand supportively. She followed me up the stairs and into my room, looking distastefully at the mess that was all over the place. Well, it wasn't really a mess, but my drawers were emptied, and everything I wanted to take was in piles covering the carpet. I smiled sheepishly and pulled out the empty suitcase, setting it on my bed.

"You haven't even started? Ellison, you shouldn't have left this until now!" she scolded, immediately picking up my clothes and stacking them on the bed.

"I guess I was waiting for you to offer your awesome packing skills," I teased, trying to connect with her again. I'd been making a real effort lately, and so had she. It was nice that we'd started to bond; it was just such a shame that it took my leaving to get us to be more than just housemates.

She smiled weakly as she picked up more stuff. "I guess you're lucky I offered then."

I grinned and sat down on the bed, deciding to let her do it all because she was a bit of a control freak anyway and I'd only end up doing it wrong if I tried to help. She smiled sadly to herself as she refolded all of my clothes, setting them in the case carefully along with all the hair stuff and makeup that I was taking. She took so much care with it all, lovingly placing everything in there, seeming to coo over each item of clothing. When I passed her my photo of us all from a family vacation last year, she smiled at me strangely.

"You're taking this with you?"

I nodded. "Of course, can't go forgetting what you look like, can I?" I joked.

She chewed on her lip as she looked at the photo. "You know, I loved this vacation. You taught Kelsey to dive. I was so proud of her for learning to do it, and I was so proud of you for being able to teach her so well," she said quietly, tracing her thumb over the picture carefully.

My breath caught in my throat at her words. She'd just said that she was proud of me. I'd never heard anything like that come out of her mouth before. She was always so prim and proper, not one for affection or declarations of love. It sounded so strange now, and I wasn't sure I'd heard her right.

"Kels is a quick learner," I choked out around the lump that was rapidly forming in my throat.

"And she had an excellent teacher," my mom added, smiling down at me nervously. She looked away quickly, putting the photo inside a T-shirt so that it wouldn't get damaged or creased by anything during the flight. "So, are you excited?" she asked.

I grinned. *Excited* didn't quite cover everything I felt about this trip. "Yeah, I don't think I'm gonna sleep tonight."

"Me either." She looked at me then with teary eyes, but she was fighting the emotion as best she could; she obviously didn't want to show me she was upset. "I'm going to miss you, Ellison. But I know you'll have a great time with Jamie. He's...well, he's good for you. I know I've been down on him a lot in the past, and that's my problem, not yours. But I want you to know that I...I like him. I like how he treats you and how happy you look and how you light up when you're around him," she admitted, nodding. A single tear fell down her face as she spoke and she quickly swiped it away as if she was ashamed of it.

The lump in my throat expanded as I tried to think of something to say to that, but no words were coming to me, so instead I reached out and placed my hand over hers on top of the shirt that she was putting in the case. I squeezed her hand softly. She looked down at our hands, seeming almost confused, before she moved hers slightly and squeezed my fingers back. It was nice. Probably the nicest moment I'd ever had with my mother.

It was over quickly, and she cleared her throat, moving her hand away, obviously uncomfortable with the intimacy. It didn't matter to me that the moment lasted for a mere few seconds. It was already ingrained in my memory, and nothing would make me forget that.

"You're really taking these shorts, Ellison? Look at the state of them," she scoffed, holding up a pair of worn-out denim shorts that I'd loved to death. "No daughter of mine is walking around in shorts with a grass stain on the rear of them."

I grinned. We were back to normal.

As I watched her toss them in the trash in a stunning three-point throw that would have made my dad and Jamie cheer in congratulations, I realized that I was actually going to miss her.

CHAPTER 28

JAMIE

I BREATHED A little sigh of relief and watched Ellie's back as she walked out of my apartment. What had transpired in the last two hours had been terrifying. I felt so vulnerable after reliving my past again. That was the first time I'd ever let any of that stuff out; no one knew most of it, not even my mother. I'd never wanted to talk about it before, I'd always suppressed it, pushed it down and tried to bury it, but right now, after telling all of that to her, I kind of felt like a weight had been lifted off my shoulders.

Ellie was probably the last person who I wanted to know my deepest, darkest secrets, but now that she knew, it was almost like it had brought us closer. The acceptance, the understanding, the support and unconditional love from her just blew my mind. The strength of Ellie's character was something that left me in awe of her. My love for her was terrifying; she literally was the most important thing in the world to me. The only wish I had was that my little sister were alive to meet her, because I know she would have idolized her, too.

When the door closed, leaving me on my own again, I realized that I was going to have to hurry if I didn't want to be late. I headed into my bedroom, zipping up my suitcase, which I'd had packed for almost two weeks. I smiled as I lifted it off the bed and put it by the door so I could grab it easily tomorrow when I had to go pick her up for the airport.

All I'd left unpacked in my apartment was the stuff that had been here when I moved in and a change of clothes for tomorrow. The most important things were sitting on my nightstand. My passport was one of the two "must not forget" items. Ellie had the tickets because she liked to coo over them before she went to sleep, so I didn't have to worry about forgetting those. The other essential item I picked up and rolled around in the palms of my hands: the little black ring box containing the engagement ring that I'd purchased recently. I smiled to myself. It was going to be a complete surprise for her. I'd already slyly asked her father's permission, and thankfully he'd agreed on the condition that we had a fairly long engagement. So, as soon as I found a nice little romantic spot in Rome, I was getting down on one knee. Hopefully she'd say yes. After what had just transpired between us, I was pretty confident that she wouldn't turn me down.

Just for good measure, I checked it for the hundredth time. Opening the box, I looked down at the ring that I'd spent hours choosing. The princess-cut diamond caught the light as I moved it, and I couldn't help but smile as I imagined it glistening like that on her finger instead of in the box. Perfection.

Snapping the box closed, I winced when I realized that she could have seen it earlier and ruined the surprise. I'd just casually suggested that she sleep in here, and the whole time the ring was sitting on the nightstand, plain as day. *What an idiot!*

Instead of putting it back, I pushed the box into my pocket. I liked to carry it around with me; it made me smile every time I bent over or crouched down and the little box dug into my leg— it made me think of her.

I forced myself to stop thinking about her now, though; I seriously needed to get to the warehouse before they all started calling me and panicking, thinking I was going to be late. After grabbing my wallet and jacket, I practically ran out of the apartment and down to my truck.

The fifteen-minute drive seemed to pass in a blur, and before I knew it I pulled up at the warehouse. I didn't want to be working tonight at all. Technically, I should have finished with Brett last week, but the thing I hadn't realized when I'd promised I would go traveling with Ellie—I actually wasn't allowed. I was still on parole. Terms and conditions of my parole meant I couldn't leave the country for another six months. It was something I hadn't even considered when I'd made the suggestion we go fulfill Ellie's traveling dream. Luckily for me, though, Brett had contacts everywhere and had agreed to pull some strings for me with the parole officer—monetary bribes no doubt—but in return I had to commit to this last job before I was allowed to quit for good. Just this last job and then I was free of it all, he'd said. Apparently he had no one else who worked like me, no one he could trust not to screw this up, and he needed his strongest team with him.

Tonight wasn't a boost like I'd told Ellie it was, tonight was something different, and not in a good way.

My hand closed around the door handle and shoved the door of my truck open just as Brett walked out of the warehouse, looking in my direction with a stern expression on his face. I flicked my eyes to the clock on my dashboard. It was one minute past eleven. Technically, I was late.

"About fucking time. Come on, Kid, where have you been?" he snapped.

I smiled sheepishly. I didn't think *"screwing the life out of my girl"* would be very graciously received. "Packing," I lied, shrugging. "I'm here now. Are we going?"

He nodded and most of his guys walked out of the ware-house behind him. I frowned; it appeared we were going in heavy tonight. Brett obviously didn't want to take any risks. Ray waved in acknowledgment but stayed inside. He didn't come to anything like this, he was just a mechanic, not too involved in anything that wasn't car related. I envied him in that respect. The ten or so guys who'd come out started heading to their respective cars in the lot.

"Kid, you're with me," Brett called as I started walking toward Shaun's car.

I sighed but nodded, heading over to his Bentley instead. "Hey, Ed," I greeted the driver. He nodded in response, looking a little nervous. This type of thing, a meeting with a brand-new client, was always a little nerve-racking because you never knew how it was going to go down—hence Brett bringing along all of his heavies.

As I slid into the back of the car with Brett, he smiled at me and ran a hand through his hair. "You have a piece?" he asked suddenly as the car pulled out.

I gulped and shook my head. "No, but I don't want one anyway."

He scoffed and reached under his seat, pulling out a black duffel bag. Dread washed over me as he unzipped it. He pulled open the bag and motioned for me to take one of the guns nestled inside.

"Brett, really, I don't want one," I protested.

He shook his head firmly, his hard eyes telling me that it wasn't actually an offer but an order. "You're coming to the front with me, you need to be armed," he demanded.

The front? Damn it!

I sighed and looked in the bag, seeing about ten guns in there, ranging in size from shotgun to small pistol. Shoving my hand in, I chose one of the smaller ones, a black handgun. I knew how guns worked, I'd been taught how to use one, but I'd never actually fired one at a real person. Usually these were carried just for show, so that people wouldn't think about a double cross. Hopefully this deal would be no different.

Tonight Brett was meeting with the head of a rival syndicate from New Jersey. The Lazlo family had mob connections and was known everywhere across the U.S. In this meeting they were trying to make various deals—drugs and guns, mostly. Brett and the Lazlos had never met up before. Brett was hard-core and well connected, but the guy he was meeting with, Dominic Lazlo, was in a different league entirely. Hopefully they'd be able to come to some sort of deal; if they could, then they would form a partnership of sorts, making Brett part of the largest crime syndicate on this side of the country.

"Why am I coming to the front? Doesn't Ed usually do that?" I inquired. Usually I would just stand at the back and look intimidating, but now it appeared that I would actually be involved in the talks, too.

Brett rolled his eyes as if I'd said something stupid. "I need this guy to be impressed with me. Having my best man there looks good for me. I don't think you understand the high regard you're held in by your peers, Kid."

I frowned, wishing this night were over with already. "But I'm not gonna be here starting tomorrow, so what's the point of me getting involved?"

His face hardened. "Don't mention that in front of Dominic. I haven't told people you're leaving, so as far as tonight goes, you're on my team to stay," he said. "I really want to form this partnership with him. If I do, then my income will practically double overnight. Not only will I have all my usual customers, but I'll have the ones that he can send my way, too. It's a two way street; usually if people come to me for guns I tell them to find someone else, but now I'll pass them on to Dominic, and in return he'll pass the boosts to me. I'll also get the benefit of a reduced-price supplier. He shifts more drugs and gets a bigger territory with people to do all the dirty work for him, and I get a higher profit margin. It's a win-win situation."

I nodded in understanding. It all sounded good and, to be honest, they'd both be crazy not to agree; there were no obvious downsides. "But what about when the orders come flooding in and you have no one to fill them?"

He frowned, sucking his teeth with his tongue. "I'll sort something out. You never know, maybe you'll be done traveling around the world sooner than expected, and you'll want to come back to work. I could make it worth your while. If this deal goes through, then I'll double your nightly boost fee, how about that?" he offered rather hopefully.

I smiled apologetically. He'd tried everything to get me to stay: money, respect, more power within his organization, and threats of violence. But none of it was enough. I wanted out, and after tonight, I was.

"I'd recommend you try and get Vincent on your team," I suggested. That night that I'd worked with him, he'd been an incredible booster. He talked too much for my liking, but I would definitely recommend the guy.

"Who's Vincent?"

"Oh right, I mean Dodger," I corrected myself when I realized that Brett probably didn't even know his real name. "Man, that has to be the worst nickname in the history of bad nicknames." I laughed.

Brett grinned and nodded in agreement. "Yeah, if it comes to it, then I'll talk to him. Maybe Ray could train up another little protégé for me, too," he mused, patting me on the knee. We lapsed into silence and I looked out the tinted windows, watching the streets whiz past in a blur. My eyes were heavy; I could actually do with going to sleep instead of this.

"You know, I'm really sad that you're leaving," Brett stated, seemingly out of nowhere.

I turned back to look at him to see a thoughtful expression on his face. "Yeah, but I never really wanted to do all this in the first place," I muttered.

He nodded. "Your dad would have been proud of you for getting out and starting over like this. He never really liked this life much, either." I looked at him curiously when he mentioned my dad. "He wanted out too, but he wasn't gonna get it. The man he worked for wouldn't have let him go easily."

"No?"

He shook his head. "No, he was too good at what he did; they wouldn't have wanted to lose his talent from their team. You definitely got that from him. I'll be sorry to see you go, and not just for your skills, either." He smiled affectionately. "I'll actually miss you a lot."

I squirmed a little in my seat, uncomfortable with the emotion he was exuding. "I'll miss you too, Brett." That wasn't actually a lie; he was a great guy, and I'd always liked him.

He smiled wistfully, fiddling with the buttons on his suit jacket. "I always thought you'd take over from me one day. I never had kids of my own, so I kind of always thought of you as my kid. If I had to hand my business to anyone, it'd be you."

I laughed nervously. "I'm too good-looking to be your kid," I joked, trying to break the intense mood.

He laughed and rolled his eyes. "And too conceited."

I chuckled. "And too smart."

He raised one eyebrow, still grinning. "Don't push it, I don't like you *that* much." Reaching into his pocket, he pulled out a piece of paper and offered it to me. "I got you a little going-away present."

I took the paper cautiously, wondering what it was going to be. When I opened it up I was confronted by a bank account number and password. "What's this?"

He smiled. "I opened you an offshore bank account to help you get started with your girl. I know you always wanted your own car garage. Well, there's enough in there to help you buy one."

I gasped in shock. "Brett, I can't take that," I protested, holding the paper back out to him.

He shook his head and pushed my hand away. "Kid, just take it. I hope it makes you happy."

"I want to go straight, I don't want to take this and owe you anything," I argued. If I took that money, then he'd always have a hold over me, I'd always be in his debt.

He scoffed. "There's no strings attached. That's yours. Just take it and spend it on whatever you want. I know you want out, and I respect you for that. That's a parting-ways gift, kind of like severance pay."

I opened my mouth to make another protest, but the car pulled up into a workshop parking lot. Immediately my business face snapped on; the deal came first, I could argue with him about the money later. I shoved the paper into the pocket of my jeans, smiling as my fingers brushed over the panties I'd confiscated from Ellie earlier.

Brett sat forward in his seat, telling Ed to turn the car around and park near the door just in case. Glancing out the window, I noted that the other people were already here. There were four expensive-looking cars parked even though it was half past eleven at night. Lights were already shining in the workshop, casting an eerie glow over the parking lot. I spotted a couple of Brett's guys getting out of their cars and heading over toward us. Another car pulled in behind us.

"Gonna put that away?" Brett asked, laughing as he nodded down at my hands.

I looked down curiously only to see that I was still holding the little handgun. Wincing, I nodded, scooting forward in my seat and shoving it down the back of my jeans, covering it with my jacket. Brett exited the car, straightening his jacket as he spoke quietly with a couple of his guys. I climbed out and stood next to him, forcing my harder personality to take over. Now wasn't the time to start thinking about how much I didn't want to be here; this was my last job as Kid Cole, so I might as well make it convincing.

"Mr. Lazlo's already inside, he has about eight men with him," Wesley announced.

Brett nodded. "Then I'll take eight, too. Tell Ed and Enzo to stay outside." He looked at me and motioned toward the workshop. "Let's go make the deal of a lifetime then, Kid."

As we walked into the workshop, I cast my eyes around quickly, taking in my surroundings, sussing out the unfamiliar people. A guy in his midforties sat at a wooden workbench in the middle of the room. His shaven head glistened in the bright light. He stood, smiling warmly at us as we headed in. He was wearing plain jeans and a pale blue Ralph Lauren polo shirt. He wasn't even that tall, maybe about five foot eight, a little stocky. He didn't look particularly intimidating at all, the complete opposite of what I imagined a mob boss to look like.

The guy next to him was obviously his son or family member because they looked exactly the same, just years apart. Seven guys stood behind them, all wearing the same threatening, menacing expression. As we all walked in, I could practically feel the tension in the air, the uncertainty and unease as everyone assessed each other with calculating eyes.

Brett spoke first. "Mr. Lazlo, it's nice to finally meet you," he stated, strutting confidently into the room—which meant that I had to go with him because I was his wingman for the night. Pulling my shoulders back, I kept my eyes trained for any sort of trouble and followed Brett into the lion's den.

* * *

Talking. Boring planning talking. My eyes were stinging from tiredness now, but I couldn't rub them like I wanted; instead, I sat straight, keeping my face in a neutral position as Brett and Dominic argued over territories and percentages of profits. I was at the bench next to Brett. Dominic and his son were sitting opposite us as they discussed things that seemed to have taken hours already. I'd had to chime in a few times about boosting, telling them how many cars it was possible to take in one night, how many staff would be needed, and things like that. Other than that I just had to sit there and look confident. In reality, the most prominent thing on my mind was the gun that was digging into the small of my back to the point of cutting into my skin. I desperately wanted to reach behind me and pull it out, but I didn't dare touch it in case the seven guys who'd come with Dominic thought I was trying something. They were already watching everyone intently, fingers twitching, as if waiting for one of us to make a move. Clearly there was going to be no trust in this partnership.

Finally things seemed to be wrapping up. Brett and Dominic were both smiling as everything was being ironed out. The more I listened, the more I realized just how good this deal was for Brett. He'd be turning over a hell of a lot more money from now on.

Brett slapped me on the back, grinning. "That's great then. I think this'll all work out exceptionally well and will prove to be a lucrative partnership," he concluded.

Dominic smiled, nodding in agreement. "Absolutely, this has been a good meeting." He turned to one of his guys and nodded. "The sampler?" The guy immediately stepped forward, setting a black leather briefcase on the workbench in front of Dominic and popping the catch. Dominic smiled and lifted the lid, turning the case to face us. My insides squirmed with unease because I'd never seen so much cocaine all in one place.

Brett smiled, leaning forward with a glint in his eye. "Excellent. You mind if I try it?" he asked, pulling out a little switchblade from his pocket. Dominic waved his hand and shrugged, obviously giving the go-ahead. I watched as Brett picked up one of the parcels, making a little cut in the side of the rectangular packet. He dug his finger in there to get a small amount and then rubbed it on his gums, nodding appreciatively. "It's definitely good quality," he confirmed. He nodded to Shaun, who was hovering behind us, and Shaun stepped forward with a black duffel bag, handing it to Brett.

I was mentally counting down the minutes now. This was almost over; once he paid there would just be some pleasantries, and then I could finally go home and flop into bed. I glanced at my watch; it was almost two in the morning. We'd been here for so long that my ass was starting to get numb.

Brett handed over the duffel bag. I didn't need to ask to know that it would be full of cash to pay for the drugs. Damien, Dominic's son, looked in the bag, rummaging through it before he nodded to his dad and they both stood up. "Well, it was good doing business with you. I'll pass your details on to the relevant people, so things should get moving quickly with the cars and stuff. That kind of thing is always in high demand. Let me know when you want more," Dominic stated, nodding at the briefcase as Brett snapped it shut and stood, too.

I pushed myself to my feet and extended my arm, shaking hands with them, glad it was finally over.

Suddenly an enormous bang sounded to my left, causing dust and splinters of wood and plaster to fly across the room. I jumped, instinctively ducking and protecting my head as a ruckus started and numerous pairs of feet thundered into the workshop. My eyes darted in that direction and I saw people dressed in black running into the warehouse, guns raised.

I barely had time to wonder what was going on before one of them shouted, "Police, you're under arrest!"

Panic made me freeze on the spot. I watched with wide eyes as more and more of them burst into the room from all sides. I groaned in defeat, knowing that everything was ruined. I was totally screwed.

That was when the gunshots started.

CHAPTER 29

BANGS ECHOED OFF the walls, almost deafening me as a gun went off near me. I crouched down quickly, ducking behind the workbench unsure what to do. I watched with wide eyes as the people from Lazlo's organization instigated a full-on firefight with the police.

"Fuck!" I hissed. I guess I'd never get a happy ending.

Everyone was shouting, gunshots were blasting, people were scuffling and fighting around me. I could barely move.

Brett ran past and took cover behind a huge metal tool cabinet. He had his gun drawn as he looked around the corner of the cabinet, sending off a couple of shots in the direction of the police.

I knew I was supposed to help, and usually if there was trouble I would be there instantly, not hesitating to get involved. This was different, though; those weren't thugs or bad people who I could beat the crap out of, those were cops. There was no way I was drawing my gun and firing on innocent police officers. I was a booster who did a few bad things, but shooting a gun at someone? Not a chance of that happening.

My wild eyes flicked over to the right. Shaun was crouched a little way away, hiding behind a smaller desk that he'd flipped onto its side. He looked terrified. He had his gun drawn too, but he wasn't firing; his hands were shaking as he looked over and caught my gaze. He nodded at his gun, but I quickly shook my head, telling him not to get involved. The Lazlos had started this; there was no way they were going to win even with our help. The police were wearing body armor; their trained eyes were making short work of the people who were fighting against them. The Lazlos were dropping like flies. I could already see Damien down on the floor; blood seeping from a wound in his neck. Dominic was kneeling over him, his face contorted in rage and grief. He let out a gut-wrenching primal scream and fired randomly at anyone who moved.

Everything seemed to be happening in slow motion; the shots were so loud that each one made me flinch as I stayed behind the desk. I debated making a run for it. There was a door off to the side. While everyone was distracted I could dash for the door and try to get the hell out of here, but I knew there was probably no chance of me making it; a bullet would get me as soon as I moved away from the desk.

Suddenly Dominic jerked, his hand flailing as he fell backward awkwardly. I gulped and watched as blood slowly trickled out of a hole on the side of his head. The smells of blood and urine filled the air as he lost control of his bodily functions. I gagged, pressing my hand over my mouth. Things were calming down now; the shots were only coming from one place.

Brett.

A couple more shots sounded, but then everything went quiet, so quiet that if it weren't for the shrill ringing that sounded from my eardrums, I would have thought I'd gone deaf. I breathed a sigh of relief that he'd conceded. Hopefully his lawyer would fix this somehow; I had no idea how, but hopefully he could make some sort of deal. I kept that in mind as I heard the sound of shuffling feet behind me.

"Show me your hands!" a voice demanded. Gulping, I instantly put my hands up, making sure they were visible over the top of the desk so that the cops could see that I wasn't a threat. Shaun did the same thing, sliding his gun out across the floor to show that he was unarmed. From the corner of my eye, I saw a couple of other people put their hands up, too—three more from Brett's team, and one I recognized as one of Dominic's goons.

"Keep them where I can see them. If you move even an inch I won't hesitate to shoot!" the cop growled.

I closed my eyes, hating this whole situation. I was in so much trouble; there was no way out of this at all. My mind flicked to Ellie as disappointment washed over me because everything we'd planned would be ruined. There was not a chance we were getting to go away tomorrow now. I'd ruined everything.

A guy in full uniform stepped tentatively around the corner, his gun pointed at me. "On your stomach! Put your hands on the back of your head," he ordered as I saw someone advance toward Shaun, instructing the same thing.

I nodded quickly, lowering myself down onto the dusty floor, my hands linking together on the back of my head. A weight suddenly pressed between my shoulder blades. I winced, groaning as the guy kneeled on my back, almost crushing my ribs. The gun was pulled from the back of my jeans as I struggled to breathe. "Do you have any other weapons?"

I tried to shake my head, but it was impossible where I was pinned to the floor. "No," I croaked.

Something snapped around my right wrist, and the click of the handcuffs made my heart hurt. I closed my eyes and silently cursed everything and everyone. When my hands were pulled behind my back, my other hand was cuffed too, and I was hoisted to my feet.

As the guy patted down my body, checking for weapons, I looked in Brett's direction, watching as a cop went over there. I saw him crouch down, I assumed to put the cuffs on Brett, but a few seconds later the cop stood back up and stepped out from behind the cabinet alone.

I frowned, confused until he shook his head. "This one's dead."

"What? No!" I cried, shocked. I immediately thrashed, catching the cop by surprise, causing his grip to loosen. I threw off his hold and my feet moved of their own accord, running six or so steps forward so I could see for myself if the guy I'd always had a fatherly respect for was dead.

As I took the last step, I saw it was the truth. He lay facedown, a pool of blood seeping out under him; his eyes, which were so familiar to me, were wide and vacant. Grief washed over me. My mouth dropped open in shock as a strangled gargle sounded in the back of my throat. Dead? Brett was dead? It hit me harder than I ever would have thought it would. My chest tightened and my hands clenched into fists as I stared at him in disbelief.

I barely had time to react before three guys crashed into me from behind, slamming me into the wall harshly. Air rushed out of my lungs quickly as they pinned me there heavily, securing me. A gun pressed into the back of my neck with bruising force as I felt the last of my hope run out of my system. I closed my eyes as one of them gave me the little speech about my rights. I'd heard it all before.

CHAPTER 30

NUMB. THAT WAS the only way to describe how I felt, like I was slipping into shock or something. I could still hear a faint ringing in my ears, and I had a feeling I'd be hearing it for a long time to come. I gulped, picturing Brett as he lay so still, a pool of blood rapidly growing under his lifeless body, staining the concrete floor. My mind was whirling, but no specific thoughts were forming; something would start to formulate and then immediately my brain would skip to something else. Thoughts of Brett, jail, blood, steel bars, and other horrifying things appeared every time I closed my eyes. The one thought that was the most prominent was of the little redhead cheerleader who I was totally in love with, and how disappointed she was going to be in me. How was I even going to begin to explain this to her?

A cop took hold of my arm and pulled me from the van that I was sitting in. I frowned and looked up at the police station. An ominous feeling settled over me as I realized that there was a good chance I wouldn't get out of here, but instead go straight back to jail. I was still on parole for Ralf's murder; technically, I could be thrown back in jail immediately for another six months, as that's how long the remainder of my sentence was before I was let out for good behavior.

My whole life had just been flushed down the toilet in one night. One night had ruined everything for me, and I would have to deal with that forever. The guy holding my arm started walking so I let him lead me along toward the blue back door of the station. As we walked in, I kept my eyes straight ahead as we approached the check-in desk, where a bored-looking cop was waiting to book us all in to our holding cells. The other boys all filed in behind me and were handcuffed to the benches along the sides to wait for their turn to be processed. Six of us were arrested tonight, three had been injured and taken to the hospital with armed guards, and nine people, including Brett, had been killed at the scene.

The cop at the desk flipped open a pad, pulling the cap off his pen. "Please state your name for the record."

"Jamie Cole," I muttered, frowning. I tuned out as the guy who was holding me rattled off my charges and the desk clerk scribbled in his pad.

"So, do you have a lawyer, Jamie Cole, or would you like us to provide you with one?" he asked, looking at me curiously.

I sighed. "I don't have one."

He nodded, ticking a box on a form before looking up at the guy behind me. "Right, let's get his pockets emptied."

I groaned, closing my eyes when I thought about what was in there. The cop behind me shoved me roughly so that I slammed against the desk. One of his shoulders pressed against my back, pinning me there while he pulled at my wrist, unclasping my watch, before shoving his hands in my pockets one at a time, dumping the contents on the desk for the clerk to process.

"One silver watch. One black leather wallet containing"—the

desk clerk flipped it open, looking in it curiously—"forty-seven bucks." He threw it into a clear plastic bag and scribbled in the pad before picking up the next item. "One set of keys. One cell phone. One piece of paper containing what looks like a bank account number. We'd better get that checked out." The other cop emptied my last pocket and laughed. I chewed on the inside of my cheek so hard that the metallic taste of blood filled my mouth. The other cop laughed too as he picked the contents up, smirking at me. "One blue lace thong. I'm thinking you have a slutty girlfriend," he teased.

"She's not a slut!" I snapped. I threw my shoulder back harshly, making the guy tighten his hold on me as I struggled against him. I wanted to grab the panties and shove them back in my pocket to protect Ellie's modesty, but with my hands tied behind my back, all I managed to achieve was a pain in my chest where the guy slammed me against the desk again.

The desk clerk smiled teasingly as he toyed with the panties before putting them in the bag, too. I was battling against my anger; my jaw was aching, I clenched it so tightly. He picked up the last item—the black ring box. "Wow, nice. Is this a real diamond?" he asked as he lifted the lid.

I nodded, not wanting to speak more than necessary.

He raised an eyebrow. "My wife would love me forever if I gave her that," he muttered, showing it to the cop who was holding me. Anger flared even more as he whistled appreciatively.

"Maybe you should buy her one then," I growled. "Put it in the fucking bag because I'm gonna need that when I get out of this shithole!"

The desk clerk laughed and snapped the box closed, tossing it carelessly into the bag. "One silver diamond ring," he announced, scribbling on the pad again.

"It's white gold," I corrected, glaring at him. I had a strong feeling that the ring wouldn't be in the bag by the time I got out of here and had to sign for my belongings.

The guy shrugged, not bothering to change the form as he shoved it toward me. "Sign here," he instructed. There was a fumbling at my back, and the cuffs sprang off my wrists. I grabbed the pen and wrote my name on the bottom before crossing out the word *silver* in the description and changing it to *white gold*. The desk clerk growled in frustration and ripped the pad and pen from my hand. "Take him to three," he ordered.

The cop behind me grabbed my arm, tugging me forward. My eyes flicked to the line of guys waiting for processing. Shaun's defeated gaze met mine. He smiled sadly, as if he already knew that he was going back inside, too. I allowed the cop to lead me along and shove me into a small holding cell. As the door slammed closed behind me, I closed my eyes, not needing to look at my surroundings to know that the room would be painted gray, with just a bed jutting out of the wall and a blue mattress on it. I already knew this place too well from when I was kept in it before.

I walked the couple of steps to the wall and leaned against it before slumping down and pulling my knees up to my chest. All I could think about was Ellie and how much she was going to hate me for screwing everything up. It was probably about four in the morning now, and I was supposed to pick her up in less than eight hours so that we could go to the airport and start our new lives. Instead, everything had changed because of one stupid night. Even though he was dead, the resentment started to build against Brett because I wasn't even supposed to be there tonight; if he hadn't forced me, then I wouldn't be in this situation now, facing jail and a life without the girl I loved. But I couldn't hate him, though; I actually really liked the guy, and although he'd done bad things in his life, he deserved better than to die in a dusty old workshop. I was truly going to miss him.

* * *

A click of the door lock made me look up and stop fiddling with the zipper of my hoodie. I'd been here forever already; it felt like hours that I'd been pacing around the room like a caged animal. The gray walls of the eight-foot cell were driving me crazy as I struggled to remain composed and not smash everything up in frustration.

The door opened to reveal a cop I hadn't seen before. "Jamie Cole, your turn for questioning," he uttered, motioning with his hand for me to walk out.

I sighed with relief that I would get to step outside the cell and see something other than the gray walls. I even welcomed the questioning because that would give me something else to think about. "What time is it?" I questioned.

"Just before six," he replied as I walked to his side. *Wow, have I seriously only been here for two hours?* It felt like an eternity since my life fell to pieces. His hand clamped on my arm tightly. "Am I going to have to put cuffs on you, or are you going to behave?"

I smiled weakly. "I'll behave." I'd always respected authority. I'd done wrong, I'd been caught, that was all there was to it, really. These guys were just doing their jobs. He nodded, looking a little weary as he guided me out of the cell and down the narrow hallway. I could hear people shouting inside the other holding cells as we passed them.

My surroundings didn't really register as we weaved through the station. Finally we got to a wooden door with a strip stuck on it labeled INTERROGATION ROOM 6. The cop opened it and motioned for me to go in.

Inside the room was a table with four chairs around it, a tape recording system, and nothing else. My eyes landed on the wall of what appeared to be mirrored glass. The cop I was with pointed to one of the chairs, instructing me to sit and saying that my appointed lawyer would be here shortly. I slumped down into the chair, unable to resist sending a little wave in the direction of the glass wall, knowing there would probably be people in there watching me.

The door opened seconds later, and a young, scrawny-looking guy in a cheap crinkled suit came in, shuffling papers as he walked, dropping most of them on the floor. I sighed. Defense attorneys really were a pile of shit, and this guy was my only chance out of here? I was screwed already.

"Mr. Cole, I'm Darren Sanders, your court-appointed attorney. I'll be representing you," he said as he bumbled his way into the room, extending his hand toward me.

I nodded, shaking his hand. "Great. This should be an open-and-shut case then. I imagine I'll be home in time for breakfast," I replied sarcastically.

He frowned, pushing his glasses up his beaky nose. "I don't think so. You have a lot of charges against you; I think the breakfast target is overly optimistic," he replied, obviously not getting my humor.

I blew out a big breath and sat back in my chair, closing my eyes. "Right, I'll let my hopes fall back down then. For a second I was confident that you'd get me off on all charges, and I would be free to go on my merry way."

The chair scraped next to me, and more papers shuffled. "Let's get started going through everything. We only have half an hour before they come in to start their questioning. I need you to tell me in your own words what happened tonight."

I sighed, deciding what I could let this guy in on and what I would keep back. Usually in this situation I would just answer everything with "no comment" so that I didn't drop anyone else in anything, but to be honest, with Brett dead there was no one to really protect anymore. Everyone would be facing the same charges as me, and we were all going down for it.

I opened my mouth to speak, but a knock at the door interrupted us. A cop poked his head in, smiling apologetically. "Mr. Sanders, sorry to interrupt, but Mr. Cole's private appointed attorney has just arrived to take over the case."

My appointed attorney? I didn't have an appointed attorney, which was why I was stuck with this little imbecile.

"Oh, really? I was called to represent Mr. Cole. Why was I called if he already had representation?" my guy asked, standing up and looking confused and more than a little put out.

The cop shrugged. "We weren't aware that he had one. Mr. Barrington has just arrived at the station and is demanding counsel with his client."

Mr. Barrington? As in Brett's attorney, the hardass? My heart leaped into my throat. Maybe there was a chance I'd be home in time for breakfast after all.

The guy who had just settled himself down at my table started grumbling under his breath about time wasters and overpriced hotshot attorneys thinking they were above everyone else. He picked up his papers and marched out of the room without so much as even looking at me again. As he stepped out, in stepped a guy I'd never met. His black suit looked tailored and expensive. His blond hair was styled perfectly, even though he'd probably been woken up to come down here this morning. He stood with a confidence and self-assuredness that came only from knowing you were better than everyone else around you.

He turned back to the police officer who had interrupted. "I expect that"—he waved his hand to the mirrored wall—"to be empty. Ensure you turn on the light in there so I can be confident that my private meeting with my client isn't being viewed," he instructed.

The cop frowned, not looking too impressed. "Absolutely," he agreed, his voice harsh and annoyed. He stepped out of the room, leaving us on our own. I stood and opened my mouth to speak, but Mr. Barrington held up one hand, signaling for me to wait. Seconds later the mirrored glass disappeared, and you could see through it like a window as someone switched on the light in there. An empty room was on the other side, chairs and recording equipment set up pointing in here. Mr. Barrington peered inside curiously before turning back to me and smiling sadly.

"I expect that you're confused as to why I'm here for you," he said, walking around the table and sitting down.

I nodded in confirmation, noticing that he wasn't fumbling with papers like the previous guy. "Yeah, I didn't call you."

He nodded. "I've heard a lot about you. Brett and I were old friends, he'd spoken of you a few times over the years. It's nice to finally meet you," he stated. I frowned, unsure what to say. Did he know that Brett had died tonight? As if sensing my question, he answered it. "I got a call from a good friend in the police department informing me that Brett had been killed. Naturally I asked about the situation, and as soon as they mentioned your name I rushed down here. Brett told me that I should look after you if you ever needed me, so here I am."

I gulped. "Oh" was all I could manage.

He smiled sadly. "I know you and Brett had a good relationship; he thought a great deal of you. He'd be saddened to know you were here right now. I understood from him that you were getting out of this life, and leaving to do some traveling. With my son's ex-girlfriend, no less." He leaned forward in his seat and clasped his hands together tightly.

I nodded. "Yeah, we're supposed to go today. I don't suppose you can wave a magic wand over all of this and get me out of here so I can still do that?" Even if he could just get me out of police custody, maybe I could try to leave the country or something if they let me out "pending investigation." Well, if they didn't seize my passport.

He frowned and shook his head. "I wish I could, Jamie. I promised Brett that I'd always do my best for you, and I will, but this isn't something that will just blow over." He sighed and reached down, grabbing a leather briefcase, setting it on the desk, popping the latch, and opening it. He pulled out a case file and thumbed through it. "They've been watching Brett for a while because one of his staff got involved in a GTA, we knew that, but I had it from reliable sources that they weren't making any moves on Brett at this time. It appears where I wasn't informed was that there was a sting operation following the Lazlos tonight, and it just so happened that it involved Brett. I think the police were very happy to have stumbled upon him in that meeting, meaning that they took down two birds with one stone, so to speak."

I snorted. So this all came about because the police were trying to arrest the Lazlos and we were all just in the way? A lucky convenience to take down a local organization at the same time? *Well, aren't their superiors going to be happy with them*, I thought sarcastically. "Well, aren't they all lucky," I said with a snort.

He smiled bitterly. "Quite," he agreed. "So, I've been speaking to the officer in charge of the raid tonight; between you and me, he's an old golfing buddy of mine, so I'm privy to a lot of things that I shouldn't be," he continued.

"Okay, and that means what?" I asked, trying to stay positive, but his slumped shoulders told me that this wasn't good news.

"Well, they had hidden recording equipment at the meeting tonight. As far as your charges are concerned, they have you on tape talking about and planning auto thefts, being present and part of a drug deal, possession of a firearm, and resisting arrest. Now, you don't need to worry about the car stuff too much, that's all circumstantial; you mention no details about previous jobs, and you don't brag about jobs undertaken in the past or mention conquests. The talk is just that, talk, so they can't charge you with that," he said confidently. "However, now that they know you're into that kind of thing, they'll start looking into other unsolved car crimes more closely to try and link them to you."

I groaned. *So because I mentioned stealing cars, they're now going to try to pin all unsolved car thefts on me? Great, just fucking great!* "So, aside from them now investigating car stuff and me, I'm actually facing drug charges, possession of a firearm, and resisting arrest?" I asked, wincing.

He nodded. "At this time, yes."

"So I'm screwed! I'm already on parole."

He reached over and patted my shoulder. "I'm going to do everything I can for you. I'm pretty confident that if I pull a few strings, make a couple of deals, I can get the drug charges dropped."

"Really?" If he could, that would significantly reduce the amount of shit I was in—well, until they linked me to the millions of dollars' worth of cars that I'd boosted!

He nodded. "As for the firearm," he stated. "You had that on you at the time of arrest?" I nodded in confirmation. "You had your weapon drawn?"

I shook my head quickly. "No, I didn't draw it the whole time. It was tucked down the back of my pants."

He raised one eyebrow, looking extremely pleased. "So you didn't take part in the gun battle?"

"No."

He smiled. "Ballistics reports will be able to confirm that you didn't fire upon the police. Resisting arrest should be easy enough to dismiss, too. But there's only so much I can do. I'm going to have to give them something in return."

"Meaning what?" I asked, confused.

A frown creased his forehead. "Well, if they start trying to link you to unsolved GTAs, then things are going to get a lot worse for you. Now that they have you on record admitting it, the slightest piece of evidence surrounding the theft of a car will be linked to you and charges will be filed. So what I'm proposing is a deal," he explained. I nodded for him to continue, eager to hear what I was hoping would be some kind of mastermind plan. "You plead guilty to illegal possession of a firearm, you tell them where you got it from, and in exchange, I'll pull some strings that will make the car investigation disappear into thin air."

I licked my dry lips, thinking about it. Either way I was screwed. I was going down for something, so I guess it was better to plead guilty to possession of a firearm than to go down for hundreds of counts of grand theft auto as well. "So what will that mean?"

He sighed. "Usually, twenty-four to thirty-six months in prison."

My body jerked at his words as my chest tightened and I struggled to breathe properly. "Oh shit," I mumbled.

He nodded sadly. "Plus your time that you were let out on good behavior," he added. "I should be able to get that all reduced, but you'll serve a minimum of a year, maybe eighteen months. But the alternative is being linked to hundreds of car thefts. I think you're getting off pretty lightly with that."

Ellie. What the hell am I supposed to tell Ellie? The thought of going inside again was terrifying. I would have no idea what to expect, considering that it'd be prison this time, not juvie like last time. Plus I would have to cope with not seeing her every day.

"A year, minimum," I repeated, trying to get my head around it. Three hundred and sixty-five days without holding her in my arms or kissing her good night. This was going to kill me.

He nodded, closing his file. "I think it's the best I can do. I'm sorry I can't do more, but I can get all the other charges dropped, I'm sure of it. Unfortunately, though, you'll have to take the consequences of that one in order for me to give them something in exchange."

I gulped and nodded in agreement, knowing that I wasn't going to get a better deal than that. I was getting off lightly here, one year as opposed to about ten. I had to take it.

"Okay," I agreed.

He smiled and pushed himself to his feet. "I'm going to go and speak to my friend and negotiate the other stuff away. You need anything?"

I need to rewind time back to when I was cuddling with a naked Ellie on the sofa. "Think maybe I could get my phone call now? I need to speak to Ellie and tell her that it looks like I won't be able to take her traveling for a while."

He nodded, reaching into his pocket and pulling out a cell phone. "Here, use this, no one will know. The number's blocked on there anyway." He tossed the expensive-looking phone at me, and I caught it just in time.

"Thanks," I muttered, dreading making this call. "Can I make two calls?"

"So long as the other one isn't to do anything illegal," he joked, winking at me.

I half laughed despite the horror that was settling over me. "No, I just want to call a friend of mine, too. He'll need to know what happened to Brett tonight." I sighed and closed my eyes, imagining Ellie's reaction to this news. "Ellie's gonna hate me."

He smiled sympathetically. "Ellie's a good girl; if she loves you, then she'll wait for you to get out." He turned and walked out the door, closing it behind him, leaving me in silence.

I knew his words were right, I knew she would wait for me. There was no doubt in my mind that Ellie would play the dutiful little girlfriend, waiting patiently for my release, visiting me every week, sending me letters sprayed with her perfume. I knew, without question, that she would still love me when I dropped this bombshell on her. Ellie was special; she deserved to be treated like a princess, not wrapped up in this scandal with a convict. She deserved better than this, much better than a loser, jailbird boyfriend.

This phone call was going to be the most painful call I'd ever make in my life, but I couldn't allow myself to think about my needs now. I couldn't be selfish, not when it came to her. This needed to be done, no matter how hard it was.

CHAPTER 31

ELLIE

AN ANNOYING, SHRILL sound was blaring near my head, making my ears ring as it dragged me into consciousness. I groaned, rolling over and stretching my hand out for my cell phone, which was vibrating on the nightstand. As my hand closed over it, I blinked my heavy eyes and looked at the clock: 6:23 a.m. A glance at the caller ID showed the words PRIVATE NUMBER.

I debated rejecting the call. If I didn't know the person, then chances were that it was a wrong number or something anyway. My head felt fuzzy, and my eyes stung because I'd fallen asleep only a couple of hours ago due to my overexcitement about today. Unwillingly, I answered it and yawned at the same time.

"Hello?" I mumbled, settling back into the bed.

"Hey, Ellie."

A smile crept onto my lips at the sound of his voice. "Hey, you," I cooed. "Do you know what time it is? Can you not sleep, either?" I chewed on my lip and sighed dreamily.

Jamie cleared his throat. "Sorry I called so early, I just—I need to speak to you." His voice sounded a little off, a little tight, but I dismissed it, thinking that he was just tired or something. Maybe he'd only just gotten home from his boost and hadn't actually been to sleep yet.

"Okay, what's up?" I rolled onto my stomach, propping myself up on my elbows. There was silence on the other end of the phone. "Jamie? Is everything okay?"

"Not really," he answered. I gulped, switching on my bedside light, immediately starting to worry that he was sick or hurt. "Ellie, I can't... I'm not coming with you today."

"Huh?" *He isn't coming, what the heck is he talking about?*

He blew out a big breath, making it whistle down the line. "I've been thinking about it all night, and I've decided that it's not the right thing for me. I thought I could do it, I thought I could give up everything for you, but I can't. I'm sorry."

His words just weren't making sense to me. I frowned, trying to work out what he was talking about. "You...don't...Jamie, what?" I stuttered, confused.

"I was thinking about what happened between us last night, when you came over and accused me of killing Sophie."

A wave of guilt washed over me again because I really shouldn't have entertained that thought for a second. I'd obviously hurt him by thinking that of him, he'd already admitted that to me last night. "I'm sorry about that," I whispered, wincing.

He sighed. "I couldn't stop thinking about it, and then it suddenly hit me: I can't be with someone who doubts me like that."

Can't be with someone... My body stiffened as I started to understand what he was saying, but my brain refused to accept it. "What are you talking about?"

"Ellie, look, this was fun, I had a great time with you. I really thought we were good together, but traveling with you would mean that I'd have to give up everything here: my friends, my work, my home. I thought I was okay doing that, I thought it would be fine, but after last night, I've realized that it's not what I should be doing." His words felt like he'd shoved a knife into my gut and was slowly twisting it.

"So you don't want to go?" I asked, needing clarification. I knew he was giving up a lot for me, which was why I had been so shocked when he suggested it in the first place. It was *my* dream, not his, yet he was changing his whole life just to do something that I wanted.

"No."

I nodded. The disappointment hit me hard. I'd been so excited for weeks, and now we weren't going to go, but I understood what he was saying; it wasn't fair of me to have expected that he do this in the first place. "Okay. I understand. We won't go then. I don't think we can get a refund on the tickets for today, but at least we hadn't booked too many nights in hotels and stuff. It's fine," I agreed. I laughed humorlessly. "I think my parents will be a little relieved, actually," I added, thinking of my mom's sad expression earlier.

"You're taking this really well," he observed. His voice shook as he spoke, almost like he was disappointed that I wasn't freaking out or something.

I shrugged, trying not to let my disappointment sound in my voice. "It's okay, I understand. Are you coming over today? Maybe you could help me break the news to my parents," I suggested, closing my eyes and praying he wasn't going to say what my heart already knew he was going to say.

"Ellie, are you not understanding what I'm saying?" he asked incredulously.

"Don't," I whispered. My eyes prickled with tears as I focused on the ceiling, trying not to let them fall.

"I'm sorry, okay? It's just not working for me. After last night I know how you really see me, and I can't be with someone who thinks that of me," he stated nonchalantly.

Oh God. "Jamie, it was just a spur-of-the-moment mistake; I jumped to the wrong conclusion, and I shouldn't have. I'm sorry, but please don't throw us away because of that, please," I begged desperately.

"You threw us away the second you thought I could hurt my little sister," he shot back harshly.

"I'm sorry, I'm really sorry. Please forgive me. We'll work through it, we can do that, I know we can. We'll stay here and just work through it, please?" I closed my eyes and prayed for a second chance. Part of me knew, deep down, that this was the end because he sounded so final and detached. He wasn't listening to my pleas at all. It was probably about time that he realized he could do better than me anyway.

"After you left last night, everything just kept playing over and over in my head. I love you, Ellie, I do, but it's just not enough, not after what you thought of me. After the boost I went to a bar with some of the boys...I met a girl there."

His words were like a kick in the stomach.

A girl? I whimpered as my mind filled in the blanks.

"I realized as I was talking to her that you and I just aren't going anywhere. I realized that I couldn't give up everything for you because we just aren't right together, not really," he continued. "You obviously don't know me at all if you could doubt me like that, and I thought I knew you better, too. That's all there is to it."

"That's all there is to it?" I repeated incredulously.

"Yeah, so I guess that's it. You take care, okay?" he said dismissively.

My mouth dropped open in shock because this was all happening so fast. I hadn't seen this coming; it was all so quick and out of the blue. One minute we were planning our lives together, and the next he was telling me it was over? My heart and head just couldn't process it all.

"Jamie, what the hell? That's it? Are you kidding me?" I asked disbelievingly.

There were two agonizing seconds of silence before he figuratively reached into my chest and ripped out my still beating heart with his words. "I slept with the girl last night. It made me realize that I'm not ready to settle down, especially not with someone who doubts me."

My whole body tightened as hurt radiated through my system. But part of me refused to believe it. Jamie was an incredible person, so sweet and thoughtful; he wouldn't have cheated, would he? "No you didn't. You wouldn't do that, you love me. You didn't cheat, you're just trying to hurt me," I whispered, silently praying that I was right.

"I'm a guy, Ellie; guys cheat. It's what we're good at," he shot back.

Each word was like the sharp stab of a knife. Tears pooled in my eyes, making my vision slightly blurry. "Jamie, no," I whispered. My heart was aching, and my chest tightened painfully as my stomach started to tremble because of his rejection.

"Yeah, Ellie. I'm sorry, but I don't love you enough to give up my life for you. I thought I did, but last night and you doubting me just made me think about our relationship. It's not working, and I was fooling myself to think that it was. It's over."

My blood seemed to turn to ice in my veins at the finality of his tone. I didn't know what to say. I opened my mouth to speak, but all that came out was a strangled sob. The two words were playing on repeat in my head: *It's over*. I didn't want that, I couldn't lose him. I was totally crazy about him. I saw him in my future. Actually, I saw him *as* my future.

"Can't we talk about it?" I begged. "We won't go traveling; we'll stay here and work it out if you don't want to give up your life. I can understand that; just don't say it's over, please?"

"Have some self-respect. Christ! I've just told you that I fucked someone else last night. I've just climbed out of her bed, and you want to work things out?" he hissed angrily.

His words made me flinch. I knew I was being stupid, right now I was behaving like a doormat, but I loved him and I wanted to work it out with him. The way I felt when I was with him made me want to forgive him for his indiscretion. He was right, I probably wasn't enough for him, but I could try to be. And the fact that he'd slept with another girl just didn't ring true. He wasn't the type of person to do that.

"I don't believe you cheated," I stated, shaking my head. "I love you," I mumbled, swiping at the tears that were endlessly falling down my face. "I'm...I'm coming over and we can talk, okay?" I swung my legs over the edge of the bed, immediately looking for something I could throw on to go talk to him. I needed to look into his eyes, I needed to hold his hand, smell his smell. I just plain old needed him right now, and I couldn't do this over the phone, I couldn't beg through a piece of plastic. I needed to see him in person and show him how much I loved him.

"Don't bother, I'm not there," he grunted.

I whimpered and closed my eyes, trying not to think about it as a wave of nausea rolled over me. "Jamie, I'm sorry I doubted you last night. I'm so sorry about what I thought. I shouldn't have done that, I should have known better. I promise I'll never doubt you again, never," I vowed. My legs wobbled so I sat down on the edge of the bed as my breathing hitched with a sob.

"Ellie—" The way he said my name, so soft and tender, just like he used to say it, made my insides churn. "We wouldn't have worked anyway, we're so different, things would have fallen apart eventually. We're not right for each other at all."

"Yes we are!" I protested. "I love you. Just meet me at the air-

port at one o'clock, please? I'll meet you there. We can go away
and work this out," I choked out.

"No. Move on and get over it. Your time with the bad boy has
ended."

The line went dead, and I whimpered as I squeezed my eyes
shut, trying to block out the pain of it. This was all so sudden
that I could barely take it in. Last night we had been all set to go
and start a new life, and today he'd changed his mind and slept
with someone else. My mind was whirling as my heart fractured
into a million pieces. The phone dropped out of my hand and I
flopped back on the bed, curling into a ball, hugging my knees to
my chest as I sobbed for the future with him that I wanted so desperately.

* * *

I just lay there for what felt like hours. My tears eventually
dried up, but my breathing didn't really return to normal as I
stared at the ceiling and went over everything that had ever happened between us. Once I'd gained a little control over myself,
I'd sent him several texts asking him to meet me at the airport,
telling him that I wasn't giving up on us and that I was confident we could make it work. Of course, he didn't reply to any
of them.

In the painful solitude of my bedroom, I started to wonder if
he ever even loved me in the first place. He was right, we were
so different—he got off on stealing cars, and I was a stupid cheerleader in high school. People like us weren't well matched at all.
Maybe we were doomed from the beginning.

When my bedroom door burst open, I couldn't bring myself to
move. The mattress bounced a little as Kelsey settled herself on
my bed, sitting cross-legged and smiling down at me. "Dad says

get up, sleepyhead, we're waiting for you so we can eat breakfast," she sang.

I forced a smile. I couldn't tell my family what had transpired this morning. I was clinging to the fragile hope that Jamie would reconsider and we'd just go away for a couple of weeks to get a fresh start. I couldn't very well tell my parents that he'd cheated on me and basically ripped my heart to pieces, because then if he *did* change his mind, they wouldn't let me go with him anyway. So, for now, I needed to try to keep my heartbreak hidden. That was going to be easier said than done, though, because my throat hurt, my eyes stung, and my head ached because of all the crying. If I looked in the mirror, I was sure to see a red, blotchy mess looking back at me.

I cleared my throat before speaking, trying not to wince as it scratched and cracked. "I'll be down in a minute, okay? I'm just gonna jump in the shower. Tell Dad to go ahead and make breakfast, I'm not really hungry anyway."

Kelsey's eyes narrowed. "Have you been crying?" she asked, reaching out and touching my cheek.

I laughed humorlessly and pushed her hand away. "Kinda," I admitted. "I'm just a little sad that I won't get to see you guys for a while. I'm gonna miss you."

She grinned then, nodding enthusiastically, obviously buying into my complete lie. "Mom's crying too, but she's pretending like she's fine and that she has something in her eye."

My mom was crying over me leaving? I didn't quite know how to feel about that after the moment we'd had last night while packing. Though maybe I was just fooling myself, the woman probably did have something in her eye...

I took a deep breath and pushed myself up to sit. "Go eat then. I'll be down in half an hour." I nodded toward the door and she grinned, immediately jumping up. I smiled at her back as she skipped out of the room, humming quietly to herself. I was really going to miss them all, that wasn't a lie. But I guess there was a pretty good chance now that I wouldn't be going after all, so there would be no need for me to miss them. That thought made me whimper and my chin tremble, so I closed my eyes and took a deep breath before heading into the bathroom.

* * *

Breakfast was…awkward. My mom was indeed crying, but pretending she had dust in her eye and that her allergies were acting up. My dad was watching me with a sad smile on his face. Luckily for me, gullibility must run in my family because they didn't push my car-crash-of-a-face issue too far once I told them my lie. I forced the food down, almost retching on each mouthful because my stomach was tied in knots.

After breakfast, I looked at the clock. It was only just before ten. Had it really been less than four hours since he'd called? It felt like an age had passed while I was alone in my misery.

I didn't need to leave for the airport until twelve thirty, so I still had a couple of hours to kill. I couldn't sit around here, though; it was driving me insane because each minute felt like an hour. My mind went to Jamie again; I really needed to see him. He still hadn't responded to my texts to say if he was going to come to the airport and give us another go. I wasn't expecting him to, but the waiting and not knowing if he'd even read them was killing me slowly. I decided to go and see him, go to his place and pray that he was there and not with some girl, as he'd claimed he was. A small part of me was still holding on to the hope that he was making that up to try to hurt me.

I made my excuses to my parents, telling them I had a couple of friends to say good-bye to before I left, and then made the short drive to his apartment. My hands were shaking the whole time. By the time I got there, I was a mess and my tears were falling again.

I trudged up to his apartment with heavy legs and an even heavier heart. I wasn't even sure I was strong enough to look at him in case he told me right to my face that it was over. I didn't want to see his beautiful face when he crushed me beyond repair. But I knew I had to do this and try to convince him not to give up on us. Raising my hand, I knocked on the door a couple of times. When he didn't answer I put my head against the wood and closed my eyes.

Had he seriously stayed out last night with a girl?

My hand fumbled in my pocket, pulling out my keys and finding the one for his apartment. He'd given it to me a couple of weeks after he moved in, when I'd started staying here a lot. I was pretty sure he wouldn't appreciate my using it now, but that didn't stop me from slipping it into the lock and pushing open his door.

I couldn't breathe as I stepped across the threshold. Everything looked exactly the same as it had the previous night. I glanced toward the sofa, swallowing my sob when I thought about the intimate moments we'd shared there last night. I would remember that forever. I could practically still feel his skin against mine, still hear our breaths tangling together as he made love to me. Everything had been so perfect, so tender and intimate, but now, as I stood here alone, the memory of it was taunting me.

Tearing my gaze away from the sofa, I let my eyes roam his apartment; the place was bare, as I expected it to be. Holding my breath, I crept toward his bedroom and peeked in. His bed was empty, still made, and hadn't been slept in. I'd come over here wanting to see for myself if he was lying to me about the girl, but now that I knew he hadn't spent the night here I wished I didn't know at all.

Pain made my whole body feel weak as I started to accept the fact that he'd cheated. The funny thing was that it didn't make me love him any less; I still wanted to be with him and work this out. Usually I despised girls like me when I watched them on TV or read about this kind of situation in a book. I'd always shaken my head and wondered how they could be so weak as to let a man treat them that way and still come back for more—but now I knew why they did. The saying "love conquers all" made perfect sense to me in that moment.

My breath came out in one big gust as I stepped into his room, almost tripping over his suitcase, which was propped next to the door. One of his favorite hoodies was tossed on the foot of his bed so I stooped and picked it up, pressing it to my face and taking in lungfuls of his delicious smell.

"Stop behaving like a stalker, Ellie," I muttered to myself, throwing the hoodie back onto the bed. "And now you're talking to yourself. Really, get a grip, woman." I shook my head at myself and turned, heading into his kitchen to find what I was looking for. When I had the pen and paper, I scribbled a note to him.

Jamie,

Please come to the airport, we can just go for a couple of weeks. Please?

I love you, and I'm sorry. Please, can we start over?

Ellie xxx

I frowned as I looked down at the paper. There were so many things that I wanted to say to him, so many unspoken words that I didn't know how to phrase properly. Hopefully he'd give me the chance to say them later on. I scribbled an extra kiss on the end before I headed back to his bedroom and balanced the note on top of his suitcase so that he'd see it and hopefully grab the case and run out the door. I sighed deeply, praying it would happen just like that. I refused to fully accept that this was over.

Fiddling with my keys, I disconnected his from the bunch and set it on top of my note. I turned and was just about to walk out when I decided that I could probably cross the line a little more. So before I left, I grabbed his hoodie from the bed, and I slipped it on as I walked out, zipping it up around me. Maybe his smell would help me get through the next couple of hours without losing my mind.

As I closed his front door behind me I whimpered when I realized that the last time I'd walked out of his apartment, I'd had the perfect future all lined up. Last time I'd headed out of this place I'd been so happy that I'd practically skipped to my car. Now, my shoulders were slumped, my heart hurt, and I actually felt a little dead inside. As I forced myself to walk away from his apartment, I sent up a little prayer that he'd come home in time to see my note and would decide to give me another shot.

* * *

The hoodie didn't help much. I still felt empty inside; tears were just making my eyes prickle the whole time I waited and spent the last of the time with my family. Stacey came over too; she was crying all over me, which didn't help my jangled nerves. I still hadn't told anyone, which was a feat in itself. The truth was bursting to come out of me, I wanted to confide in Stacey and have her tell me it was okay, but I couldn't do that because I was still waiting to hear from Jamie.

My cell phone went off a couple of times, and each time my heart would leap into my throat as I immediately thought it was him, only to be disappointed when it was friends calling or texting to wish me a safe journey.

When it was finally time to leave and the cab driver had loaded all of my cases into the trunk, I stood on my front lawn, bidding a teary farewell to my parents, sister, and Stacey. I'd spun a lie that something had come up with Jamie's family so he was meeting me at the airport instead of picking me up. Again they bought the lie, obviously having no reason to doubt me or him. As we hugged, my mom lost her battle against the dust in her eye and all-out sobbed, begging me to write often and call. I swallowed, trying to remain in control, trying not to think about the fact that if Jamie didn't turn up at the airport I'd be hailing a cab home again in a couple of hours. My good-byes were shadowed with grief as in the back of my mind all I could think about was him and the last words he'd said to me on the phone.

After I'd hugged everyone a billion times and made watery promises to call as soon as we landed, I finally got to climb into the solitude of the cab. As the driver sped us away from the house, I didn't look back; instead, I pulled out the tickets that I had in my carry-on luggage and looked at the names printed on them.

"So, where you off to?" the driver asked.

I looked up to see him smiling at me politely in the rearview mirror. "Um...all over. Rome first, but my boyfriend and I are planning on backpacking around for a bit." I noticed how my voice trembled on the word *boyfriend*.

He nodded. "Sounds great. I went to Rome once—" I tuned out as he started telling me about all the sights I needed to see when we got there. I nodded along, pretending to listen as he drove. Thankfully, he was one of those cabbies who rambled on and on with no real interaction needed from me, so I got away with not really listening to him.

When we pulled up outside the airport, I dug in my purse and paid the fare before pushing open the door and stepping out. Dread washed over me as I looked at the bustle of JFK airport. People were walking in and out in a constant stream, but I couldn't really see their faces. Nothing seemed to matter to me apart from the fact that none of them was Jamie. Something bumped my leg, so I snapped out of my daydream and looked around to see that the friendly cabdriver had gotten me a cart and had already loaded my luggage on for me.

I smiled gratefully as a wave of loneliness washed over me. I'd never been to this kind of place alone before; I had no idea where to go or what I had to do. "Thanks."

He nodded. "No problem. Have a great time, and remember what I said about the Colosseum," he called as he headed back around to his side of the cab. I nodded in agreement but actually had no idea what he'd said about it at all.

After standing on the curb for a couple of seconds plucking up my courage, I lifted my chin, gripped the handle, and pushed the luggage cart into the airport. Jamie would turn up, I knew he would. He was an incredible person, and he'd give me a second shot, I was sure of it.

As I walked in, I gulped. I'd forgotten how enormous the airport was; I had no idea how Jamie would even find me when he did arrive. I decided to stay fairly close to the terminal entrance just in case. Maneuvering myself over to the side, I took a seat on one of the hard metal chairs, discreetly checking the monitors to see that our flight was still on time and that we had to check in at gate A3. There was still an hour before check-in closed for our flight; he had plenty of time before we had to go through security.

My eyes scanned everywhere. Every time I saw a guy walk past who had brown hair, my heart took off in overdrive, only to be disappointed over and over. I chewed on my lip as a middle-aged couple sat down in the empty seats next to me; both of them were grinning and laughing, obviously happy to be going on vacation. Their happy smiles made me die a little inside while I was waiting there for a guy who might not even turn up.

I could imagine the looks on my parents' faces when I returned home today. I could practically hear the sympathetic words of support that would mean nothing because of the heartbreak I'd be feeling.

One o'clock came and went. After what felt like forever waiting and watching the clock, my heart sank when they appealed over the loudspeaker for any remaining passengers on our flight to go to the check-in desks. Realization suddenly washed over me; it was like someone dumped a bucket of cold water in my face. He really wasn't coming. I'd built my hopes up, planned my life with him, I'd sat here totally expecting him to show…and he wasn't going to. I was a fool, a complete heartbroken fool.

Putting my head in my hands, I bent forward and sobbed like I had never sobbed before. It was over, just like he said. I was alone. I'd blown it; my one chance with the adorable, beautiful boy and I'd completely blown it because I hadn't trusted him. I deserved this, I deserved to be alone.

Everything else seemed to fade away as I cried and cried. No one offered me support—or if they did I didn't hear them through the sound of my grief crashing in my ears. I gripped my hands in my hair, welcoming the sharp pain in my scalp so that I could try to focus.

I sniffed loudly, swiping roughly at my face, drying my tears as people around me stared openly with a mixture of sympathy and nervousness. I guess my sudden outpouring of tears scared them or something; I couldn't bring myself to care.

His words on the phone earlier were replaying over and over in my head: "*I don't love you enough to give up my life for you.*" Why had I let myself hope that he would come? Why had I pretended to everyone this morning and carried this pain around on my own? Why had I fallen so in love with him that it felt like my world was crashing down around me right now? It was like I'd fallen into darkness, a dark and ugly place that I didn't want to be in but had no way of escaping. A weight was pushing down on my chest, making it hard to draw breath as the devastation and hurt just kept building and building the more I thought about it.

Home. I need to go home.

Just as I gripped the handle of the cart, ready to stand and go hail a cab so I could cry myself to sleep, a hand touched my shoulder.

"Ellie?"

Relief washed over me. I took a deep breath and turned in my seat, the stress and tension leaving my body because his being here obviously meant that I got another shot, a second chance, and there was no way I was wasting it. Jamie and I were meant to be together, and I'd prove that to him.

EPILOGUE

THE SUN WAS streaming through the windows when I slowly started to drift into consciousness. I squeezed my eyes shut at the brightness of it, moaning as I rolled over and buried my face in the pillows. A thin line of sweat covered my skin, caused by the humidity in the room.

Huffing out a big breath, I pushed myself up, already hearing the sounds of the shower running, which explained the empty bed and the lack of soft snoring in my ear. When my feet touched the cool tiles of the floor, I closed my eyes and sighed before grabbing the bottle of water from the bedside table and forcing myself to get out of bed and start the day.

My gaze settled on the open double doors and the little balcony beyond. Needing fresh air, I walked outside, taking deep breaths, trying to stave off the hangover that was fighting to take over.

Smiling to myself, I leaned my elbows on the metal railing, casting my eyes over Florence as it started to wake up and get a little busier.

Florence was much nicer than Rome, in my opinion; it was calmer, more chill and not as busy.

When the smell of coffee wafted over from one of the quaint little cafés that were hidden in the back streets, my mouth instantly started watering at the thought of a tall vanilla latte with extra foam. I headed back into the room, still hearing sounds of the shower as I threw on a pair of denim shorts and a pink stretch T-shirt. I scribbled a note saying I would be down in the square and set it on the bedside table, then grabbed my purse and left the room on a coffee hunt, not even caring that I hadn't showered or brushed my teeth.

I weaved the familiar path to get to my desired destination, the Piazza della Signoria. The square was fairly busy, even though a quick glance at the clock on the expansive building told me it wasn't even ten a.m. I smiled to myself and walked across the huge square, letting my eyes rake over the statues that were dotted around.

My stomach gave a little squeeze as I approached the café that I loved to death because they did the most incredible pastries. It was fairly busy already, but I managed to grab the last outside table, which had the most perfect view of the square and the benefit of shade, thanks to an umbrella.

The waitress came over immediately, taking my coffee and pastry order, then I sat back in my chair and relaxed as I watched the people walk past going to work, or the tourists as they cooed over everything and took pictures.

"*Mi scusi.*" I turned to see a kind-faced older lady smiling warmly at me. "*È libero questo posto?*"

I winced, smiling apologetically because I had no idea what she'd said. "I'm sorry, I don't…um…*Non parlo italiano?*" I prayed that was right because, as beautiful as the Italian language sounded to me, all I knew how to say was *no thank you, where are the bathrooms*, and *how much.*

She laughed and nodded. "Ah, you are American, *sì?*"

I grinned. "Sì."

She motioned toward the chair opposite me. "May I sit with you?" she asked in thickly accented English.

"Oh! Yeah, sure!" I agreed, blushing because of course that's what she was asking me. Now I felt stupid for not understanding.

She smiled gratefully and pulled out the chair, sitting down. "It is too hot to sit inside, no?"

I nodded in agreement, leaning back as the waitress brought my coffee and pastry, setting them on the table in front of me. The lady at my table smiled and placed her order as I stirred in my sugar.

"You are alone in Florence?"

My head snapped up at her question. I was unsure how to answer. I shrugged. "Sort of" was the only thing I could think of to say. She looked at me curiously, obviously waiting for me to continue and explain, but I didn't want to; it was too hard to say out loud.

"A *bella ragazza* like you should not be alone," she replied.

I smiled weakly but turned my attention back to people-watching in the square so that she wouldn't continue to talk to me. My mind wandered to Jamie, even though I had forbidden myself to even think his name. My chest tightened and my breathing came out a little shallow as raw emotion started to build up inside me. I tried so hard not to think about him. That day was still so fresh in my mind that the pain of having my hopes dashed time and time again made my heart ache, even after three weeks.

I hadn't heard from him at all. Jamie had asked his friend Ray to come to the airport and meet me that day. Just as I had gotten my hopes up that everything was fine, that I would get a happy ending with him, my dream was crushed again when I turned around and saw that it wasn't the love of my life standing there after all.

Ray had given me this long, sympathetic speech about how Jamie had always been afraid of commitment, about how he'd never settle down and it wasn't my fault.

It had hurt so much that I could still feel the painful squeezing of my heart as I pictured Ray's sympathetic expression as he cupped my elbow, holding me steady when my knees weakened. That expression on his face had made me realize that I wasn't ready to face it yet, I wasn't ready to tell people that the guy I wanted to spend my life with had rejected me and crushed me beyond repair. Looking at Ray while he smiled with understanding and tried to make me feel better, I knew that I needed to get away and make a clean break. So that was exactly what I did.

I'd dried my tears, forced a smile, shoved Jamie's plane ticket into Ray's chest, and told him to tell Jamie that he was an asshole and that he was welcome to the tramp he'd bedded last night. Then I'd lifted my chin and marched over to the check-in desk.

I'd hoped that by putting some distance between us, I'd leave my grief and problems behind. It didn't work. The heartbreak had just followed me to Rome and overshadowed the beauty of everything around me. I was so lonely and broken that I didn't leave the hotel room for four days, and then, on the fifth day, I'd ventured out to the market and run into someone—*literally* run into someone—who'd seemed to make it a mission to make me smile again. It was working, a little. Each day got just that little bit easier, and just that little bit less painful.

My family had been less than supportive when I'd called them. As soon as they found out I was alone in a foreign country, my dad was ranting that I had to get on the first flight back. He'd threatened to fly out and get me if necessary, but thankfully, I'd avoided that so far. We weren't exactly on good terms at the moment. Every time I spoke to them they argued that I should come home, that it wasn't safe for an eighteen-year-old girl to travel alone, that they'd only agreed to the trip because of Jamie coming with me.

I hadn't told them the full extent of what had happened, I'd simply said that we'd broken up and that I'd decided to still go. The plan was to go for two weeks, because that was how long Jamie and I had booked the hotel in Rome for, but my new friend had persuaded me that I needed to see Florence before I went home. So we'd been here a week, and then I'd somehow been convinced that we needed to go to Venice, which is where we were heading tomorrow. At this rate I couldn't see myself going home anytime soon.

Sighing, I stirred my coffee absentmindedly, letting my thoughts wander to dangerous places where I really shouldn't allow them to go. I thought about Jamie's kisses, his smile, the warmth of his hand as he caressed my cheek, how his hard body would wrap itself around mine while I slept. I could almost still taste him on my tongue if I thought about it hard enough.

Over the last three weeks I'd allowed myself to call him only once, hoping that he was regretting his decision and that he missed me too—but that call was pretty pointless because his cell phone number was no longer in use. No one had heard from him at all. Stacey told me that my dad had gone around to his place wanting to "speak" to him about me, but that apparently he'd moved out and his apartment was already rented to another tenant.

A chair scraping on concrete snapped me out of my reverie, and I looked up into the grinning face of Natalie, my new little traveling buddy. I smiled back as she nodded down at my coffee. "You order me one of those?" she asked, her voice a little husky, probably from all the drunken singing we'd done in the karaoke bar last night.

"Nope. Didn't know how long you'd be in the shower for; you know you spend hours in there," I joked.

She grinned and waved for the waitress, putting in her order, too. She sat back in her chair and blew out a big breath as she adjusted her huge black fashion shades and smoothed back her damp brown hair. "You suffering this morning after drinking so much?" she asked, laughing.

I shrugged. "Not too bad, actually. You?"

She nodded, lifting her shades and fixing her bloodshot eyes on me. "Not taking these off today, that's for sure," she replied sheepishly. Both of us ignored the Italian lady at the table, who was now engrossed in her book anyway.

I'd been with Natalie for just over two weeks now, and in that time, we'd become great friends. She was a little older than me at twenty-two, but we had a lot in common. She was American too, and had just finished college and wanted to travel before she got a job. She was on her own as well, so when we hit it off in Rome we decided to stick together and explore for a bit.

"You were talking in your sleep so much last night," Natalie grumbled. "At one point I actually considered smothering you with a pillow, but then I realized that spending time in an Italian jail probably wouldn't look good on my résumé."

I laughed and smiled apologetically. I'd always thought Jamie was kidding around when he told me I talked in my sleep. "Sorry. What was it about this time? Alien abduction?"

She sighed and shook her head. "No. You were talking about him again."

My stomach twisted in a knot. "Oh."

She reached across the table, taking my hand in hers and squeezing supportively. "It'll get easier, I promise," she assured me. "Besides, the guy was obviously a moron for letting you go in the first place, so it's his loss. I don't swing that way, but if I did, I'd bang you."

I laughed because this was just what she was like; she always knew how to lighten the mood. "I don't know whether to take that as a compliment or be slightly worried about sleeping in bed with you tonight," I replied, fighting the tears that were pooling in my eyes.

She grinned wolfishly. "I'll try my hardest not to jump you, cross my heart," she vowed, crossing her heart with one finger.

I smiled and tuned out as she started to ramble about what we should do today, on our last day in Florence. My mind wandered to Jamie and I glanced at the little bracelet on my wrist, the one he'd given me for my birthday. Deep down I knew I should take it off and throw it into the river in some sort of metaphorical gesture that I was moving on and was over him, but every time I thought about removing the bracelet from my wrist, it made my heart ache even more. Maybe one day I'd be able to take it off and let go. Maybe Natalie was right, maybe one day I'd stop thinking about what I'd lost, and I'd see the beauty in everything again. I sighed and looked up at the blue sky, just praying that day would come quickly.

JAMIE

I sat at the table, waiting. Waiting wasn't one of my strengths at the moment. Huffing out a big breath, I tried to settle the apprehension that had taken root at the bottom of my stomach. But it was no use; I'd been a ball of nerves for the last three weeks, since I'd been arrested.

My eyes stung, so I rubbed at them with fisted hands. I frowned when my mind wandered to Ellie again. Thoughts of her were both torturous and beautiful at the same time. Memories of her made my heart ache and my palms sweaty. I hated myself for hurting her, but I was confident that I'd made the right choice in setting her free. I loved her too much to make her wait around for me.

In hindsight, though, I knew I shouldn't have been as harsh to her as I was. I'd told some gut-wrenching lies to her on the phone that day—ginormous lies that had almost choked me. They still haunted me. But I knew I'd done the right thing. I couldn't let her set foot in a place like this to visit me; she was better than this, much better. That knowledge didn't make it hurt any less, though. In fact, I felt lower right now than I'd ever felt in my life, and that included when I'd lost Sophie.

My nerves were frayed, and I couldn't stop my leg from bouncing on the spot. Around me, other inmates, each sporting the same orange jumpsuit that I was wearing, sat at their own tables. A commotion caught everyone's attention. Every face turned toward the heavy metal door at the end of the large room. A hopeful and excited expression covered even the hardest and most weary face.

Today was visiting day, and for the second time since I'd been arrested, I had a visitor.

I stood, shuffling on my feet, rubbing a hand over my prison-standard shaven hair, watching people walk in. Ray was second to last to enter. He looked good. Maybe a little tired, but still good. When he spotted me, his posture loosened, and a grin stretched across his face as he began to weave his way cautiously through the room.

When he got to my table, he stepped to the side and pulled me into a hug, slapping my back just that little bit too hard to be comforting.

"Are you all right, Kid?"

I resisted the urge to roll my eyes. Apart from my lawyer and the guards, no one had called me Jamie since I'd been arrested.

I nodded, shrugging nonchalantly. "Yeah. You look good," I replied, stepping away and sitting in my hard plastic chair.

He smiled weakly, taking the seat opposite mine. "Yeah." He shifted, twiddling his thumbs. "How's it going in here?"

"Fine." That was hopefully a good enough answer to placate him for a while.

"And Shaun, how's he doing?" he pressed.

"He's doing all right. There's a couple of people here that he knew from the outside so he's keeping his head down with them and staying out of trouble," I answered. Shaun was doing good, really; he'd made a couple of acquaintances that benefited us both because we could join a group rather than be on our own, vulnerable and easy targets. We had each other's backs. So far, there had been minimal trouble, which was good. I knew it wouldn't last forever, though. "How's your wife and daughter, and have you found a new job yet?" I asked, wanting to change the subject.

He frowned. "The family are good. And no, I haven't been looking for a job yet. I've had a couple of people approach me about coming to work for them, but I've decided to take a break for a while." His frown deepened. "Brett's funeral was last week. He'd have been proud that so many people showed up to pay their respects. The place was packed full."

I smiled sadly, feeling that dull ache in my chest grow more acute. I'd missed his funeral. That hurt. "That's great that he had a lot of people to see him off."

Silence fell over us as Ray looked at me intently, his eyes boring into mine as if he was trying to read my mind and tune in to my feelings. "How are you really?"

"Coping." That wasn't a lie, somehow I *was* coping. I didn't know how I was, but I was managing to hang on to my sanity and not let the depression get me.

Sighing, I decided to broach the subject, bring up the only thing that had been on my mind since it happened. I sat forward, clasping my hands together. "So, where is she now?"

He sighed and settled back in his chair. "Florence," he answered. "But she's going to Venice tomorrow."

I nodded, processing the information. "Is she doing better, or..." I trailed off, not wanting to know the answer but needing to.

Ray shrugged, fiddling with the cuff of his sweater. "She's doing a little better. Natalie said that she's still upset, she still—" He stopped talking suddenly, gulping and shaking his head as if he didn't want to say it.

"She still what?" I prompted. I needed to know if she was okay, I needed to know she was safe; that information was the difference between life and death for me.

He looked at me apologetically as he answered. "She still cries for you and talks about you in her sleep."

I groaned, closing my eyes, hating myself. It wasn't supposed to be like this, she wasn't supposed to hurt. "Tell Natalie to up the act a little, take her to see more sights, spend more money. I don't care how long it takes or how many places they have to go, just tell her to help her," I begged.

Ray's sister-in-law, Natalie, had been at loose ends since she finished college. She was bored and wanted to see the world, but had no money, while I had more than a hundred thousand dollars in the bank and the girl I loved was alone in Rome. Once I'd come up with the idea and pitched it to Ray, it hadn't taken much convincing on his part to get Natalie to agree to a stealth mission to cheer Ellie up. She got to travel, no expense spared, and I got the peace of mind to know that Ellie wasn't alone in a foreign country.

Ellie didn't know, of course. I'd told Ray that it had to look like a chance meeting between the two girls, that they both needed a friend and traveling buddy. From what I'd heard, Natalie had run through a market and almost knocked Ellie over when they met.

So far, my plan was working out perfectly. Apparently, according to Ray's regular phone calls over the last three weeks, the two girls had become great friends.

In time, Ray's sister-in-law would stop my little girl from hurting over me. That was worth any amount of money to me. And in the meantime, I got regular updates on how Ellie was doing.

"I brought you a couple of photos. Nat emailed them over to me yesterday. I left them with the guards for you," Ray said quietly.

I smiled gratefully, already wishing I were back in my cell so that I could have them, hold them, and see her beautiful face. The only things I had of Ellie's to remind me of her were one picture that Ray had found in my apartment when he cleared it for me and a note that she'd written to me the day we were due to catch our flight and start our new life together. She'd left it on top of my suitcase, along with my spare key. The note was a little dog-eared now. I read it several times a day, and it never ceased to make my heart race.

"Thanks, Ray. You've been great, you know."

He waved his hand dismissively. "It's the least I could do. So, any news on a date for your sentencing?"

I nodded, rubbing at the back of my neck where the rough prison-issue jumpsuit scratched at my skin. "Yeah, it's in about a month."

Arthur Barrington was pushing to get the case moved up sooner. I'd already pleaded guilty to illegal possession of a firearm, but the courts were busy with other cases, so my sentencing was dragging on and on. I knew I would be in here for at least a year, though, so I guess it didn't really matter when they confirmed it. Mr. Barrington had done his part as promised; he'd negotiated with police to drop all other charges against me and Shaun. How he'd done it I had no idea, but the guy must have a lot of friends in high places and have called in a lot of favors. I was currently serving out the remainder of my sentence for killing Ralf while I waited for my new sentence to be added into the mix.

My lawyer had also done his best to keep my involvement in the raid hidden from as many people as possible—and that specifically included his son, Miles. I couldn't have it get back to Ellie that I'd lied to her to set her free—at least, not until the time was right. The press hadn't printed our names; they had bigger fish to fry, considering that the Lazlos were there that night, too. No one was interested in the small people like me and Shaun, which worked out to my advantage.

Ray nodded, sighing. "I sure wish there was something I could do to help you, Kid. You don't deserve to be here, you're a good guy."

I smiled at the warm tone of his voice. "You're already helping me. The only thing that's important is her, so just keep your eye on her for me, that's all I need." Ellie's happiness was the only thing I had left in this world; I *had* to know that she was okay after what I'd done. I cleared my throat, needing a change of subject because thoughts of her were painful. "How are those Yankees doing?"

He laughed quietly, and conversation changed to easier, lighter topics until the buzzer sounded, signaling the end of visiting time. A frown slipped onto Ray's face as he looked at the clock mounted on the wall. "Shit, that went too fast," he mumbled.

I stood, actually a little grateful for the time to be up. Making conversation and pretending I was fine was hard and exhausting. "Time flies when you're having fun."

He smiled sadly as he stood and stepped to the side of the table, pulling me into another hug. "Just keep your head down and stay out of trouble," he instructed, looking into my eyes.

"Will do," I answered. At least, I'd *try*. Thing was, in places like this, trouble was sometimes unavoidable. "I'll call you in a couple of days and get an update. Tell Natalie to spend whatever she wants, buy Ellie some stuff, get her drunk, I don't know, just tell her to cheer her up, okay?"

"I will. I'll see you next week, yeah?" People were leaving now, and a guard stepped subtly to the edge of our table, silently indicating that I was to leave, too.

I shrugged. "Sure." *Lie.* I wouldn't see him again now; I could get updates over the phone. I couldn't sit through another hour of polite chitchat while I pretended I wasn't dying inside.

He smiled, looking a little relieved, so he obviously bought my lies. "Take care of yourself."

"I will. You too, and take care of your girls," I instructed. I didn't want him to have to feel what it was like to lose a girl you loved. This was agony and I wouldn't wish it on anyone. I turned and marched toward the convicts' door at the back of the room, following other inmates.

After another thorough search to make sure we hadn't been passed anything during the visit, we were finally allowed to go back to the cell block. When the guard handed me a flat manila envelope, a lump formed in my throat because I knew what would be inside.

I headed back to my cell quickly, weaving through the populated area, not making eye contact with anyone and ignoring Shaun, who called out to me and waved me over to the table where he was playing cards with some other inmates. I shook my head quickly in rejection, holding up the envelope as an excuse as I marched purposefully up three flights of metal stairs and finally made it to the cell that I shared with the skinniest man I had ever met.

Thankfully, my cellmate was out somewhere, so I flopped on my bed and took a deep breath before opening the envelope and pulling out three photos.

A groan left my lips at the sight of the first one. Ellie was sitting at a little table, drinking coffee. Her hair was pulled up into a messy knot at the back of her head and her shades were tucked into her hair. From her expression, it seemed as if she hadn't realized that the photo was being taken. She looked beautiful, so incredible that it made my whole body ache. She wasn't smiling, though, and the gray eyes that I loved so much looked closed off and sad. The photo broke my heart a little more. All I wanted was to wrap her in my arms and do everything in my power to take that sadness from her eyes.

The next photo was better; someone else had obviously taken it as there were two girls in this one, standing side by side, arms linked as they smiled and posed in front of a fountain. Ellie had on little denim shorts and a loose blue T-shirt that hung off one shoulder, exposing a thin hot-pink strap that I knew belonged to her bikini because I was the one who bought it for her.

I shuffled to the last one and gasped in shock as my body jerked involuntarily. She was wearing said hot-pink bikini in this picture. She stood by the side of a pool, doing a silly pose, one hand on her hip, the other on the side of her head as pouted exaggeratedly. She was obviously laughing and joking around for the photo. My eyes raked down her body, taking in every inch of the skin that I knew like the back of my hand. She looked incredible, and I knew this photo would keep me awake at night, but I loved Ray for putting it in there for me. I traced the line of her leg with one finger, wishing I could actually feel the softness of her and the warmth of her skin. I would give anything to be in this photo with her.

Loneliness settled in the pit of my stomach as I rolled to the side, my eyes just roaming the picture, taking in every single part of her all over again as memories of her flooded my brain. Knowing she was so far away was torture. Knowing there was a good chance she hated me for what I'd said to her, knowing I'd broken her heart, caused me actual physical pain.

"Just a year, little girl. In a year, when I'm out, I'll win you back," I whispered to the photo. "I will." I nodded with determination. I *had* to win her back. Ellie was my life; without her there was no point to anything. I'd done what I felt was the honorable thing in setting her free so she wasn't waiting for me and could live her life, but as soon as I was out I'd do everything in my power to make her mine again. Ellie and I were meant to be together, destined even.

Until she was in my arms again, I'd be counting the days, planning how to regain her trust and make her mine again. Because in the end, prison was nothing; it was being without Ellie that I wasn't sure I'd survive.

Jamie Cole made a choice. A choice that cost him his freedom...and his heart. Now he's a man with nothing to lose—until Ellie Pearce comes back into his life.

Everyone says you can't fight fate. For Jamie and Ellie is this their second chance—or their final goodbye?

Don't miss

Worth Fighting For

Available Winter 2016